VOICES OF THE SOUTH

OTHER BOOKS BY PETER FEIBLEMAN

NOVELS

The Daughters of Necessity

The Columbus Tree

Charlie Boy

NOVELLAS

The Only Danaid

Fever

Along the Coast

Eyes

PLAYS

Tiger Tiger Burning Bright

Cakewalk

MEMOIR

Lilly: Reminiscences of Lillian Hellman

WITH LILLIAN HELLMAN

Eating Together: Recollections and Recipes

OTHER NONFICTION

The Bayou Country

The Cooking of Spain and Portugal

Creole and Acadian Cooking

A PLACE WITHOUT TWILIGHT

A Place

Baton Rouge and London

Without Twilight

by PETER FEIBLEMAN
With a New Afterword by the Author

LOUISIANA STATE UNIVERSITY PRESS

Copyright © 1957, 1958, 1986 by Peter S. Feibleman
Afterword copyright © 1997 by Peter Feibleman
First published by the World Publishing Company
LSU Press edition published 1997 by arrangement with the author
All rights reserved
Manufactured in the United States of America
06 05 04 03 02 01 00 99 98 97   5 4 3 2 1

Library of Congress Cataloging-in-Publication Data

Feibleman, Peter S., 1930–
   A place without twilight / by Peter Feibleman ; with a new
afterword by the author.
      p.   cm. — (Voices of the South)
   ISBN 0-8071-2225-4   (pbk.)
   I. Title. II. Series.
PS3556.E4P57   1997
813' .54—dc21   97-15673
                                                           CIP

The paper in this book meets the guidelines for permanence and durability of the
Committee on Production Guidelines for Book Longevity of the Council on Library
Resources. ⊛

By way of dedication, may this book in some measure
come to replace that bunch of hollow glass grapes
(with a different perfume in each)—

FOR JUDITH

PF

Mallorca; September, 1957

CONTENTS

SIDE ONE:

No Movement

FISHING that afternoon, Dan said: "Cille."

"Yes, honey." I was real tired. The air was all fevered with summer, and so full of wet even the leaf shadows felt heavy. And that was one of Dan's question-asking days. Not a fish, neither.

"Cille. How do people know what they going to be when they grow up?"

"Foo," I said. "Most of them don't, I guess. Unless they *want* to be something. And even then, maybe."

Little Dan squirmed around on his bottom. He told me: "You got a mosquito sitting up over your left tit."

"That ain't no way to talk," I said. But I looked down and swatted.

"Cille."

"I'm still here."

"Know what let's don't be?"

"What?"

Dan said: "Niggers."

"Honey, why don't you just shut up and fish? And keep still, you shaking the worm clean off that line."

"Let's make a pretend."

"What?"

"Let's pretend we ain't niggers."

"How you going to pretend that?" I said, "you better think up some other pretend."

"Why?"

"Just because," I said.

The sun softened behind a cloud. I had been waiting. I leaned over to my right, and rubbed the inside of my arm across my forehead. There was a way I could do it that the sweat wouldn't pour down onto my skirt. I missed, though.

"Cille."

"Lord," I said, *"what?"*

"Clarence going to be a . . . what he says?"

"Might."

"What you want to be?"

"Honey, a woman. Just a *plain woman.*"

More time.

"Cille."

"Sweet Jesus above," I said.

"Cille."

"I'm listening."

"Know what I want to be?"

"No."

"Want me to tell you?"

"You going to anyhow, ain't you?"

Dan rolled his eyes down and pushed out his jaw. "Not if you don't want to know."

"Okay," I said, "okay. What? A fireman?"

But he said: "No. I don't want to be nothing. I ain't never seen a thing I wanted to be. So I just don't want to be nothing at all."

". . . Then what did you want to pretend for?"

"For fun. I just want to pretend about *not* being a nigger. But I don't want to *be* nothing."

"Well, don't worry," I told him, "you going to find something to be soon as you get a little bit older."

Dan lay back against the levee, with his pole on top of him, and squinted at the sky. "I ain't worried," he said, quiet; "because I plain ain't going to look no more."

Out by the River, about a quarter-mile down from the bridge, was where we used to play. Dan and me. Clarence was a lot older, and anyway, he always had his things to do. It took a good while to get out there from Mama's house, so we would only go on Sunday afternoons, after Sunday school and church and something to eat. Mama held the washing down on Sundays, when she could, account of the Lord.

We first took to going in the spring two years before our father died, when I was ten and Dan was eight, and Clarence was fourteen and a half. Course, we were so young then that Mama made Clarence ride us out on the streetcar and fetch us afterwards too—but he wouldn't stay with us in between. Clarence was a person to hisself. Dan and me picked that spot because the levee was high there, and if anybody ever drove along it, the chances was they couldn't see us down below. So that was the spot I stood when I first saw the River, and after I saw her there, I never would go anyplace else. And Dan didn't care.

Queer, Mama letting us go out there at all. Only, I think she wanted to get us away from our father on his Sundays off. And she didn't want us to be with anybody else (except Adelaide, which wasn't going to happen if I could help it), and she didn't want us playing around the neighborhood (for fear we might make friends or get mixed up with the St. Thomas Street gang), and besides, she must of figured we *had* to play sometimes.

Anyway, she let us.

But that is just one lone time, of the times I remember. One loose piece, without a number or a sense by itself.

And you got three kinds of times that stay with you.

First are the ones you keep outside: some, because you can tell they made a difference; some, you don't know why. These are the times that changed things most and least—not always for you, but for the people you love and the place where you live. They hold their real colors, long as they can.

Then, just below the skin, you got the second kind. They come back up to the surface if you smell a certain smell, or see a thing in a way you saw something else before. Like when you look at the sun and you recall a different sun that was important to you once. But most of those times won't come back completely: you see a brand new house with its last brick still drying and you sure you ain't seeing it for the first time; or you go someplace you never been before, and you already know it; or a flower has a separate smell from all the other flowers, and even the touch of its petals reminds you of . . . ? They are the strange, halfway times—the ones that wasn't quite bad enough for you to have buried them clean—the ostrich-times in a backwards world, where you can only see the heads. They have wispy colors that jump and change, like plants moving under water.

Last are the bad times that mattered. The rosy, rotten pearls you got deep down, from when you coated over a grain of something you didn't want but couldn't get rid of. They are hard and shiny, and they will reflect any color you ask, in their pink smiles. Mostly, they only lay there. And you pretend to forget them, but you really know —you can feel the shapes inside, waiting. They don't cause no pain, because you got them slicked over, but you can feel them. It's them that makes your body jerk at night, or makes a flush below your stomach when somebody says something that shouldn't be important. It's the fear of them makes dreams twist crippled and slink away before morning, to leave you with just a sour wonder back of your tongue. The trouble is, you have to keep on slicking; you can't ever let them be. Because something you let slip in during the day might act like acid and dissolve a pearl while you sleep. That is what makes you wake up screaming: when one of them dissolves and leaves you with the same old grain scratching in the same sore. You say a real pearl wouldn't act like that? Course it wouldn't. You can't make real pearls. You ain't an oyster.

Lots of your times are made up of all three kinds, and the different colors will mix and fade no matter what you do. But that's okay, just so you know. Once you take them out and study on them, you can put the colors back together, without feeling bad. See: blood always runs *some* kind of red. And green is as good a color for you as yellow or blue, just so you know how it's made. What you can do is know those things.

All you can do is know.

I

Out of twenty-three years, the first part of my life I can remember is the part before it all started to go wrong. Back where nothing *could* go wrong: while our father was still alive. Back there beyond all the hurting—when every breath had a secret reason—before the first big hurt that showed me how.

And the quiet nights, when we sat on the gallery with our father, under the one electric light bulb that hung on a cord too short to swing if a breeze was just a breeze. Sitting in the shy mother-air that felt around us, blind and gentle, to see if winter was hiding there or had really gone; body-rocking, slow, so the pregnant air could touch you all around and make sure; loving the green promise in the air; believing that promise was for you too. Believing.

And listening to our father sing and tell stories and talk and read.

I wonder could anybody else ever imagine the way we felt, or why we felt that way. Because the why is the important thing. It wasn't *where* we lived that poisoned us, ever. It wasn't even *how.*

Only: *why.*

Back of town, one house down from the corner of Millicent and St. Thomas, certainly wasn't no special location. Most all the colored people lived someplace like that, a little better or a little worse. If your tongue just showed too pink against your cheek, you lived someplace like that. Course, while I was still trying to find a spot to blame for everything that happened, I used to say our house brought bad luck. I said that account of it was shoved a couple jumps further back from the others on our block, like it was out of line. But one day, when I went walking up and down through the whole neighborhood, it came to my mind how all the houses looked about the same. They still do, too. Nothing ever got a chance to change—not in those houses.

Gray is the color. Gray slats of splintery wood to make the sides, full of pinhead holes at the end of squiggly, rough paths a fingernail long, where worms shivered and went in. Shingles for the roof, a darker gray; the roofs are always cracked, and sometimes off-center after the winter's ice—like somebody who puts their only hat on at a raw angle, hoping you won't take no notice of the oldness nor the rips. And galleries. You can count on the galleries. They are made of the same wood as the sides, but everybody whitewashes them to look smooth. That lasts about two weeks. By then, they are all streaked with dust and pasty brown, and they would of looked heaps better if you just let them stay natural gray in the first place. Course, if you put the whitewash on in the summer, it bubbles, and if you put it on any other time, it cracks till you can play tick-tack-toe on it, and anyway, it loosens and flakes off all by itself. The wood gets tired of the whole mess, and raises its bristles—so you still end up having to watch out for splinters, only now they got whitewash on them, so they harder to see. Don't pay any of it much mind, though: *everybody* whitewashes their gallery. And everybody's got one. Galleries are a yard wide, and they run the width of the house. Plenty of those houses don't have no bathroom, but they all got galleries.

We had a bathroom, though. Sure. Course we did. Mama picked her house for that, so we could be clean. So at least we could be clean.

I know just how Mama must of acted when she and our father first went in to look at the house. They couldn't help but decide on something quick, because they didn't know a single person in New Orleans, and they had lived in a boardinghouse for two nights. The hundred and fifteen dollars they brought with them from Atlanta was a heap of money then, but it was all the money they owned, and our father without a job yet, and Mama with Clarence only five months old. And they had already looked at two other houses. So they couldn't of waited much longer.

I bet Mama didn't like the four feet of dirt that set the house back from the others. It must of been high with weeds, and lumpy under her feet. But Mama always walked light:

Up those three steps to stand on the gallery with our father, while some agent pulled back the screen door to unlock the wood one behind it. I know how she stood then: stiff—not turning her head, so the agent wouldn't put her no questions—scared to move, but seeing everything. Seeing the screen door was warped and the solid door too, and knowing they would always be that way because warped wood can't be fixed. Not liking his attention if the agent stepped aside to let her pass; not liking the way he looked at her, if he looked at her. Holding her breath while she set one foot over the stoop and followed it up into the house. And suddenly in a kitchen, the first room. Standing quiet as ice, with only the fingers of one hand moving like a trapped spider around and around the baby blanket to the edges of her shiny black purse. And her eyes zipping quick from side to side, and back over each thing.

Seeing: the sink on the wall to her left, with a window above it so she could wash dishes and watch out over the gallery and across the street; then the corner, and another window on the other wall, facing the next house; a real little oil stove right by it, to cook on; the back wall, and a potbelly coal stove for heat, with a black pipe going up through the roof; the wood table and its four chairs, maybe hugging tight together in the center of the room; the wood floor, with spaces between the slats that would have to be filled; two more doors, one on the back wall, and one on the right.

Mama would of held still, seeing all of that and liking it. Not minding the dirt, or the smell of mildew, because she always loved to work things clean. But approving of a big kitchen for the first room, to live in.

Then she would of gone into the bedroom on the right to see the two thin beds in it and the single windows on both outside walls, one over the gallery and one looking out on the empty lot next door.

And then through there, into the bathroom. A real bathroom—without no sink, but with a toilet, and an iron bathtub that had four curved legs made to look like the legs of some big bird, each one holding an iron ball in its claws.

Back through that bedroom, through the kitchen, into the only other room, where she and our father would have to sleep. And a back door leading off there into the middle of the block where everybody burnt their garbage.

I wonder if Mama said yes right away; or if she went out on the gallery with our father to think about it, and maybe to sneak a half a minute of deep-hummed lullaby for only the baby to hear. The price was high, but the down payment was all right, furniture included. And the house was all right, because it had the thing Mama always wanted—the thing she must of kept back of her mind all the way in the train from Atlanta—the thing that was going to make them both clean and free, with free kids, in a free world: a bathroom.

They took it the same day. They paid a hundred dollars down and moved right in, with four suitcases full of the household stuff they'd brought from Atlanta instead of clothes, and a broom and a mop and a bucket they had to buy separate, and thirteen dollars and twenty-nine cents. They slept in the back bedroom because it only had one bed then, but before night, Mama got our father to board up the back door. It was the first fixing she made him do in the house, account of she said she couldn't rest in no room with an outside door. So it was closed up before I was born even. As if that could of helped Mama to rest.

The only other person in the family we ever knew was Cousin Wila, and she wasn't a blood cousin anyway; she just liked people. Mama and our father met her one day at a wake, and they got to be friends. But Cousin Wila didn't want to feel she had any real friends she wasn't related to, so she always carried around a long piece of paper with her family tree on it, and the minute she met somebody nice, she would pull it out and give it a once-over. Then, if she really liked you, she could always fit you on it someplace. Our father got to be related right away. By that time, the tree was already so big he could only be a fifth cousin six times removed up in the left-hand corner. But she put him there just the same, with a side list for Mama and us three—and we all called her Cousin Wila afterwards. Cousin Wila never got married, and she switched jobs so often around the whole South, she wasn't in town much. She wrote us post cards from most everywhere, but I only remember her coming to the house for two visits—both before our father died, when I was little. She'd had a nerve cut in her neck when she was a baby, and one side of her face was twisted down. I remember taking a notice of that, and of the way her eyes blew up so big behind the thick glasses she wore. And I remember liking it when she picked me up and held me. But I never really knew her till I was grown, when I left Mama's house.

Mama never got tired telling us that all our other family was dead, even before we knew what dead meant. Course, she would get around it by saying: "gone up to the land of the Lord." She kept us all pretty confused, because the loving voice she used when she said: "land of the Lord" made it sound like a place you went for your health. I didn't catch on till the day our father told us the story about how Mama's mama passed away. He was liquored then, and when Mama found out, she nearly slapped him.

I forget exactly when I began to feel through to the truth, but nobody ever told me outright, so it probably just knitted together slow in my mind. Our father was the one who gave me the first pieces. Once every so often he would let things slip—like talking about his brother, and about one of Mama's sisters, in a way that made me think they might still be around somewhere. Our father was a man plain couldn't keep the truth to hisself.

But by the time I saw how Clarence must of been the one *behind* the truth—the first wrong egg in a dry-rot nest—Clarence already knew, and he was gone.

What I still don't know: how did we look to other people, when our family was together? What did people think, *really?* What would they of said, if they didn't have their faces to hide behind?

Supposing we stood in a line—Mama and our father, then Clarence and me and Dan. They would of seen:

First, Mama. So black she generally looked dusty. So black, ashes turned white on her hand. She had a perfect little body then, but the wrinkles all over her face seemed to pull her down shorter than she was. Mama had wrinkles far back as I can think. It was like she was trying so hard to live that she couldn't, and her face creased with the strain. Only, Mama liked for her face to be creased. She didn't want people to see her no other way. She told me she wanted people to see the real her, not just the outside—and I believed that before I was old enough to know it was just the opposite. We never saw her when she was asleep; she wouldn't allow none of us in her room then. Even our father had to keep the light out there at night. And she got up every morning before the sun did. For a long time, it was my biggest wonder if Mama kept those wrinkles while she slept.

But anyway, the wrinkles didn't make no difference in her color. Mama's color was close as black can get to night on something alive.

Our father wasn't so dark, but he was deep brown. With him it was that look of milk chocolate left out under the summer sky—the kind of skin that has a light of its own. Our father: plain Serge Morris, without no middle name. Maybe his face was too wide to be what people called *handsome*—but it was clean-slashed and whole—and for me, *handsome* would of been a poor, useless word around him.

He was a good head over Mama, and the richness of his color helped you to forget how thin his body shrank inside his clothes. You only got an idea when he moved sometimes, testing out with his feet before he put his weight on them, like a newborn animal with long, knobby legs. Then you looked and saw how much room he had in his pants. But it was more than his color that fooled you. There was something solid our father had—something his body was built around, like a wood crate around a hot stone. After people knew him, and specially if you loved him, you didn't take much notice of the crate, and you certainly didn't believe in it. You just couldn't believe the stone would keep so hot in a contraption like that. Because the solidness was inside there, and you got waves of its heat. And you plain forgot about the skeleton being on the outside.

The only extra flesh our father had was this oval-shaped bellow in front, where his stomach had settled down to make a home. That was where the stone lived. Sometimes he would cross his hands over it and look way out—and then I would know that nothing was impossible long as a man like our father could be alive. And I remember how strong he was: watching him lift the whole potbelly stove full of coal clean off the floor till the pipe broke, one day when Clarence lost his pencil under there. I remember wanting to do things for him—so he wouldn't go and give away the strength he had; so our father could go on forever. What I disremember is whether I just did that because I saw him so thin. Or if it was the last year, when his color went suddenly bright, and I felt his warm stone start to go mushy—forcing too much heat through all of him—using itself up to go out.

But our father wasn't even halfway between Mama and us three for color; the line broke with us.

What people *said* was that some kind of miracle had made us come out like we did. But their eyes squeezed thin and their faces blanked out when they looked at Clarence. Because Clarence's skin wasn't even much darker than the white men who worked all day in the port without their shirts. And the difference was in his tone more than his darkness. On a hot day, you had to see him away from the sun to catch the soft shadow that was really brown. It was a color made people squint and cover their eyes to see better. The color that looks not-quite white next to a white man, and not-quite colored next to a colored man. It was just a not-quite color in a place where you had to be something.

And Dan and me wasn't more than a shade behind him. Even our noses kept near as narrow as his—much too narrow for people on our side of the fence.

But it wasn't a miracle. It was our father's grandmother, and his great-grandfather, both, and our father told us that. Course, when he told us about each of them being a yard-child, I was too young to know exactly what he meant. And he wouldn't explain it much, he only said a yard-child is born with mixed blood. He said we should always remember it though, and I did. And the year after he died, I went next door and asked Jewel. Jewel said: "A yard-child means when a nigger girl slave went and had her dress lifted by some white man on the plantation and then got pregnant and wound up with a baby. Then they called the baby a yard-child." What our father said was that blood like that can stay in a family long as it wants to. But it's got to come out sometime, and when it does—it plain comes out.

The thing people seemed to mind even more than Clarence's color was his looks. Clarence was always beautiful. And he had it in a way that was different from anything anybody around town ever saw before. His skin held a fuzziness when the light played on it, and I can recall wanting to touch-feel where the bones came to a high curve under the outside of each eye, like the tops of bubbles just before they break. His eyes was slit longer than any I ever saw, and the heavy lids doubled the surprise of the wideness when he looked up. It wasn't a girl's face, any more than a real cat's is—but when he got to be about sixteen, Clarence started to use it in a funny way. Suddenly, a smile was waiting around his mouth and back of his eyes. A smile that was really a sneer turned in the wrong direction. It made him look like a too-beautiful girl who knows what people want her for, and is going to use just that to make them sorry. But maybe Clarence had to act like he did; maybe he thought his looks was the only thing he had left to give his color a place in the world, after he lost the one thing that was his life.

He had Mama's body, but shaped to a man: round and hard, with a big chest that cut down to a waist he could circle with his own hands. His legs pulled out smooth from the hips, with two long balloons of muscle in each. And you could see his shoulders heaving and bunching through any shirt he wore. All of Clarence's muscles sang when he walked. "Clarence the Tiger," our father called him, "Clarence the Tiger-Cat born in the city." The wrong city. Because everybody, even the white people, turned away-and-back when they saw Clarence. And when he got older, some of them didn't turn away at all.

Nobody ever got a chance to tell me I was pretty, but maybe somebody would of if it hadn't been for Clarence. Except for him, and the way Mama kept me dressed, I might of really showed up on the block. But I ain't once met a person could show up around Clarence.

The white blood didn't settle right in Dan. He started plain, and he got kind of big-faced and ugly when he was thirteen or so. Then that eased down and went back to plain again. The color just never looked alive on him: it had a dry yellowness to it. His face stayed wide as our father's from ear to ear, but the skin was drawn too tight across, and his nose didn't take up enough room there. It could of been a strong face, though—our father lent him that. Dan was cutest of the three when he was little. Course, I can't remember Clarence being very young, only he couldn't of been cute as Dan, he was always too perfect. The thing Dan had was an eye-shyness, like he was calling out to you all the time. And if anybody but Mama rested their hand on him, the beginning grin that happened made you grin to see. But those things didn't last.

In our three faces, only a thickness to our lips and the kinks in our black hair hadn't been touched by those dead white fingers. And we kept them to remind us and everybody else that we wouldn't ever be what parts of us looked like, even though we could never look all like what we were.

But what did people *think* when they saw our whole family together?

I remember how they acted to us kids, most of them.

The white people didn't want to treat us no different than they would any other colored person, but they couldn't help it: we were so light, they plain had to take us into account. And then it was like they had to make more of a point of pushing us apart than if we had been dark—like they had to push down on us harder to make the separation.

And while the white people was doing that, lots of the colored people treated us as if we were white. Specially when they got mad. Course, they got mad pretty easy, because they had a lot to get mad about. They could take out on us what they couldn't on a real white person: we were enough on the other side—and enough not—to be different without being dangerous. Then some of them sidled up and made friends, with a smile that meant they really wanted to be light as us—not like the *blacks*. That burned me worse than anything, I could of knocked those ones. The colored people eased off on us when we grew up and they saw we lived the same as them. But somewhere in the backs of their minds, a lot of them never seemed to stop thinking we might of found a way to get born like we did on purpose.

And sometimes, even the white people would look at us with strange eyes.

Mama said our blood and our color made the cross which God put on us in this life. And she said if we could just *get through* this life, we would have a home in the next one. She was trying to teach us not to expect a rightful home in this world; wanting us to twist into a triple daisy chain that could dance to its own music, so we wouldn't need the world any more than it needed us; trying to teach us not to care about this life—just to live it—not to care.

And how can a mother teach her kids *not* to care?

We learned what she meant, though. And the others like us learned. There was a family with light kids three and a half blocks down on St. Thomas Street, and one beyond them—they got taught not to make friends too. It was the first lesson you had, when you didn't belong to either part: when you didn't *belong* anywhere. We learned to be outsiders everyplace we went, and we only had ourselves to grow up with.

But Clarence was number one, in time and looks. I think the truth was, right after he was born, our father's family and what was left of Mama's got ideas about the baby's color. Even if they all knew the real reason—maybe they didn't believe that was enough. And then, probably, everybody else in Atlanta got to whispering and wondering. All I know for sure is, when Clarence was five months old, Mama and our father left everybody and everything there, and came to New Orleans to begin a new life. They covered their tracks some way, and they forgot about the past, or tried to. Because they both had dreams, and they wanted to go to a new place where they could let them out into the open, without worries nor fears. But they never got rid of the worries, and the dreams was made of fear. And on through too many years—closed in and waiting—those fear-dreams curdled and went bad. See: that is where the poison came from.

I guess I'll never know what would of come to pass if Mama had just let the world teach us our lesson. It would of been hard, sure—only not as hard as what she did. But Mama couldn't let us find out from the world how to live. She was too scared. So much, she wrapped us in her wings and crushed down. So scared we might get hurt, she did the hurt herself. Sometimes, broken love can be worse than the thing that breaks it—and sometimes it can even be worse than no love at all. Or is the mother bird who never comes back to a nest that's been fingered better than the one who does come back to kill her young? I don't know. When a mother is so scared for her babies she can't think—what does a mother do?

Mama tried to put it all on Jesus. "The Lord is the knower, and He is the powerful One," she would say. "Go along His way, and thou will come to no evil." (Cross Him, and look out.) But then, Mama always had religion, bad. It was the door on her fear, and it got thicker as the fear grew. Only, grew ain't the right word. Spread, maybe. Maybe you would say it spread, like a cancer, till it lived under the skin in every inch of her body—till it knotted the knuckles in her hands and glued her shoulder-bones together, so she stooped for breath.

But that was afterwards. Everything was afterwards: none of it started to happen till our father died.

Our father was a different kind of a person. He was real—loving-real. He was something of a real man.

It's funny I never saw him cook; I never even tasted anything he made. But people said there wasn't a cook in town could come near him. And it wasn't because he had any secret recipes—he just knew how to put food together to get as much of any dish tasting exactly the way people craved it as he had to. Course, Mama was good as you might want herself, but I don't think she could ever of done regular for a couple hundred people at one time, like our father. Probably one of the reasons he was so fine was he hated doing it so much. It was just a nasty business with him. Sometimes when he came home from the restaurant at night Mama would have to make him a sandwich, because he hadn't eaten all day. And when he ate it he wouldn't look at it—he got so he couldn't stand the sight of food close up. He worked in the same restaurant for nine years before he got Cousin Wila to find him a job in a private house. He stayed there for a year, and then he went to another restaurant. After that was when he started quitting regular to go someplace else—always because somebody told him it would be better. But there was only three or four top restaurants in New Orleans, and when he finished with them, he began to get less and less money. It was when he was thinnest that he went back to his first job, and then they didn't pay him much as they had before, account of he'd worked in too many other places. That was two years before he died, when he started drinking. It took him a whole eleven months to get fired for it.

But our father wasn't truly scared of anything, not even Mama. No, the fear took a different way with him.

Afterwards I let myself wonder why he started drinking like that. Course, I was too young to know, in words—but maybe I felt the reason. Anyway, I kept a count of everything Mama told him, even when I knew she was wrong. "Months and months of liquor," she used to say, "you got months and months of liquor in you, and you going to drown in devil-water for the Lord to flush you clean." She said it all through that last year, day after day. Then he got his attack and died.

But the Coroner's doctor *told* Mama it wasn't only liquor had killed our father. He said: "Ma'am, a man plain can't drink hisself off the map. Not in that short a time, leastways."

Mama wouldn't argue with the police. She said: ". . . Can't?"

"No, ma'am. Not in three years. Why, if all the drunks I know . . ."

I said: "He wasn't no *drunk*." It was a word meant something bad to me.

The doctor asked: "What, little girl?"

"Shut your mouth," Mama said, low. Her hand turned into a lump on the table.

"Well," said the doctor, "you just keep in mind, ma'am, if he didn't have nothing wrong with him in the first place, the liquor wouldn't of done what it did."

Mama clamped her mouth together and looked down.

The doctor got on his feet. I couldn't figure why he mopped his face with a handkerchief, it wasn't the hot time of the year. Then he tucked his shirt in, and turned to Clarence. "Well, son," he said, "looks like you the man in the family now . . . ain't you, boy?"

Clarence took his shoulder from under the doctor's hand, and made a sound like a hiss. "What *man*?" he said. "And what *family*?" He cut out quick through the door. But he didn't swing over the gallery railing, like always, to pad away so silent you never knew he was gone. That day he walked careful down the three steps, dragging his feet after him.

With my eyes on the doctor, I listened to the Cat drag his feet.

The other thing Mama used to tell our father was about his drinking being the fault of *"them books."* She said that because he got a hold of them the same year he started on the liquor.

And maybe the two did have something to do with each other; only, not like Mama thought.

Somebody left them in the restaurant, and never came back. But nobody there had any use for them, and they was too old to sell. So after a couple months, a waiter tripped over one and spilled a plate of soup, and the restaurant owner got mad and threw them both at our father.

They didn't seem to mean much of anything to him for the first few weeks. He just left them on the floor of the closet in his and Mama's bedroom. Then, one Sunday, Dan and me came back from the levee and we found him sitting holding them in his lap. The top one was open, and our father was staring up the air with a new look on his face. For a time after that, he only took them out on the gallery late at night, after we were in bed. I was supposed to be asleep, but I watched from the window. He sat real quiet, mouthing each word to hisself, voiceless. He only got away with it about an hour every night, before Clarence opened up his bed in the kitchen and complained on account of the gallery light—or Mama just got tired keeping awake in the dark, waiting on him. Then he would close them and hold them tight in the bend of his left arm while he turned out the light and went in.

Course, there wasn't nothing at all strange about our father sitting out on the gallery, only he hadn't ever stayed so late. But always when he came home from work, and on his days off, I can remember him sitting there and singing at us and telling a story. Sing *at* is right, too, because he tried not to give the idea he was doing it *for* you. He just sort of did it. While the big summer mosquitoes and the gnats sailed over our heads, he would talk, and sing a while, and tell a story or talk again. He never looked at you then; he concentrated on the camphor tree near the corner. And the only way you could tell he was doing it for you was that he stopped doing it if you went away—and if you came back, he would start off again at that exact point. He had a batch of songs he could riffle through in his mind, to pick out the one he wanted. The story was nearly always the same, though. He might start it different, and it might have different names, or different people sometimes. But it was only a different story once or twice; most generally he came back to the same one. Clarence put up with it, and anything our father did would of been all right with me. Little Dan used to get upset, though, when he'd been listening all anxious with both ears, and then it started to get familiar.

"*Stop*," Dan told him, "now you *stop*."

"Why?" said our father.

"You going to make it the same story."

"Well?" said our father.

"Well, *don't*," Dan said.

"I can't help it," said our father, "if that was the way it happened."

". . . Couldn't of happened that way *all* those times."

"Why not? Now, who is telling this story?"

"You is," Dan said.

"You want to tell it?"

"No. But I plain don't want to *hear* it that way."

Then our father might change it around and make up something else. Mostly not, though. Mostly, the story stayed the same.

It wasn't till a little more than two years before he died that he started reading to us. First, he only did it once every week or so. Then it got to be more and more often—maybe the more he drank. And finally, it was always—every night of the world—except in winter. He came home from work about seven-thirty, with his coat over his arm and his food and the liquor in him. Mama had already fed us. He went inside, and if he was *really* liquored, he would bow to her. Otherwise, he wouldn't pay her no mind at all, unless she was in a good or a bad mood enough to tell him good evening, and then he would answer her back the same thing in a long half-whisper. He put his coat on a hanger in his closet, as careful as he was liquored, and if he brushed it off too, you knew he couldn't hardly stand up; he went and unlocked the two *books* from the special drawer where he kept them, and came and sat in the gray wood rocking chair on the gallery, where Dan and Clarence was usually waiting.

I waited earlier. Soon as I saw him round the corner onto Millicent, I ran to him. He stopped walking when I got near, and he said: "Yooooop," not finishing the word till I was in his arms and swinging up, higher than his head—then down, laughing, to kiss him and be kissed, and on my feet to hold his big hot-earth hand all the way to the house. I went right with him to the closet—to unlock the drawer with the key that was always in his pocket—back out to the gallery. I waited for that all day long. I think, in a way, it was what I lived for.

One of the *books* was named *Alice in Wonderland; Through the Looking-Glass. By Lewis Carroll,* and the other was *John Keats, Poetical Works.* But our father never called them *books,* and he wouldn't let us do it neither. Our father said when a man writes a thing like that, when he tears his soul from his guts and puts it down on paper, then the thing ain't a *book;* it's the man hisself. It's the everlasting soul the preachers talk about, saved from death and from time, and kept from heaven, so every person that ever lives can always know what it is, inside the body, that makes a man. And sitting there on the gallery, our father said those two gentlemen was with us closer and more than they'd been even with their mamas when their lungs could still use breath—and the least we could do was to call them by their right names. So they was just Mr. Carroll and Mr. Keats.

Mama wouldn't ever come out on the gallery when Mr. Carroll and Mr. Keats was there. She claimed a lot of reasons: that it was against the Lord to believe you got a soul before He did; that there was bound to be slews of bad thoughts hidden in amongst those big words nobody could understand; that our father was so liquored up he didn't know what he was talking about in the first place, and nothing that was any good could stand to come out of his mouth with alcohol on it. But I think the real reason was that the way our father talked about those two white gentlemen being actually out there on the gallery communing with us kind of gave her the creeps. It was the reason she allowed it, anyway. And there was enough *thees* and *thys* and *thous* thrown in with the poems to remind her of the Bible, so she figured it couldn't really be all bad. She sat on her kitchen chair behind the screen door, sewing, and she said she never listened, but I knew she did.

Mama had a thing of her own, though. Two things: the wind-up victrola she brought with her from Atlanta, and her record, "Thank God for a Garden." She would play that any time during the day she felt like it, whenever it came to her mind. I got so sick of "Thank God for a Garden" I used to dream about it. Sometimes I still do. I don't know which was worse: the lady soprano who sang it, or the violin that tried to stick with her. Her voice was so high and squeaky, if the window was open, she could collect a whole pack of stray dogs sometimes. Course, the violin helped too. It was just as high as she was, and the two of them sort of wavered back and forth up there, off-key. Then, the victrola was old, and it had what our father called the "pernicious everlasting hiccups," so it made the whole thing just that much nicer.

The song went:

"Thank God for a garden,
And for the fish in the sea;
Thank God for a garden,
He made them for you and me."

I disremember the other part, but it wasn't much different. Our father always said if the man who wrote *that* was willing *his* soul to mankind, Jesus could of stayed off the cross.

Once when our father was real liquored, he came home from work early and staggered into the kitchen while Mama had the record on. Must of been six o'clock or so, because we were still eating. He jerked the record from the victrola without taking the arm off first, and the needle shrieked up and then thumped on the turntable and scratched harsh there till it slowed down and quit. Mama had a forkful of turnip greens part way in her mouth, and she held it right there, her jaw set open. Our father raised the record in his right hand. You could see he meant to smash it on the floor. He threw his head back and looked down till the whites of his eyes shone in milky moons, and then he stuck his chin out and turned to Mama. But Mama didn't say a word. She didn't have to. She just sat, with her mouth carved over the turnip greens. They say some people have eyes that go right through you. Mama's didn't. Mama's got as far as your insides and spread around there. Our father used to say when she took to looking like that, she could stop a Jax beer truck. Anyway, she stopped him. He let his hand come down, and he slid the record over the table to clink on the milk pitcher. Then he bowed low to Mama and weaved into the bedroom. He was so long hanging his coat up, I knew he was brushing it off. We heard the screech of the springs when he fell on the bed.

Mama lifted the turnip greens out of her mouth, and picked up her plate. She went over to the old bucket we used for an ash can, and she dumped all the greens and scraped the plate clean. One of Mama's rules was that you never threw food away, unless it was poisoned, or unless you got a sign that somebody close to you just died. So we all knew what that meant, far as she was concerned.

"Pray for him and for his soul," she said. "And pray for your own souls, for God to deliver you from all sin, and from weakness, and from *al-co-hol.*"

We sat and made a silent prayer for our father, while Mama prayed out loud. Mama's prayer lasted a good fifteen minutes, and before she was finished, our father called in from the bedroom to say he would like it a whole lot better if she would please put the record back on. But it was scratched pretty bad, and Mama went out the next day and bought three of them, and hid two in the house.

The most important thing our father and me had together, besides the way we both felt about "Thank God for a Garden," was our love for his reading from those two gentlemen. Dan and Clarence didn't mind it none, but I don't think it ever hit them very deep; not like his story or his songs. It was just something strong in back of them— something to lean on, but something they took more notice of when it finished than while it was there. I was the only one to keep a notice of it from the first day.

When he read a poem, our father wouldn't allow no stopping to ask what anything meant till you had the sound of it all in you. Because he said if you broke off to do that then you couldn't really sense it. And a poem was a sensing-thing, so it wasn't made to go straight into your head; only if you felt it first. Like a song, but with the music inside the words instead of the other way around. In the beginning you had to hear it over and over, till you got the music out to love. *Then* you could wonder.

Slews of times, there was a word our father didn't know hisself. I could tell because he would see it coming, and slow up, and press down on the beat till that carried him through. I could hear it in his voice: he used the pulse of the poem to keep him from stumbling.

Anyway, to start with, he would only read from those two gentlemen when he had the right feeling (that he didn't used to need liquor for), and if Mama was in a let-live mood. It didn't get to be regular till after that bad winter, when I was eleven, and Dan nine, and Clarence fifteen and a half.

Course, our father never even talked in the winter nights. Winter was for Mama; that was her time. It was when she could shut us all in, and have us there, safe from everything and everybody—except herself. Only, I don't remember it for her. I remember it by our father's eyes, moving, switching, blinking, never still. We all stayed there with him waiting in the kitchen where five people's breath and body heat mixed together to hold thick around us; our father with an open newspaper he had already read, waiting, waiting for the winter to pass. And most of all, I remember that one bad winter, when a baby dog somebody had thrown away crawled under our house and started its life there. (Hearing it scrounge around trying to get away from the cold; wanting more than anything to take it in and warm it; knowing it could smell the food, and not being able to swallow myself; seeing the question flush wet in Dan's round eyes, and knowing the answer that was waiting in Mama's.) Waiting. All of us, waiting.

And then early spring, and the promise of newness, and the wide life. The dog was still there—mean now, but still there. We hid scraps from Mama and saved them to throw at him. But he never would come near any of us. Not after that winter.

And one night when our father came home, after he opened the screen door, he tightened his hand over mine. I knew something was up. And in we went, and out we came with Mr. Carroll and Mr. Keats.

Clarence was sitting where he always used to, on the railing. He had one foot up, teaching Dan how to double-knot a shoelace.

Mama was in her chair on the other side of the door, cooling off after supper and shelling black-eyed peas for the next day's lunch. She said: "Serge, I ain't in no capacity for that this evening."

Our father sat down and stretched. He told me: "Hunch up on my knee a while, Lucille, till it gets tired."

I climbed on.

Mama stood on her feet. "Maybe you didn't hear me," she said. "I *hope* you didn't hear me."

"I heard you," said our father. "And Mr. Carroll and Mr. Keats done heard you too."

I was beginning to be able to tell one liquor from another on his breath. This time it was gin. When it was gin, it wasn't no use to argue with our father. If he had a feeling-point, that is.

Mama said: "You is in a *condition* again."

Our father smiled.

Then she gritted out: "On top of everything else I married, I got a man ain't fit to touch his own children."

But he kept his smile. "If I didn't know it was love that was killing you," said our father, soft, "I sometimes think I would do it myself."

"Clarence," said Mama, "take my chair inside."

Clarence did.

Our father opened Mr. Keats and read:

> " 'Two or three posies
> With two or three simples—

> Two or three noses
> With two or three pimples—
> Two or three wise men . . .' "

"Simples," said Mama, "and noses, and pimples. Teaching them things to children."

Our father looked up. "You going inside?" he asked.

"The Lord knows I am."

"Yes. Just watch you don't step on Mr. Carroll." Our father had him laid out on a handkerchief next to the rocking chair.

Mama jumped. "I ain't stepping on nobody," she said, "what I can't see with my own bare eyes."

Our father sat and waited.

Mama told him: "I am going inside for one last time, but . . ."

"I think," said our father, "you better get yourself used to going inside, if you don't like the company out here on this gallery."

"Ain't nobody going to be on my gallery that I don't . . ."

"I think," said our father, "this gallery might be pretty crowded from now on."

"Not if I burn them *books* once and for all. Ain't nobody going to crowd up on my gallery if . . ."

Our father said, quiet: "I don't think you better do that." His voice had the same funny ring as when he first told us about those two gentlemen.

Mama bent over and picked up both pans—the one with the peas, and the shallower one with the pods. She handed them through to Clarence, and then stiff-legged in and pulled the screen door to behind her. It popped open again, soon as she let it go; it always did, since the spring first broke.

Our father never stopped smiling while he finished the poem.

After that it was different. Even the next December was different. Because we all knew Mr. Carroll and Mr. Keats was just keeping out of the cold, same as us. And for me, it was because the soothing liquor had begun to take that winter-wild blink out of our father's eyes.

But the spring nights—the wonderful, easy spring nights, two years before the scissored end of our father's life that started ours. All of us together then, a real family: our father and me; those two gentlemen; Dan and Clarence; and Mama inside. Mama in her right place. Mama like she should of been—hazed off—there and not there. Keeping watch, but half checkered-out behind the screen, so the closer to her you sat the less of her you could see—like a sometimes dream you can believe in when you know you are only dreaming.

And the moon with us. Truly with us. Palest green, throwing crooked shadows on the lap of my skirt from the swollen wood fingers of our bush that was aching to bloom. (That white-flowering bush nobody knew the name of when it grew like a weed one winter in the mouth of the empty lot next door.)

I remember sitting, holding the moon in my lap, and knowing it was on my face too. Leaning back against our father's legs, and letting my eyelids down to feel the moon touch there. The real moon—the realest thing of all, because it could touch but couldn't *be* touched—stroking me cool into its strong sleep.

Hearing some cricket's voice drift out of my mind as it called one stupid, squeaking question to the green moon.

And our father's deep, gentle voice—liquor-slow—telling me:

" 'Asleep! O sleep a little while, white pearl!
And let me kneel, and let me pray to thee,
And let me call Heaven's blessing on thine eyes,
And let me breathe into the happy air,
That doth enfold and touch thee all about,
Vows of my slavery, my giving up,
My sudden adoration, my great love!' "

It was the year after that our father lost his job.

Two men from the restaurant carried him home. He was laughing, happy, to hisself, and he had been sick on the lapel of his cook's linen jacket. They brought him in, one of them holding his ankles, and the other's wrists looped under his armpits; his own coat was folded over his stomach, clean. Our father hung down so loose they had to bump him up the three steps and across the gallery to let him rest on the kitchen floor.

Mama dropped her spatula and swung fast to face the blank wall next to the stove. She put her hands behind her hips, with the elbows sticking out, and she raised her head high before she said: "Right on through is the bed."

The two men took our father in and laid him out over it. Then they came back and fidgeted near the front door. One of them had the white jacket bunched in his hand.

Mama held like she was. Finally, she told them: "Thank you kindly. Now get out."

The men did, quick and stumbling.

I went to Mama and slipped between her and the stove. I was going to tell her not to cry. But she wasn't crying. I stood and watched the look on her face—the angry, hateful look that pointed out at one sharp spot too small to be true—the look I didn't understand yet then.

Five days later Mama started to take in washing. She got as much work as she wanted right away, too. Mama hated dirt. She could leave stuff better looking than if it came from the store, and when word got around from one customer to another, soon she had to turn laundry away from some of the richest white families that sent it over with a maid. She could afford to turn it away then because our father had a little money saved up from his fifteen years' work, over and above what was needed for the monthly payments on the house, and he took some out of the bank each week. That was all right, he said, because soon as he found work again he would put it all back. Only, our father never found work again.

I washed too, but Mama wouldn't let me help her with the ironing at first. I was only eleven, and ironing was a thing she always liked to do herself. Besides, I was going to school.

School was my other love, after our father. There was only one more light girl in my class, and she was pretty awful. But I didn't mind her, and I didn't mind the way they looked at us, because school meant too much to me. It was where I could find out things— where they *wanted us to learn*. Not like Mama, trying to keep the world away from us, hating it if we ever asked questions about anything, teaching us that wondering was bad. Course, our father wasn't that way, but even he couldn't really explain a thing if Mama was in hearing distance, without having to whisper. School was where you didn't have to whisper. Or feel bad. It was where you didn't even have to ask: where you *went* to get *told*. School meant learning was right, because the more you got, the more they praised you. And if you did want to ask, they didn't think it was dirty there—even though they had too many kids in a class for you to be able to do it much as you might want. So I saved up my questions, and I pieced them out maybe twice a week. And the day I knew it was my turn to ask, I would skip all the way. Getting the answer to one of my questions at school made me feel good inside, and it made me feel something close to free.

Till our father died, and Clarence and me had to quit so he could get a full-time job and I could help Mama take in more washing. Mama made Dan quit then too, just for the good of it. Course, Dan didn't mind about school. And I don't think Clarence minded much about our father's dying, except for what he had to do because of it. But I lost my two loves at once.

Our father went out almost seven times a week, after Mama began to work. He said he was only looking for a job, and I think he really started out with that on his mind, in the morning. Only, when he came home, he was generally in the condition. And after a while, the condition changed. His body got to be so sogged with liquor, it couldn't un-sponge—and he softened, living in a kind of lazy haze, drifting along to death. Course, Dan and me couldn't really know that was what was happening. We only felt his strength melt all into this warm buzz, like a fresh morning's idea under the heavy, bug-aired sun that hangs late to play out the end of a summer's day.

I think Clarence knew, though.

Clarence said: "No, I don't want to talk to you. I plain won't talk to you, like you is."

"*Are,*" said our father, "like you *are.* Should practice to talk right, whoever you going to talk to."

Clarence told him: "I don't give a whang in hoot and hell."

But he did. He was close on to sixteen then, just finished the eleventh grade at school, and he could talk awful well when he wanted. I think he could really talk a lot better than our father, because our father quit school when he was ten. With Clarence it was more than the years, though. He was just as famous at school for his brain as he was for his looks. And he spoke about someday being a *scientist.* Nobody had ever heard of a colored kid expecting to be a thing like that, leastways not around where we lived. Not many kids even stayed in school up to the eleventh grade. By then the classes was cut down from fifty-seven in mine to only three in Clarence's. All the other kids his age was working. Clarence worked some too, delivering papers, only he stuck it out at school. And worse still, the word was that he could tell you more about numbers and things than either Miss Sater, the Monday-Wednesday-Friday teacher, or

Miss Petit, the Tuesday-Thursday teacher. People said it wasn't right to have a mind like his. Even the teachers said he could of been finished school two years ago if he'd wanted to. But Clarence didn't want to. He kept right on asking for extra homework and borrowing books to study on his own. Then, he was so quiet, most everybody got the idea he looked down on them. I guess he did, in a way. He sure wouldn't have nothing to do with any of the girls who eyed him around, and he studied by hisself all through the summer.

So there was heaps of reasons people took a dislike for Clarence: he was too light, and he was too beautiful, and he was too stuck-up, and his mind was too quick, and he knew too much. The thing was, you never could be quite sure *how* much, with him. He even gave me the feeling sometimes he was trying to talk wrong on purpose around us. I think that was what scared people a little.

Our father said: "Seems to me you been acting kind of cut-off lately."

Clarence swung away, sitting in his place on the railing. He was copying numbers called *algebra* out of a book onto a piece of paper, with that extra-sharp pencil he always carried. Clarence did a lot of numbers, and he was special about his pencil. He kept the point so fine it chipped if you looked at it, and then he really raised Cain. That was the only way you could get a live rise out of Clarence, if you went after his pencil or one of the books Miss Sater loaned him over the summer. Otherwise, he kept what he felt pretty much to hisself. Clarence was the strange one, even then.

Summer was curling in its own heat: I remember the crickets whiling up the baked air. Must of been real late in the afternoon, because Clarence was long back from delivering papers, and his bike was already cleaned off and leaning against the wall in the kitchen. That was the summer he paid the last installment on it, just before it broke down.

I was there, and Dan too, but not Mr. Carroll nor Mr. Keats. Mama was inside cooking supper. I could smell her unlid the stew all the way out on the gallery.

Our father said: "Ain't no call to get set up like that. Ain't nobody said a fool thing. I just asked you how your studies was going."

"Ain't," said Clarence, still making numbers.

"Ain't," said our father, "is a perfectly *good* . . . *living* . . . *word.*"

". . . Is?"

"English language done changed, son. Like *thee* and *thou*. *Thee* and *thou* went out, and *ain't* came in."

"That's right," Clarence whispered, "they even teach it in school."
Our father squinted at him. "They might not," he said. "But they
don't teach a lot of things in school."

". . . They teach *ain't*," said Clarence. He turned his paper over
and copied something on the clean side.

Our father started again: "If you went on studying hard . . ."

"Studying. In that school."

"Good enough for Lucille and Dan."

Clarence said: "But not for me."

". . . School's got two teachers."

"Two *whole* teachers."

"And don't the teachers talk right?"

Clarence made a careful number on the paper. "Prissy," he said,
"not right."

Our father frowned hard to think through his haze. "I was going
to say, if you studied lots, maybe they could send you on to some
other school."

Clarence went on figuring.

"Must be some school would fit you."

"A few. One over in Dallas."

". . . For colored people?"

Clarence said: "For colored people."

"Good," said our father, "then that's the place to go. Soon as you
finish up here."

Clarence laid his pencil exact along the center of the book, and
put his hand over it. Then he leaned around to look at our father.
"Course," he said, "costs money."

"That don't matter none," said our father. "If you want it with your
guts, that don't matter."

"And who is going to make a living for everybody around here?
With his guts?"

"Don't you worry none. I can still get work. *I* can get it."

"Sure. How . . . long you planning to be around to get it?"

Our father made a whishing sound through his teeth. "I'm just
taking money out the bank to give myself a rest. Do I look like I'm
dying?"

Clarence stared at him.

"Well. *Do* I?"

Real easy, Clarence said: "What I always liked about you is, you
tell a good story."

Our father backed the look for a second. Then his head sank

down slow, as if it was weighted. "I'm glad," he said. "I was beginning to think there wasn't nothing you liked about me."

"Yes," said Clarence, "you tell a good story. Even the same story
you always tell. I like it."

Our father coughed and kept staring at the floor.

"I mean that," Clarence said. And he did. You could tell by his
voice. The way he was watching our father then, I almost thought
Clarence might of wanted to reach out and hold him. But he turned
back to his book, fast, and picked up his pencil.

Dan asked: "You mean the story about Florabelle?"

Clarence was lost in his numbers, and our father was studying
the floor so hard, I said: "Yes, honey, that's the one."

"I like that story too," Dan said, "even when I'm plain sick of it.
I really like it. I like the part when they go riding in that horse-and-
buggy, and the wind brushes up her hair. I just like it when the wind
brushes up . . ."

Our father's voice came sudden, from somewhere out of his
stomach. By the time it hit the air, it was a growl. It said: *"Do* I look
like I'm dying?"

Clarence must of been doing some hard figuring, because he had
to take a couple seconds to finish. Then: "Not dying," he said.
". . . Dead."

(Mama yelled: *"In to eat now."*)

"Who's dead?" Dan asked.

"Nobody," said our father. He raised his head and shook it in
jerks, like a person coming up out of water. "Nobody. Ain't nobody
dead. Nobody."

"What does dead mean?" from Dan again.

I grabbed him by the arm. "Don't pay Clarence no mind," I said,
"he's just talking about those numbers he draws all the time. Better
go in and clean off some of that dirt before Mama sees it."

But Dan told me: "Look, Cille . . . look how cold your hand is
in the summer."

Our father sat forward. His face went fierce with the effort when
he said: "One thing you got to know, Tiger. One thing, only one
thing. Just remember this: whatever you want to do, you do it.
There's a way. There's always a way. There's a way, there's a way.
Be what you want to be, in this life. Always . . . in *this* life. *Be that.*"

Folding his paper, Clarence asked: "What did *you* want to be?"

"Oh," said our father, "not like me."

"What *did* you want to be?"

Our father slumped back and let the buzz come in again. "Shhh," he said, rocking there. "Hush . . . Not like me."

(Mama: *"I said in to eat."*)

Clarence got up. "I knew there wasn't no use talking to you no more, like you . . . *are*. What you care what I want to be? What you care about anything?"

"Care?" Our father's eyes closed, and his voice burned, deep: "God, I care. All I ever did was care. Boy, you can't take that away from me. Mother-child, not that, oh no indeed, not . . . that too."

"Clarence, you quit nastying him," I said. "Boy, you stop."

But by the time I finished, he had already curved past me and gone into the kitchen.

Only, see: Clarence knew.

Dan was too young—he was only just ten the year our father left us. Too young, that is, to know what things was *supposed* to mean. And too young not to feel what they really meant.

The first thing, the big thing Dan couldn't understand, was why the world was such a careful not-place. Why it was always *don't*.

Mama told us: "Don't play with them black kids, they might could pick on you for being so light—Don't talk to no white kid, ever—Don't use bad words like the kids use at school—Don't stay on after school, come right home—Don't ask no questions, only the Lord knows all the answers, and He don't like for you to ask—Don't be thinking too much—Don't go believing in yourself, believe in the Lord—Don't be dirty—Don't be sick—Don't *be* . . ."

—And more, always more. Every day there was a new one.

When the outside world is a don't, you got to have an inside world: you got to *have* a world. Clarence had his studies, then. I had our father and school, and washing, and three men to help Mama tend. But Dan didn't like school: he couldn't forget the don'ts long enough. Course, he did have our father. For a while.

The afternoon when Dan wandered off the gallery must of been around a month later, at the end of that summer.

Mama was inside ironing, or he wouldn't of dared. I had just finished helping with the wash, and I was sitting next to our father, on Clarence's part of the gallery railing. Clarence was delivering papers.

Some boys from the St. Thomas Street gang had been playing fast tag on the corner across the street. They was all closer to my age than Dan's, but I could see he was getting ideas. He kept walking up and down the three steps off the gallery, and each time he would finish a little further away from the house, standing and watching. Then he would come back and do it again.

I knew how bad he wanted to play, but Mama had ruled out the St. Thomas Street gang. They had a bad name, and there wasn't one of them near as light as us—and anyhow, it was plain *no*. That meant I couldn't tell him to go on and get in the game. But I wasn't going to tell him to stop, neither.

When he got as far as across the street, a house up from where the kids was, he didn't come back. He put his hands together behind him, and made like he was all interested in hopping on one foot and kicking a stone along the sidewalk. I knew what he was aiming at; I turned and faced the other way, towards the corner of Farnay. Didn't seem like those kids was going to hurt him none, and he wanted it so bad.

I listened to our father read, and I ran my eyes down the jagged cement of our sidewalk, past the empty lot. Mama's other pleasure, second to her bathroom, was living on a street with actual cement sidewalks. They had them all around our neighborhood, even though the streets was just gravel and dirt and crushed oyster shells, bumpy with ruts. I used to wonder if the streets only looked so terrible bumpy in a place as flat as New Orleans. I bet it's the flattest place on the map. And not just the city—the whole countryside is flat. We learned about mountains and valleys at school, and from the picture show when we got to be old enough to go; but before then we had to be satisfied with sneaking a couple quick looks at that great big hill the WPA spaded up in Audubon Park so the white kids and the animals could know what one was. Apart from that hill, though, and the levee, the only really *un-*flat thing I could locate around town was our sidewalks. They was more than bumpy. They had cracked and buckled a long time ago to let the crab grass stretch, and when it didn't rain you could walk easier in the street. Those sidewalks are mostly gone now, and I never did figure out why they got put there in the first place, unless somebody was planning on building a district for white people to live in, and then had their mind changed. The only bodies who walked our sidewalks on a dry day was Mama and the ants. I asked our father why the ants did it, but he said they went around carrying pieces of bread that weighed up to five times as much as theirselves anyhow, so you could never really tell what an ant might do. Mama did it because she said if the Lord meant for sidewalks to be put there for that, then that was what you did on them. Not someplace else.

Anyway, I was watching the sidewalk, and our father was reading from Mr. Keats, something for a gold god name of Apollo. Then he began on a long poem I already knew the sound of, and I got lost in his voice. Our father had a voice you could do that with. It rolled and tingled and hushed up the day. First, it was something you held on to, and then it was all over you—a world of itself. It was morning and midnight in one, the sun around the moon, and it was the only thing that was important, while it was.

When a poem was long, and nothing happened to stop him, our father pushed the beat of it right *into* the day. Then the buzz of the bugs, and the crickets' rasp—even a locust's scream, or the inch-and-a-half noise a half-inch tree frog makes—or a bicycle bell, or a dog that coughed in the distance—anything and everything sucked clean out of the slow air and fell together around the beat in our father's voice, till his voice was all you could hear, and the day was his too. But then, if something did happen to stop him, in the middle of a poem, it wasn't just a voice that let up. It was the only middle of things: the magnet-beat of *be*, turned off. And all the sounds zoomed out again, running free now, louder than their natural selves. They clashed wild against each other, out there in nothing. They ran, clashing, and each one trying to find the rightful place that it held before our father taught them all a new beat and a new meaning. But they couldn't ever find it, those sounds; not unless our father started again where he'd left off.

Because when our father's voice stopped, there just *wasn't* no more meaning to what was.

Mama said: "Everybody out there?" She was standing at the window.

The voice cut off, and our father turned to look at me, with his lips pointed round.

"More or less," I said. I listened for Dan or the gang. They were gone.

"That ain't no kind of answer. Where's Daniel and Clarence?"

"*Clarence* got to be a big boy now," our father said. And I knew then that he had seen Dan slip away, same as me.

Mama asked: "Meaning what?"

"Working," I said, fast, "out with his papers."

"Working, or just riding around?"

Clarence had this habit of coming back to where we lived, after he got through delivering the evening papers to the white people, and then passing us right by. Sometimes he would do that two or three times, always looking straight ahead, without even turning to see which of us might be on the gallery. It was like he couldn't make up his mind to stop the bike and come home.

I waited to answer Mama, because our father had his mouth open to say something, but he only shut it and shook his head.

Mama said: "I done asked you if he was *working* or *just riding around*."

"Don't know," I said. "Must be working, I ain't seen him since he left."

"He got Daniel with him on the handle bars again?"

"He's working," I said, "sure he's working. You can still see the whole sun over Miss Roberta's house."

Our father said again: "Clarence got to be a big boy now."

"When you said that before, you hear me ask *meaning what?*"

"Oh, he can suffer along by hisself."

Mama said low: "He still *my* boy, Serge."

"Yes he is," said our father, "that he is."

Mama asked me: "He take Daniel with him?"

"Not since you told him not to," I said.

"Where *is* Daniel?"

"Playing."

"*Where?*"

I looked over the length of the gallery to the empty lot next door. But I tried to keep from telling the lie with my mouth. I said: "Only a couple places he can play."

"Well, you keep your eye out and let me know every so often like I told you. He don't have Clarence's pencil, do he?"

"No, ma'am. Clarence got it with him. Clarence can really ride around a long time steady."

"I know all about him. I'm talking about Daniel. You just keep an eye out, and make sure he don't snitch that pencil when Clarence comes back. You know what went on last time."

Our father said: "Mr. Keats is holding his breath."

". . . *Why?*" When Mama got took by surprise, she believed it for true.

"You just bust in on him," said our father.

"Bust in *on him?* I talk in my own house *any time of the day.*"

"That you do," said our father.

"Making like them *books* is real."

"They are . . . realer than real."

Mama said: "One thing you can just tell Mr. Keats. Tell him I found another bottle in my closet, and tell him I emptied that bottle and put bleach water in it." (Mama allowed our father to keep one key around the house—the one to his private drawer—and she only let him have that one because she knew he wouldn't hide no liquor in with those two gentlemen. He hadn't learned to slip his bottles under the gallery yet, and she located about one a week under something. But anyhow, our father did most of his drinking outside when he went to look for work, and he never even let us see him uncork it.) "Tell that to Mr. Keats," Mama said. "Tell him *that* while he still holding his breath." She walked back to her ironing.

Our father sighed, twice. He waited for the air to clear, and went on with the poem. It didn't have but a page more, though, and he put down Mr. Keats and picked up Mr. Carroll. Then he remembered he had skipped the poem I liked best of Mr. Keats; he grinned at me and took a hold of him again.

Lord knows I didn't want to leave our father there, only I was getting worried about Dan. I knew by the late light he must of been gone way over an hour. The sun was beginning to go big and flat—deep orange, with a watery rim—getting ready to slide down out of sight.

Then I heard Mama winding up her victrola, and I knew there was going to be trouble about something, any which way.

Our father read :

"'I stood tip-toe upon a little hill,
The air was cooling, and so very still,
That the sweet buds . . .'"

Mama played:

"*Thaaaaank* God for a garden . . ."

Our father shut his eyes and shuddered. He screwed up his face, and sat on through the record looking like he just swallowed upwards of a tank of Pluto Water. But he sat through it all right. Only when Mama put the needle right back at the start, that was too much. He got up and steadied hisself on the railing a second, and went over to the screen door and opened it. He asked: "Would you mind for me to close the window and this other door a time?"

Mama waited for one of the parts where the lady soprano stops for breath, and lifted the needle off. "Why?" she said.

"Well," said our father, "I was kind of feeling a draft out here?"

"In *that* heat?"

"You are so right," said our father, "worst way to catch a cold."

". . . Seems to me you being funny."

Our father swayed forward and frowned. "You mean laughing-funny?" he asked. "Or plain peculiar?"

"Whichever," said Mama, "just leave the door be like it is. Anybody going to catch a cold can come inside here."

Our father felt his way back to the rocking chair and sat down. We both waited, but the record stayed quiet. And it looked like there wasn't going to be no trouble about that, after all.

Soon as our father began to read again, I stood up to go and look for Dan, and soon as I stood up, I saw him. He was running around the corner from St. Thomas. When he got nearer, he spotted me there, and he slowed down to a shuffle. Then I took a good look at his pants and shirt, and I figured you couldn't really do much about a trouble-day, once it got started: he was messed all over with this dark brown. When he was a little closer, I saw what the brown came from.

I told him with my head to hurry up, and he came and sat on the first step.

I put my hand on our father's arm. He stopped reading after a minute, and I said real quiet: "Dan is sitting down there."

"I figured he was."

"Can you see him?"

"I can't see him," said our father, "but I can smell him."

"Got his clothes awful dirty."

"Hisself? Or he been playing in it? Or both?"

"Not hisself," I said. " 'Horses', it looks like."

Our father said: "Good. A man's got to start somewhere. Horses, or somewhere else. A man got to start from the ground up."

"Dan," I said, "you get on your feet right exactly where you are, and stick your head in between the railings."

Dan did. And seeing his face there, I knew whatever came to pass, it was worth it. Dan was just through having a good time. His cheeks held a shine that was more than the sweat, and there was a hope back of his eyes. A baby hope. All alone, he'd gone and found something that didn't live in Mama's house, and it made me glad to look at him.

He said: "I played a *game*."

"Good," said our father, "what kind of a game? What's its name, your game?"

Dan said: "Dead."

"That ain't so good," said our father.

". . . Why?"

"Well, couldn't you give it some other name?"

"Dead *is* its name," said Dan.

Our father watched him. "How you play it?"

"Well," Dan said, "first thing, I laid down. And then they all covered me up."

"Who-all?"

Dan pushed up his shoulders and made a face like that was a stupid thing to ask. "Everybody else," he said, "who was playing the game."

Our father said: "So you was *it?*"

"Not *it . . . Dead.*"

". . . You know what that word means?"

"Sure. Like I told you. Means you got so much manure on top of you, you just lay there, and you don't care."

Our father smiled. "Surely," he said. Then he asked: "Do you have to always play it in horse manure, or could you maybe play it with grass next time?"

Dan thought some. "I forgot to ask. But I don't think so."

"Why not?"

"Because," said Dan, "grass ain't horse manure."

Our father said: "I see your point. How long the game last?"

"Well . . . like you want it. They covered me up, and I stayed there a while, and when I made up my mind to get on out, they wasn't there no more."

"How long was that?" asked our father.

". . . Don't know. How long I been gone?"

"About an hour and twenty minutes."

"Which is more," Dan said, "the hour or the twenty minutes?"

"The hour."

"That's how long," he said.

"Lord," said our father.

Shy, Dan told him: "Do you ever want to play, I could teach you."

"Look," our father said, "I only got one comment to make. Next time all you-all play, why don't you let some other kid be dead for a while? And you run on with the gang."

"Sure thing . . . sure. They only let me do it because I wanted to join up. And account of the color my skin's got."

"Well, you just let somebody else do it next time. And you tell them you got the best looking skin anybody ever saw."

"I already told them," Dan said. "I told them. And I kept uncovering my face."

". . . Good."

Dan put his hands around the railings, and stood tall as he could. "See," he said, "the thing is, while we was playing . . . I wasn't by myself *alone* . . . I was by myself . . . *with them*."

"Good," said our father, "good for you. Good."

The time they was talking, I had moved sideways to stand in front of the screen door. Now I thought I could feel Mama right behind me. But I wasn't sure, and I didn't want to look around.

Then she said: "Lucille. Stand away off this door." She was there. I took a step to my right.

"More," Mama said, "I'm coming out."

I scraped over a little further, and the door pushed open.

Next to me, Mama said: "I want to know who is *them*. And what am I smelling?"

With Mama there, Dan figured he had to cry sooner or later, and he might just as well get started. So he did.

"Move yourself out where I can see you, and answer my question."

Dan walked around, bawling, to the front of the steps.

"Lord Jesus above," said Mama, "help me not to believe my eyes."

Our father said: "Let him alone, now."

"Lord Jesus above . . ."

"He's all right," our father said. "He has to begin."

"Begin . . . *Begin?*" She moved forward.

I got in her way. "Don't hit him, Mama," I said, "Mama, hit me, it ain't his fault. Mama . . ."

Our father was on his feet again, standing there without even holding on to the railing. "Ain't no hitting going to happen," he said. "*What you been doing?*"

"Playing," Dan wailed, "playing. It was just a game."

"*A game? What game?*"

Our father said: "He told you, just a game. Don't matter what game."

"*Matter?*" Mama's hands was opening and closing. "You see what them kids put on him?"

"I see."

"*Well?*"

"Well," said our father, "Dan is more like *my* son. *Dan* is plain *hard to disenchant.*"

Clarence braked his bike sudden in the middle of the street, and walked it up to the house; he leaned it against the gallery. Then he slid a hand in his pants pocket and stood with his weight on one hip, watching.

Mama wheezed her breath out. "Get in here," she whispered.

Dan came up a step and put his knuckles in his eyes and really let go.

"Stop your crying. I don't allow no crying in my house. *Stop your crying.*"

Dan choked, but he got it down. ". . . Going to beat me?"

"No," said our father, in that voice, "she ain't."

"Move in here. *Move.*"

Dan came up another step, and then another, slow, getting both feet on each one before he tried for the next. He waited at the top, like he couldn't decide whether to run past Mama, or right into her and hide his body in her skirt. Some kids are born knowing a woman won't hit them if they cling to her hard enough. Course, Dan knew better than to try a thing like that with Mama—but he was still young as you have to be to figure the world might of changed in an hour.

Mama's hands was gripping for him, again and again. "You . . . get in here."

I stepped back and pulled the screen door out wide to give him a clear way. Must of been what he was timing for, because the second I did it, he started running. He went past Mama with his head scrounched down and his arms up over it. But just as he passed her, she reached to grab his arm, and Dan yelped and fell over into the kitchen. He got up fast, and went around behind the table. He wasn't crying now, or even whining, not after what Mama told him. He kept it down to a steady whimper—almost as if something inside was trying to talk that didn't know the words.

Our father asked, quiet: "You done hit that child?"

Facing me, Mama said: "I didn't. But I do what I want around my house."

"No," said our father. "*Not all. Not while I'm here.*"

Mama swung her head to look at him up over her left shoulder. I couldn't see her face then, but I knew what it looked like. "Oh," she said, "is *that* what you here for?"

As she stepped into the kitchen, I let the door swing to behind her. Our father waited, his eyes on the door. Then he said to hisself: "*Hah.*" Only it wasn't a real laugh.

From below, Clarence said: "Better sit down before you fall."

"He ain't going to fall," I said.

"Wouldn't be the first time."

"He *ain't* going to fall," I said.

He stood there while Mama undressed Dan. Before she took up the scrubbing brush, she stuck her hand out the door with Dan's clothes. I took them from her and went around and rinsed them good under the faucet back of the house. I put them to boil on the garbage-dump fire. When I came back, our father still hadn't moved.

Clarence hadn't either; he was watching our father. I walked up behind him, and he said: "Will you look at that? Learn something new every day."

"I told you," I said. And I went on up and stood with our father.

We waited together while Mama scrubbed Dan all over for the third time, till his skin was so sore, she had to grease him before he could go to school the next day. She put him to bed right afterwards, without his supper.

Then, after she crossed back into the kitchen, our father went inside. He teetered some, starting out, but he made it all right. (He hadn't been gone very long that morning, and the liquor was wearing off anyway.)

Clarence carried his bike onto the gallery under one arm, and set it there to be cleaned later. He still kept the other hand in his pocket; it was holding to the cloth now. "Late to eat," he said. ". . . Latest we ate this year." He looked through the screen into the kitchen, and he almost didn't move his mouth to ask: "Why don't that man leave her alone?"

Our father had turned the light on, and he was close up to Mama. He was saying something about finding work the next day, and ". . . *our* house" something. Then he went in to Dan. We could hear him better there, because he sat on the gallery side of the bed, next to the window. He said: ". . . Danny . . . got me right here, boy. Don't you worry none . . . be all right. You always got me, Danny. You always got me. Always."

Clarence took his hand out of his pocket, and opened the screen door. As he slunk in, body sitting loose over the hips, he rasped: "*Always.*"

He threw the door wide, and let it bang after him.

It clapped back twice, once loud, and once like a smaller echo. After that, it opened up its usual crack, and the iron hook rattled and jumped on what was left of the scaly whitewash for a second more.

I turned clear around and looked at the houses and scraggly trees across the street that kept me from seeing the last orange sun die down the day. Over the treetops, three dark clouds lay on their stomachs, reflecting some of the red and gold heat, watching what I couldn't. Then a piece separated off one of them, like a pinch of cotton, and fell a ways, catching the real fire. It burned there in blood-flame, the kind of color that shines so deep you know it can't last long. I kept still, feeling the house against my back. Mama's house—full now, except for me. And Mama's kitchen, with the thin light from its sad yellow bulb. I wondered what it would be like up in that cloud, burning in that color, high over the screaming, dying sun.

But I couldn't wonder long. I couldn't even watch the dark come, hissing-quick like always—too quick for any soft, middle glow between the day and the night. (Our father used to say: "We plain don't get no twilight down here in this flat land. What can you do in a place without no twilight?")

Mama called: *"In to supper."*

So I never got to watch the razor-turn of light into blackness that summer's-end night. And I didn't think to look for one again till long after our father was dead.

He did it when the next winter had just passed. He left us two weeks into spring.

It was a Tuesday afternoon, a holiday for something; not much after lunch.

Our father had just got through telling all of us his story, and he was reading from Mr. Carroll. He hadn't told the story in a long time, and I sometimes think I never heard him do it quite like that last afternoon. But most probably I only think so because of the way I remember the whole day: bigger than natural, but blurred and smeared around itself—like looking through somebody else's glasses.

On into the second part of *Alice,* our father began to stop once every so often, and clear his throat with a rumble that heaved and then cut too short down inside his chest someplace.

The first time it sounded, I sat and waited for him to go on. Then.

I saw that Clarence had quit figuring in his numbers, and was look-ing up—bone-still—still as any animal will get when it first hears some strange noise.

The second time, our father stopped halfway through a line. It was something he never did, not even for Mama. And the sound he made broke into three separate gurgles that he couldn't find enough air to finish. He pushed up straighter in his chair, and went back to Mr. Carroll, glowering like a man has a right to if his body starts to let him down on a very simple, very important, everyday job.

I turned to see Clarence watching him full-on.

Our father read slower and slower—pushing through. But the beat was off. When he finished, I was short of breath too: I had been straining with him.

But then our father tipped Mr. Carroll to one side, flipping him forwards, and he started to read again.

Slow and harsh and even, Clarence said: "You doing it on purpose. You dirty sonofabitch." Something about the way he said it reminded me of the time I saw him kick a hurt tree toad Dan had accidentally stepped on, just because he got mad watching its pain.

I got up. "Doing what?" I asked.

Still to our father, Clarence said: "Whatever." And he swung away so fast he practically fell off the railing. He didn't take up his num-bers, though. He sat with his back to us, stiff, looking out at the camphor tree.

Our father went right on into the poem in the middle of the last chapter. The one that begins:

" 'They told me you had been to her . . .' "

He was through most of it when his fingers stretched out and began to jerk so hard Mr. Carroll dropped to the gallery floor. Our father swallowed. But he caught his breath again, and he said a couple more lines from his own memory.

The furthest his lungs would take him was:

" 'Don't let him know she liked them best,
For this must ever be . . .' "

After that, he hicupped and slipped down in his chair. Then he arched his back real hard, with his legs stuck straight out in front of him. Just before he shut his eyes, he made a different gurgle, that might of been a laugh, and he said: "All right, now. Tell your Mama to get her ass out here. I'm on my way."

He didn't turn to me specially when he said it—or afterwards. Maybe he couldn't.

Dan got into the kitchen before I did, because I had trouble moving. I finally made it, though, and we shouted together at Mama. But death is the one thing that never made Mama jump. She dried her hands on her blue and white dish towel, and walked around the table and out the screen door. Dan and me was already there.

Clarence hadn't twitched. He hadn't even turned around to look.

And our father was where we had left him; only he had his eyes open now, and his back wasn't arched no more. And he was dead.

That was it. Simple as that. An end and a start to everything.

I hadn't ever seen a dead person before, but I knew right away. I knew because our father's hot stone wasn't sending out a wave to me. I knew because he was hanging off that chair, legs splayed wide, looking plain silly: I knew our father couldn't look silly.

But it wasn't the strangeness of death that scared me into trembling while I waited there; not in *his* body. No, I just got choked from wondering how anything could possibly of happened to stop our father for always—before he could finish a poem.

Of all the clashing sounds I heard around my new life, first was the clatter of Clarence's pencil, next to Mr. Carroll, on the floor.

2

THE story our father told, he generally told like this:

"*A true love story.*

"When New Orleans was a baby town, there wasn't no St. Thomas Street, nor no Millicent Street. It was a little bitty town then, and a whole lot prettier than it is now. Up the levee, they had plantation houses big as a city block. And there was long white columns and upstairs galleries on most of the houses in town too. Course, St. Charles Avenue wasn't the white people's fine-living place, like today. Then they did it in the Garden District. You go walk through the Garden District now, and it looks all disgusted and broken down. But not then. Then it was really something. With the high-gull white of the houses blinking back at the morning sun—and the ivy hugging there to keep them cool—and the dark green shutters. And the winter-grass clipped so even and straight it looked like sheets of glued emerald mash, put out there to glisten and dry. And flowers: so many flowers the colors jumped all over each other to get out. And every lady had a separate silk dress to match every flower in the District. And they had horse-and-buggies, and some people had two. Everything was new, and very different from what you see around town now. Everything but the people, that is. The people was just exactly the same like they are today.

"Now, at the time I'm talking about, in one of the biggest, finest houses in the District, there was a young man living whose name was Dennis. Dennis' family was the most important family in six streets, and they didn't like to let theirselves forget it none. They had two buggies, and three horses (in case one got sick), and you couldn't even of counted the help inside the house, and two gardeners outside it. They had everything.

"Well, one day, Dennis was standing on his lawn, eyeing the buggies pass, and wondering what to do, when he just chanced to look out over the neutral-ground at the house across the street. Now, Dennis never had no truck with the people across the street—not because they wasn't okay (he knew they was okay, or they wouldn't be *living* across the street); but only because all he ever saw of them was one old lady who kept pretty much alone. Which was why, when he saw a half a girl's face in the window, he just thought that half of the old lady looked a heap better on that day. But when he leaned over a little Dennis got a surprise. Because the face watching him was so lovely, he plain couldn't believe it. And the face stayed right where it was.

"Dennis studied on it. Only, the more he studied, the better it got—so, after a time, he figured he better just cross over to the neutral-ground, and see what did it look like from closer up. And he went. And that was when Dennis got the biggest surprise of all. Because that was when he saw the first thing he'd ever seen in his whole life that looked better from someplace else than it did right from his own front lawn, and it had looked pretty good from there.

"But before he could do anything more, the girl reached her hand out, and quick flipped the curtain to. And Dennis was left watching nothing but a closed window with a closed curtain behind it.

"Now, all this went so fast, Dennis wasn't sure afterwards if he really saw what he thought he saw or not. The only thing he was sure of was that he better find out, and quick. So he figured some, and he got hisself a plan.

"The next morning, Dennis dressed up fine and doused the out-

side with cologne water, and then he slipped in and borrowed a pair
of his mama's best gloves, when she wasn't around. He put them in
his pocket, and crossed the street and rang the doorbell. Course, the
butler knew him to look at, so he didn't have no trouble there: Dennis
got took straight on into the front room and left to wait.

"After a time, the lady of the house came sailing in under her hoop
skirt like they all wore; only, it was made of black silk, because she
was an old lady. Dennis pulled the gloves out, and he told her as
how he'd found them on the sidewalk and thought maybe they belonged to her—or even maybe to somebody else who might live there
too. Well, the old lady said she didn't think they was hers, and then
she felt of the material and took a good look and said, course, they
might be hers, or they might be her niece Florabelle's, but there
wasn't no sure way she could tell right now, account of Florabelle's
being asleep. But anyhow, she said it was real nice of Dennis to take
the trouble to come in, and if he wanted to leave the gloves till later
and send somebody over, she would try and find out who did they
belong to, or not.

"Course, Dennis said that wasn't no trouble to speak of, and he
wouldn't bother to send nobody, he would just come on over in
person later and see what was what. The old lady said if that was
suiting him, it would pass by her, and Dennis got on out.

"While he was walking down the walk, he had a sense like the
hair on the back of his head was creeping there. And when he looked
around, Dennis thought he saw one of the long lace curtains on the
second floor untwist and fall to. But he couldn't be sure, and he
didn't see nothing else.

"That afternoon, Dennis poured on some more cologne water and
went back. The afternoon butler put him in the same front room.
Only, this time, it didn't look like the same room at all. Because this
time Florabelle was there.

"She was sitting in the chair by the window, facing the wall, with
a thick quilt pulled tight around her up to her waist, knitting.
And even though Dennis could still only see half her face, he knew
it was the same half he had seen that first day—and it was really
something.

"She was all feathery white, with a black eye cut deep across, and
a black eyebrow that curved way high over it, soft as fur. She had her
head tipped down, and there was a shadow of a fan down to her
cheek from her lashes. In back, her hair spilled clean over the chair
to the floor, shiny and thick as sun-melted tar, and her white face

under it. She was so white she was blue. You could see the veins
stand out under her skin, and you got the feeling if you went up
closer, you could see a lot more—but if you went up *real* close, maybe
she wouldn't be there at all. And there she was. Knitting.

"Well, in one quarter of a second, she moved her head and looked
right at Dennis, right full at him. And Dennis felt a heat ball start
in the center of his spine and go running on up to his neck, and then
it turned to a cold ball and went back down again. Because the left
side of Florabelle's face was just as beautiful as the side Dennis knew
so well. Except for one little thing. One silver patch, shaped like a
baby mullet, and stuck up under her left eyebrow.

"In the left side of her face, Florabelle was blind.

"Now the old lady was standing next to her, and she got busy
telling everybody who everybody else was, and then she told Dennis
to go on and sit down. But Dennis wasn't good for nothing. He just
stood there being a turnip and staring at Florabelle. And Florabelle
caught the stare in her one good eye, and pitched it right back at
him, till she figured enough was enough and looked away at her
knitting again. And that was when Dennis plain had to sit down.

"Then the old lady said as how it was so nice of him to bother hisself to come all the way over just about those gloves, when it turned
out they *did* belong to her after all. And she thanked him and said
whenever he ran across anything of that nature out on the sidewalk,
he should just bring it right in, because there wasn't no telling what
could get lost out there. But Dennis just kept on looking at Florabelle, with his mouth shut. And the old lady kept on talking about
one thing and another. And Florabelle kept on knitting and not
looking back.

"About a half-hour passed, when the butler came with coffee and
watercress sandwiches, and served Dennis and the old lady at a big
table that was in between them, and then served Florabelle at a
little table right next to where she was sitting. The old lady was still
talking. And so far, Florabelle hadn't said one solid word.

"But when she finally did, just to answer a question, it was worse.
Account of she had this voice that was smooth as the feel of sweat
on your naked body, and delicate as the sound of tinsel, and clear
as a spider's web made out of glass. And when Dennis tried to talk
afterwards, his own voice came back at him like a hacksaw working
on a piece of steel.

"Dennis was in a fix. What's more, he *knew* he was in a fix. Because he knew that Florabelle's only having one eye didn't make no

more difference to him than another lunch with brown betty for dessert. And that was a bad sign.

"Well, the afternoon wore on, and the old lady kept blabbing, and Florabelle's knitting got to be really long.

"She sat in her chair, with the quilt pulled up to her middle, watching her needles. She never left off making the same fast in-and-out movements with her hands, and she never did get up. She mostly stayed the same, but once or twice Dennis would catch her looking at him while he listened to the old lady—not raising her head, just looking at him—and her eye would flash out from under her lashes like a black sun playing behind the palm fronds. Only, when he caught her doing it she always looked back at her knitting so quick, Dennis was left with a swallow of coffee halfway down and going in the wrong direction. And nothing to do but sit and watch how her hair dropped forward in big swirls from her shoulder to make blue shadows on her face.

"Finally, after about three hours and five cups of coffee, the old lady excused herself and went out to take a leak.

"Dennis worked his toes up and down in his shoes, and hunched up. He said: 'Miss Florabelle.'

"Florabelle kept quiet, but she seemed like she was listening. She always seemed like she was listening. But she only changed the needles around and went on.

" 'Hey, Miss Florabelle,' said Dennis. 'You ever go out?'

"And Florabelle quit knitting. She just clean lay off. She put her hands together, and dropped her head down till her hair practically fell in her lap.

"Dennis got a knot in the region of his watercress sandwich. 'Well,' he said, 'do you? Miss Florabelle? Do you ever go out?'

"Florabelle kept on staring down at the palms of her hands, and waited.

"Well, Dennis got to feeling all feet, like a doodlebug. Course, then he got mad, account of nobody can feel really dumb without getting mad about it. So he was just going to clear out of there, when he saw the light from the window shining in Florabelle's right hand. There was a little puddle of water in that hand—and while he was looking, he saw a drop fall and make a splash in the puddle. And Dennis knew that out of her one eye, Florabelle was crying.

"Then he was stuck.

"He said: 'What is it, Miss Florabelle? What did I do, Miss Florabelle, honey? I'm sorry,' he said, 'you just forget what I asked.

You want me to shut up?' he said, 'I'll shut up. You want me to go away? I'll go away.'

"But when he said that, Florabelle took and put her head in her hands, and plain started to sob.

"Just then, the old lady got back from the toilet. 'What-all is wrong with *you?*' she said. Then she turned to Dennis. 'What-all is wrong with *her?*' she said. And she looked like it better not be what she was thinking.

"Dennis said: 'I don't know. Honest to God, ma'am, I only asked her did she ever go out.'

"But the old lady looked a heap better. 'Oh, sure,' she said. 'That's all right, man.' She went over and stood by Florabelle, with a hand on her shoulder, and she said to Dennis: 'You better take off now; you can come back tomorrow do you want to.' And when Dennis was almost through the door, she said: 'Hey, man.' Then she glanced down at the top of Florabelle's head and back at Dennis. 'She can't walk,' she said.

"Dennis didn't get it right away. Not that there was much for him to get, he just didn't get it. And when he did, he only grabbed his hat and his gloves and his cane, and made haste getting hisself right off those premises.

"And Florabelle's sobbing followed him clean through the closed front door.

"All that night, Dennis sat and thought. He was in a worse fix now than before. Because the more he thought, the more he knew that it didn't make no difference at all to him whether Florabelle could walk or not. And that was a bad sign.

"The next afternoon, real early, he went out and hitched up his papa's horse-and-buggy. Then he climbed on it, and drove it around and stopped in front of Florabelle's house. He went on in.

"Florabelle was sitting there, same as before. But she didn't look up at him when he came in. So Dennis didn't say nothing either; he sat down and waited for the old lady. And after a while, the old lady came trotting in and sat down too, just as if nothing had happened, and started to talk.

"Well, Dennis let her. And when she took time out for a slug of coffee, he stood up. 'I would like to have the privilege of taking Miss Florabelle for a ride,' he said. 'In my buggy.'

"The old lady, as you can imagine, practically tossed her coffee. 'You done gone a ways out of your head, man?' she said, 'or ain't you heard what I told you yesterday? *Which?*'

" 'Yes,' said Dennis, 'I heard.' And he swung around and looked at Florabelle to see was he going to have to fight with her too. But Florabelle had her head raised up, and she was staring straight at him, and she was smiling. And maybe you would of seen a thing in her eye that was a little more than a smile. Dennis saw it. 'Yes,' he said, 'I heard.'

"The old lady took a look at Dennis, and another at Florabelle, and then she sat back. 'Listen,' she said, 'don't get me mixed up in no problems, please. I got enough to take care of, and I have just led one long life. So do whatever you want, but please don't give me nothing else to think about.'

"But Dennis wasn't paying no mind to her. He was watching Florabelle. 'You going to need a sweater?' he asked. 'Or you all right just like you are?'

" 'I'm all right,' she said, 'just like I am.'

"Dennis said: 'I'll have her back in a couple hours.'

" 'Kindly take three,' said the old lady, 'they are small.'

"Florabelle wrapped the quilt tighter around her bottom half, and fastened it real good.

" 'You don't need that quilt,' said Dennis.

" 'Yes, she do,' said the old lady.

"So Dennis went over and picked Florabelle up in his arms. 'Three hours,' he said. 'Or maybe more.' And he carried her out and put her in the buggy.

"The first part of the drive they took out to Lake Pontchartrain they didn't hardly talk none. Dennis kept the horse at a real fast trot. And Florabelle dropped her yard and a half of hair over the seat behind her, combing it, and letting the wind brush it way up—sparkling black on the air. She watched the sky, and smiled some, and her silver patch shone so hard it sizzled. Then Dennis saw that even though the sun made her skin whiter and more transparent, the blue shadows was gone.

"Once they got out there, Dennis took her hand a while, and he kissed her, real light. Only, when he tried to talk to her afterwards, she put her fingers up to his mouth. And from that time on, she wouldn't let him talk at all.

"Now, there is a funniness about men: they never know when they got a good deal till later on. Right when they *got* it is when they have to go and try to double it. That is why men wait to take the biggest chances till they have the most to lose. Because when they ain't got nothing, there ain't nothing to take a *real* chance *with*.

"So, when the three hours was almost up, Dennis knew he couldn't let things drag out no more. Things had got just too good.

"By then the sky was opening up and blazing out like a September watermelon you let fall on the ground. The sun was so hard-bright you couldn't look up, and the water was worse. Dennis couldn't even look at Florabelle without squinting, and when he did she stood out so sharp she seemed like she had a double edge. And her beautiful silver patch would of fried any egg three feet away.

"But while Dennis was getting all red-honey skinned, the way white people get from the sun, Florabelle wasn't even turning pink. She stayed pure white, like the whalebone comb she ran through her snaky hair.

"She was sitting there with both arms raised straight up. And Florabelle didn't even have no little sweat-rings below the pits. She was perfect.

"So Dennis couldn't take no more. He wound the reins around the knob on the front of the buggy, and edged over to her. 'Florabelle,' he said—his voice had a peculiar twang, as if he was trying to play it down.

"Florabelle let her hair fall back, and turned to him real quick.

" 'Miss Florabelle,' he said, 'I want to . . .'

" 'Don't,' she said, 'sugar, I done *told* you: don't talk.'

" 'No,' he said, 'I got to now. I want to ask you . . .'

" 'Don't ask me nothing. *Please.* Sugar, don't you talk.'

" 'I got to,' Dennis said. 'We come to where I plain got to.'

"Florabelle shivered. Then she took a hold of his ears, one in each hand. She leaned close to him, and her eye was sad, like she had to fight about something she really knew was already lost. She asked: 'Ain't you happy this way? Why you got to talk? Don't talk, sugar.'

"Dennis put his hands over hers, and pulled them down in his lap. 'Sure, I'm happy,' he said. 'Course I am. I'm the happiest I ever been in my life. *That's* why.'

"Florabelle kept her eye on him. But she let her hands go limp in his, and Dennis felt that they was almost cold. 'Listen,' she said, 'listen to me: if you happy . . . if you want to go on being happy like this . . . then, sugar, just *be* happy. Don't say nothing, because there ain't nothing to say. *Just be happy.*'

" 'I can't,' said Dennis. 'Honey, I can't.'

"Florabelle turned away from him out to the Lake, and she drooped a little. She began to cry, very easy, without making no noise. 'I know. Nobody can. I know, sugar, don't you ever worry. Nobody can.'

"Dennis gripped harder, trying to squeeze her alive again. But she was ice-cold. 'Florabelle, honey,' he said. 'Miss Florabelle, honey. I want to ask you . . . *will you marry me?*'

"Florabelle winced like he'd hit her, and stopped crying. Real slow, she pulled her hands back. When she got them free, she looked at him. And there was a lot in that look Dennis never forgot.

"She reached behind her, and undid the bow that held the quilt together. Then she started to unwind it from around her body.

"Dennis saw what she was doing, and he saw her face. 'Why you doing that, honey?' he said, 'don't diswrap yourself . . . I don't care . . . don't do it, honey.'

"But Florabelle went right on.

" 'Don't,' said Dennis. 'Honey, don't.'

"Florabelle gave it one last swirl, and it was off. And when that was done, she reached and hiked her skirt up to her middle. Dennis looked down at her—and his chest cracked like it was going to break in on him.

"From the waist down, Florabelle was a fish.

"Now, Dennis' voice would of turned off like a spigot if he'd made to use it. But he didn't. He just stared at where the tiny little green scales at the end of her tail kept getting bigger the further up they went, till around her hips they was big as a silver dollar. And when he got up that far, he stared back down to where the smallest scale was, at the tips of the fork. And he could see where the sunlight made the tail all gold-green and blue-green and yellow-green, and even sometimes red-green—and it would flash at him, first in one color and then in another, like a million fine-cut diamonds was stuck there, winking out. Matter of fact, it was a pretty good-looking tail as tails go. Only, Dennis was not feeling very appreciative at this particular time.

"Then he saw that Florabelle had been watching him. And that was when she put her cold hands on the back of his neck, up in his hair, and leaned forward and kissed him on the mouth. And even though her lips was cold as the deep Lake water in the winter, it was a burning cold—like dry ice—and when she pulled away, she left little heat waves blazing up in him, like the waves that come when the Lake boils white after a storm.

"When Dennis could see again, he saw she had her arms behind her, working at the snaps on the back of her dress. After she was finished, she crossed them over her head, and grabbed the big puffs at the shoulders. And when Dennis got a hold of what she was going to do, he bent away from her and squinched up his eyes, without even thinking, and took the edge of the buggy and held on tight. He heard the swishing of the silk when it was lifted, and all kinds of feelings went running through him. But finally, he sat up straight, and he made up his mind he was going to turn around and look at Florabelle right in the eye. Because he was going to tell her . . .

"But before he could, the buggy gave a jerk to the left that made him sway way out over the side; the horse neighed; over below the cement steps leading down to the Lake, there was a loud splash, and then the sound of the water when it fell back in a spray. And then there wasn't no sound at all except the throb of Dennis' own blood in his own ears.

"So that was how Florabelle left him. Ain't no use in explaining you how Dennis didn't find but a pile of clothes next to him, or how he called out to her, because you can pretty well figure all that out for yourself. She didn't answer him, and she didn't come back. Way out, where the water makes a mirror for the sun, he thought he saw a trail of foam heading towards the Gulf. He *thought* he saw it. But Dennis wasn't really sure of anything else for the rest of his life.

"And that was that. Dennis stayed where he was, and yelled out to the water, and waited—but that was that. Later on, black fluff-head clouds came up out of nowhere and plastered theirselves all under the sky, and a wind whipped across the top of the water and sent it splashing over the steps. The sun gave up and quit, and things got poorly colored. And Dennis sat on. Every quarter-hour or so he called: 'Florabelle,' out onto the waves. But the wind was against him, and there wasn't nobody could of heard him, would there of been somebody to hear. Which there wasn't.

"Along towards evening, when the sun paints up the Lake from the sea, and the gulls scream in, Dennis took the reins and started his horse for town. But he wasn't halfway there when he turned and came back to the place by the Lake wall, and stopped and sat some more. He didn't call this time; he sat looking out till he couldn't see but only the underlit clouds over the black water. Then he started up again and went back to town.

"When the old lady saw him come in alone, she pushed back the curtain and looked at the empty buggy. Then she hunched over and took Florabelle's knitting from where it was on a table, and started winding it up. 'You look hungry,' she said, 'why don't you go home and eat?'

"Dennis swallowed a mouthful of nothing. 'What is she?' he asked.

" '*You* ain't one-eyed,' said the old lady, 'you saw what she is. Man, don't come around here asking no fool questions this time of night. Go home and eat.'

" '*Where* is she?' asked Dennis.

" 'Ain't you hungry?' said the old lady. 'You look like a man that was hungry.'

" '*Where is she?*' Dennis said, louder.

" 'Which way did she swim?' said the old lady.

" 'Out to the Gulf,' said Dennis, 'I think.'

" 'Then more than likely, that's where she is,' said the old lady.

"Dennis sat down real sudden. He said: 'How come?'

" 'That is a great question,' said the old lady. 'One great big fool question.'

"Dennis got up again. 'Listen,' he said.

"But: 'Listen *you*,' said the old lady, 'you been having a big time.'

"Dennis dropped his mouth open.

" 'Ain't that right? Ain't you been having a big time all this time?'

" 'That's right,' said Dennis. 'So what?'

" 'So you done had it,' said the old lady, 'now go on home and eat.'

" 'What you going to do?' asked Dennis.

" 'I am going up to bed,' said the old lady, 'on account of I am horse-tired.'

"Dennis said: 'Florabelle . . .'

" 'You forget about Florabelle,' she said. 'Man, go on home. You come over here on your own call. You have a good time. You get happy. But that ain't enough for you. No, you got to find out what it was made you happy, and why, and try to latch on to it. Now you lost it. Don't come back here asking no fool questions, man. Go on home and learn how to separate succotash.'

"Dennis wiped his coatsleeve across his forehead. 'That poor girl,' he said, 'that poor, poor girl.'

" 'Poor nothing,' said the old lady, 'she just doing what she got to do. Now you do the same.'

"Dennis said: 'Her poor lost eye.'

"The old lady hiked up her shoulders. 'Wasn't my fault,' she said, 'I always told her you never can trust no swordfish.' And she headed out for the hall.

" 'Hey,' said Dennis. 'Please. I love her. When is she coming back?'

" 'She ain't,' the old lady called. 'She ain't, man. Don't you know? She ain't.'

"And that was the last Dennis ever saw of the old lady. Because about a week later, he watched them carry a little black coffin out of the house and shove it in a coach and drive it out of the District. Then not long afterwards they put the house up for sale—and before Dennis could think, somebody else bought it up and moved in and changed it all around till it didn't look like the same house at all.

"And every afternoon, Dennis drove out to the Lake front and waited. Sat, and waited. There was good days and bad days and cold days and hot days—Dennis was out there. He didn't forget; he didn't let it fade. But he didn't call to her, because he knew she wasn't there. When he was thirty years old, his papa died, and when he was thirty-eight years old, his mama died. Then he had his own house and a lot of money. When he was forty-five he caught pneumonia from sitting in the winter by the Lake, and for a while, he was so sick he couldn't even get up to do his necessaries. But soon as he got well, he was back in the buggy sitting out there and asking for it again. And that was the way it was.

"He never got married, and he never even went with the same girl twice. All the mamas in the District tried to get him for their daughters, but he would just look at them and smile and go out and sit by the Lake front. Nobody ever asked him why, and he didn't ever tell a soul.

"After a while, he was sixty. He was still pretty good-looking, because he hadn't used hisself for nothing but sitting and suffering. But he was old. Only, he took to counting the years from the time Florabelle lit out to sea, instead of from his birthday, so he didn't even remember how old he was.

"On the day it was forty years since she swum away, Dennis rode out to the Lake early in the morning. When the fog went up, it was hot and bright and clear, same as forty years before. There wasn't no wind, and the sun made heat waves shimmer up from the cement steps, so the water looked like it was wavering back and forth. Dennis closed his eyes, which was tired, because he'd been a long time looking with them. He slept a while, and made a pretend, and woke up, and slept again. The day got hotter and the horse got to fidgeting, and Dennis went right on sleeping with his pretend. Along in the afternoon, he got out and fed the horse, and he ate a sandwich and went to sleep again.

"Course, in his pretend, Florabelle was with him. She swam back the same way, and she was more beautiful than before. He took her in his arms, and explained how it didn't make no difference to him her being what she was, she never should of left him. And when he carried her up to the buggy, her tail changed to legs, and the fork to two of the littlest feet you ever saw. And when he got her in the buggy, he lay her down on the seat, real easy. And then he always woke up.

"The sun got hottest about five o'clock, just before it swelled big. Dennis stood on his feet and stretched the sleep off, and sat back down. Most of his shirt was sticking to him, and the sweat was running down where it could, inside and out. The water was so sleek and glossy you could of cut it with a knife, but you couldn't watch it. Dennis wrinkled the skin all over his face, and looked at the horse, to keep from getting a headache. Then he saw it.

"First it was just a fuzz in the side of his eye, and when he turned to stare at it, it wasn't there. But when he looked back at the horse, there it was again. Then it got bigger. Only, he still couldn't see it except like that.

"It was a place where the water had broke up and foamed, way out. And instead of settling down like water does when something breaks the surface, it stayed foaming, and it got nearer. It was a path of foam in the water.

"Dennis watched the horse, and saw it. He took to rumbling in his gut, and then he got the palpitations, but he held on under the seat and kept from shutting his eyes. Sometimes it looked like it wasn't moving at all, and then it was nearer. That's how slow it came.

"Course, in no time at all, Dennis' eyes started to water. He dried them but they just got to burning and watering again, and he had to shut them a while, and they burned even more. When he opened them, he could look right out across the water and see it, and so could the horse. It was coming straight for the buggy.

"Dennis knew it was Florabelle even before he saw her clear. So by the time her tail flipped high and shone out and sank under again, he was already jiggling so hard the buggy creaked. It took her more than two hours from when he first got a notice of the foam. She was still swimming when she touched the steps and looked up and saw him.

"Dennis plain couldn't keep the tears from pouring out, and he was shaking so much he couldn't talk. He sat sobbing out loud, and looked at her. And Florabelle pushed the hair off her face with the back of her arm, and looked back.

"She was indeed a mess. She was sixty too and she looked it, and older. What there was of her hair was stringy, and all knotted with seaweed, and generally wet. Her face had shriveled up like a raisin, or like your hands get when you leave them in water too long—and her fingers was calloused and knuckled, with a slippery sheen to them. Two little tiny pieces of seaweed was hanging down off her old silver patch, but they was hard to place, because the patch was the same color. She didn't have but one tooth left in her head, and forty years under water hadn't done that one much good. Even her tail had lost over half its scales, and the part that was left was kind of a greasy gray. Florabelle had more or less had it.

"But Dennis didn't care. She *was* Florabelle, and she was back. He waited till the shaking eased down to where he could talk, and he asked her:

" 'Why did you do it? . . . Florabelle. Why? . . . Did you think I cared what your bottom half was like? . . . I never would of cared . . . Why did you do it? . . . I loved you all my life. All my life . . . You shouldn't of done it . . . I loved you, and I always waited for you. I knew . . . I knew you would come back . . . But why did you take so long? Florabelle . . . *Why* did you do it? . . . Do you think I care if you can't walk . . . Do you? . . . Do you think *I* care if you half-blind? . . . Do you think *I* care if you half-fish?'

"But Florabelle bared her tooth and cackled up at him.

" 'Lord, sugar,' she said. 'It ain't none of *that*. It's that I'm one-tenth Negro.' "

First Movement

MAMA bought a good new iron with the rest of the money our father kept in the bank. There was just enough, after she paid to bury him.

She had to put up all the money for the funeral, because she never did let our father join a lodge, and the monthly payments on the house was too steep for him to sign up with one of the burial associations.

Mr. Carroll and Mr. Keats got put in our father's coffin. Mama was scared to throw them in the garbage, and that was the only way she could think to get them out of town.

Our father's funeral cost eighteen dollars and fifty cents. The funeral parlour put out printed sheet-ads telling you the prices. The eighteen-fifty funeral was the *high-class* type and there was a *deluxe* type for thirty-nine ninety-five, and a *special-deluxe* type for fifty dollars. On all three you got a nice funeral service, and some kind of a coffin, and the down payment on a grave, and a real embalming job done. On the *special-deluxe* you got seven hymn-singing mourners included, who followed the whole thing around looking like they lost their last pair of pants. (The Mr. Jameson that lived on the corner of St. Thomas and Shay was one of them. He got so he couldn't get that look off his face, and he still has a collection of filthy-dirty stories he tells and then laughs hisself sick without ever cracking a smile.) The only trouble with the *special-deluxe* type was it about doubled in price, because you had to invite all the hymn-singing mourners to the wake first, and they could sop up more liquor and peanut butter than seven empty cans you put sponges in.

Anyhow, Mama couldn't afford no better than the *high-class* type. We didn't even think there was going to be much of a wake: you can't go very far on a dollar-fifty's worth of Coke and salami. And there wasn't hardly anybody to invite, because Mama didn't have more than four people she spoke to, and none of our father's friends was ever allowed in her house before, except the two who carried him home that time, and they never came back. But there hadn't been nobody to die around our neighborhood for a long time, and people kept piling in and bringing their own liquor. So it did get to be quite a party. Mama kicked them all out about four in the morning, account of they was pretty far gone by then, and they wouldn't stop going in the bedroom and trying to give our father and Mr. Carroll and Mr. Keats one last shot. Wouldn't of made much difference to those two gentlemen, but our father's coat was getting sort of saturated with raw whiskey, and it had to last him through the next afternoon when they buried him.

That was the first and the last day Mama ever put up with that many strangers in her house or drinking, either one. But it was the end of a long strain, and fear always eases off a while when you sure what you have to do. Besides, Mama wanted everybody to know how much she appreciated our father's letting hisself get into the Lord's hands. The part that made me mad was she could of allowed him a little liquor around before, instead of waiting and giving it all to him after he was dead. She sat there next to Reverend Segrette and prayed for our father's soul, with a hard, thankful look, till the Reverend got so pie-eyed he couldn't sit up no more, and she had to take him in and lay him out on the bed next to our father. Clarence stood by Mama, but Dan and me sat off in the other corner of the kitchen. We watched everything, and let people pat us on the head, and we knew it was a fine party and that our father would of liked it that way.

Cousin Wila was working out of town, so she couldn't come; but she sent fifteen dollars to the Upward Brass Band, and they showed up around eleven in the morning and played for the whole funeral. They was the best band around at the time, and the marches they played on the way to the graveyard was so swell that all kinds of people kept second-lining the parade from behind, and we were near fifty altogether when we got there.

The colored graveyard where they buried our father is even and brown, with chipped cement slabs and headstones, covered with dirt. There ain't no mausoleums. Just rows of graves. In the *high-class* row they don't carve nothing on the headstone; Mama figured she could do that when she had the money, though. They leave the bodies there for twenty years, and then if you can't afford to buy the grave for good, they take the bones out and use it for somebody else. Mama made us promise if she died before she got the chance we three would put up enough to buy our father's plot and hers too before the twenty years was up. And while we were praying, we thanked the Lord for giving us the chance to buy our father his own private grave. The Reverend led the prayers, till Mama took over, and I liked the way he talked, in this sad, heavy voice that had a purr to it. Course he was pretty hungover.

When the coffin was in the ground, the band leader really started to hep it up. They did that so well, there was a good twenty second-liners more by the time we got near Mama's house. I think the whole Upward Brass Band felt pretty sorry for Mama, seeing her left alone with three kids and all. Anyway, they followed us back right to the door.

Through the next week, Mama sat on her gallery in our father's chair, and played "Thank God for a Garden" one solid hour every day. I don't think I was ever quite that mad with God. It was like Him and His record had finally won out.

Mama's Bible says: "In the beginning, God created the Heaven and the earth." If you want to believe that, you welcome to. What you can't believe, though, is that there was any real beginnings about your own life. Because there wasn't. And there ain't. And there won't be. Only bridges. You got born in a mold of a world, and maybe the mold changed, or, if you lucky, you did. Maybe somebody or something crossed over to someplace else. Maybe you learned a feeling, or forgot a habit. Say forgot; say learned; say crossed; say changed; say bridges. But don't say you began, because you didn't. No, ma'am. You are strictly old material. New is just for people to think with, not for the world or for life. And first times ain't beginnings, Mr. Columbus. The wonderful wonder of life is that it can't begin or end, once it's here. It can only repeat and go on.

The flow of the five years between our father's death and my leaving New Orleans is gone for me now. Splotches are all that is left—humps of times that rise up out of the darkness like islands in the swamp. Five whole years in Mama's house—the quicksand house—sinking. When I was the only one who wasn't going down in her clutch. Wanting to pull against her, for my brothers, and not knowing how; having to watch it happen. And the terrible, wild feeling I got, more and more, that it was me had to make good for what our father did. Me alone, to fix his leaving us and to take his place in the house. Only me, Lucille Morris, born at twelve to clean behind our father's coffin and save his loving soul.

Through five years. And I was the lucky one. Because whatever hold it was Mama had, she just had it with Clarence and Dan. Course, I loved her too, maybe even as much as they did. Except, I could stand off and love her—off where I could see her at the same time. So when I got older, I got to understand her. But Clarence and Dan was too close to Mama, and she stopped them from seeing anything else. She took them to her and blocked off their life right where it had sucked. Then, when they wanted to get away and be on their own, they had to hit at her to tear free. And when you move away from something like that, you do it backwards, like a fly off flypaper: you got to look at what you leaving instead of where you going. And you plain can't know where you liable to wind up. But Mama made them do it. She taught them. She taught them with her eyes; she taught them with her voice. And she taught them with her hands, that wandered and picked all day long to hide their own shaking.

Through five years. Then, for me, the newness of the world when I left home and first had to find out about my own self. And for all of us, all of the things that happened afterwards—the things that had to happen after those early times had past. After Clarence got taught his lesson, and Dan his. After I found out that I was useless-born, from the passing of every second of every breath of every blessèd hour.

And the splotches of times are all that is left now of five gritty years.

I

NOBODY picked a special day for us to quit school, after our father's funeral. We stayed out for that, and none of us ever went back. Cousin Wila wrote telling Clarence to hold off on work till she saw what she could do, and in no more than a couple weeks, she fixed him up a job being assistant gardener for these people on St. Charles. (Clarence didn't know beans about gardening, but Cousin Wila said he should just dress dirty the first day, and then keep his mouth shut and learn from the other man.) It was a double job, with two separate families that lived across the street from each other, and the idea was supposed to be when Clarence got old enough, he could switch to butlering or chauffeuring for one of them. He was only sixteen and a half then. Dan was ten; I was twelve.

Clarence already knew he was going to have to take on a full-time job. I remember his face when he helped lower our father's coffin into the grave, and the set smile he started to have that day, while all the others was crying and carrying on, and praising the Lord. And I remember the way he walked away afterwards, keeping next to Mama but not touching her, dusting his hands again and again.

Before Clarence took the job, Mama asked him in the kitchen one morning if he couldn't get some kind of work connected with all the studying he'd been doing that might pay better. But Clarence just got up and unhooked the window screen and spit out a big blob of saliva, very still and careful. Then he shut the screen and came and sat down again.

Course, Clarence never had been one to answer Mama much. He'd been in her hold ever since he was little, same as Dan and me, only he didn't act like we did about it. I couldn't really figure if he kept a hate for Mama or what. There was days he fixed everything he might think of to grate her. And it wasn't just that he did whatever he wanted, he used to grate her on purpose: sometimes he would go out of his way to get her upset. But if I, or Dan, or anybody else ever did or even said anything that might fidget Mama—Clarence would come out of nowhere and be right there to fight for her.

He didn't exactly act different than before, but a while after our father's death the Tiger-Cat started to get a certain swing to him. And he could make the round, hard muscles of his body go almost cushiony when he wanted. Then, he had this way of flipping his head around to see what you might be doing—and suddenly it wasn't a boy watching you, at all. Never lasted more than half a second, but you got it.

I think, even while our father was alive, I began to get the feeling there was something about Clarence that Mama knew, and that he knew she knew. You could sense a change in the air whenever they was together: a kind of disgust and a love for each other they had that was tighter than anything I ever felt. Course, it didn't make no difference to me, but it did to Dan. When he was little, he would come in the same room with them, and right off make a play for Mama. But even if she picked him up or patted him, she kept her eyes around Clarence. And when Dan got bigger and really caught on, he would walk out and leave them alone.

The thing was, when I or Dan did a bad, Mama gave us hell. She smacked us, or kept us in, or worse. But not with Clarence. She could just look at Clarence, and whatever it was she didn't like, that was enough. She wouldn't lay a hand on him, or even yell at him, ever. Just a look. She and Clarence had that.

I remember once, not much after he went to work, when Clarence helped me deliver two big boxes of laundry Mama and me had done. It was in the afternoon, on his Sunday off. Late enough for the bugs to be settling into the weeds of the empty lot next door, starting their chitter and pout-cries for the light they knew would go soon. Clarence saw me leave the house with those boxes, and he came up behind me and took one.

You never could tell when Clarence was going to be there with you. Or if he was, how he might be going to act.

Walking along, he said: "Where we going?"

"Just over to that Miss Mornet's, on Melbourne. She takes it to the people she works for."

"*Miss* Mornet can't pick it up herself?"

"She does, usually," I said, "but she's sick."

We walked on a piece, and Clarence didn't say no more about her. I did, though. Clarence could always give you the feeling you had to apologize for people.

I told him: "Miss Mornet brings us an awful lot of work."

"Sure," he said. "And then gets paid twice what she hands Mama for it."

I gave up. Clarence had his own ideas about things.

I began to try taking two exact steps for every one of his, but my box was too heavy. Then I reached and grabbed some moss off a low branch we passed under. I used to like to scrape the gray off a string of moss and dig my fingernail into the green center.

A lady passed us, on my side. She must of been about forty, medium-dark and real pretty. I remember her because of the way she stared at Clarence—almost hungry. I thought that was a silly way to stare at a person. But Clarence didn't even take no notice.

Then I thought of a thing. "Hey," I said, "Tiger."

He told me: "My name is Clarence."

He hadn't ever minded that name before, it was what our father generally called him. Anyway, I said: "Hey, Clarence."

"What?"

"Your bike bust again?"

"Been bust."

"When you going to fix it?"

"When I get ready. Might sell it."

"What you going to sell it for?"

Clarence said, hard: "*Money.*"

I let that ride too. I didn't know how to tell him what I really wanted, and everything else was plain silly-talk. Course, when I just about made up my mind I wasn't going to say it at all, it plopped right out: "Clarence," I said, "I loved school same as you."

He turned and cut across the street, in the middle of the block. I had to run some to catch up with him.

After I did, he said: "You better forget about school."

"I don't want to forget."

"Forget it," he said. "You might not want to do a lot of stuff."

"Clarence. Would you . . . ?"

"Would I what?"

"Teach me . . . things?"

"What things?"

"Numbers and things," I said, "like you know."

"I don't know *nothing.*"

"Yes, you do," I said.

"No."

"*Please*, Clarence."

"Look," he said, "forget it. Nothing you learned at school is going to do you any good. Shut up and forget it. Just going to make you unhappy, and it won't help you for one stupid day in ten times the life you got to live. Just do your work and shut your mouth and forget it."

". . . Like Mama says."

Clarence snickered. "Mama always did know what she was talking about."

I asked: "What *you* going to do, Clarence?"

"About what?" He knew what I meant, though. He started walking faster.

I told him: "*You* ain't going to forget it. You was figuring again this morning, I saw you."

"Money," he said, flat, "I was figuring money. That's all I got to figure."

"How about all those numbers you used to could keep in your mind? You going to throw them right out of your mind?"

"No," he said. "I don't have to. All I got to do is just put a little dollar sign in front of each one."

"Clarence, ain't you going to be a *scientist*, like you said?"

"I might be what I might be, someday. Now, I told you to mind your own business."

"No," I said, "you didn't tell me that."

"Well, I'm telling you."

". . . Clarence."

"*What?*"

"I can't run no more."

"*Lord*," he said. But he slowed down to where I could walk. "Clarence-I-just-want-to-know-one-more-thing."

"Shit," he said, "you worse than Dan." Then: "Well, go on . . . get it out."

I asked: "Why you done started talking different?"

"Different than what?"

"Than the other way. You used to talk better than anybody, when you felt like it. How come you changed?"

". . . I talk the way I got to talk."

"Why? Why not the *right* way?"

"The right way is wrong."

"Wrong for who?"

Clarence said: "For a nigger."

"Why?"

"Because it is, that's why."

"Who says?"

"The white people says and the niggers says, both."

"You mean the white people where you work?"

"Them too."

"Did they *say* that?"

"Look," he told me, like he was explaining something to a little child for the umpteenth time, "Cille, look: you got to be *one* thing in this world, see? *One* thing or the *other*. If the white people want a nigger to shovel up the dirt in their garden, then they plain want a nigger, that's all. They don't want nothing else."

I said: "I bet a *scientist* would talk like you *used* to."

"A nigger ain't a scientist," said Clarence. "A nigger is a gardener. After you know what you are in a place, you just go and be it."

". . . Maybe they would let you talk right, if you asked them nice."

Clarence said: "You mean for Christmas?"

"For true, maybe they would."

"Cille," he said, "don't ever ask nothing, nice. You a nice kid, but keep that to yourself. That's your secret. Don't go around giving out no kindness, and don't ask for none. Just do your work, and make sure you get paid for it."

"I still don't understand about *you*," I said.

Very patient now: "What don't you understand, honey?"

"You didn't start talking like us on account of this job, or . . . anything that happened now. You already been talking this way for longer than a year."

We were waiting on a corner for a streetcar to pass. Clarence turned and stared at me. "How you know that?"

"I heard you."

". . . How old are you now, Cille?"

"Twelve and three months."

"Well, don't get too smart," he told me, "for twelve and three months. And don't get used to thinking, if you want to stay happy."

"Clarence," I said, "I ain't happy."

Then his face twitched, and he swayed toward me so close his eyes looked bigger than the day. He said: "That's your second secret, honey. That's just your second little secret. You can be *unhappy* and you can be *nice* now, both. Now, while you got the time. But keep those secrets, and don't let nobody else know. Keep them both to yourself, while you still can. Because they much too good to last. You going to be working so hard to eat in a couple years, you plain won't have time to be one of them."

But Clarence couldn't scare me. I stared back at him, and I said: "Our father told you a person could be anything he wanted. Our father told you that."

"What father?" he said.

"Clarence," I said, "you ain't near as nasty as you make out."

He reared back and looked away down the rusted car tracks. "You remember him saying that?"

"I remember most everything I ever heard him say."

Clarence kept his face turned when he told me: "I wouldn't, if I was you." Then he swung his body in the same direction as his face and padded off ahead of me down the dusty street.

Sunday school was worse than nothing. Dan and me had to go, though. Mama made Clarence take us there and wait for us, to make sure. After it was over, we three went home and picked up Mama and went to church. The whole thing took about four hours out of every Sunday morning.

I had lots of reasons for hating it. Sunday school taught you the same as Mama did: believe in the Lord Jesus, and believe in the Other World Heaven, and believe in the Other World Hell, and learn and believe in all the sticky little details everybody knows about all those things they never saw—but don't get curious about *this* world, because nobody's supposed to know a thing about it. And don't go asking yourself if God did create the heaven and the earth, why he got so good and holy about one, and then turned around and made such a crapped-up mess out of the other. Don't ever ask why He put you here; just get baptized and stick with Him, and then grit your teeth and see it through. Learn: every part of your body and your touching-world is full of dirty things and dirty ideas; don't expect to get all clean till you get out. Learn: every part of life that's fun is liable to be dirty and probably is, except praising the Lord. (Course, you can't really praise him for when a person gets born on this earth. So what you do is save it and have one slam-bang blessing party when the person dies and goes up to heaven.) Learn to do right by the Lord just like you was making a deal with Him. Because if you do, He will do right by you. And if you don't, oh brother.

I hated feeling dirty. I hated not having a place to find out about *my* world. And worst of all, I had a sense that the things they taught at Sunday school might of had something to do with our father's death. It was exactly one year before he died, right when he lost his last job, that he left off going to church and never went back again.

But I went to Sunday school, because Mama made me. Our father and his school was both gone. Mama, and hers, was all that was left.

Dan liked Sunday school. It was the only thing he had that wasn't on Mama's don't-list. He was cute about it then, too. He would sit and listen to the Bible stories so hard, he practically squirmed when the preacher's wife took time out to breathe or cough or look around the room. I was sure for a while he thought the Lord Jesus Christ was king of the cowboys.

He asked: "Was the Lord Jesus a white man or a black man?"

"Hush up," Mama said, quick, "don't ask questions."

And that spoiled that. He still liked Sunday school, though.

Church got to be the only reason Mama would leave the house, because I was the one did all the shopping. Around ten o'clock Sunday morning, she took a bath and put on her dress. Then she got her Bible, and sat in the kitchen if it was winter, or on the gallery if it was summer, and waited for us to come back from Sunday school. When she saw us, she locked the door and came down, and we usually walked all the way. She wouldn't let us take the streetcar, unless it was raining.

In church, she put Clarence next to Dan on one end, and she sat next to me on the other. She kept the Bible in her lap. She held it there, running her fingers over the cover till the gold letters was plain worn away. And when she prayed, she held it against her breast.

Mama could let go in church what she couldn't anyplace else. She was always the loudest praying person in three rows, and she would swing from side to side to the hymn singing till I had to brace myself against her if I didn't want to get knocked on the floor. She got just as excited as the preacher did every time, and whenever there was a new soul to save Mama had hers saved again too. I don't know how many times the same person can really be converted, but I think Mama set some kind of a new record in our neighborhood. Reverend Segrette always said church wouldn't be church without Alva Morris, and he knew if he ever went more than a couple Sundays without finding a soul to offer up to the Lord, he could always count on her.

Sometimes Mama didn't want to wait for Sunday, and she would make Clarence read to us from the Bible during the week, after supper. I never listened much, account of it was always around the time of day our father used to be with us, and that was all I could think about. And from the siren-whine Clarence got under his voice, I was pretty sure he had his mind on the same thing. Mama must of known too, only she just had to let Clarence go ahead and do it any way he wanted, long as he spoke clear. Because Mama loved the Bible more than anything else. And Mama couldn't read.

Some of what I told Clarence when we had that talk really got through to him, because he did start to give me lessons twice a week or so. He kept it up for almost a year. He taught me a little about spelling, and more about numbers. And he even let me look at a few of the books he still borrowed someplace. He gave me problems and things to figure by myself, and he always looked at me peculiar when he saw how quick I did them. (But once, a year later when I was past thirteen, he gave me a whole bunch of problems he knew was a heap harder than any I ever saw. After I brought him the answers to those, he sat and looked at the paper a long time. Then he folded it up and tore it into as many little pieces as he could; he walked over and put all the pieces in the stove fire, without dropping one. And he never gave me another lesson again.)

Dan didn't learn to write very well. He could put down a word the way he heard it, though, and he could read enough to get him by when he cared about doing it. Only Dan didn't care about it much. The thing Dan learned best was that he wasn't supposed to care about anything at all.

One day, five months after our father died, I was washing, and Mama ironing, in the kitchen. It was August, and the weight of the sky made my whole body open up and go flabby. I couldn't keep the sweat from dripping into the suds no matter how much I wiped my forehead, and the prickly heat was up inside my legs right into the crotch, and it was killing me. I had to stop once every so often and rest there, leaning over the sink and biting my lip not to scratch.

"Cille, you quit, che," Mama said. "You sit down a while."

"I ain't tired," I told her, and I wasn't. It was just the heat.

But when Mama said to do something, she wanted to see it done. "You go on over there and sit and breathe a while. Breathing is a very important thing for a person, and breathing is something you never did too much of. That's why you get winded so easy. Now go on over there and breathe some. Go on, do like I say."

I would of liked to finish the washing and get out, only there wasn't no use in taking up that kind of a point with Mama. So I went and sat in front of the screen door. It was just the same there as anywhere else, with the sun on the gallery and no air outside. But I slid forward in the chair and opened my legs wide, and the burning-itching eased off a little.

Dan was sitting on a chunk of the curb, playing with a stray she-cat that used to hang around the house. I could see him fine from the door. He had four or five acorns strung on an old wire, and when he rolled it between his fingers, the acorns danced. The minou wasn't much interested, but she would bat at it from time to time. Dan was used to being alone, and when he had to he could play like that for hours, stuff that would bore any other kid wild.

This open car came around the corner, skidding and splattering a little in the dry gravel and the dust. It was going pretty fast, and the man who was driving had to swing hard to the left to make up for the skid. There was a lady next to him in the front seat, and a young bald man in the back trying to keep his legs up. They was all white. I don't know what they was doing in the colored section, except maybe to fun up a dull day. Anyhow, they was laughing and not paying much mind to where they went.

They didn't mean to do it, and it wasn't all their fault, because the minou got panicky. Only instead of taking to a tree or something, she ran out right under the wheels and got squashed. Dan yelled, but too late, and it probably wouldn't of worked anyway: the man stopped the car and got out, and still wasn't exactly sure what might of took place. The cat was mashed across the middle, practically broke into different pieces. By the time the man went around to see, Dan was there trying to pick her up.

"Leave it where it is, kid," the man said, "ain't nothing you can do."

But Dan went right on trying to peel her out of the street.

"Oh, Mildred," said the man, "give me a quarter to give to this little nigger boy."

The lady in the car was all yellow and curly, and she had on a dress the same color as her mouth. She fished in her purse. "Is it a pussycat?" she said, "or what-all is it?"

The bald man behind her had one shoe off, scratching his foot. "Sure," he said, "you can always tell when it's a cat. A dog just makes one bump, but a cat hits twice. Sticks to the wheel."

"Don't talk revolting," the woman said. "I ain't got a quarter. How about a couple dimes?"

The bald man said: "Anyhow, what kind of a nigger is that? Looks like he been dipped in lye."

Dan let the cat alone and sat back down in the street. He wasn't crying. He asked: "She's dead, ain't she? Is she dead?"

The bald man leaned across over the fender and looked down. "If she ain't," he said, "you got two now."

"Shut up, Willard," the driver said. "Here, boy. Here's twenty cents. You can buy a cartful of strawberry snowballs and more cats too."

Dan didn't even look up.

"Come on, now," said the man, "take the money."

"He's holding out for the quarter," said the bald man. "They all do. Niggers get taught to do that before they can walk. Even pasty niggers."

"No, he ain't," said the driver. "Come on, kid. Take the money, I told you." He held the dimes over Dan's open hand, but it was kind of bloody so he just dropped them in it from high up.

Dan got on his feet and shuffled over to the curb. He was crying now. He looked at the bald man in the back seat. "You big shit," he said.

The man stuck one leg in the air and bust out laughing.

"Oh, come on," said the lady, "I want to go home. I really am *pained* by the whole *episode*."

"You killed her," Dan said, "you big shit." He didn't shout it, he said it kind of low. But he meant it.

The bald man went right on laughing. "Little kid's got balls," he said. "Funny color balls, but balls."

"Get in, Edward," said the lady. "I *told* you not to drive through the nigger district." She asked the bald man: "Are you going to sit there and let him call you that?"

Dan reached back and threw the dimes at the bald man's face. They missed him, and tinkered down against the side of the car. The man stopped laughing. "Hey, nigger," he said, "watch what you doing."

"Leave him alone," said the driver, getting in. "He don't know no better. Kid's upset."

The lady lifted one eyebrow way high, only nobody was watching her. She said: "What are *you*, a *altruist*?"

The car rolled away. Dan went over and kissed the cat, once on each half. Then he saw two other kids coming down the street, and he started to pick up the dimes, for Mama.

"Look at him," the man in the back seat shouted, "what did I tell you?" And he said something else, but by that time, the car was too far away for me to hear. I could see the lady laughing again when they turned the corner.

I would of gone out to Dan from the first, only Mama had been standing in back of me with her fingers digging into my shoulder since she heard the car skid. I looked at her afterwards. She was so scared, her mouth was fixed open, and she couldn't move. She still had a half-ironed slip in her right hand, hanging loose on the floor.

I tried to signal to Dan, but it wasn't easy with Mama right where she was, and he didn't see me. He came up the steps, sniffling, and he had his bloody hand stuck straight out with the two dimes in it, bringing them in to give to Mama. He opened the screen door hisself, and before he even saw her standing there, Mama came to life.

She grabbed him by his shirt collar and she lifted him clean off the ground over where I was sitting. Dan's shirt ripped down, leaving powdery white specks all through the ray of sun that came in the window. One of the dimes fell in my lap; the other banged against the wall, and slipped down behind the stove. Mama was so angry, she couldn't talk or hit Dan. She held him for almost a minute, and she kept looking around the room, as if that could help her.

Then she saw the gunny sack standing in the corner. She jerked Dan over and knocked it down, so the potatoes rolled out on the floor. They bounced around and got under everything. There was just potatoes all over the floor. She put Dan between her knees, and took the empty sack and slipped it over his head. Then she picked it up from the bottom, and shook him in upside down, like she was casing a pillow. Dan never opened his mouth.

Mama reached and got a cord out of the kitchen table, and tied the mouth of the sack. She took a knife, and cut two holes below the cord, next to Dan's feet. After she finished, she put the knife down, and hiked him up, and carried him outside. Around the side of the gallery, right under where one of the clotheslines attached, was where she left him. I watched her from the side window. First she tried to pin him on the line, but Dan was too heavy, so she put him on the ground, in a shady place. When she came back she was panting, and her jaw was set.

She picked up the slip from under the chair where she had dropped it. It was all dirty on one end. She held it out. "Wash it again," she said.

I said: "But, Mama . . ."

"*Wash it,*" she said.

So I took and put it in the sink and washed it again. I couldn't see Dan from there, but I kept thinking of him out in that heat in the gunny sack, and I started to cry. Only, I was sweating so hard, Mama didn't catch me.

She left him there two whole hours. Once I thought she was looking a little sorry, and I dried off my hands and headed out to him, but she said: "*Lucille.*" And I had to come back.

When she got ready, she went out alone and brought him in. The knot was so tight she had to cut the sack open. Dan had been sick at his stomach inside, and he was unconscious. It was hard getting him out, but she wouldn't let me help her.

She cleaned him off and put him in bed. He was sick for two days, and she tended him. She didn't even let me in there except for the bathroom, and to go to bed at night, after Dan was asleep.

When he was well enough, Dan came and sat at the table with us. Mama still hadn't said a word to him about the accident. She served Clarence first. Then me. Supper was redbeans and rice; Dan liked redbeans. She took an extra big scoop and put it on his plate. Then she dipped in again and gave him the whole cut of fatback. She stood by him a few seconds. "If I ever catch you saying them words or talking sassy to white people again," she said, "I will kill you, and it will be a kindness."

Then she sat down to eat, and never talked about it no more. I don't think she forgot it, though. And I don't think Dan did either. But he ate the redbeans and the fatback too.

2

MAMA wasn't as scared for me as she was for the boys. She watched me pretty careful, and she checked on me whenever she got the chance, but it wasn't the same. There was just a feeling around the house that Lucille could take care of herself. I could, too. Even later on, when I started to think I didn't have a real self. Even when I tried not to take care. I plain could: I had to. It was like something strong got born inside of me that wouldn't let me give up.

I must of been what they call a tomboy for a good long while. Or maybe not so much a tomboy as sort of a not-girl. Not like Jewel or Adelaide, and they was the only girls I saw around after I left school. Not like anybody; no girl nor woman I looked up to enough for that. And no time to try and find one, even if Mama would of allowed us new friends. No time at all.

Early every morning, I went to the market to get the food for that day. Mama used to go with me when I was real young, but soon as I learned how to get the best of the cheapest stuff, she let me do it alone. She trusted me with the money because she knew I wouldn't spend a penny more than I had to, and never on myself. And she knew that sometimes the market people would throw in a little lagniappe when a kid my age did the shopping. I liked doing it, after I got used to hearing people pass remarks about my color every so often. But Mama kept a count of how long it took me to go to market and come back again, so I couldn't stop and talk along the way.

When I came back there was cleaning the house, and folding Clarence's bed to take it out of the kitchen, and the washing to do, and then I helped Mama fix lunch. After lunch, more washing. After supper I was usually too tired to do anything but go to bed.

Maybe once a week, I would finish the afternoon's wash an hour early. Then, if Mama was feeling good, she would let me go over to Adelaide's house. Adelaide was the only girl—was the only person— Mama ever let us be friends with. That was just lovely, because I couldn't stand Adelaide.

I liked Jewel a lot, but she was on the don't-list. She lived right next door to us, between Mama's house and Adelaide's, so it was hard to sneak in and visit with her without getting seen by somebody on one side or the other. And Adelaide was a tattletale. I thought Adelaide was a fart.

Jewel was three and a half years older than me, and she was cooking in this house on St. Charles. Her mama died the day she got born, and she lived alone with her father. Jewel was kind of lumpy when she was little, but she got curvy when she got big, and she couldn't keep the men off no matter how hard she tried. Course she didn't try very hard. She sure always was nice, though. Used to get pregnant from time to time, but nobody paid her much mind. She got rid of them a-mile-a-minute for a few years, instead of having them, account of she never could save enough money. And that was how all her trouble started. But anyhow that was later. The thing was, Mama said if she ever caught us over at Jewel's, we could just stay over there, she didn't want us coming back to no house of hers.

So Dan and me always kept pretty much together, when we wasn't with Mama. We didn't ever have Clarence, mostly.

What I couldn't take in Adelaide was her being so prissy and cute-frilly and stuck-up. And worse even, I was plain sure she'd only started making friends with us because she was jealous of our color. I guess I didn't really know enough about people then to try seeing through to the why of them. But maybe not. Maybe I would of got through to Adelaide, if Mama hadn't pushed me at her so strong.

Mama must of sensed right early that I was a different kind of person from herself, and from the few people she approved of enough to say hello to at church. I always did. I didn't know what I *was*, but I knew I was different: I knew what I *wasn't*. Course, after our father died, it was a long time before I saw anybody that didn't seem to me like they was wasting breathing-space.

I think, in her secret mind, Mama kind of admired me for being different. She didn't love me for it, though. She didn't really know how to feel about me. I never got into trouble or caused her any worry, like Clarence and Dan; I generally did like I was told, and I always helped out everyplace I could. And still, Mama knew she couldn't handle me. I minded what she said because that was the thing to do, not because of any particular way she acted. I was her best-behaved child, and I was the one she couldn't understand.

Mama understood Adelaide, or she thought she did anyway. At least Adelaide felt right to her. The sense I never got over was that Mama would rather of had Adelaide for a daughter. We were the same age.

Adelaide wasn't quite as dark as Mama, but close enough, then. It wasn't till she grew up so tall that her skin pulled out and got a little cream under it. She had a real sweet face, and long, thin bones in her body—and she was always skinny and delicate till she stopped growing to fill in some. Only, I plain didn't go along with the delicate-business. Seemed to me from the very first she was just trying to be special.

But Adelaide got brought up to believe she was special. Her mama did special hand embroidery for a shop in the French Quarter, and made a heap of money on it. And her mama really was what you might call delicate. She was always coming down with something, even before she got the last thing that kept her laid up for so long. She was lighter than Adelaide. I remember her always being in bed, with too much face powder caked into the sweat, and an old gris-gris charm hanging on the wall by her feet, and a little white towel next to her so she could keep her hands dry for the embroidery. She and Adelaide lived by theirselves, and the story was that Adelaide's father died a long while back. Jewel always said she figured that for a fib.

Anyway, Adelaide spent most of her time trying to make people think there was something extra about her—better than all the other people in our neighborhood. Mama fell for it. And because Mama did, Dan did. It was so seldom Mama said yes about anything or anybody, Dan thought Adelaide must of dropped off a cloud. He even tried to make up to her a couple times, but what with Adelaide being my age and a stinker to boot, she wouldn't even make friends. She went for older boys, like most girls do, but they had to be special boys too. Jewel said Adelaide didn't really like boys, and I knew what she meant. It was a way Adelaide had of picking them out very careful, like something you buy at a store, for what she thought they might be worth to her. The summer when she was fifteen, she got herself a boy friend who was going to a university. I don't know where she found him, but she used to come up with that sort of thing. She used to make out she was a highly read girl. Which wouldn't of made no difference, only she wasn't, so she had to get stuck-up about it. And her being stuck-up and her being cute and her being prissy, the three things she had for a cover, was the same three things that kept everybody and me from knowing the special hell—the only truly *special* thing—little Adelaide had to live through. But that was later too.

Sometimes I would make like I was going over to see her so I could get out and see Jewel without Mama's knowing. It wasn't easy, though; I had to do it when Adelaide wasn't home.

Jewel was a year younger than Clarence, but some of her men friends was a lot older. She didn't start getting pregnant till she was seventeen. Jewel kind of liked me after a while, and she tolerated me even before then, account of she had it on for Clarence. So did Adelaide. So did most all the girls who ever saw him. But Clarence was a funny one.

Jewel's father was crippled, so he couldn't work. The railroad company gave him some kind of a lump pay-off back when he was a porter and had his legs cut away under a train. But it wasn't much, and it got used up the first year Jewel said. So she went to work, and got enough money for them both. Her father must of really known about her, about the way she laid around; he didn't say nothing, though. Course, he didn't get his mind all back on kilter after what happened to him. First Jewel started to do it because she was too young to get a steady job, and then she never stopped, I don't know why. Must of liked it, I guess. She never complained none. Not then.

Once Jewel mentioned to me that she had seen Clarence standing on Tulane Avenue with two white women. I went and asked him, but he said she was a dirty liar and a couple other names, and if he ever heard about my going over there again, he would tell Mama. So I didn't let on to Jewel that I'd spoke to him about it, but anyhow I told her he was very intelligent and had some very good associations from his gardening job. But she looked kind of strange, and said as how *that* kind of associations was the kind Clarence could of did without. And she said: *"Gardening* job . . . ?"

3

SUNDAYS with the River.

When the dandelions came out we collected them and made a big pile on the near side of the levee, and Dan would bury me under them. Sometimes he left my head free, and sometimes he buried it and only left me a space to breathe. When I got out of my blouse, he wanted me to take my skirt off too, so I would be all naked under the dandelions, only I never would. If there wasn't enough dandelions, we used goldenrod.

In the early years we had a pretend: I was Dan's mama, and I was sick. He spread me out on the grass and examined me everyplace. Then he mixed up a medicine out of River water and more mud, and he treated me with it on the end of his finger. But I got sicker. It was supposed to be winter, and we were on the North Pole. So Dan always decided what was wrong was I had got too cold. Only he never decided that till after he tried the finger treatment. Then he would lay down on top of me to keep me warm, because we had been put there on the Pole by a bunch of pirates who left us clean out of blankets just to be mean. Dan would lay still for the longest time, and he wouldn't let me move or even talk. He just lay on top of me with his eyes half closed. Then when the bugs got bad, and I had the sweat pouring off me and plain couldn't take it, I would push him off. That was the part he liked best. He was strong and he always grabbed me around the middle and hung on. Sometimes I had to hurt him to make him let go. But he never got mad.

The summer levee was burnt all yellow and brown and dusty by the sun. If you pulled up the crab grass, big chunks of dust would come up. You had to tear it out, because crab grass has a fierce hold, but if you did it right you could get a piece a foot long. There wasn't many trees out there.

There was a bunch of white boys used to play on top of the levee. They had a white man who drove them in a station wagon that said "Billy Club" on the side, and I think he was like a teacher or something. He had a sled tied on behind the station wagon, and he would drive them along the cowpath up there, following the levee. One of the boys stood out on the sled holding the end of a rope, and they went along till that boy fell off or got tired, and then it was somebody else's turn. Most always he fell off. When the sled picked up pieces of cow dung and threw them up at him, they near died laughing. We could see them coming from way off, and we would lay on our stomachs and hope they didn't see us, and watch. They never would of given us a thought, but once the boy on the sled fell off right above where we were laying, and they had to stop there. Two or three of them got down and pointed us out to the rest. Then they all got to shouting. You couldn't hear what they said, but you could get it from the sound of their voices. And they must of been using pretty dirty words, because the man tried to make them shut up. But they didn't want to, so he started the car and left a couple of them standing there, and they had to run to catch up with him. Then he slowed down, and every time the boys was almost there, he started away and left them behind again. So they all got to laughing about that and forgot about us. A ways along, he let them catch him, and one of them stood out on the sled again, and they drove off, still laughing.

"I ain't never going to work for no white man," Dan said.

I told him to keep quiet.

"I ain't," he said, "they can come and get me and bash my face in like they did Tenet Stevens. I ain't never going to work for no white man."

Tenet Stevens was a delivery boy for a white grocery. He rode the bike that belonged to the store while he was making deliveries, and one day some white boys stepped up and made him let them take a ride. Then they got to throwing the groceries around, and they broke a box of eggs. So Tenet got mad and lit into them, and they bashed his face in and broke the bike. He wanted to go back to work when he got out of Charity Hospital, but the store wouldn't take him. That's why some white stores don't like to give colored kids much work, they say they never last long.

I said to Dan: "What you going to be, President of the United States?"

"No," he said, "I just ain't going to work for no white man." Dan used to have this habit of repeating a thing five or six times when he knew you didn't want to hear it.

I said: "You just go right on saying that."

Dan did.

I told him: "You just watch Mama don't catch you, that's all."

Dan said it again.

"You say it once more," I said, "and I'll slap you right on up to Baton Rouge."

Dan started to sing. "I," he sang, "Oh, I . . . Oh, I ain't . . . No, I ain't . . . No, I ain't a going to . . . No, I ain't a going to work . . ."

I stepped up to him.

"I ain't said it yet."

"You better not say it, neither."

He didn't want to back down: "How far away is Baton Rouge?"

"Say it and find out."

"I would say it did I want to," he told me, real nonchalant. "But I plain don't feel like it." And he reached around and pinched me way up on the back of my leg, and cut out across the levee.

We generally buried the poles in the same place, and when we felt like it we took them over and fished in the River. You wasn't supposed to fish there, only nobody ever stopped you. You couldn't catch but just catfish, and you almost never got one. Dan never did. He used to get peeved when I had a nibble, and he would go up and slide down the levee so rocks and dirt would fall in the River and scare the fish away from my hook. I caught one two or three times, though. Catfish make pretty good eating, but you can get a bad sting from their whiskers.

If you go up on the bridge and watch down at the River, it looks the longest ways; but if you are on the ground and watch up at the bridge, it don't look so very high. We just sneaked up once, because they didn't allow you there. Dan got scared. Dan hated high-up places.

I used to hear people say the bayous across the Lake in the swamp are like little rivers. But when I saw them, after I left Mama's house, I found out they ain't. The bayous have trees, lots of them, with moss so heavy it looks like it's pulling them over into the water. Cypress trees, with their knotty knees sticking up out of the wet, looking dead-alive—like a praying mantis looks when it sits still for hours, and then picks up one leg—just one leg—and stretches it out in the air. The bayous have more fish, too, and worse slimy things. I remember in the spring when the gars got to running, and the black water boiled high with those dark-shined bodies. And the bayous have snakes, and alligators, and even little spiders to run over them; spiders so light they make dry dents in the water.

That ain't the big difference, though.

A bayou is gloomy, and the further up you go, the gloomier it gets. Way up, where it narrows, the trees sometimes cross overhead and shut out all the light. (Once, I saw a heron there, standing in the water looking at me, looking back.) And the water is clear and dark, and it feels empty, like tap water. You can't talk to a bayou like you can to the River. A bayou is just a thing.

The River was born alive, and she moves like she was solid—a whole of a piece—taking new dirt to her body and always, always growing. Her water is so thick with mud it looks like it's hardening from the bottom through. And there ain't no animals to bother you, because the River is big enough for everybody.

But I don't think any person could ever of loved the River like I did, in all the time of the world. I can still feel the strange wonder that came to me when I first saw her. I must of stood there and looked for about five minutes. I plain couldn't believe it. Dan kept tugging at my arm, saying something, I don't recall what. Then I took off all my clothes and dropped them on the ground next to me. And when I was standing naked as the sun, I walked right into the River. Dan yelled at me—we hadn't neither of us been in swimming anywhere. But I was sure that didn't matter, even before I stepped down and found out with my touch what I already knew in my mind must be true: that her water wasn't no hotter nor colder than my own blood, and we felt right together. And when I got down inside her, she held me up like what I was—like one of her own. She held me and she moved me along in her way, so slow, so slow and thick and easy, it seemed as if the land was moving, and I was just staying still there under the sky. But I knew, I already knew how it would be. I knew the second I ran over the levee and stopped on a breath halfway down, to see that big long woman, that gut-bucket mother

River—the only *real* woman I ever saw—with exactly the same color as my stupid skin.

And I never left off loving her. And I don't think I ever will.

While Dan and me was still little, we played games on the near side of the levee till we plain had to fall down to get our wind back. But the older I got, the more I wanted to cross over and fish, or just sit and do anything that kept me touching the water. Because I knew time would catch up with us soon, and then I wouldn't be able to stay near the Sunday River any more.

The day I remember best was in the beginning of the second summer after our father died, when I was thirteen, and Dan eleven.

I had a hook in the River, waiting to see if a catfish would pass by and be hungry. It's hard to find them hungry. She feeds them all right.

Dan was fishing too. Only he couldn't sit quiet long enough.

I'd been noticing ever since Christmas how tightened up Dan was getting. He had clean lost his knack for sitting in one place, hour after hour, playing one lone game by hisself. He couldn't even keep his body still, he jerked and moved around all day now. He kept running into the kitchen and running out and changing his game every five minutes. Then if he did sit down, he would get a queer frown on his face, and then a whoops-de-doo expression like he just remembered something. But, quick as he got on his feet, he forgot it. And he would wander off to something else. It wasn't the same as any kid will bust out all over the place, discovering new things. I would of done it with him if I'd thought it was that. No, it was more like a person will turn a house upside down, looking for a certain thing they know has to be there. I wasn't sure just what Dan might be looking for, but whatever it was, he couldn't find it. He couldn't even remember it.

Well, he fished for a while. But he never stopped thinking he saw the cork edge down, and he would pull the pole up so fast the hook swung way back over his head and got stuck in the levee. At the rate he was going, if he ever did get a bite, that worm would of been question number one to some fish for the rest of its life.

"Che," I said, "the only way you going to kill a fish doing like that is if it swims on out to the Gulf and then dies of curiosity."

"I don't want to kill one," he said, "I plain wouldn't want to *kill* one."

He kept at it about two minutes more, and then he got tired staying where he was. So he got up and went a piece further down and started over again. Only, he didn't last long there either.

"Ain't no fish in this here River," he called, "it's all a waste of time."

But I wasn't going to quit. I made signs for him to shut up. Catfish can hear.

Course, he yelled back: "Let's us go over and play tag."

I said no with my head.

Dan shouted: *"Got him,"* and jerked his line out so quick he fell flat on his back. He stood up and looked down at the water. "Missed him," he said.

"You didn't miss him," I said, "he missed you."

Dan took his pole and wrapped the line around it and stuck the hook in the cork. Then he left it there and ran up on top of the levee.

There was a catfish nibbling on my bait; I didn't let on, though, for fear Dan would come down and scare him off. He was only playing with the worm. I could tell, because the cork didn't go down —just bobbed there on the surface, making circle ripples in the water.

"Come on," Dan yelled. "Cille. You might come on. You ain't going to catch nothing."

The cork went down and up, twice. That fish couldn't make up his mind to swallow.

Dan took hold of a little rock and threw it at the River. It landed right next to me, and I stopped it from going in. If he scared this one off, he was going to get strangled.

But the cork went all the way down, and I jerked about six inches to the left. I could feel him struggling then, so there wasn't no problem. I just let go the pole, and grabbed the line, and pulled him out.

Dan came skidding down the levee. "Did you get him?"

I had him laying on the grass, flipping. The blackest catfish I ever saw.

"That must be the one ate all my bait," Dan said.

I knew he hadn't had a nibble, but I didn't say so.

"You step on him light," he said, "and I'll pick the hook out." Dan couldn't stand to see a hook in anything. He wouldn't even hook his own worms. Come to think of it, I don't know why Dan ever did any fishing at all. Seemed to like it though.

"You watch you don't get stung," I told him.

It ain't easy to step on a catfish, they much too oily and rounded. My foot was slipping off. And the harder I stepped, the more slippery he got.

"Watch out," Dan said, "you mashing him."

I picked up my pole and held the point of the butt down against his side. Dan lay flat on the ground in front of him and looked in his mouth.

"He swallowed it," he said. "Poor fish."

"You going to get it out?" I asked, "or you going to lay there?"

Dan took and put a finger on the catfish's mouth. The fish made a gasping sound, and he pulled his finger back. "Swallowed it real deep," he said. His voice was high, and I was sure he was going to cry.

I squatted down and felt for the rock behind my foot.

"What you going to do?"

". . . Bump him on the head so he don't feel nothing."

"You going to kill him now?"

"Don't you cry," I said, "I'm just going to bump him on his head a little so he don't feel nothing."

Dan's chin was shaking. "Put him in the water, Cille."

"He can't live with that hook inside him," I said, "not even in the water."

"Don't kill him." Dan started to cry.

I said: "You go on up over the levee. I'll call for you when I get it out." I was going to kill the fish and throw him back in the River. But Dan knew. He turned his back and stuck his fingers in his ears.

I brought the stone down on the fish's head. A catfish is hard to kill. I had to do it again and again.

"*No*," Dan shouted, "*no*."

I put my fingers deep in the fish's mouth and felt for the hook. It was too far down. So I took the other end of the pole and stuck it in the soft part under his belly, and ripped him open far as I needed. A lot of dark blood blupped out. I went on quick so Dan wouldn't have to see it; I pulled the line taut to find where the hook was, and got to working it free.

Dan sidled around and looked down over his hand. "You killed him dead," he said, "you stinking fool."

I tried not to pay no attention till I had the hook out on the ground.

Dan said: "You fool. You dirty stinking liar." He still had his fingers in his ears.

"Wasn't nothing else to do," I said, "you wouldn't want him to suffer."

"Ass-fool. You didn't have to kill him dead," Dan said. He kicked out at the fish's body to push it back in the water. That was when he got the hook in his heel.

I still can't figure exactly what Dan might of felt then. He never was a sissy, and a little pain wouldn't of scared him. Anyhow, the hook was just a tiny ways in the rindy part, where his heel was all calloused over: couldn't of hurt him none at all. Maybe he did it because he was crying before, but I don't think so. It was something else.

He started to scream, loud and hard. So hard his voice broke, and he had to gulp and force it out again. Screams, one right after the other. He wouldn't stop. And he wouldn't take his fingers out of his ears. The funny thing about it was, he'd stopped crying, and he had this lost, staring look, almost as if he didn't see me. That was the thing I didn't like—the feeling he couldn't see me and couldn't hear me, and didn't want to.

And I got worried somebody might come around there. Then it would of been bad.

I shouted at him, and shook him, but he could as well of been made out of cotton. When I saw he was standing on the hook, I knelt down and took his foot. He plain let me. I was only a second getting it out. Where the skin is that tough, you can rip without sensing it, no more than cutting a fingernail. And he didn't even wince; he didn't move. He just went on screaming.

Then, when I wasn't sure what else to do except maybe grab Dan in my arms or smack his face—he stopped of his own accord. Sudden as he'd started, he stopped. And stood there shaking all over and looking out into space. I patted him, and I tried to hold him afterwards, but it was like he didn't even know I was there. It was funny. It was like Dan had got so scared by some horrible secret thing he felt or saw, he wasn't really there hisself.

He stayed the same way for about fifteen minutes. I left him to go bury the fishing poles, and then he let me take him by the hand and lead him over the levee. I put his shirt on and his shoes. He was still shaking pretty bad.

By the time I got him home he had quit, but he kept on with that stare, and he wouldn't talk none. I never said a word to Mama, and she didn't take no notice. She was pretty mad about something else, I remember.

The next morning, Dan had forgot all about it. He ate his breakfast and went out to play, and he even seemed a whole lot easier than before. Most of the tightness was gone, and he sat on the steps and played quiet all morning without getting up once.

I still didn't like it, though.

4

DON'T breathe, try not to move, in the summer. Don't do anything, just be. Stand there. Don't lay down, because the side you lay on will get all wet. Hold your arms away from your body and stand with your feet apart. Don't get yourself pregnant for the summer. When you work, go on, work, but don't think about it. Do what you got to do, that's all.

In the winter the wet turns cold, and it always freezes. Always. There is a note in the paper saying it's the coldest it's been on that particular day for one hundred years. Course, in New Orleans they bury all the water pipes shallow, about six inches underground, because the flat land is really swamp-flat and too soggy underneath for pipes—and because it ain't ever supposed to freeze so deep anyway. Then, when it does, you get no water for a while. The ice swells up inside the pipes, and they bust. After about two weeks, the water company comes and lays new ones in exactly the same place. They don't put them any deeper, because it still ain't ever supposed to freeze so deep. It was just an accident; it won't happen again. Not till next year.

You think the same thoughts every year. In the summer you think summer thoughts, and in the winter you think winter thoughts. You are always sure it's the first time you ever thought them.

Like playing Parchesi. You can play fifty straight games of Parchesi, and the next one is still going to feel like a different game. You fool yourself: you believe you on a terrific *new* game, just because the positions get mixed or somebody else gets ahead. Or maybe you took to using the red chips instead of the yellow ones. You forget you starting from the same place, and going in the same direction, and sooner or later you will end up in the same goal. Might not be this game. Might not be the next. But you will. It might take you ten minutes or twenty minutes or even a half-hour—but that won't change the game. Because, honey, you are still playing Parchesi.

But you won't believe it. You *can't* believe it and still do it. Or supposing you could, who wants to see herself pushed around like a Parchesi chip? Everybody likes to think they got a little to say about how they going to live, even if they know it ain't true. And you do always get a chance to roll the dice before the next move. *Something* could happen.

It could so.

That's right, that's the way. Forget what you already sensed, go on, kid yourself. Laugh and have one good time. You might just as well, you don't know how to play nothing else. What else you going to play?

Starting from the time I was thirteen and got the curse, Mama turned me upside down every Sunday night, and looked in between my legs. She always said she could tell right off did I ever get a mind to do something dirty. I guess she figured that would keep my mind from wandering on my parts. Course, the way it worked, all I could think of was *who* I wasn't going to do nothing *with*.

Which was mostly why I took to going over to Jewel's. I thought I might pick up a couple details from her—some of the stuff I wanted to know. Not because I counted on going wild, I just wanted to find out how things was. You couldn't even scratch your personal self at Mama's house, and Adelaide got so cute about it, she acted like she kept her money there. Matter of fact, I think she did.

Jewel never did get cute, but she wasn't much help neither. She learned to loan it out to men kind of like you learn to eat with a fork instead of with your fingers, and she didn't give it no more importance. I think, over half the time, she didn't even enjoy goofing off. Just sort of a habit she got into. But she was a good friend, and she didn't take no more notice of my color than she did of anything else.

Anyway, Mama sure got me going backwards. She said what I had down below was dirty to look at and dirty to touch, except twice every day with a washrag, and dirty in all the ways you could imagine and dirty all the time. She used to stand by me when I scrubbed it, to make me turn my head up and not watch. And when I asked her what the curse was for, she said it was how the Lord reminded a woman once every month that she had to keep on taking the right kind of care of a certain part of her body. (Jewel said that made sense to her.) But I used to sneak into the bathroom, and open my legs, and look in this broken piece of mirror I found on the street that Mama didn't know I had. Then I would wonder things. Only, Mama made me believe that even thinking about my parts was so filthy-dangerous, I plain didn't want to touch them.

Course, according to Mama, thinking was bad no matter what you did it about, except the Lord, and then it wasn't thinking, it was thanking. For a garden. Otherwise, thinking about the world was awful, and doing it about yourself was worse, and doing it about your personal self was plain criminal.

She tried everything she could, not to ever let me know I was pretty. And it worked. She always dressed me the same: a high middy blouse, and a plain brown skirt she made, and easy-walkers just like Dan's. For Sunday school and church, I had a sack dress always made of the same dark brown material as the skirt, with brown shoes like Dan's Sunday shoes. My coat, when I had one, was cut without a waistline, and it was brown too. Long as Mama could, when the dress got too small, she would let it down and open a seam on the side to put an extra piece in. My hair had to be combed straight back in a bun.

The real reason she dressed me that way was to make up for my color. She didn't want me thinking I was particular around the other girls on the Lord's day. Course, most of them didn't have but one dress either, but it was always frilly and starched and fancy colored, and their mamas primped them up real sweet. So I felt even more particular and out of place.

One of the few times Mama ever smacked me was when Adelaide let me try using her mama's hot-comb to get the kinks out of my hair. Mama said changing any part of my looks was against the Lord, because if He had meant for me to be pretty He would of made me different. Then, when I told her whose hot-comb it was, and how Adelaide always used it on her own hair, Mama just said Adelaide had to have a special care of herself account of the way she was. But I wasn't special. Only peculiar.

She wouldn't let me date like all the other girls. Not till two years later when I was fifteen, and then it was timed better than a boxing match. (I didn't know any boys anyway, and I had to start off with the turn-backs Adelaide sent over for me; the best of them could walk.)

So I used to sneak over to Jewel's.

When Jewel wasn't there, her father always was. He had a cart like a pencil-seller's cart Jewel put together for him out of three boards and an old pair of roller skates she got someplace. She was trying to save up enough money to buy him a wheel chair. He used to sit in the front room facing the door, and when somebody came in he would put his hands over the stumps of his legs and grin real shy —like Dan when he did a bad. He didn't hardly ever talk.

Jewel mostly hadn't the time after her job to come home and cook meals and clean house too. So whenever I got a chance, I went over and scrubbed everything down for her and gave her father his supper. Jewel always left it on the stove. He could get around okay by hisself, only he wouldn't in front of anybody. He got pretty used to me, though.

When I did something for them, cleaning up or serving him his supper, he didn't use his voice, but he nodded up and down at me or put his hand on my arm, and I knew what he meant. He treated Jewel like that too, and he never asked her for one thing, he just took what she gave him. She said it was hard on her, because if she forgot to fix the food there wasn't no way she could find out about it, he never would tell her. She said he got his strangeness right after the train accident, and he stayed the same ever since.

Every so often, Jewel brought a boy home. She told me sometimes, and everybody knew. She claimed her father didn't understand, but I think he did. I think he understood a lot, and he could of talked if he'd wanted to. Only it just wasn't his place to say anything.

I told Jewel: "Yesterday I couldn't open my mouth."

The day before, I had passed her on the street in front of Mama's house, and Mama had been watching.

"Lord, che, that don't matter," she said. She started to fan us up with a palmetto-shape fan she had, made out of cardboard.

It was around five o'clock on one of the days she lost her job. We were in her bedroom. Jewel's house had three rooms, like Mama's, only backwards. She was drinking a Coke, and I had this bowl of chipped ice in my lap, and I was sucking on a piece. I'd already been there a good while that day, because I'd sneaked over an hour or so before she got home, and washed all the dirty plates.

"You shouldn't ought to come over here so much," Jewel said, "somebody going to find out."

I said: "I don't give a whang." She knew I did, but what could I say?

"You wash *all* them dishes?"

"Sure."

"I swan," she said.

Adelaide's mama was watching us from her window. She kept her bed placed so she could see out. The sun was on her, and you could tell the face powder she used was way too light a color. It made her look like all the skin was peeling off. I was afraid she might tell Adelaide I was with Jewel, only I didn't want to let on it mattered to me.

But Jewel saw me scrounch away from the window, and she looked around. Then she slid over and pulled down the shade. "That old bitch," she said, ". . . always laying there."

"Adelaide claims she's got diabetes."

"She ain't got nothing I know something wouldn't cure her of," Jewel said.

"Adelaide claims she does."

"Like you tells me, Adelaide been claiming a lot of things."

"That's true. Well, what *you* think is ailing her mama?"

"I don't think. Something a mite peculiar over there, though."

"Like what?"

Jewel said: "Oh, you don't ever want to be too sure." She had her right arm up with the fan, and I could see the long triangle bleached white from the pit down to her waist, where she had sweated the print clean off her dress.

"Hey, how come you lost your job this time?" I asked her.

"Shoot," she said. "Mrs. Wirth."

"She the lady you was working for?"

"Uh-huh." Jewel wasn't really in such a bad mood, only it was too suffering hot to talk. The sun came right through the green shade, sucking it back out and pasting it against the sill.

But I wanted to know: "You quit, or she let you go?"

"I ain't never quit on no job."

"Why she fire you?"

Jewel yawned. "Don't know for sure."

"Course you know," I said. "Why?"

"Got her grated, I guess. Going to have a baby."

"She is?"

"No," said Jewel, "I am."

I sat up. "Hey," I said, "you never told me."

"Didn't know it myself till a couple weeks ago."

"How you find out?"

"Doctor."

I looked down at her. It didn't show yet. I asked: "How did Mrs. Wirth find out?"

"She saw me throw up," Jewel said, "and she asked me."

" . . . Che, what you going to do?"

Jewel stood on her feet. "Doctor says I best get rid of it. Don't much like to." She pulled her dress off and lay back down on the bed. (Jewel didn't used to wear but just a cotton brassiere and panties, no slip.) "Doctor says with nobody to take care of it and all. And the money. Course, ain't going to be cheap no ways." She put the back of her hand over her eyes. "Reach me a piece of ice, che."

I gave her one. "How come she fire you," I asked, "on account of that?"

"Don't know. Said first she wanted to help me."

"How help?"

"Shoot," said Jewel, "give me this big long talk. Told me I shouldn't ought to be scared about it."

"*Was* you scared?"

"No." She giggled. "Who, me?"

"So anyway, what happened?"

Jewel saw I wasn't going to let her alone till she explained me all about it. She stretched back and grabbed the iron bedposts, one in each hand. "Che," she said, "I swan. You the end."

I waited. Jewel was pretty if you looked at her like that, from down below. She had a tight little waist, but there wasn't a bone on her. Her face was all rounded out and chicory, and it glistened there, even without the light on it. There was a sweat line on her upper lip, but she didn't look puffy the way people do when the heat cases them in and dries them; she looked steaming, like she gave out her own fire to set back the summer.

She licked around her mouth. "Mrs. Wirth come to sit with me in the kitchen. Wanted to know who-all made the baby. Said she wanted to help me do right, account of my not having no ma nor nobody to teach me. I was supposed to tell her who done it, and she was going to help me find him and make him marry me. Must of thought this was the first man I ever been with, because she said she knew that lots of colored men like to fool around with poor innocent young girls like me, but anyway, this one wasn't going to fool. Said:

" 'Jewel, now it all depends on you, and on your ability to come out and tell the truth. Now you be honest, and nothing going to happen to you. Honesty and truthfulness is the most important things in this life, except for charity, and charity is just what I got here for you. And I am going to help you plain fix your broken life all up and make it happy, and put you on the right road. So you tell me who this man is, and I will help you to find him, and we going to get you a husband, and everything going to be all right. It just ain't fitting that a nigger man should be allowed to grab a young girl's heart and walk off with her innocence and get away with it, whether she's a nigger or not. And if he married, you tell me that too, because then he going to have to pay for the support of the baby.

Now, I am going to give you back the peace of God, so you be a truthful good girl with me, and don't be afraid to tell me the name of the man who is going to be the father of your child.' "

"Did you tell her the truth?" I asked.

"Sure," Jewel said, "told her I didn't know."

"What she say?"

"She got all hurt up. Thought I didn't want to tell her. Said I didn't put no trust in her because she was white, but I should understand she is a white person that wants to help the poor people who is colored and don't know no better. Said I had to find it in my soul to be honest and tell her exactly who this boy was, and not cover up for him just on account of I am in love with him, because love is a wonderful thing, but you can't never trust it loose. Told me to push my love away to one side, and show up the buster that got a hold of my innocence."

"*Lord*, che, what you do?"

Jewel leaned up on both elbows. "Well, honey, I felt kind of sorry for her. She wanted to know so bad, I sort of thought I had to tell her something. So I tried to be nice. I told her the *whole* truth, just like she wanted me to. I said:

" 'Mrs. Wirth, ma'am, like I say, I don't know. I really ain't just exactly certain *who* it was. But I certainly *hope* it was the one bought me that nice fish sandwich.' "

". . . So what she do?"

"She fired me," Jewel said.

"Why?"

"Don't know," she said.

She got up and went into the kitchen for another Coke. They had a real icebox. Course, it wasn't electric, it worked by putting a hunk of ice in the top part. Nothing stayed cold much longer than it did in the barrel we used.

My legs was cool from the bowl. I stuck my hand up under my skirt and felt of the skin.

Jewel called: "You want one?"

"No," I said.

"Got two left."

"No," I said, "thanks." Then I remembered her father. I put the bowl down and went in the other room where he was sitting. "You want a Coke, sir?" I asked him. "How about an iced Coke to keep out the heat?"

He leaned forward a piece and let his hands fall over his leg-stumps, like always; he grinned at me. I thought it was a new kind of grin, till I looked and saw he had his teeth laying out on the arm of the chair.

"Don't put him no questions, che, just give it to him," Jewel said, from the kitchen. She held me out an opened bottle, and I took it and slipped it up in his hand. His fingers closed around the middle, but he only let it stand there, without drinking. He was watching the bubbles.

I went back in the bedroom and lay across the foot of the bed.

Jewel came in. "I'm sweating up a breeze," she said. She lay down crosswise, like I was.

"Jewel, when you going to get another job?"

"I get one, don't you worry none about me, che."

". . . Did you tell your papa?"

"He don't take a notice of nothing no more." She sounded angry.

I said: "He can't help it."

"Course he can't," Jewel said, "you bringing me news."

"How come he pulled hisself all in like that?"

"You get hurt like he did," she said, "you pull yourself in too."

That made sense. Then I saw Jewel had her hand over her belly, where the baby was. "Don't let the doctor hurt *you*," I said, "doing what he does."

Jewel laughed loud, and her voice gave off a high ring to stay in your ears, like the last note of a bell. She said: "*Can't* nobody hurt me, honey. I got the hurt pushed in when I was born. It was the only thing my mama had to leave me."

I could see she was feeling lousy now. Her eyes was shut, and her head swung over the edge of the bed. I took the empty Coke bottle out of her hand and put it on the floor. "I guess I'll go on home," I said.

Jewel didn't open her eyes. "Sure, che," she said, "you go on home."

I got up, and stood a minute, but I couldn't think of much else to say or do, so I left her there.

When I was in the other room, she called: "Thanks, honey." She meant for washing up the plates.

"That's all right," I said.

I passed in front of her father, still sitting with the Coke in his hand, watching it. He must of been thinking, he hadn't moved or drank any. Soon as he saw me, he quick put it up to his face and wet his lips a little. Then he pushed his tongue out over them and took the bottle in both hands and nodded up and down, grinning again.

After I passed him by, I looked around and I saw he was still grinning; but he had stopped his head halfway through the last nod, like a tin dancing-doll that quits with one foot in the air when the spring winds down.

I took a careful peek out the back door. Mama wasn't looking. I ran, fast.

"Do I ever have a baby," Adelaide said, "I would most enjoy for it to be identical twins." Lord knows where she got that from.

I wasn't sure what identical twins was, and I would of laid eight to one she wasn't either. I kept my mouth shut, though.

Dan and Clarence was with us on the gallery—Clarence standing up, and the rest of us sitting on the steps.

Adelaide had spotted Clarence there on her way back from the drugstore with a package, and made believe she was coming over to talk to me. She saw Mama in the window, and waved and said: "Good evening, Mrs. Morris."

"Evening, che," Mama said.

Adelaide knew Mama thought she was a good thing. She came over and sat next to me. "Good evening to all," she said. "My," she said, "ain't it hot, though? Why, I just thank my lucky stars every time the sun *de*scends." Adelaide copied most of her talk out of the toothpaste ads and songs and the pictures.

The mosquitoes was getting bad, and she was sitting so close I couldn't get my hand out to slap. I moved over.

Then I saw the way Adelaide's hand was picking at the skirt of her pretty blue dress. A little like Mama's might do—just picking there. I think if Mama hadn't given me such a natural dislike of her, I would of known then that something was beginning to pan out a little wrong for Adelaide.

"What is that book you are reading, Clarence?" she asked. Clarence was reading this book.

Dan said: "It's a *science* book. Ain't it, Clarence?"

"How *interesting*," said Adelaide. "I don't believe I have ever read a *science* book. Would you be so kind as to lend it to me when you are finished?"

Clarence didn't hear her.

"I got me a book about toads you can have," Dan said, "it shows all the different kinds of toads . . . ? I found it myself on the floor in the streetcar."

Mama stuck her head out the screen door. She said: "Would you-all like a glass of lemonade, Adelaide?"

"Why, Mrs. Morris," Adelaide said, "listen at you: *lemon*ade . . . *Adel*aide. Why that sounds so nice, I think I will just have a glass. Thank you very much."

That was the kind of remark, I thought, would of driven our father to the nearest bar.

The light was getting bad, and Clarence went over and sat on the railing.

"Are we disturbing you with your reading?" Adelaide asked. (Are *we* disturbing you.)

"He don't even know you here, yet," Dan told her. "When he picks up a book . . . "

"Oh, yes," she said, "I know just how he feels. Why, Mama says when I get to reading there ain't a single thing in the world will *consume* my *attention.*"

Dan said: "I could get you that book about toads . . . wouldn't take me but a second."

But she made a face to me and didn't answer him. Mama brought her out the lemonade, and we sat some more. She was waiting for it to get too dark for Clarence to read. Then she got this dreamy look and pulled the line about the identical twins.

Dan never did know when to keep his mouth shut. "What is *idical twins?*" he asked. He couldn't even say it right.

"I*den*tical twins," said Adelaide, "is when you get these two twins that one looks just exactly like the other one. Like having two separate babies that you can't tell which is which." I should of known she wouldn't come up with it if she hadn't got it explained to her first.

Dan lifted his shoulders. "I ain't never seen two babies didn't look the same to me," he said. Which took care of her. Dan could do that from time to time.

"Well," said Adelaide, swinging back fast, "like they say, two eyes see what one eye don't." She made that one up.

I sneezed.

Adelaide said loud: "Why, I just *knew* there was something I had to tell you, Cille, and you doing that plain reminded me of it. You acquainted with this girl, Jennie Dentine, who been living up in New York City for three years now? You *ain't?* Well, anyway, she came back for two weeks with her mama to sell all the stuff they got here, so they can go back up to New York City and live there for always, and I got to talking to her, because me and Jennie was always such good friends before she left the first time, and you know what she told me?"

"Not likely," I said, "if I don't know who she is."

"Well, Jennie told me she is doing *modeling* work up there, you know, posing for pictures and things? See, Jennie is real light, and she has a real thin *nose,* and she says they are just looking for colored people up there to do that kind of work, and you know what she told me? She said, 'you know that boy, *Clarence Morris?*' And I said, 'why, yes, I am acquainted with him.' And she said, 'why that boy could get into *modeling* work so easy, he plain wouldn't know what hit him.' And she said, 'they ain't got nobody up there near as good-looking as *Clarence Morris,*' and she said, 'with *his* face and *his* body, there just ain't no telling how much money he could make up there, and if somebody would only do him the *favor* of *telling* him, why he could make more money than anybody.' So I said, 'why you know,' I said, 'it's funny you should say so, because I have always thought *Clarence* was one of the best looking boys of my acquaintance, and I just consider him *one of the nicest people I know.*' So I just thought I would drop on by and tell you, Cille."

"You better tell me the whole thing over again a little louder, honey. He didn't quite hear you that time."

"Why heaven for*bid,*" said Adelaide, "I wouldn't want to disturb him with his *reading* . . . You just tell him for me, che, and tell him *I* said so, will you?"

I let it ride.

"Cille?"

"Sure," I said, "I'm game."

For a couple minutes we had a little quiet. Then Adelaide started in again. "I have got a third cousin," she said, "which is *remarkably* lucky. I would just like to be so *remarkably* lucky as my third cousin. He has won four different lottery prizes."

Nobody asked her what the prizes was, so she told us: "Now the last time, my third cousin won a piano. Course it wasn't a very big piano, but it *was* a piano. It had keys."

That's a help, I thought.

Adelaide saw me watching her pick at her skirt. She put her hand up to her hair. "I just don't know if I like *this* dress or not," she said. "Do you like *this* dress, Cille?"

"It's a pretty dress," I said.

"Why, do you really think so? My mama made it for me last week. Course, blue *is* my favorite color. What is your favorite color, Cille?"

I looked up at the spread basket sun, turning watery, and I thought of another time. "Orange," I said.

"Well now, that's a funny color. I just can't imagine such a horrible thing as a *orange* dress."

"Not for a dress," I said.

"You don't happen to have a orange dress by any chance?"

"Adelaide," I said, "you know I don't."

"Well, that's a weight off my mind," she said, "I mean I wouldn't want to think I had went and hurt your feelings."

"No, honey. We don't have no feelings around here."

"Now that's a funny thing to say. You upset about something?"

"No," I said. "Seems to me you the one been acting upset."

"Who, *me?* Che, you say the funniest things."

I knew I was closing in, though, because then she started to get nasty:

"Know, che, it's a shame you had to quit school that year, just before everything become so *interesting*. Why I would of *died* did I have to leave then. I didn't even miss a *day*. Why, *that* was the most *interesting* year of *all*."

Dan told her: "Clarence gives Cille lessons at night."

"*Clarence* does?"

"He used to," I said.

"He don't no more?"

"No. He don't no more."

Dan said: "I didn't know that."

Adelaide wanted to know: "When did he quit?"

" . . . Month ago."

"Why?"

"Adelaide," I said, "he's right in back of you, why don't you just turn around and ask him yourself."

"Well, if you feel that way about it. Course, personally, I was glad when I quit school the year *after* you did. I mean that last year was the most *interesting* year for *me*, and after that everybody says it was plain dull what they taught you. I mean the things you want to know after you start to grow up you can get a lot better from your *friends*. Don't you think so?"

"I don't know, Adelaide," I said, "I don't have any."

Dan asked: "Why you quit school too, Adelaide?"

" . . . Why, because I *wanted* to." Adelaide's hand was back working at her skirt.

Dan said: "That was when your mama got to ailing so bad?"

She got up, quick. "My, it's getting late," she said.

"Certainly is," I told her.

Clarence shut his book and stretched.

Adelaide said real quick: "I was going to *tell* you not to go and strain your eyes, Clarence."

But Clarence was still off somewhere on his own. He was most always like that.

Mama came and stood in the door, to get some air.

Adelaide practically shouted: "*Want me to leave the glass right here, Mrs. Morris?*"

"Lord," I said, "Oh, Clarence."

He didn't look around, but he finally woke up. "Yes?"

"Guess what," I said, "we have got company."

" . . . Oh, hello, Adelaide, I didn't know you was here."

Adelaide told him: "I just think it's the most marvelous thing I ever saw the way you *concentrate* yourself."

I could see her point.

"Well," said Clarence, "didn't have no choice. Somebody done kept their radio blasting for the last hour."

"That was *not* a radio," I said. I must of snickered.

Adelaide asked me: "Wasn't that you I saw the other day going into Jewel's house?" She did it on purpose.

I knew without turning that Mama was standing stiffer. "No," I said, "I don't ever go over there."

"I could of swore it was you."

I stood up tall and looked at her.

"Well," she said, "must be near time I should be getting on home."

Clarence asked: "How's your mama's diabetes?"

Adelaide put a finger in the front of her dress, and pulled at it. "Why, thank you," she said. Then, quick: "Clarence, Cille has a message for *you* from *me*. Bye, Mrs. Morris." And she grabbed her packages and ran off.

I watched after her, and I started to think there was something wrong even in the way she had left. Adelaide didn't used to run at all, ever.

But Mama said: "Lucille. You bring yourself in here." She backed away from the door.

I went up on the gallery next to where Dan was sitting.

Clarence asked: "What's that girl been going on about?"

"Oh," I said, "modeling. Got a friend says with your body and your face, you ought to be able to make a heap of money."

Clarence belly-laughed sudden, and a little too long, I thought—it wasn't all that funny. He pushed his big muscled arms in the air. "Does she?" he said. "*Does* she now?"

Dan said: "Adelaide didn't even tell me if she wanted my book about toads."

I put my hand on his head as I went in. "Never mind, honey," I told him.

I knew I was going to get it from Mama; and I did.

5

CLARENCE claimed he had just quit his gardening in the beginning of the year when he was eighteen. But he didn't even say that till Mama caught on to his giving her more money every week, and asked him. And then he never told her where he worked, only that he had quit for a new job with better pay and a future. He said the new job had to do with servicing white people, just like anything else—but he said there was no way of explaining exactly what kind of work it was because it changed from one week to the next, and sometimes got so different you wouldn't know it was the same thing at all.

He made a whole lot of money, and just like he told us, it was always getting better. He paid all the monthly installments on the house by hisself, and gave Mama money separate. Only, he didn't keep regular hours, and he took to coming in awful late and switching over to Dan's bed when we went in the kitchen every morning so he could sleep some more. And there was days he didn't even go out till the evening. But he wouldn't stand for no questions, and Mama plain had to get used to it. She pretty much did, till the night Clarence brought two new suits home, with two shirts and three ties and a pair of shoes and socks, because he said he had to look right for his work. Then she got to asking him so much, he did different things: he started to go out and come back at the same hour each day; he paid her the same amount of money on the same day each week (a little less than he'd been giving her before, but plenty enough); and he got his new clothes together and went and kept them someplace else (where he worked, he said), so Mama never had to look at them again. All that calmed her down again.

But I would see him from time to time in the middle of the morning, sitting in the drugstore with a cup of coffee and a newspaper. And once, I had to go downtown to get a special kind of soap Mama needed that they didn't sell around our neighborhood, and I saw him buying a ticket at a picture house. When I told him about that, he was standing outside eating an apple, and he threw it on the ground so hard it exploded. He told me if I didn't tend to my own business and stop following him around, he would really fix me with Mama. I explained twice how my seeing him there was just an accident, but he only turned and walked away. It reminded me of what our father said the day Clarence got so mad only because I ran after his bike down the street. Our father said: "Course he was mad for true, honey. *Course* he was. You plain can't go stepping on the Tiger-Cat's tail."

Just over the Canal that marks the city limits is the big white cemetery. It don't take you but twenty minutes to get there from the center of town on the Cemetery car line. From there on, if you cross the bridge, and then turn to your right and go straight out, following the Canal, you get to the Yacht Club by the Lake.

Dan's twelfth birthday fell on a Sunday, and Mama made Clarence take him and me out to see the sailboats they keep in the Club. She couldn't give Dan nothing else, so that was his present. (But Clarence bought him a whole new suit of clothes for church wear, and a yo-yo to play with, the only toy he ever had.)

On the streetcar, Dan got all excited about the trip being his birthday present—Lord knows why, we'd already been there once before when nobody knew. He kept trying to make a gag of putting his foot in front of the seat where the "Reserved for White Persons Only" sign was. The car was around half-full, and they had pushed the signs back till there wasn't but two seats for colored people, with six or seven of us crowded in there. So Dan's kidding made less room for everybody, and before he was through one lady had called him a "snot-nosed quadroon bastard" as she got off, and another lady kicked him. Which didn't bother Dan any, but it made Clarence and me sort of edgy. Course, Dan knew better, only I think he wanted to start enough fuss so he could tell somebody it was his birthday. And he might of, except Clarence made like he didn't know him, and I finally got him quieted down.

You can either switch cars with a transfer at the Canal, or walk. Dan wanted to walk, so we did. Then he wanted to stop and look at the entrance to the cemetery. We wouldn't of paid him no mind, but it was the only birthday Mama ever let him do something special. Clarence had a face like he was going to put up with the whole thing long as he could.

The cemetery has a high, dark-green metal fence that goes all the way around it, and a curlicued double gate at the entrance. They say it covers hundreds of acres, it must be the biggest cemetery anywhere. There's a pond with goldfish and ducks, and a little bridge across it. And there's the old part, with all the mausoleums, and the new part for when they learned a way to bury people without the swamp water getting into them. Right behind the entrance is a pink marble house that could be either a mausoleum or a monument. The house has two white columns, and it has a white marble bathtub with something chiseled on the outside in a foreign language.

We stood on the curb and watched the people going in and coming out.

Dan couldn't keep his eyes off the bathtub. He asked: "Is that where they got the dead man?"

"No, it ain't," I said, "is it, Clarence?"

"Certainly not," said Clarence. "Lord."

"Looks to me like it is."

"You got a thing on about being dead," Clarence told him. He did, too.

He wouldn't walk on out to the Club for the longest while. He wanted to go right in the cemetery and look at the graves, and he knew they don't allow colored people in there. And he kept asking questions. Like: "How long does a man stay dead?"

"How long was you before you was?" I said. But he didn't catch me.

"How long before he turns into a skeleton? How much time do you get a dead man before he turns into a skeleton?"

"Not long," I said, just to shut him up. I could see Clarence was getting his fill.

But you couldn't stop Dan. "What turns him?"

"The water turns him," said Clarence, "if he's in the ground. And if he ain't, the bugs do. Now come on out and see the goddam sailboats."

Not Dan. Once you let him get started, you had it. "What color is a skeleton?"

"Oh, shit," said Clarence, "white."

". . . A white man's skeleton or a colored man's skeleton?"

Clarence pivoted around slow and looked down at him out of his eye-corners, a little like Mama. Except he was smiling. "Quit asking questions," he said. And there wasn't no answering nor mistaking of that voice. It was Mama's voice.

The Yacht Club ain't so much, from the outside, anyway. We sat on the cement steps by the Lake, and watched the boats go in and out this drawbridge. The men who run them are all rich white folks from town who do it for fun when they don't have no other way to get through their time, and they sure can make it a serious business. They wear white caps with braid, and stand up and blow whistles and shout orders like they thought they was admirals or something.

Dan took off his easy-walkers and put his feet in the water, but I didn't want to, because most of the boats waited to empty till they came back from sailing, and all kinds of garbage had collected in a wide, scummy line below the steps. We saw four different crabs come up to eat at it.

There ain't no waves on the Lake, unless the wind rises, and even then nothing like the Coca-Cola beach posters. Course, that's the ocean. No, the Lake water is flat as the land. Plopping-flat, heavy, sitting on its fat self with its bottom spread, and plain *there,* is all. Not a thing that cares; not a live thing. Not part of a rolling place that cradles you up to the sun. Just not part of a place where you can matter.

Dan thought the Lake was all right, but he wasn't raving any. Clarence had an early date with somebody (he wouldn't tell who), and Dan didn't raise no fuss when we got ready to leave.

But on the way back, he kept stopping to look in the cemetery fence. You couldn't see much of anything from there but trees, and the shine of the mausoleums way off; it was enough for Dan, though.

Time was getting on, and Clarence driving to go. Finally, he made me promise to meet him at the St. Thomas car stop at seven o'clock, and not to tell Mama about his leaving us. I said okay, so he gave me carfare and let us stay there by ourselves. It wasn't much later than three-thirty in the afternoon.

Dan followed the fence along, bit by bit, running his hand over the iron railings. I would of known what he was studying on, only I wasn't lending him much attention. There was a string of Jankee barges going down the Canal, and you could see the big shiny black men on them, playing craps, and some singing. I waved every time a barge passed, but they was too busy doing nothing. When I turned around, Dan wasn't there.

It was queer right then. I knew where he was: I saw the two railings loosened at the bottom and the space under a shrub where he'd gone. And I knew what they might do to a colored kid they found in the cemetery. But I wasn't scared like I should of been. I tried to be—scared and angry the way Mama was when something went wrong. But the feeling wouldn't come. It's been like that with me a lot since, but I think then was the start. It's queer because a little thing can get me all edged up, but let something come along I *ought* to get fussed about, and I don't: I can't. Not till later.

I only waited to see there wasn't anybody watching, and I followed Dan in. Inside, through the bushes. And on into the high grass where it bent over a dirt path that passed by, leading to the mausoleums. It was the old part of the cemetery. Dan was standing with his back to me, looking out at the little town of marble houses with the crosses and the angels on top.

Sometimes you expect a thing a certain way. When they won't let you in somewhere, or there's a thing you ain't allowed to touch or see, you get to imagining how it must be, and for you that's the way it is. You don't make the dream on purpose—you don't even know you making it—it just happens. Because they ain't built the right kind of fence yet for a person's mind.

It happened to me with the cemetery. I knew they never would let me inside, so right off I got an idea for my own self of what it must be like. What I set up was a sort of combination of the green gate with the too-pretty pink house and its white bathtub—and the cold gray graveyard where our father is. I thought the white cemetery would be a little like the colored graveyard, only lots bigger and lots prettier and lots more expensive, with the mausoleums and the monuments standing staring at you like old policemen.

Course, it wasn't like that at all.

I stood behind Dan, and I even forgot I was supposed to get him out of there.

The first thing you see is the high winter-grass, still shifting in curved lines from the last breeze. Nobody tramples on it there, and it grows to six, seven inches some places. Then the trees. Hundreds of trees. Oaks, and maples, and weeping willows, and right in front of me, the biggest magnolia tree I ever saw, cracking with flowers.

Maybe it was the magnolia that made everything carve out, fresh and living, like it did. You couldn't really believe in anything being dead there. But maybe that was only on account of I saw it all from behind the smell and the white of this one tree.

The hardest white and the hardest black have blue in them. Blue is the color shaves things down to a pureness. And because of blue, I used to think a pureness was a wholeness—I used to be afraid. Till I saw the River, and took a careful look at a magnolia.

A magnolia flower is a special color white. It ain't cotton-white and it ain't paper-white; it ain't cloud-white. It ain't cream-white nor sky-white nor, least of all, pure blue-white. It is all the whites there ever was, in one, because it is its own beginning: the first pregnant, gentle white, that began with the world—before God had a chance to get the colors from it—waiting, and bursting to let them out.

And the flower is firm and big, bigger than a man's hand. Not one of those delicate little flowers like a camellia or a pansy. It has a wood stem you can't hardly break off, and its petals are so solid, it looks like you couldn't kill it no matter what you did. (But you can take a pansy, a baby butterfly pansy, and practically squeeze it without doing it harm. And all you have to do is stroke a magnolia for it to turn brown.)

You can't smell a magnolia from up close, it's too strong. Like if you went into a room that was all painted a beautiful red: the walls, and the tables, and the chairs—everything. You wouldn't like it, and after a while, you couldn't see red. That's the way it is with a magnolia. If you hold it too close, it's so strong, first it smells bad—and then it don't smell at all. The best things are the only things you can't take much of.

You got to smell a magnolia like I did then. Standing a ways back from the tree, with the wind against you, having to sniff for it. When it comes, it comes in touches and thin streaks, and it's so good it leaves you dizzy and empty, waiting for the next one.

And that white, and that smell. Looking out over the wavy green, and the brown, and the gray stone standing there. Taking Dan by the hand; jumping over the tall grass to the path, not to trample it. And following the dirt way to the mausoleums. The hush silence.

We didn't talk none. It wasn't right to talk. We plain had to be quiet. Not for the dead, but for the life—the quiet strength of the life, growing. We walked on half soles, breathing light. And whatever it was, it made Dan older—turned him inside out. Then Dan had me by the hand, leading me out there, driving forward with a real thing he wanted to do and a real place he wanted to go, no matter what came afterwards. I think for those two minutes out of one afternoon out of his whole life, my brother Dan had something he really *wanted* to live for.

The dirt way led to where the mausoleums started, and broke into blocks of paths: streets for the marble houses, where nobody walked. Then we saw the pots of dead flowers banking some of the iron doors, and we knew people had been there.

And everything went back to like it was.

Dan pinched my thumb; he was Dan again. He said: "All them is for the dead people?"

"Sure," I told him.

I knew we had to get out, quick. But I knew we had to see it, too, now we were there.

Dan asked: "How they got them?"

"In boxes," I said, "it's just the same."

"I don't see no boxes."

We were talking low as we could, but it *was* for the dead now. And for the people who left the flowers, and for the guards.

I looked in one of the cross-bar doors. He was right, there wasn't no boxes. That was just another idea of mine, the way I had thought of it. "They must have them in the walls," I said. You could see some writing chiseled on the walls.

"How many dead people in one of them?"

I wasn't sure, so I started walking straight down the path to where the mausoleums came to an end. I didn't think it was right to take a guess, not about that.

Black, white, pink, brown, gray; sometimes solid, sometimes streaked. Houses spaced apart, with bushes and low trees. Houses everyplace you looked.

"How come they got so many?"

I said: "All the people who died."

"*That* many people done died?"

"Everybody dies," I said.

". . . You going to die?"

"Sure."

"Clarence going to die?"

"Course," I said, "I told you."

He held off a while, but I knew it was coming: "Am I?"

"When you real old. Everybody does."

"No," he said.

Wasn't no point in arguing with him. I did, though, just to talk: "You got to. It ain't so bad."

"I ain't going to."

I kept my mouth shut.

"Cille. I *ain't* going to."

"That's all right," I said. "Don't."

We passed a black marble house with two big black jars on either side of the iron door, all streaked with white. Even the steps and the floor inside was streaky black marble. But I looked up and saw the angel on top; it was solid. Solid white.

"*Cille.*"

"Shhh. What?"

"Why do people die?"

"Because," I said, "it's plain natural."

". . . Well, why do people *live* then, Cille?"

"Look at that pretty bunch of yellow flowers over there," I told him. But it didn't work. "Cille. *Why* do people live?"

"Honey," I said, "I don't know."

We came to the last line of mausoleums, and stopped. In front of us there was a strip of mowed grass, and then the line where the new cemetery began. They had them in the ground there, like our father. Only, the graves was spaced so far apart, didn't even look like rows. Some of them had headstones with figures and things, and some was squared off, with extra-fine edges. Everything was clean and smooth and polished, and it all seemed like it had been dusted just that morning.

Dan wanted to go out there, but I was scared of the guards, because I didn't see one good place to hide. I looked across the new cemetery to where this line of trees began, and on up to where the graves wound around back of it. Nobody. But then I knew I had seen a bright spot move somewhere, on the gray and white of a stone. I pulled Dan flat against a mausoleum wall, and waited, watching back over where I had looked before. I could feel the marble burning on the side of my neck; it must of had the sun on it all day.

I couldn't find the spot, and I ran my eyes faster from left to right over the graves, hoping it would jump out at me again. Then it moved, and I saw it: a redbird sitting on one of the headstones, fluffing up its wings. I stepped out to the path and let my breath go.

Way on the left, just back of the first graves, there was a high bush between two headstones. We could hide behind that.

We ran to it. Dan was ahead of me, and he slid in against the leaves. I sat close next to him, so we both were shadowed by the bush and by the headstones too. And that way, we each of us had a grave.

The one next to Dan was pink; it had a fancier stone, with two angels on top. Dan put his hand on the sunny part of the marble and patted it. "This one's mine," he said.

Then he saw what I was looking at: on the other side of his grave, before the next, was a thick clump of sugar cane. Each cane was a smooth, ripe yellow, turning to green only where it went into the ground.

Dan reached in his pants and pulled out his pocketknife. (He'd found it one day going out to the levee, and scraped most of the rust off with a rock; we always kept it hid under the gallery, so Mama wouldn't know he had it.)

"If you do," I told him, "they going to catch us, and if they do, I hate to think."

But he was already crawling over his grave. He lay on his belly and hacked at a tall piece. Sugar cane is tougher to cut than it looks, and his knife wouldn't of made much of a dent in your finger. He finally got it, though, by bending and peeling it with his hands at the place where the hacking made it weaker. Then he pushed it over to me and crawled back.

I took the knife from him and sharpened it good on the edge of my grave, and I began slicing the cane into half-inch pieces. I gave the first to Dan, and put the second in my mouth. When I had cut about fifteen my hand cramped, and I lay the rest of the cane against my headstone. The pieces made a pointed pile in my skirt, not very big, because Dan was already on his fifth or sixth. They was still a ways from ripe inside, and there was a green taste mixed with the sweet. But they was warm and juicy, and when you bit down on a new one it made your mouth fill with saliva. We sat and sucked and spit out the chewed pulps. After I had enough, I cut some more to take home.

I didn't even think what time it might be, till I got a mind of the locusts. And after that, it was a minute before I thought to look up and see how low the sun was. I just hadn't really seen the half-shadow that was creeping over all the graves around us. The sunlight was only clear on the tops of the trees way behind our heads.

I put the pieces of cane in my handkerchief, and stuck that back inside the front of my blouse. When we stood up, we saw how the whole cemetery was twice as big as before. Shadows do that.

We ran up the path, through the mausoleum city to the edge of the winter-grass. Then I stopped. I thought: we ain't ever going to get out of here—we ain't *never* going to get out.

Because when I looked at the solid line of trees ahead of us, I knew I had clean forgot to mark the place where we first came in.

I choked, and spit out the piece of cane I was keeping in my cheek. Dan said: "Lordy-Lord."

"Don't cry," I said. "Hum."

". . . Can't."

"Hum," I said.

"I can't. Cille . . . I *can't.*"

But then I grabbed his wrist and ran straight on up the shadowy dirt way. It was all right: I remembered the magnolia tree.

The time couldn't of been so late, because when we got to the St. Thomas car stop a half-hour later, Clarence wasn't there yet. We stood and waited for him, munching on the cane. We weren't hungry, neither of us, but there wasn't much else to do.

Adelaide passed us across the street, and turned her head like she didn't see us. She had another package from the drugstore, taking it to her mama. Dan was going to call out to her, but I made him not.

We popped camphorberries with our feet, and smeared them on the sidewalk. A streetcar came and went by, but Clarence wasn't on it.

A few blocks up the street, a long black Buick stopped. Wasn't no special reason I saw it, except I was looking in that direction. A man got out on the other side real quick, and slammed the door. The car made a wide turn and doubled back, raising a dust cloud all across the street. Then it turned again at the next corner and was gone. I wouldn't of took a particular notice, or even gone on looking, except that it was a classy car, and I could of swore the man at the wheel was a white man. But Dan didn't see it, and it was out of sight before I could tell him.

The man on the street came out of the dust and walked on down toward where we were standing.

It was Clarence.

That was the first time I ever saw him dandy some. Or if I had seen him do it before, I didn't give it much thought. Because that was when I first came to think there was a swing to it just a little something like a woman.

The funny part was, I'd seen lots of boys trying to walk like girls, specially around the Quarter—and they always got all of the bad points, and none of the good ones. I plain hadn't ever come across a man could imitate a woman so he didn't look like a man imitating a woman. Course, once or twice I'd seen one doing a real studied good job, and maybe making it sort of like a city whore. But then, a whore is doing the same kind of pretend. No, all the men I'd ever seen try it must of figured the number one thing to do was to get rid of their backbones and their guts. And after they did that, they either swayed too much or walked too brittle. So, even if they had all the outside looks, they never got the *force* of a woman into it. Just the shell tricks. Clarence wasn't trying that way. He wasn't trying at all; he plain had it. And it wasn't much, only down around the hips, and the way his legs swung out. It was a way of stepping as if he didn't want to crush the camphorberries. But the little bit Clarence had was the real thing.

He was staring right at me, only he was his usual daydream self, and he didn't see who it was. When he caught on, his gait broke and he almost tripped. Then he covered by leaning down to tie his shoelace tighter. When he straightened up again, he started to walk like always, like a man. And then I got a frown inside. Because I suddenly sensed a trick-something about that, made it exactly as much like a man as the other way had been like a woman.

But I told myself: Cille, you being stupid: that's the Cat.

(And I *was* being stupid. Stupid not to let myself wonder. Stupid not to let myself think. Stupid not to let myself remember that the only thing really *male* or *female* about the way a city cat walks—just depends on who stroked it last.)

"You-all fifteen minutes early," Clarence told us, when he got close enough.

I said: "We weren't sure what time it was." I decided to shut up about that car.

There was a red place on his cheekbone, below the eye. It was on the spot where the light used to play; the spot I always wanted to feel with my fingers.

"Where you get that?" Dan asked, pointing at it. "What happen to you there?"

Clarence reached up and touched it. "I fell," he said, and fast: "who gave you the gum?"

"Not gum," Dan said, "sugar cane. How you fall?"

"I fell down. Got another piece?"

I reached in my blouse and pulled out some pieces, and gave them to him.

"How?" said Dan.

"Off the streetcar," Clarence said. He looked at me, but I looked away. He must of known at least I could see he hadn't been on the St. Thomas car, not coming from that direction. He put the cane in his mouth, and we started to walk to Mama's house. "Where'd you-all find this?"

Dan didn't think: "Growing out in the cemetery." By the time he realized what he'd said and stopped walking, Clarence was already standing still.

Clarence asked: "*What* cemetery?"

I kept quiet for about a quarter of a minute. But then I remembered he couldn't tell Mama: he was supposed to be with us all afternoon. "Didn't nobody see us," I said.

Clarence was getting blood-colored. "You goddam fool kids," he said. He grabbed my wrist and made me open my hand. I had about three pieces of cane there, stuck together. "You got this out of the white cemetery?" He turned to Dan. "Where?"

Dan dropped his head and tried to dig a hole in the ground with his heel.

Clarence said louder: "*Where?*"

Dan glubbered: ". . . Growing in between two of the graves out there."

"Growing in between two of the graves out there," Clarence said. "*Growing in between two white graves.*"

I thought he was going to bust, and smack us or something. I thought he was so mad he was choking. But he wasn't. He was laughing, or trying not to: chuckling, way down deep. And it was a dirty chuckle, like when somebody tells a filthy-dirty story.

Dan looked up and saw him, and began to giggle out loud, wanting to make a joke of the whole thing.

Then Clarence cut short and cuffed him so hard against the back of his head, he practically knocked him down. "If you-all ever go out there again," he said, "I'll talk to Mama. I swear I will. You know I will. And what she don't do you, *I'll* do."

We knew; we kept quiet.

"Okay," Clarence said. He headed for Mama's. On the way, he spat out the chewed cane, and put a fresh piece in his mouth. He didn't talk, but I could tell he was chuckling again. Not making any sound, I could just tell.

He went on walking—chewing the sugar cane and laughing inside.

6

JEWEL was almost eighteen when she had her second abortion, the one that made her so sick. She stayed in bed near four weeks. I tried to get over much as I could, but it wasn't easy, because Mama had found out. Course, the whole neighborhood knew about it, but nobody else tried to help out or even went in and ask how she was. Except the grocery boy that delivered her food, and the doctor, and the preacher. The doctor went every day to take care of her and bring her medicine, real sweet-like, only I think the baby's being his had something to do with it. The preacher went to see her because word had got around that she was dying; but she was a whole lot better by that time, and he happened to have a pack of cards with him, so they played a nice game of pinochle instead.

For the first two weeks she had to do the cooking on a hot plate next to her bed, and she couldn't make much but fried meat or eggs, and *pain perdu*. She said her father surprised her by bringing whatever she needed from the kitchen on the side of his cart. Then he would take it back, and he even learned to wipe off the plates and put them under the faucet.

And one day, Jewel told me Mama had been over there, while we were all at Sunday school, with a bowl of hot soup, and some boiled peppergrass to rub on her tummy. Mama hadn't spoke a word to her; she only put the soup and the peppergrass down and went away. But I liked that.

Jewel said she wouldn't of minded the pain any, only it was having to hurt just to be empty, and the plain empty feeling afterwards that she hated. She never admitted it, but I knew Jewel had wanted that baby. I could tell because she let the doctor give her all his medicine, but she wouldn't take a penny from him, and she had to spend most every bit of the money she was saving for her father's wheel chair. And she did admit how it was the first time she'd ever turned down money from a man.

Soon as she could, Jewel found another job and went to work again. She said she was going to be more careful from then on, but it was only five months before she got pregnant again. It was like she couldn't stop. And she just had to have another abortion.

Everybody said Adelaide's mama must of really had diabetes after all, because she up and died that winter.

We didn't find out about it till the next day, when Clarence came home early and told us. Mama made us all wash and get dressed in our church clothes, and she did the same. Then she locked the door, and we all went over to Adelaide's.

Adelaide hadn't been around to visit with us for a long time. Sometimes we would see her pass, going to the drugstore and back, but she never stopped over no more.

When we walked into her house, she was sitting by herself on a chair in the kitchen, and right away I knew it was a different Adelaide than I ever saw before.

She had on a plain dress, without any of the frills she usually wore. But it wasn't just her dress; the frills was gone from Adelaide too. She was quiet as quiet could be, sitting there and holding time for the funeral. And she didn't care what anybody did, and she didn't care what anybody said—and, strangest of all, she didn't care what anybody thought. She was nice to us, and nice to the people after us, but it wasn't a practiced nice like before. Course, it was something she did from her outside, the way it always had been; only now, she did it without caring or really even knowing. The same face for everybody—the same smile. She never once got up or offered even a Coke to a single person who was there. None of the people found out in time to bring their own drinks, and Mama sent Clarence to the grocery store for some stuff to serve them. But if Adelaide knew that, she didn't say thank you or ask how much it was. She just sat on her chair and let people do what they wanted; she took her rest, and she let life go on. It never got to be a real party, because Mama wouldn't allow Clarence to buy anything with alcohol in it, but Adelaide didn't care. She kept her mama's coffin closed, and when the hour came for the funeral, she waited till the pallbearers was on the street, and she followed the coffin out of the house.

Two things kind of bothered me about the way Adelaide acted that day. One was the hush she'd let slip over her voice like a soapy glove, changing the tinkle it had before to a whine that was soft and dull, so near to her mama's voice that for a while I thought she must be doing it on purpose. The other thing was the way she sat there, keeping to her own quiet self—waiting—and the whole time, flashing a secret stare at Clarence and every other young man in the room, with this expression on her face almost as if she might of wanted to spit. It was the same expression I'd seen on some women at the market, when they looked over the cheap cuts of meat: knowing it was all a little bad, but knowing they had to be satisfied with a piece of it to take home and doctor up with garlic and hot spices enough so it would get past a set of wiggling noses and waving tongues, on into the stomachs that wasn't quite so delicate because they only needed it to live.

Clarence was the one nipped her on the bleeper.

Walking back from the funeral, I said to him: "Queer the way Adelaide acts."

"How queer?" he said.

"I don't know. Like she might be waiting for something. Funeral's a funny place to act like you was waiting for something."

"Foo," Clarence said, "it ain't like that."

"What ain't like what?"

Clarence told me: "Waiting is something you plain got to do sometimes, no matter what else might be going on. You plain can't change your skin any other way."

And he was right—that was exactly what Adelaide had started to do.

She dropped the specialist-cutest-little-cream-puff-around-town act. She dropped it cold, and the next day I saw her—on the street about a week later—she just said: "Hello, che," and pushed my arm, and clipped off without even looking me in the eye.

For almost a month, she wouldn't talk to a soul. She wouldn't even take up Mama's offer to come over and eat her meals with us. Right after the funeral, she went out and got a maiding job, and she stuck to it and lived alone. People said something was awful strange about her only giving a *high-class* type funeral like that, without even a real party, after all the embroidering money she must of got from her mama. But Adelaide left them to wonder, and went to work. And she kept her front door shut till she had time to grow her new skin.

I sort of had a hope we might be a little more friendly, now that you could see there was a real person going around in Adelaide's clothes. But the real person didn't last very long, because it wasn't strong enough to live out in the air. And Adelaide started to grow the layers back, like a fungus. Her eyes filmed over, and the person inside dried up and made her mean. From then on, in bits and pieces, she started getting more and more like her mama—like anything with a dried core.

And one day, she opened up her front door, and had a young university man in for a piece of Melba toast and a cup of very weak tea. Because in just one month, Adelaide had found a fresh way of keeping herself special.

7

THE summer after he was thirteen, Mama let Dan go to work. Clarence got him a job delivering for a fancy flower shop, and what with tips and all, he started bringing home close to five dollars a week right away.

I was awful glad for him. Dan had been turning quieter and spongier for more than a year. While the other boys his age was already out working and smoking like men, Dan never did a thing but sit around the house and sift through his own thoughts. He always minded Mama to the word, without ever asking why; he minded her so perfect, I think it even began to worry her after a while. He didn't have any of the kickback Clarence had, and his quiet wasn't a hard, holding-off quiet, like mine. I did what I had to because it was what had to get done at the time, but there was always a million other things I would rather of been doing, and having, and being. But not Dan. Little by little, *no* began to mean plain *no* to Dan. It didn't just mean don't do—it meant don't wonder and don't be. So if Mama gave him an order, he went and did it because it was the *only* thing: everything else was blacked right out, for him.

I began to catch him in little stuff. Like when he left his knife to rust under the gallery. I called his mind to that a couple times, but he just shook his head and sat down on the steps, waiting for Mama to give him some new order. And one Sunday, when Mama sent us out to the levee, she said: "You-all make sure you don't get no mud on your clothes, I got enough work to do here," the same as she had been telling us, on and off, all our lives. But when we got out there that afternoon, Dan wouldn't even take his shoes off. He found a flat rock in the levee, and cleaned it off, and then sat on it and watched the water slide by for three whole hours, till the time came to leave.

He still kept a saving-day, though. Around once a week, he would get up in the morning with that old way he had of walking around like he was looking for something. And it would last right on through to the night. Those was the days he plain couldn't keep still: there wasn't a thing anywhere could hold him for more than half a minute, without his jumping up and wandering off again, like a finger had snapped someplace in his mind. But it was always too quick; he never quite got it. The snap didn't leave any aftersound, and Dan plain couldn't remember where it had been.

A little before summer was when he got the worst. Dan was so quiet then, you didn't take no more notice of him than you would of a shadow that was in a certain place at a certain hour of the day. He had a corner of the gallery where he sat all morning, and a part of the steps where he sat all afternoon. If Mama told him to do something, he would get up and do it, and go back to his place. Day after day, the same. Except the one day—the once-a-week day—that was always so different. Too different. Because Dan was exactly as tight then as he was loose the rest of the time.

It was as if the blacker Mama painted the world for him, the brighter his one little mystery-spot shone. One lone star, in a night where even the moon was clouding away. But a star that was still so faint, he could only feel it there—only see it out of the corner of his eye while he stared into the blackness. Account of every time he looked right at it, it plain disappeared.

I could sort of tell what was going on inside Dan; we still kept part of the closeness that had started when our father died. Only, he wouldn't let me in near enough to feel *with* him, or help. And in a way, I guess he was right. I guess, whatever might happen, a man's star must be the kind of a thing a man has just got to locate for hisself.

But I *was* glad when Mama let him start to work in June.

For the first weeks, he looked scared when he went out in the morning. He hadn't been around people much, or even out alone, since four years before when we all quit school. So every morning, before he started for work, he would breathe deep and kiss Mama and me goodbye forever. I would of thought it was cute, except it meant more than cute to me. It meant Dan was finally getting out of Mama's house, to be with real people in a real world. I might of known that Mama wouldn't of let him go unless she was sure he'd never get free.

Then, in the hottest passing of the summer, Dan got a little like Clarence in his way. Sometimes he couldn't find enough to do to make Mama happy—fussing her, and loving her up, and even bringing her dead flowers from work. And a minute later, he would rear back from her sudden, like Clarence when she rubbed him wrong, only without no reason at all.

What I took a dislike to wasn't when he made up to her, though, or even when he shied away. Those was only the old clothes Clarence handed down to him. No, what I didn't like was when Dan was his-self alone: when he wouldn't let Mama or anybody else touch him at all—shrinking back inside and staring that blank stare, the same stare I had seen once before. And he wouldn't do it regular, only I got the feeling there was a pattern to it just outside my knowing. He was like a piece of rubber in Mama's hands. A rubber you stretch out to where it's going to break, and then let go one end. Sometimes it stings your wrist, but most often it flicks out in the air at nothing and pulls in short, hanging down and jumping a little—useless.

Anyway, sooner than the fall could start its zipping-up of life, I saw that Dan's new world wasn't going to help him. Because no matter how new the world was, nor how many new things was in it, for Dan the old don't-rules still held—and they held *him*, like cement. He couldn't forget, my brother Dan. I guess he was always a man that couldn't forget—or forgive—what he thought was true.

So Mama stayed with him. No matter where he went, no matter what new door he opened, there was her black hand to stop him. And Mama meant right. The terrible part is, Mama meant right.

But here is what she did: she wouldn't have him hurt in a hurting-world—so she took the world away from him. She wouldn't have him *hurt*, so she never let him *be*. And Dan's fight was over before it began.

Course, I didn't know then. I tried not to, anyhow.

Only, I couldn't take that stare—the stare Mama let slip by. When Dan looked at me that way, it made my stomach sink. I remembered it even when I hadn't seen it on him for a week. When he was out working, it would come back to me; I plain got it under my mind. And it would pop up in stupid places.

Like the night I went flash-hunting on the sly.

It was around the middle of October. I had just been on the second date Mama had ever allowed me, with a boy name of Unifont. I can't recall Unifont's last name, but the chances are I never knew it. He probably didn't even need a last name, with a first name like Unifont. He was one of Adelaide's rejects back from when she was thirteen. She just took a good look at that and sent him right over. From then on, he came around every couple months till Mama finally gave in and let him take me out to the drugstore down Millicent Street for a soda. I don't know what I had left to expect from a date, after everything Mama always told me, but little as it was, Unifont plain didn't have it. Course, he was nice enough, I guess. He was mostly glasses and one *long* stutter. The stutter bothered me for a while, but after about an hour I figured it was just as well, because he didn't have nothing to say anyway. But the next day I got to thinking, and I couldn't really believe it was his fault. The way I saw it, I had been waiting so many years to have a date with a boy, I had clean forgot how to behave. So the answer I came up with was, if the date had turned out *that* bad, it must of been *my* fault. Not Unifont's.

The next Saturday we went on a date, I was good and ready. I had spent the whole week thinking up questions to put to him and things to tell him, and getting the conversation all planned in my mind like I was going to make it go. I'd even paid a visit to Adelaide, in case she knew anything about him, but all she could tell me was he had two older brothers he didn't get along much with, and they was both passable-nice, and a good bit darker than Unifont. Wasn't a whole lot to go on, but it was something. The only other facts I knew about him was what I saw: my own age; a color somewhere between mine and Adelaide's, a little bit closer to mine; kind of dumb or kind of shy, or both, or maybe neither one—it wasn't easy to get at him through that stutter. But I decided *I* was going to take him *out* from *behind* the stutter, and see if I couldn't make Mr. Unifont a friend of mine. So I got everything ready in my mind, and took another notch in the belt of my old Sunday dress, and did what I could about getting my hair a ways up off my ears without Mama seeing me. I only had an hour and a half to be with him, no further off than the drugstore, because those was Mama's rules then. But that hour and a half was going to be a real to-do.

And it was.

We sat at the soda fountain, and he ordered a lemon-Coke, and I had a chocolate ice cream.

"Unifont," I said, "I want you to tell me all about yourself."

Unifont asked: "Wha-wha-wha-wha-wha-what?"

"Man, now you stop being so nervous around me."

"I ain't ne-nervous," he said, "I just stu-stu-stu-stu . . ."

"I know," I said. "I know. But I think you awful nice, and if you think I'm nice too . . . well, the only way we going to really get together is if you tell me enough about you and I tell you enough about me till we both have something to say about each other, so we can be *friends*."

". . . You do?"

"I do what?"

"Think I'm nice?"

"Sure I do."

"Gee," he said.

"There," I said, "you talking better already. That's what we got to be like . . . just talk easy here till we plain get used to being together."

"Gee," he said. "I ne-ne-never knew nobody like you."

"You think I'm nice?"

Unifont grinned.

"Why? . . . Now, come on, you just tell me why you think I'm nice. Easy, now."

"You really want me to?"

"Course I want you to."

"Well . . . I went ov-ov-over to Adelaide's that day to give her a me-me-message from my brother, and she sent me over to your house."

"That's how," I said. "Now why?" He was doing real well, and I leaned forward so he wouldn't see I had my fingers crossed under the counter.

"You se-serious about wanting to know why?"

"Sure, I told you I was."

"Well, the reason I like you be-be-better than anybody is on account of your color."

I uncrossed my fingers. "Oh," I said.

"I mean, I just do-don't like a *dark* nigger. I don't know why, I just do-don't."

"Oh," I said.

"See: I just do-don't think a nigger ain't got some white blood in him is wo-worth much, you know? I mean not like *us*."

"Sure." I pushed my ice cream to one side.

"Ain't you hungry?"

"No," I said, "I ain't hungry."

"Cille, can I ask you a pe-personal question?"

"Huh."

"Was your pa-papa a white man?"

". . . No."

"I just asked you on account of your mama being so much darker than yo-you."

"Sure."

". . . What you studying on?"

"Nothing." (I was trying to think of a way to take the new Unifont and put him back behind the stutter.)

"Cille."

"What?"

"Da-Dan getting to look funny, ain't he?"

"*Funny?*"

"Well, you know."

"No," I said, "I don't."

"Well . . . you *know*. Kind of ugly-like."

"He ain't ugly," I said, "he's just growing up."

"How you mean?"

". . . Unifont, you got brothers?"

"Ye-yes, I do."

"What's your brothers like?"

"Oh, yo-you wouldn't go for the-them."

"I kind of think I might," I said. "I kind of think I *might*." That did it. Unifont said: "Wh-wh-wh-wh-wh-why?" We sat a while, talking about his brothers. Then he told me how they had a real Ford car. His two brothers and both their dates was going to drive out to the country that night and go flash-hunting, and one of them had asked him did I want to come along; but Unifont had said no, my mama didn't let me associate with just *every-body*. And the way he told me about it, after all his other talk, I practically had steam coming out of my ears. So I got up then and asked him what time his brothers was going. And when he said around eleven o'clock, I just told him I would be standing on the corner of St. Thomas and Shay, at a quarter to eleven, and I walked right on back to Mama's house.

Later on, I felt pretty stupid. But I knew I wouldn't be able to look at myself in the mirror if I didn't go ahead and do it, after saying I would.

Dan was the only one I let on to, and he didn't make no comment. We both had a pretty good idea what would come to pass if Mama or Clarence found out.

That night when I went to bed, I unlatched the window screen. Mama's clock worked all right, and I kept a careful mind of the hour after she took it in her room at nine o'clock. When I knew it was around ten-thirty, I got up and dressed in my washing clothes. Clarence hadn't come home yet, so I stuffed two of Mama's laundry cartons in my bed, in case he crossed through to the bathroom. My bed was in the shadow, and Clarence wasn't one to notice things much, but I couldn't see taking a chance. I knew Mama wouldn't get up for anything till six o'clock in the morning, unless she heard a strange noise, and I wasn't going to make any. I squeezed Dan's hand, and he squeezed back. I was glad it was too dark to make him out. I crossed over and sat on the window ledge and pulled the shade down over me, slow. Then I pushed the screen away and slipped down onto the ground.

Soon as the car stopped for me I was sure I had done a dumb thing. It plain wasn't the way to start being with people, sneaking around like that at fifteen—and I knew it. The others in the car was already cutting up and having fun. We were six all together, so I had to sit on Unifont's lap. Then, aside from the fact that I hadn't felt knees like that in my entire life, Unifont didn't help much, because he was as out of place as I was, being three years younger than his brothers and all. I tried to laugh and get into the swing of the night right away early, but I felt silly, and it showed. Both of the other girls was just waiting for the chance to think I was different anyway, after they saw my color under the street light, and it wasn't long before they cut me out and got their boys talking about things and people I didn't know. I asked questions for a while, but when I saw it wasn't no use, I leaned back on Unifont and shut up.

We drove out to the country, and stopped close to a marshy place with trees. I was beginning to think the flash-hunting was an excuse, but they got gasoline torches out of the back of the car, and some spears they had filed out of old pieces of iron from the freight yard. Soon as the torches was lit, the boys took a good look at me up and down, and I remembered I still had my hair pinned on top in pigtails. That, plus the way I was dressed, would of discouraged a hungry elephant. But the other two girls looked real pretty. Anyway, they gave Unifont and me the torches, and we all started out.

The whole night was weird. There was a little lake in the middle of the marsh, and we walked along its edge, trying to keep our shoes dry. Unifont and me held the torches up high, and when somebody saw a frog or a fish, we quick pulled them down and shone them in its eyes. It would freeze there, looking back at the light. Then the boys could spear it, or if it was close enough, put their hands right down into the water and grab it: it wouldn't even wiggle until it felt the touch.

We did that for over an hour before the boys wandered off someplace to be alone with the girls in the darkness. I had figured on as much, and I was just counting the minutes till I could walk on back to the car and dry my shoes off good. But by then, Unifont had dropped his glasses in the lake and fallen in hisself looking for them, head first, with the other torch. So I had to fish him out and lead him back by the hand, because he never did find his glasses, and it turned out he couldn't even see a tree without them. Then he was embarrassed to squat down on the other side of the car and give me his clothes, so I took a hold of him and spread him face down over the hood, and pressed out as much water as I could like that. He was drier by a half-hour when the others came back, but he was still awful muddy. But the boys had a pile of newspapers stuffed in the back, and I got four and doubled them on Unifont's knees after he was in the car, and held up my skirt while we drove back.

My first night out; my first drive in a car; my first chance to be with people. And the strangeness didn't come from any of those. It didn't come from feeling apart like I was, or from thinking what Mama might do if she found out, or from knowing flash-hunting was against the law, or from having to take care of Unifont. It was what took place back of the lake.

In that wild dream of orange fire, and black shadows swishing and jumping and smashing across, and no sound—we came to a spot where we had to circle behind a clump of trees that grew out over the water. I was last, holding my torch for the rest. I picked my way careful, and when I stepped up on a log to keep clean of the mud, a raccoon ran out from under a bush and held cold, his muscles quivering under the fur. He couldn't look away from the light, and he couldn't move. And watching him there, I was like ice too. We stood and stared at each other.

The boys called to me, and one of them came back to see what was going on. When he caught sight of the raccoon, he began to creep up—easy—noiseless. As he moved, he lifted the spear and pointed it.

I wanted to save the raccoon, only my body wouldn't work, and he was the same. I tried to think of running away, or throwing a stick; no use, and the boy was almost there. When I parted my lips to yell, my throat hardened.

The boy stopped about three feet away, bending forward. Out of the left side of my face, without looking away from the raccoon, I could see the muscles knot in his arm. And then I knew it was all okay: I knew it wasn't going to happen. I just stood quiet, and opened my hand, and dropped the torch.

The wet mud sizzled and the night crashed in, turning everything back to filmy white under the moon. The boy swore at me, and I nearly fell backwards off the log. But even before I bent over to pick up the torch from where it was spluttering between two roots of a tree, I knew the raccoon was gone.

I remembered, though. I remembered the way he looked at me: his body bristling, quivering—planted there. And those shiny, round, blank eyes that reflected the fire, with nothing going on behind them.

I remembered because that was the way Dan looked.

8

IN the winter of the year. The same year; a new winter. Three-inch adhesive tape, bought by the strip and stuck over the jagged line on the kitchen window. Newspapers stuffed around the sill, and under the door at night. Trying to keep the weather and the world outside. Not knowing you sealed the poison under your bed and in your closet and in yourself. Sealed it in, not out.

But don't worry. Work is worry enough, so just work hard.

Tape up your house. Keep the wind and the freshness from getting at you. It's the only time of year there is any real wind, but let it go. Breathe the same air you breathed yesterday. Eat the same food. Smell the same smell. Be the same, the same as yesterday and like last year and like ten years ago. The same as your grandma, in different clothes. Live. Live, live into your soul. Stew there; you got a good excuse: it's cold out.

With the rain, Millicent Street makes ice-mud. If you walk on it, you crunch the dirt and the ice and the pebbles and the oystershell flakes all together. Then a warmer day comes, for everything to thaw out, and in the street you got a running stream of gook. When *that* ices over again, you *can't* walk on it.

The rain freezes on the camphor tree, and the wind cracks the end branches. They break off and blow on top of the house. You can hear them at night.

Next, ice is suddenly pushing from between the boards of the roof, blessed there to stretch out, and spread over, and crack it all across. Put a pan down. And put another over on that side, and one in the corner. Put five down for when the ice goes to water and drips in. No use fixing the roof till April.

If you own more than one dress, watch the mildew don't get at it. The mildew that seeps in with the wet to make fuzzy black spots on the walls, and the food, and anything you leave it. Watch the mildew.

. . . Mean to tell me you finished your work? *All* your work? Well, okay, step on out. But don't stand still too long, the wind remembers you. Patch the tear in your coat, and move. Go somewhere. Go anywhere.

Go and watch the best of the white folks having to make do with the same winter, over on St. Charles. By the corner of Doraine you can see their biggest house, with its lawn that covers half the block. Lungfuls of gardenia bushes every six feet, in white velvet clumps; soft azalea purple in between. A bird fountain. A pug-low white column with one perfect round gold ball sitting on it, the shade and the sheen of a Christmas-tree ball, only ten times as big. If it's cold enough, somebody will walk down and take that ball in. But they always leave the fountain going, and it freezes into a single hard spurt. The birds still come down to peck at it, you don't know why.

But you can't stand there wondering—your nose and your ears and your feet already ache. Better just take your heart home, before the cold slips inside.

Mama and me was doing the day's wash; Dan was in our bedroom with the door closed. Clarence was out working.

The potbelly coal stove made Mama's whole house pretty warm whenever we lit it for hot water, and the little oil stove helped some too. We bought coal once a month, and stored it in the bin back of the house. Thirty pounds for each week was usually enough to keep the stove going three hours in the morning and another three in the afternoon, every day except Sunday. Mama never lit it on Sunday. I don't think she would of used it at all if we didn't need the hot water for washing. But oil cost too expensive to heat all the water we needed, so Clarence bought us a five gallon can and filed it around the bottom till it fit exact on the flat lid of the potbelly. We always kept that can full when we worked, putting as much water back as we took out each time, and it stayed hot a good while after the stove quit. What was left over went for the dishes, and sometimes there was even enough so one of us didn't have to use cold water in the bath.

Clarence used to talk about having a special attachment put in to heat the tap water for the kitchen. But the attachment was electric, and Mama said it would make the light bill run up so high, if Clarence ever lost his job, we wouldn't be able to afford it. Anyhow, it cost thirty-eight dollars and fifty cents just to buy and install— and I don't think Mama liked knowing Clarence could save up that amount of money and still give her much as he did every week, when she never even knew where he worked.

The cotton fog had mostly burned out of the morning, but hunks of splotchy-white clouds stayed to mess up the highest blue, like yesterday's milk curdling in the sky. The time was around ten o'clock. I had gone out twice to hang up wash on the line, and back in the kitchen a thin cold-shell cupped over the warmth that spread from the stove.

Mama was stirring the beans with one hand, and ironing with the other. I don't know how she could do that, without ever getting one touch of grease on a shirt or a blouse. When I asked her, she would get all tickly proud and tell me: "Everybody got to know how to do *something.*" She was a real good cook, too, in her own house. Course, there ain't a colored woman in New Orleans don't learn how to fix up cheap food to get the natural bad taste out. But Mama was better than most. She taught me some, only I couldn't get that last flavor in like she did. She took care of it with the back of her mind—always knowing just when to add the garlic or the bay leaf—and I never saw her burn even a piece of bread.

"Thank God for a Garden" was going strong, and Mama wouldn't allow you to talk over it, if you could of. When the victrola was wound up full it was good for one and a half playings; the last part of the second sort of died off. She had it right next to her, and she would reach over with her stirring hand and wind it up again and put the needle back on, keeping the iron moving across the shirt the whole time. The other side of the record was "Ave Maria," but Mama never got a shine to it. I always told her it moved me a lot, so I could turn the thing over once in a while and get "Thank God" out of my ears.

The lady soprano started off-key, like she was going to get that off her chest before she really buckled down, and I used to wince every time she hit the first note. After Mama gave the record about six straight playings she let it rest a few minutes, to say: "You can get a lot of good out of that record."

I don't know whether you could or not, but if you could, we got it.

Then she said: "Scrub, Lucille, don't scrape. You likely might fray the lace clean off that chemise." I probably would of, I was pushing down with my shoulders and my back. "Let up for a minute," she told me, "ain't much left to do this morning."

"Just as well keep on till I get through," I said.

"No, che, you sweating. Cold sweat ain't good for the body."

Wind was running past the house. You could hear it, clean and new-wet. There was a sometimes sun, too, jumping out from behind the clouds and splashing color over everything.

Sunlight is the color of freedom. It's the life color. If you want to

know how life began or what God is, stop figuring. Just go out on one
cold, bright day, and stand in the sunlight, and look up. If you don't
get it that way, you ain't likely to. I did what Mama told me: I quit.
I went over to the window. "What you looking at?" she asked.
(What *was* I looking at? Hard to tell.)
"You hear me talk to you?"
"Things," I said, "the sun on the air."
Mama stood the iron up on its end, and raised her head. "Child,"
she said, "I know just what you mean. It makes you think how the
Lord Jesus made the grass, and the trees, and the flowers, and the
fruit . . ."
There we were, back thanking Him for a garden. I turned around
and leaned against the sill. "Iron cord's worn open," I said, talking
fast to keep her mind off the record, "wire shows through."
Mama stooped over for a good look. "Tape it up, che, while it's
out-plugged. Got to keep electricity to itself all the time."
I opened the table drawer and took what was left of the adhesive.
There was only a little strip, doubled together, but it was enough. I
unstuck it and cut it lengthwise with the scissors. Then I put two
ends of the pieces together, and wrapped both pieces around the spot
where the cord was frayed deepest.
"Where's Dan?" Mama wanted to know.
"Still in the bedroom."
"How many more days that flower shop going to keep closed for
repairs?"
"Only till day after tomorrow."
Mama waved a puff of lint off the ironing board. She said: "What-
all he doing in the bedroom?"
"He's just in there," I told her, "he ain't *got* nothing to do."
She was ironing the wrinkles out of a shirt cuff. Mama could
finish a cuff in three passes if she had to. "No good for a person to be
in a room by hisself too much," she said. "Like your grandfather.
Thinking too much is against the Lord." She was feeling good,
Mama almost never talked about her family, except to say how dead
they was.
Mama's mama must of been kind of a loose character, I think.
Course, none of us ever knew her. The way our father told it to us,
seems both our grandfathers was born slaves, and then got emancipated when they was a year old or so. But the one on Mama's side
never could get hisself a decent job like he wanted after he was
married, even though he was famous all over Atlanta for being the

best educated colored man in town. Or maybe it was because of that. Anyway, after a while, our grandma started going out to see how she could do, and right away she made a whole pile of money. Well, she put her money in the bank, and it was her pride. And it was probably our grandfather's pride too, because he up and quit looking for the right kind of work, and took to sitting around and spending much as he could get his hands on. And when our grandma stopped him spending, he went right on sitting. Then, I don't know whether he figured out how she might of made the money, or if he plain got tired sitting, but anyway, he stood on his feet one morning and went away and never came back. Mama was pretty grown up by then, and she and her sisters was all out maiding. Our father married her a couple years later, and our grandma went up to the comfort of the Lord, according to Mama, but the way our father told us I got the idea she more likely boozed off. Same thing, I guess. Our father was kind of liquored hisself the day he told us about it, and didn't any of it make much sense to me till I sat down and thought it over after he was dead. When I did, though, it fell right together: it sort of accounted for Mama's being so religious, and so much against liquor, and so scared. Scared for what her mama might of done; scared about what her papa did; scared by what her husband wound up doing. And in case that wasn't enough, a flush of white blood in her babies to scare her for what we would do someday.

I said: "I sure would like to of known our grandfather." I thought maybe I could get her to talk about it.

Mama was finished with the shirt, and she put it on one side and took a pair of drawers from the basket. She shook them out and lay them on the board.

I tried again: "I think of him as a sad man."

She wet her finger on her tongue, and touched the bottom of the iron to see if it was hot enough. It was. Before she put it down on the drawers, she looked over at me, and I knew I had to shut up about that.

I turned and watched back out the window at the stump of our bush—the white-flowering bush that died the year after our father.

Course, I was sure Mama was going to do it now, only I thought there might be something I could say would put her off a little. But the handle was already wound up, so all she had to do was push the lever and put the arm on. I screwed up my face, waiting.

Thaaaaank . . .

I went back to the washing. I used to get so I couldn't help scrubbing up and down in time to the music:

> *Thank*—beat, beat—*God*—beat—for a *gar*—beat, beat—
> *den*—beat, beat
> *And-for-the-fish-in-the-sea*—beat, beat, beat, beat, beat
> *Thaaaaank* . . .

Mama played it through nine times. Then she wound up for the next two, and shut the victrola. I was finished, and drying my hands on a dishrag.

"Do that in the sink," she said, "you dripping all over the floor. Got less sense than a black-eyed Susan."

The skin on the tips of my fingers was all wrinkled and loose, like squishy paper. I was thinking it was funny how the more water wets you, the more it dries you out.

Mama looked over at the bedroom door. "What is that child doing shut in there all by his lonesome?"

I didn't know, but I thought it was a little strange myself. The bedroom hadn't ever been one of Dan's places. I said: "You finish up ironing, I'll go see."

But: "No," she said. "I find out."

So when I got there she was close behind me.

I took my time opening the door, and I rattled the handle first so he would hear. There was a chair leaning against the other side; it fell away. Mama reached over my shoulder and pushed. She would of knocked me out of her path, only I stepped forward too quick.

The bedroom was empty. But I saw Dan right from the doorway. I still don't know why he went to all the trouble of the chair, and then didn't even shut the door to the bathroom.

He was sitting on the bathtub, and he was so surprised he couldn't move. He didn't try to cover what he had been doing; he just didn't move at all. The picture fell out of his hand, face up on the floor.

I made myself as big as I could in front of Mama, so he would have a chance to get up and turn around or something. But right away she stuck her arm out and shoved me aside, and stepped into the room.

She was quiet for a time, looking. It didn't sink in very fast. Then her whole body like to got taller, growing with the horror and the fear. Her breath began to sound as if she might of had something in her throat. There wasn't hardly enough air for the words. "Stand up," she said, low. "Stand up . . . stand up, you . . . stand up."

Dan inched to the side along the bathtub edge.

"You stand up." Mama was whispering. "You . . . put your feet on the floor and stand up."

Dan couldn't.

"Stand *up*," she rasped.

Dan hunched over and let his weight find balance on the floor. One hand went to his pants, trying to push hisself back inside.

"Put your hands to your sides," said Mama. "Put your hands down and stand straight . . . up."

It would of been better for Dan if she had hit him—better than that face and that shaking voice. I saw him lean against the wall to keep his knees straight. His pants was still open, and his parts hanging there, shiny and wet, and limp now.

Mama walked forward as far as the bathroom, her body knotted, holding back a little—like a person who is going to see a fearsome dead thing. She leaned way down over the picture, not believing, not wanting to believe it. Then she swung her hand over it and picked it up by the corner; she held it in two fingers, away from her legs and from Dan, and she took three long steps behind her.

I looked at the picture, tilted in the air. It was a page off some old calendar, torn at the top and smudged. The girl on it was fleshy and beautiful, and she was practically naked. A white girl, with long hennaed hair.

Mama said: "May the Lord have mercy on you. May the Lord have mercy on you and save you."

The muscles in Dan's chest started to tremble under his shirt.

"Where you get this?"

He kept quiet.

"Where you *get* it?"

No answer.

She took a deep breath, and yelled: "*Where?*"

Dan choked out: ". . . Found it."

"*Where?*"

"In . . . in a . . . ash can."

Mama raised her free hand and stroked her own forehead. Then she let it drop down again. I think she must of made up her mind then not to speak about the girl's color.

She said: "You know what happens to men who do what you been doing? You know what happens? They go crazy, that's what. They go crazy. You plain going to go crazy." Her voice sank deeper; she talked slow: "You sucking all the brain juice down your spine and letting it out, and you going to go crazy. *Crazy . . . crazy . . . crazy mad.* All the insane people in the world done started like that, just like you. All them people sucked out all their brain juice and threw it away, sinning by theirselves. And you plain going to go crazy mad like all them . . . How many times you done that?"

Dan opened his mouth, but nothing came out.

"*How many?*"

". . . Not . . . much."

"It ain't so," Mama gritted, "you lying to me."

He shook his head no.

"How you know to do that?"

He had no voice. But he tried to say: "I . . . saw . . ."

"What you see? Where you see?"

"On the street . . . a man . . ."

"Doing that?"

"Yes, ma'am." He sighed the words out so light you could barely hear.

"Now, listen," Mama said, talking low again. (I was thinking: don't talk like that, not like that. Shout at him, or hit him, but don't soft-peel him alive.) "Now you listen at me. If you want a chance to keep from going crazy out of your head, don't you never dare to do that again. I going to pray to the Lord Jesus to help keep you from going crazy this time. And if you ever do it again, the Lord will tell me, and I going to know it. And I going to come with a razor and cut that part of you right off to stop you from going crazy."

Dan's face twitched once, and then went loose. His eyes dulled over like a shade you pull down. He stared blank.

That's okay, I thought, I don't mind it now . . . you just shelling in because you can't take no more . . . that's okay . . . that's okay.

Mama prayed: "Oh, Lord. Keep my son Daniel from going crazy for what he done today. Give him some more brain juice for what he has threw away, Lord. In your kindness, keep him from going crazy. Amen."

He shuddered, hearing her. But his face could of been painted on him.

"And if I ever catch you with a picture. *Any* . . . *kind* . . . of a picture . . ." She lifted the calendar page and hit it between her hands, crumpling it. When it was a small enough roll, she put one hand on either end and twisted it backwards, till it broke in two—as if she might of had a live rat inside, snapping his neck. "See what I did to *that?*"

Dan stayed the same.

"Go in the kitchen and pull the window curtain across and wash yourself with hot water," Mama said, "and pray."

But he couldn't budge. He shook, but he plain couldn't budge.

I thought: waiting for the spear, like the raccoon . . . look at him . . . just like the raccoon.

"Go in and wash. Go in and wash off your sin."

Dan stood and watched her.

Like the raccoon. I knew Mama had forgot about me; I slipped in front of her and put my arm up to my hair so he couldn't see her eyes.

Dan jumped, and ran around us out of the room.

"What you doing," Mama said, "*you?*" She slapped me quick across my face.

I didn't answer. I turned and walked to the kitchen door, wanting to cry. Not for the slap, for him. Only I was too empty inside to cry.

"Stand right there," Mama ordered, "till he get through."

I stopped where I was; but I could see Dan huddled over the basin, still shuddering.

Mama kept her body very straight, and called, singsong: "I will cut it off before I let you go crazy. I will cut it off. I will cut it off."

For a long time she didn't turn around or move. She stood in the bedroom with her back to the doorway, and her arms stiff at her sides—each hand crumpling a tight paper ball smaller and tighter. She held her head high, praying.

9

RIGHT after that day, up until Christmas week started, Dan was even quieter. He went to work, and came home, and stayed in the house. He sat around the kitchen mostly, helping to shell peas or peel potatoes. I tried getting close to him, but there just wasn't anything to contact. If I winked or smiled or passed a remark so Mama wouldn't hear—no matter what I did—he looked back with the same watery eyes. It was as if he had went all soft.

I waited for a chance to be alone with him, but I don't think he wanted it. Mama switched us and put Clarence to sleep in Dan's room, and me in Clarence's bed in the kitchen. So I wasn't even with him at night.

Then I saw that the softness had gone; Dan had found some comfort to keep him alive. Not what he was looking for, I don't think. But it stopped his looking all the same, and it made a big change in him.

He began to act like he knew what he was doing—like he *had* a thing to do. And whatever it was, Dan made his deal with God and settled for it. He didn't sit for hours in one place, and he didn't get his once-a-week day either. He was pretty much always the same: fidgety, almost sneaky, generally with something in his hands. He wouldn't watch you in the eye for very long, even if you talked to him. And he got that blank face down to where he could pull it whenever he liked. He would be listening to you, or he might be answering a question—suddenly you knew he had shut hisself off, and he didn't want anybody else. From then on, he had his own secrets and his own life. It was when I really lost my brother: when Dan started to grow up.

About blaming:
Before spring of the same year I got my first wonder of all. And I got it just in time.

Sooner or later, everybody likes to know what they are. Some people can find out by plain going ahead and being it. They either run across the spot in the world that fits them right—or they bend their shape around till they fit into the best spot they see along the road—or, if they big and strong enough, they shape the spot around to fit them. The point is, *they fit*. So, happy or not, at least their blood has a home to dry in. And happy-or-not is a part of life. It's the people who don't fit that get a disgust round their blood, to make up for the home. The people who can't be happy, or not, or anything. The other people.

Washing Monday, washing Tuesday, washing every day away behind Mama's closed door, in Mama's empty world, I never had a chance to see why *I* didn't fit. I only knew I didn't. And I figured if I ever got out of her house, into the true world, it would be plenty soon enough for me to know if I had a true self to go on with. Only, shut in like I was, I couldn't exactly *live* while I was waiting. And when a person can't live, a person starts to wonder.

So I got to wondering.

The first thing I did it about was the thing that mattered first, and most, in my whole life: our father. I remembered the way he looked before he died, and I remembered the doctor telling Mama afterwards how liquor wasn't enough to kill him in just two years. Then I thought about what Clarence had said to him that last day on the gallery. And the more I thought, and the more I remembered, the more it seemed to me that our father really might of slipped out of the world on purpose. But why? Because he couldn't find his spot—his *one* spot—a man like our father? "Be what you want to be," he said, "there's always a way." *Always* a way. Then where was his way?

Next was Clarence. He knew what he wanted to be, and he knew he couldn't, not the way he was headed. And still, he *was headed* somewhere. Only, where? He said: "Soon as you know what you are in a place, you just got to go and be it." Be what? What did Clarence know?

And now Dan. My little brother Dan. Now even he had a secret.

But something about my brothers kept me from believing in either one of their secrets. Something was off; something was wrong for both of them.

I asked myself what it was, and why it was wrong, and who we could blame for making it like that. Who set up the world against them—against all of us? *Who?*

Mama? No, she couldn't help what she did, and her mama had passed the fear on to her.

The white people? They had mamas to teach them too. The colored people? They had mamas, and they had the white people.

Whose *fault* was it, and who could I hate?

But I knew too that before I could even sense a hate, I would have to forget our father. Because he was a man never hated anybody as long as he lived. Except maybe hisself.

So I thought: now hold on a while, honey. Everybody on earth must have a reason for everything they do, if you only go back and look for it. It might be the wrong reason, but that don't stop it from being a reason. And a person can keep traveling back on that chain practically forever if she wants to, from reason to reason, from colored to white, from mama to grandma to great-grandma. Only just how far back is she going to go? *Who* is she going to blame?

Then I thought: no, you can't. No, ma'am. You plain can't stop anywhere you want along the line and point your finger at somebody and blame him. No, you got to go all the way back, if you started. And the only one you can really take to count is the One who *thought up* the whole mess in the real beginning.

But I got stuck again. Because I said: supposing it ain't His fault neither. Supposing it wasn't such a mess then. Maybe He had a lot of assistant angels who bitched it, monkeying around with people's colors and things. That would make it just another good idea, gone to pot. And even so, how can you say an angel was wrong, just because he liked to play with colors?

Che, I said, the big trouble with you is you *trying* to find fault. You should have to invent a bigness like the world, out of nothing, without making no mistakes. That's what.

And I thought: maybe our father knew. Maybe he found out he couldn't ever blame a single person for anything in this world except hisself. And maybe—*just maybe*—our father was the first in the family to find out that you can't even blame God.

10

ONLY one thing was left to happen in those five years.

It was almost summer. Hot, anyway. Only not suffering hot, you could still breathe and walk around without feeling the sky close in on you. It was the part of the year when you always think summer ain't going to be so bad this time.

I was over sixteen then, and almost as tall as I was going to be. Dan had passed fourteen, and Clarence was not quite twenty-one.

Dan was set in his job by then, and Mama and me was used to not having him around the house except at night. He worked from nine to seven, riding the flower shop's bicycle for small orders and helping out on their truck for the big ones, and he made seventy-five cents a day plus carfare and tips. Some weeks he brought home much as eight dollars, so Mama generally let him keep a quarter for hisself.

Clarence went on working wherever it was he worked. He hardly read any more, though, and he almost never did his numbers. I don't think he could of forgot about wanting to be a scientist, ever. But somewhere along the line, he plain had to give up.

I dated regular that year, and I had two boy friends, eighteen years old. They didn't amount to anything serious—both kind of boboes, I thought—but still and all I had come a long way since Unifont. And I liked one of them all right. Course, the way it always is, it was the other one was crazy about me. The trouble was that the one I liked's brother was married to the one who liked me's sister. Meaning I couldn't play around with them both, the way the other girls did, till I finally fished out the one I had wanted in the first place. Because I wouldn't but pass a remark to one of them, when the other would up and throw it back in my face. Anyway, what I did in the end, I quit trying to copy how the other girls treated their boy friends, and I just acted *straight* and *sincere*, like I felt. So I lost both of them.

As we three grew older, the lightness of our color let off being such a big problem. Our people still took a first notice, but they mostly forgot after they knew us. They let it slip into the backs of their minds, anyhow, and we buried it too. Working people got a lot more to do than be silly, if they work hard enough. It was different with Clarence, but then it always had been different with him, and he never stopped being the most beautiful man I ever saw.

Clarence was the one bucked Mama for me. He was home on an evening I went out for a date, and when he took a fresh look at the old brown sack-dress I was wearing, he stared me right out of the house. Then I think he must of had it with Mama that same night before I came home, because she looked stormy, but she didn't say a word the next day when he brought me the package of new clothes. There was two different dresses—a cream-tan print and a solid blue; a darker blue fitted dressy coat, with square black buttons; a pair of black patent-leather pumps, with half heels; a purse made out of the same leather with a comb and a mirror inside; three little handkerchiefs with blue edging, and a rayon slip, and a set of rayon underclothes. When I opened the box, I tried to keep from crying, but I couldn't. Clarence got mad at my wanting to thank him, and Mama just examined each thing real careful and then went back to the stove. So I took the box in the boys' room and put everything away in its new place, and I washed my face in the bathtub. But I had to sit down on Dan's bed anyhow, and it took me most of an hour to stop the tears.

Three afternoons later I had a date to go walking, and I got dressed in the blue dress. I combed my hair into a higher bun, and I lifted as much of it off my ears as I thought I could get away with. Then I put on the shoes, and practiced with them for a long time up and down the room before I opened the door and almost fell on my face into the kitchen. When I got my balance, I stood straight and looked at Mama. Clarence and Dan was there too, they was all waiting. Didn't any of them speak, but I could get it from their faces. Even Mama bit her lip and started to stack plates very fast to hide the shine in her eyes. When my date came for me fifteen minutes later I was still standing there, and nobody had opened their mouth even once.

After we went out, though, Clarence got up and followed us onto the gallery. He put his hand over my wrist and swung me around behind him. "Cille," he said, "you be careful now. You always be careful." I didn't answer him; I just leaned up and kissed him on the cheek. And Clarence snatched his face away and jumped back inside so fast, I practically fell again. But I was always happy I had been able to kiss him that day.

The morning before it happened, we had rain, and by night the air was circling. That is one of the things I can still feel. The air that rose off the wet ground, up my skirt with its cool, and around down my neck asking the skin to move there. Air so light, if you stood quiet and tried to feel it, you couldn't. So light, I didn't even know I had a notice of it then—didn't know till a year later when I thought back. Frightened, restless air.

I was walking back to Mama's house, with one of my two boy friends—the one who was love-simple about me. They hadn't neither of them dropped me yet.

We had been to the pictures, and he'd held my hand through the entire feature. He was one of these boys with sweaty hands, and I was all for getting back and latching onto a bar of soap.

Besides, he had tried to kiss me in the dark. Course, I wouldn't of minded, if he hadn't waited to do it till just when Clark Gable was kissing Lana Turner. But if there was one thing used to grate me, that was it. And a lot of boys would try to kiss you like that, when one star got to kissing the other star. All I could ever think of was either he is trying to make believe I am her, or he wants me to make believe he is him, or he just plain got the urge from watching them. And any way of the three I took it, I didn't like it.

So I walked on, feeling the air without knowing.

He asked: "You mad at me or something?"

"Lord, no," I said, "what am I going to be mad for? You get these weird ideas, William Jones." His name was William Jones.

"Oh," he said, "I thought you might be mad or something." That was the kind of conversation he held. And the other boy wasn't a whole lot better.

We went close together, and he kept brushing up against me.

I figured he wanted me to take his arm, but number one: he had put
me in a bad mood, and number two: I was still acting fine, and sweet,
and a little thick, like I thought a girl should.

The next thing he told me: "It certainly does look like rain." Just
like that, *wham*. It certainly does look like rain. It didn't, either.

"Yes, it certainly does," I said. I couldn't really of cared less what
he talked about, just so he wasn't going to start rehashing the
picture.

"That was an interesting picture," he said.

"What time is it?" I asked quick.

William Jones said: "Around ten o'clock I liked the part where
she tells him she's been bad but she still better than his dead wife
is did you?"

I sighed.

"Did you like that part?"

"Course."

He looked at me out of one little eye. "You sure you ain't mad or
something?"

"Sure I'm sure. I done told you I ain't."

We crossed the street, and turned the corner down Millicent,
William Jones bouncing. Another reason I didn't want to take
his arm, he bounced a lot and he walked fast. A hold on William
Jones was a little like the handgrip in the Tulane streetcar, without
the nice noise.

"I certainly hope it don't up and rain before we get to your house,"
he said, and then again: "it certainly does look an awful lot like
rain."

I thought: he must be doing it on purpose now, he ain't that
dumb; yes, he is dumb, but he ain't *that* dumb.

It was a transparent-clear night. The only clouds up there
looked like smoke. They was so thin, the stars came clean through
them and stared at you. The moon curved a little over half, but
bright, and you could see where the other half ended. And the
only rain for miles around was strictly in William Jones' head.

But watching the glitter of the darkness, I got sort of sorry for him.
I figured he didn't mean to be aggravating, like he was. So when he
came near to the house, I thought I might as well kiss him goodnight. I turned, and held my head up. "See," I told him, "it didn't
rain."

"Sure didn't," he said.

I couldn't think of another comment to make, but I held the position. We stood there a while, and I stretched my head further up.

"Neck hurt?" asked William Jones.

"No," I said, marching to the gallery steps. "You want to come in?"

"I only thought . . . account of we was sitting over to the left in the pictures . . ."

"Yes, indeed. You want to come in?"

"Okay," he said.

Sure he does, I thought. Course.

I didn't understand then. I didn't understand why you had to talk about the weather and the pictures and a lot of other foolish stuff, if you really wanted to talk about something else or maybe not to talk at all. Seemed to me if a person couldn't say a thing, he plain couldn't feel it. So I wanted William Jones to say: *Look, I like you*, if that was what was on his mind.

I guess I just hadn't learned yet that it was going to be up to *me* to look for the truth.

The kitchen light was on, and Mama sitting under it, darning one of Dan's socks. Dan stood facing the wall. The boys' bedroom door was open, and Clarence was in there.

I could tell from the way Mama's mouth was turned that there must of been something passing around she didn't like.

I said right away: "I invited William Jones in to have a drink."

"A drink?" Mama said.

"A Coke, or whatever we got."

Mama pushed a smile, and her bottom lip twitched. "Good evening, Mr. Jones. Do you want to sit down here with us, you welcome to." She was really upset.

"Everybody calls me W.J.," he said, "excepting Lucille."

"He mean for me to correct you?" Mama asked me.

"No," I explained, "he means for you to call him W.J."

"That's right," said William Jones.

"Oh," Mama said.

William Jones sat down to the kitchen table, and I went for a Coke. Crossing over to the ice barrel, I saw Dan was still standing with his back turned. He hadn't spoke a word, and it kind of irked me. I knocked him with my shoulder, and asked: "You know William Jones?" Dan knew him, we lived close together.

He said: "Hello." But he didn't turn away from the wall. And his voice had all the edge off it.

William Jones said: "Hi, Danny."

We were lucky, there was one Coke. After I washed my hands,

I poured it out over some ice I had rinsed off, and put the glass on the table.

Nobody talked. William Jones sipped at his Coke.

I looked around the room, and then at the screen door. Course, the spring coil was busted again, and the door hung open a couple fingers, like always. It opened out onto the gallery, so you couldn't put a chair or anything against it, unless you was leaving the house. You just had to let the flies come in, and the mosquitoes in the summer. The screen was ripped in four or five places anyway. Mama had pasted a square of wrapping paper over each one with rice water, and then sewed them on. They was dry and mostly coming off.

When you stand outside a lighted house at night, you can see in better than the daytime, and you think they can see out the same. But they can't. I was thinking about that.

Clarence came from the bedroom, and nodded at William Jones. He got a cup of hot water from the can over the potbelly, and stood that in the sink. Then he took a comb out of his back pocket, and wet it, and started combing his hair.

"You ain't going out," Mama said. She didn't ask it, she said it.

Clarence wet the comb again, and used it some more.

"I said you ain't going out."

He shook the comb dry as he could, and put it in his mouth while he smoothed all the water drops from off his neck. After that he went back into the bedroom.

Mama dropped the wood egg out of Dan's sock, and put her hand inside to test the spot she had darned. She was breathing hard, you could hear her.

William Jones held his glass upside down, trying to get the last slivers of ice that slipped around the bottom. They wouldn't fall, but he saw I was watching him, so he put the glass down. "I hope you-all got some more Cokes. I certainly hope I didn't drink up your one last Coke."

I told him: "We got some more in there."

"No, we don't," Mama said.

William Jones sat up. "Hey," he said. Just hey.

Mama made a ball out of the finished sock; she tucked it into her sewing basket. Then she stuck her needle in the strawberry pincushion, and leaned across the table to William Jones. She said, loud: "Mr. Jones, my son got a letter from the government of the United States. My son going to go in the army."

Dan turned, and flattened back against the wall.

Clarence stepped into the doorway, smiling. Not a nice smile. "Your son," he said, before William Jones could talk, "don't know yet if he is going to go in the army, or if he ain't going to go in the army. He don't know yet. He plain do not know yet." Clarence talked nasty and even, letting each word have the same force.

Mama told William Jones: "My son think maybe the government of the United States going to wait on him to make up his mind?"

The smile on Clarence's face was extra there. He walked backwards, shutting the bedroom door.

I was going to follow him in, but:

"Keep out of that room," Mama said, "you keep out." She got up and threw the door open so it banged against the wall. "Ain't nobody going to slam no doors I know about," she said.

William Jones was on his feet.

I put my hand out to him. "Go on home, honey," I said.

"Sure. Hey, I'm sorry."

"Go on home."

He wanted to say goodnight to Mama, but she had forgot all about him, so he just waved to Dan (who wasn't looking either), and tiptoed like a cartoon mouse around the table. One of his shoes squeaked a little when he walked, but it squeaked more when he tiptoed, and the slower he went the louder it got. He shrugged at me as he went out. You could hear him halfway down the block.

None of us moved.

Mama said: "How you figure, you think maybe you too good to go in the army?"

"Maybe," Clarence said, from in the bedroom, "I might be too good."

". . . You going to do like I *say*."

Clarence laughed.

"Don't you dare to laugh at me . . . You *got* to go."

"I got to do like I want to do."

"You want to make me unhappy?"

"You wouldn't of known about it," Clarence said, "if you hadn't fished through my pants and found the letter, and then made Reverend Segrette read it to you."

"You got no right to hide nothing in this house."

Clarence walked past her, and sat in her chair. He reached in his shirt pocket, and took out a cigarette, and lit it. He knew Mama wouldn't allow him to smoke in front of us.

146 A Place Without Twilight

"You think you too good to go in the army," Mama said, "you plain think you too good."

Clarence blew smoke at the light bulb in a funnel-shape stream.

Mama leaned over behind him and shouted in his ear: *"Too good, too good."*

He sucked at his cigarette again, and she grabbed it out of his mouth and threw it in the sink. A little part of skin ripped wide open on his lip; he set it between his teeth, and then bit it clean off.

She told him: "Ain't nothing you can say nohow. The army ain't going to pay no mind to what you say."

Clarence looked around at her, and turned back. The smile was still on. "If you think that, what you getting so riled up about?"

"I want my son to do right by his government. I want my son to be a man. I want my son to do right by his *soul.*"

Clarence pulled out another cigarette and played with it in his fingers. Real soft, he said: "You a little late on that one."

"What you going to tell them?" The scared sound was in Mama's voice now.

"I done told you, I don't know yet."

"How you think you going to get out of it?"

"I got friends."

"What kind of friends is them?"

"Friends; where I work."

Mama threatened: "I find out where you work and go talk to them."

"Find out." He said it the same way, like a threat.

"Oh, Lord," Mama said, "make my son a man to know his duty to Thou."

"To Thee," Clarence said.

"You swerving in your duty to the Lord?"

"I ain't got no duty to fight for no white people."

"This here is your country."

"*This here* is the white people's country."

"Don't talk like that," Mama whispered, harsh. "Don't you never talk like that. It's dangerous to talk like that."

Clarence whispered back: "But it ain't dangerous to go into the army."

Mama sidled around and sat in the other chair. "Reach me a glass of water," she said, "my child is killing me."

I went and got it.

"You ain't dead yet," Clarence told her. "You going to live for a long time. You going to be ashamed you lived such a long time." His voice was knuckle-hard, like the call of a blue jay.

Mama drank the water, choking on it. "I done always taught you . . . I don't know why you acting like you is . . . I done always taught you to do right. For every single day of your twenty and one-half years of life . . . I done always taught you."

"That's seven thousand four hundred and eighty-two and a half days," said Clarence. "Gone bye-bye."

"Always. I done always taught you never to think you was too good to do nothing for no white person."

Clarence was so mad he was struggling inside to hold on; only you had to know him to sense that. He said quick, so it would be out: "I done a couple things for a white person *you* wouldn't do. But I might not fight for one. I just might not."

Mama jumped back; she knocked the glass onto the floor. It didn't break, it rolled across to the stove leg and stopped there. *"What you telling me?"* She was shouting, but she'd bent double in the chair, holding the pain with her hands. *"What you wanting to tell me there?"*

Clarence stood up and let the unlit cigarette drop away. "I ain't telling you nothing," he said, "I ain't telling you nothing but I don't like to fight for no white man. That's all. I ain't telling you nothing more than that." He sounded to me like he was trying to backwater. I got the same feeling then I used to have when I was little—that something had passed between them. Some secret they each kept a part of.

"Trying to hurt me, making up them lies."

". . . No lies."

"Wanting to hurt your poor old Mama with them *dirty lies*."

"No."

"Lies, lies, lies," she yelled.

Clarence said: "No. Oh, no you don't."

She stared at him for a full half-minute. Then she shut her eyes. She told him: "You going to get killed . . . I know it . . . No matter what you do, no matter . . . where you go . . . you going to get killed . . . you going to get killed . . . you going to get killed." She sang it to him, deep and heavy, and the tune was close to the old lullaby I hadn't heard her sing since we were kids.

That was when Dan started to throw up. He was right next to the sink, but he did it down on hisself and on the floor. He stood looking at Mama, and he did it like a thing apart. I don't think he even knew it was happening.

Clarence lost his hold. I could tell soon as he had, because I was watching his smile. And suddenly, while I watched, it wasn't a smile any more. It was a snarl. His mouth hadn't moved, and you never saw the change. But you could tell. When he talked, the Tiger-Cat's voice slashed out fierce: "You rather see me killed in the army than someplace else? You rather see me killed *that way?*"

Mama didn't answer. She couldn't, she was crying. It was the only time in my life I ever saw Mama cry.

"Well, would you? You rather see me go in the army and get killed *there?* I won't do it. I won't go in the army unless I goddam well want to."

Mama called: "What did I do? Dear, sweet Lord in the Heaven up above, what did I ever do?" Then she told Clarence: "You ain't all of a man."

"Might not be," he said. "*Might not be.* And maybe I just might tell them a little bit about that. They won't take me . . . if I tell them about that."

"*My son ain't a man. Not all of a man,*" Mama called. Then: "Tell them what?"

"*You* knew." Clarence was shouting now. "*You knew. You knew* it all along. *You* knew even before *I* did, so don't make like you surprised, *you knew, you knew, you . . .*"

Mama screeched: "*What you going to tell them?*"

He waited till the sound of her voice had died out, and he answered quiet, practically spitting out the words he said them so careful: "Now, what you think I'm going to tell them? You tell me."

Mama pushed me away, and got up. She swallowed three times, swallowing the hurt, swallowing her guts back in. Then she breathed a jerky breath, and talked to Clarence like he was a little tiny baby. But she didn't look at him. She was looking a ways to his left, at his shadow, when she said, gentler than I'd ever heard Mama speak: "You get out of here. Get out of my house. You do what you want, but you get out of my house now. And don't ever come back. You infecting all my children."

They both held like they was: Clarence looking at Mama, and Mama looking at his shadow. Clarence's mouth had shut, and the smile and the snarl had both disappeared. There wasn't nothing on his face. Even the blood had left it; his smooth skin was all ugly, and pasty, and gray.

Then they both moved at exactly the same second—sudden as two acrobats that had counted, each to hisself, for the right click. Mama buckled stiff into her chair. And Clarence took one long, slinking step, and was gone outside.

The screen door fell back easy, but it caught and stayed shut: like something had pushed it to, and was holding it there. I plain couldn't see why, after so many years, it had finally closed tight with the spring broke.

We all three watched the door. In the empty lot next to us, a locust was croaking his rhythm up the night. It was the only sound out there.

Dan retched to the beat of the locust.

II

WHEN Cousin Wila wrote saying I should come and work in her job, maiding for a family that lived across the Lake, I never once thought Mama would let me. It was nine months since Clarence had left. I was a ways past seventeen.

Cousin Wila was about forty-five then, though she wouldn't of admitted to it, I don't think. She had started working for these people as a cook, and then she came to be tired of that and she got another cousin of hers name of Celeste to come and take it over for her soon as the maid up and left on some account, and she got herself made maid. Then after a month or so she claimed she was plain tired of maiding too, so she gave notice she was going back to her home in Biloxi for a rest, and wrote to Mama did I want to come and take her place.

Cousin Wila was always the same: she would get tired real fast of each job so she could change over to the next one, and leave it to somebody on her family tree. She must of passed through half the state like that, and every time she switched she would move a different cousin of hers in. Our father used to say she was trying to get enough personal family working in enough houses on a one hundred per cent basis so that when she got really old she could call just one strike and make a fortune. I don't know how she got all the other help to leave, but she sure could do it. She would go through a house like a herd of termites, and in less than six months, wasn't nothing but family working there. I think the thing was, with her face so twisted around, Cousin Wila never planned on getting married or having any babies of her own, and maybe giving a lot of young kids a chance sort of helped make up to her for that.

In her letter, Cousin Wila explained all about the people she was working for. She said they was rich people, and fine, and they lived across the Lake in a big weekend plantation house they had put up on Bayou Liberté. By way of showing us how rich and fine they really was, she told us how they had built the house specially so it would look real old and crumbling down, like it had been getting what she called *antique* for the last hundred years. She said their family used to own a real plantation house a long time ago, but it burned down and they sold the land. And this house was supposed to be a copy of the real one, only not so big. Cousin Wila said they used to keep another house going in New Orleans too, and drive back and forth to Bayou Liberté every weekend—but they had to stop on account of the health of this old man who was the lady of the house's father, and who was so sick the doctor said he couldn't live in but one place at a time, and not in the city. So the lady of the house had to figure a way for him to stay across the Lake, and the only way to do that was for her and her husband and her husband's brother to move on out there with him. But both of the young gentlemen had some kind of a business going in New Orleans, and they drove in three or four times a week anyhow, and kept an extra apartment in the city. Cousin Wila said the reason everything got so complicated for the poor people was because what they was really doing was waiting for the old man to die and leave them all these millions of dollars he had. She made a special point of that in her letter, so Mama could see it was the best kind of white family, but she didn't have to: everybody knew Cousin Wila didn't ever pick but the best houses. She had accumulated a pile of references three feet high, and our father told us whenever she went to apply for a new job you got the feeling it was the lady who was showing the references to Cousin Wila. She stayed careful that way because she said after all she couldn't have nothing but the best for her own relatives.

She always put everybody's birthday down next to their name on her family tree, so when she saw I had got past seventeen, I came to be next on her mind. By then, Cousin Celeste and Cousin Ernest the gardener was good and settled in their jobs. (I found out later Cousin Wila had kind of a problem getting Cousin Ernest in, because these people kept a mean old Cajun working all the time in the garden, and he didn't speak any language but one called patois, so Cousin Wila couldn't really get at him to find out why he might like to quit. But one day while she was still cook, he got awful sick with a bad stomach upset and decided it was a whole lot safer back in the swamps with his own tribe.) The other colored person who worked in the house was Charles Leroy Merrill, butlering. He had been there before Cousin Wila, only he was lucky and she took a shine to him, so he just got pasted on a new branch of the tree. Mademoiselle the upstairs maid was white, and different, and didn't count.

Anyway, when Cousin Wila's letter came, I didn't even think about going, what with all the washing we had now. And how was Mama going to let me leave the city, when she was still watching me so careful she wouldn't allow me to stay out of the house later than ten-thirty at night?

Something changed her, though.

Dan had given notice of quitting at the flower shop to get better pay someplace else, only when they saw he was really going to leave they gave him a twenty-five cent raise. They liked him there because he did good work and held serious. Mama said he should stay on then, till he was old enough for Cousin Wila to place him in a private house around town. He'd learned to make better tips anyway, and with the raise he averaged about twelve dollars a week. Dan was near fifteen and a half years old; the new man in the family.

Clarence never came back. Not even for his clothes. He didn't even send anybody. And Mama wouldn't speak his name or allow it to be spoke in her house, after the night he left. That night she sat for two hours, staring at the tight-shut screen door. Then, she got up and went over to it; she put one hand in front of her, fingers straight, and with the inside first-joints she pushed steady till the door popped open its little space into the night. And the only thing she said to me and Dan: "The Lord Jesus seen fit to take one child of mine to his rest. We going to pray for his soul now, and we going to forget about him. The Lord is all good."

But after we prayed with her, nothing. His name was gone with him, and his old clothes belonged to Dan, and Mama only had two children left. I guess she thought he was cleaner gone and finished that way, for Dan and me. He wasn't, though. He was more there than if he had been talked about. Only instead of being there simple, like Mama's favorite child and our brother who had left us —he was with us in a kind of a tender fear: something we loved, but didn't know and couldn't say, like a dirty word for a beautiful thing. I used to dream his shadow came back at night after Mama slept. Not the shadow she had stared at when she told him to go. Not a shadow like anybody's. It was a white shadow.

And one night I dreamed the Dennis and Florabelle story the way our father told it to us, all through. The story only got mixed at the very end, when Florabelle came back. Because there I was, waiting for her with Dennis on the steps next to the Yacht Club, and then instead of swimming in, she came on a great big sailboat sitting next to this king and flipping jewels in the air. When she got close to where we were, she jumped overboard, and the king sailed off fast. She plopped a while in the water-scum, with her hair hanging down over her face, stringy and wet. And just as she said: "It ain't *that*, honey . . ." she leaned back till the hair fell away. But her body fell away too, and suddenly I was standing looking through the water at a real tiger with Clarence's face, laying dead on the muddy bottom in the bottle tops and the mushy cardboard and the filth—some crabs already picking at his bloody fur. After that it didn't seem at all strange in my dream when I saw how Dennis had changed to Mama.

The day William Jones told me Clarence had gone into the army, I made him tell it again like he was saying it for the first time, outside the screen door so Mama would hear. She was cooking, and I knew she heard because she stopped stirring the grits and stood holding the wood spoon up in the air. She was praying to herself, I think. Then she turned half around and looked at William Jones through the screen in a way that cut him off in the middle of a word. But when she had him quiet, she asked him to come in for lunch. And she put his chair where our brother used to sit.

A month from the time he left, Clarence started sending an envelope with a thirty-dollar check in it every week. Mama opened the first one, but after I explained to her what it was, she tore it up and got the mailman to mark all the next: "Return to Sender." When she'd sent four back, they stopped coming. The checks was on a New Orleans bank.

And that was the end of our brother alive with us. The end of his person, leastways. For me the Tiger-Cat never ended—years later I could still hear his soft padding outside the house after dark, coming home quiet not to wake anybody. Dan felt him too, I could tell. It was only for Mama that Clarence had stopped living the minute she told him he was going to get killed.

So Dan got a raise.

After I read her Cousin Wila's letter, Mama put it away without saying a word, and I thought she forgot about it. I was just going to remind her I should write and thank Cousin Wila anyhow, when she took the letter and went to see the preacher with it by herself. He must of written the answer that same morning, because Cousin Wila's next letter came a week later, registered, and inside was the dated ticket for me to go.

Mama talked to me a long April day. She said she was putting me in Jesus' hands and in Cousin Wila's, who was a fine woman. She said she knew I was the strongest of her children, and she wanted me to have a chance. I think that was true, but I think she wanted to be alone with Dan too. Maybe she thought we would forget Clarence easier if we were separated. Or maybe she might even of felt the thing that was wronger in Dan than it had ever been in Clarence—felt it, deeper buried, but wronger. I hope not; I hope she never felt it. Because if she did, then she must of really known that it was her had helped put it there, same as with her other child. And she would of wanted to dig it out and make it right this time. I hope not because she couldn't ever of made it *right*. Not Mama.

She cut down on the washing to where it wasn't too much for her alone. She had seventeen dollars saved up, and she said there would be enough with that and what she and Dan made to hold them over till I was settled and could send some. When Clarence left, there had been five more monthly payments on the house to go; but we never got the bills. Clarence always knew how to clean up after hisself, when he had to.

Then we made everything ready for me to take the next Monday's train to Caytown.

I said goodbye to Dan, alone, the night before. I tried to, that is. There wasn't no system you could use to get at him any more. He blinked at me, and even smiled—but all I saw in the darks of his eyes was my own little head looking back. And the stare was practiced now, so you couldn't just wait for it to pass.

Then I left. I just took a laundry carton with my clothes inside, and put my coat on, and went down to the station with Mama and Dan in the early morning fog, and I left. It was that way. Nobody cried. Nobody wanted to. We stood on the platform—Mama ashamed to be there, Dan fidgeting to get to the flower shop—the three of us out of place together in the open air, with real people running up and down, and without Mama's house around us. Mama had told me everything she wanted to, so there wasn't much left to say except goodbye. Steam came out from under the train over our feet, hot and full, then rose up and mixed with the fog to make a high cloud around us. It smelled bad and morning-new, but I liked it. It smelled like used water that was burning, if you could burn water. And it smelled like a quick, last breath before the beginning. We didn't go into the Colored Waiting Room, because we kept thinking the train was going to leave. But we waited almost an hour before it did. I got on just before, and Mama sneaked a wave at me with her hand against her side. She was too ashamed to holler or get ready to walk along the platform the way the other people was doing. Dan stood next to her, and he seemed to be watching something, but I couldn't tell if it was me or the train. Then my car shook down the string from the engine and pulled away about two feet—and his eyes didn't follow—and I knew he wasn't watching anything at all. When the train made its second jerk, I couldn't see them no more.

What you really want to do is have a piece of pig iron inside you someplace. Inside, where the hurting things that stick will get their points dulled or cracked off before they can do you any harm.

Or just stand and scream the hurt away.

Anyway, not like me. Whatever happens to me, I never let it in till afterwards. And then when it does hit, I feel it worse than if I had opened up in the first place—because by that time I ain't ready for it. No, the people who scream and yell the second something gets at them do all right. Use your yelling then. Ain't nobody brave, there are just some crusty people know how to hold the pain and store it in a skin-pocket, by itself. But that just puts it off till the next day, or the next week maybe. Or maybe it don't work for a long while, and then the person has got herself all covered with the different sized blisters of a year's disgusts. Course, when she ain't expecting it, some fool friend comes and accidentally pops one of the blisters. And the poison from that one burns all the others open. So all a person's poison mixes together and washes around outside her body, seeping into her internals and splashing out on her acquaintances—which hurts her like hell, and which just looks kind of stupid. That ain't no way to do. Something sticks into you, let it, and scream like a chicken right away; you can take the edge off a pain screaming.

But if you are really smart, you will sit quiet and start growing a hunk of live pig iron. What I mean is, don't shell up. Get hard from the bottom, like the River; make your thickness deep. That's all you need to live along. That's all.

Second Movement

I

A TRAIN is a thing feels like it should take you longer away than just one hour and three quarters from New Orleans to Caytown; a train is too much of a machine. Maybe that is why it seemed even then as if I was going on to a new part of living. Because the train bridged the break, but it sort of made it too. There wouldn't of been so much of a difference if I had gone by bus or some other way.

I sat by the window, and this fat lady wearing a new, creamy, unnatural-pink angora sweater sat down next to me. The colored section of the train made a whole car, and it was almost full when we started. The seats was of wood and tilted back, same as a streetcar only wider, but the fat lady kept trying to get herself set leaning forward. I could tell she was doing it not to crush the angora sweater. She couldn't take the strain more than five minutes, though, before she had to lean back and breathe. Over her shoulders was a brown coat that she wore like a cape, without putting her arms in the sleeves; a thick layer of angora hairs had come off and lined the inside pink down to the waist. Looking at it made my nose itch.

We went slow out of the station, weaving and changing in about four different tracks. I thought we would go along Elysian Fields, because I had seen trains come in there. But we left a shorter way, cutting across below the Canal bridge, by the dairy that has the big white pasteboard milk bottle sticking up on top. We stopped once just before there, long enough for more people to get on than there was seats, so a few had to stand up or sit on their suitcases. Then we got started again and went straight on out into the country.

It was cold for April. The space between the double-glass window held a thin film of its own fog that turned to droplets when the sun came up, and made tiny rings where they dried on the wrong side of the glass for me to clean. There was specks of soot inside there too, blown through some crack from the long carbon cloud that swung over the train flapping in the wind like a black stocking tied to the engine. I watched out the window and put my head up against the glass, but it wasn't cold as it looked, and the white splotch I made was just from the sweat on my own forehead. I have this ability that I can sweat almost any time of the year I get dressed up and shouldn't.

The fat lady couldn't get comfortable. She was short, and when she sat straight her feet didn't touch the floor, so her legs went to sleep or got crampy. Then when she pushed her bottom out to put her feet down and rest her legs, only the tops of her shoulders could touch the back of the seat, and she got an ache in her spine-muscles. I wanted to pull my laundry box out and make a footrest for her, but I was scared to hurt her feelings. Only, when we got going some, it began to edge out all by itself with the movement of the train, and I hooked my heel around one end and pushed it under her. I don't think she knew what it was, on account of not being able to see down, but she put her feet up on it and breathed a whole lot better. Then right away she spent about a half-hour trying to get her legs crossed at the knees.

We passed brown crumble-land, all flat, and mostly shaded by the moss that hung thick as a gray carpet woven through the green of the trees. Many times, we crossed over muddy little branches of the Mississippi—sad, wiggly fingers of clay that searched along for the mother River and looked like they would harden and die before they reached her. I wondered how they had got separated so far, and why, and watching them I began to feel afraid and empty myself. You could see boys some places, catfishing in the slow water.

No matter if a person is already sure she don't have a place, she still has to get convinced of it when she first steps into the world. And the knowing comes soon as you cut out from under and start to move: you feel naked. That is the scariest time of all—when you sense yourself begin to slip around without a base. It is the time when you got to be heaviest in all your life, with only weight to hold you down till the right roots have a chance to grow and take hold. It is the tricky time. Because if you ain't careful, you going to let yourself sprout all over with the wrong feelers—the phony roots—the fast-growing ivy that reaches up and wraps around your own body. You got to turn a steady eye on those ivy roots: they choke off the real ones, and they never get into the ground.

The fat lady said: "Lord." She had a fudge-bubble sheen from the dry heat inside the train, and she would sigh so deep her big breasts pushed up angora to tickle her under the chin and make her scratch. She looked to me like she wasn't getting enough air.

One single arm of the early sun crossed over both of us and fell in the aisle; it was swarming alive with pink fuzz. I coughed, and then I sneezed.

"Bless you, che," said the fat lady.

I did it again.

"Double-bless you," she said. Then: "In Europe they got these trains you can open the windows on them."

I couldn't talk because I was holding down another sneeze, but I smiled, sort of.

"All over Europe," said the fat lady. "*Hold on* . . . Well, triple-bless you. My son is in the army, which is in France, Europe. And I got one letter from him in which he explained to me how all over Europe they got these trains you can open the windows on them."

"That must be a comfort," I said.

"Just what it is," she said fast, "is a comfort."

We were coming near to the Lake. Outside, all the trees had thinned away, and tall razor grass grew in patches over the sogged earth. The sky was full of thick, heavy clouds, waddling around trying to get under the sun.

Then I took to watching the telephone wires. I was beginning to find out how, if I watched anything for a long enough while, it seemed like it had a pattern and a purpose. These telephone wires looked as if they was climbing up and up, wanting to break free and run wild to heaven. Then, each time a telephone pole came along, it slapped them back down so hard it made them droop towards the ground. Then they would start up again. That was their pattern; from where I sat it was just the only why of telephone wires. They drooped—they curved—they started up easy—they zipped faster—and on the exact second when they was going to be free——wham, another pole came along. The funny thing was the way I could keep on watching without getting discouraged or plain disgusted. Because even though I really knew the wires wouldn't ever make it, I always thought: come on, maybe this time. And after about fifteen minutes, they got to looking higher to me, like they was *almost* there. But, wham. Well, if you going to get fooled by something that has half a mind, I guess it might just as well be hope.

Up—wham—droop; up—wham—droop; up—wham—droop. And the chuckling of the train on the tracks underneath me. I kept expecting it was all going to make me sleepy, but it didn't. What it did, it gave me something to study on while I was thinking about something else. That was a good thing, because I used to have a habit of foolish-staring somebody right in the face while I was thinking my own thoughts, which was not a good thing.

The fat lady said: "Going all the way to Biloxi?" kind of loud, so I figured she probably had already said it once without my hearing her.

"No, ma'am, I'm getting off at Caytown." I felt silly being on a train just to go to Caytown.

"You-all live in Caytown?"

"No, ma'am, I live in New Orleans."

"I live in Biloxi," she told me, "but I got family in New Orleans. I got family all over, if you follow my train of thought. I got this one son in France, Europe, in the army. And I got my married daughter living in New Orleans, and I got my other daughter just married a man in Biloxi, and the man which she married says they ain't going to live but a little while in Biloxi till he can make enough money to go someplace else with a future. You got family in Caytown?"

"No, ma'am, I got a job there."

". . . Job?"

"Maiding," I said.

"Funny place to go and maid, Caytown. How come you got a job there? Now, I always been the type person, I always wanted to move on to a bigger place than the place where I was. I used to say to my husband: 'Daniel,' I used to say, 'how come you couldn't just as well work in a garage in New Orleans instead of working in a garage in Biloxi?' I used to tell him: 'Daniel, let's get on out of this little bitty city, and let's us go live in a big city where you can get the same kind of work there as you got here, only the difference is we going to be living someplace with more people, and more jobs, and more everything.' Course, I was really thinking about the children, if you follow my train of thought. And Daniel always did think I was absolutely right, let me tell you. 'Marbelle,' he would say, Marbelle is my name, Marbelle Bone, well he would say: 'Marbelle, I know you absolutely right is what I think.' He got hisself this job all lined up, too, and we really was going to move, excepting he died just a week before. Course, he couldn't then. Naturally."

I told her: "One of my brothers is named Daniel."

"This son of mine which is in the army's name is Daniel, too. After my husband. My mother-in-law wanted to name him Euphrates, for this very important river they got, but I wouldn't let him to be named anything else but what my husband was. My mother-in-law went right on calling him Euphrates, just the same, though, even though I kept explaining to her that when I had a girl it would still be plenty time to go around calling anybody Euphrates. But she wouldn't pay me no mind, because she said she had already fixed up the name for when I had a girl, which was to be called Tigris, on account of this other very important river they got by that name. Course, she passed away before I got pregnant again. Thank God: can you imagine anybody going through life being named Tigris Bone? How come you got a job maiding in Caytown? Or did I ask you that?"

"My cousin Wila found it for me," I said.

"Cousin *Wila?* You wouldn't be specifying to a Cousin Wila which is a person about my age or a little younger, and which lives in Biloxi when she ain't working in practically every first-class private house there is in all Galilee?"

"That sounds like her."

"This Cousin Wila I am talking about is the one which located the daughter of mine in New Orleans' husband butlering in one of the best houses on St. Charles, and which was fixing up a location for my other daughter when she up and decided to get married. I mean my daughter, not Cousin Wila."

"That's the one," I said.

"Well, now, I am so glad to meet a actual somebody which is related to Cousin Wila. We actually ain't far back as I can figure. What you say your name was, honey?"

"Lucille Morris," I said, "but I don't think we really related to Cousin Wila. We just sort of *call* her Cousin Wila."

Marbelle plucked the angora sweater away from her throat with a finger and a thumb of one hand, to get a little air in. When she let it loose, the puff of hair that came off held in front of us for a second, and we both watched it float away. "You neither? Caytown, you say, she got you this job?"

"Yes, ma'am."

"I can't help to wonder sometimes," said Marbelle, "if Cousin Wila is a very fine woman or a agency." She pushed her chin in and blew down over the roll of fat around her neck. Then she stretched the sweater out and let it flop back a few times to make a breeze. Each time she did it, the air flushed fake-pink, and big hunks came away in her fingers. She went on: "Well, no, now. Cousin Wila does all right. I be doing all right if I can help my kids to set up, and then just leave them alone, that's what. Trouble is, you give too much. You plain want to give too much, and then when you done give it, you got to watch the kids get married and be happy and not need you to give no more. I ought to find a thing to do like Cousin Wila, that's what. Instead of going from one child to the other making out they still needed me for something."

Marbelle was talking down into the sweater, but I heard the hardness that caught around her voice.

She pulled her head up and looked at the roof of the train. "No, don't you tell me, it's true, like I say. If you want to learn how to love, first you got to learn how to give, and then you learn you can't give it all. No, you got to keep something to give from . . . you got to keep the strength and the home inside you. Don't you ever give that, honey . . . don't you. And if you afraid or you wondering how to live . . . if you full of not-knowing and changing . . . you keep that too. You keep the stomach of the good to give *from* it, and you keep all of the bad *not* to give it. And you send your kids out free. Then you be a kind of a person."

She was beginning to sound upset, so I figured I better be the one to skip the subject: "Cousin Wila . . ."

"Cousin Wila . . . is a person," Marbelle said, and she shut up for a while. After we got out on the Lake, she said: "My daughter give me this here genuine angora sweater, and she told me she didn't like to see me sleeping on the bed in their kitchen. Course, they ain't got no other place to put me. Last year, she give me a pair of earrings, and she told me it was better in Biloxi for my health. Next year . . ." Marbelle cleared her throat six separate times, and sat rocking back and forth, with her bottom lip stuck out. Finally, she said: "It's a pretty sweater, ain't it?"

"Yes, ma'am," I said, and I felt of it. "It sure is a pretty sweater."

". . . Your mama alive?" Marbelle asked.

"Yes, ma'am, she's alive. She's in New Orleans with my brother Dan."

"How old your brother Daniel?"

"Just fifteen."

"That's old enough," said Marbelle, "to start being a man."

A man. Something in the chuckling of the train was trying to remind me of . . . ?

Marbelle wanted to know: "You got no more family?"

"Yes, ma'am. Yes, I got one other brother, Clarence. Clarence is twenty-one and seven months."

"Twenty-one *is* a man," she said.

Then I got reminded. It was what Clarence had said when Mama told him she wanted her son to be a man who did right by his soul. He had said: "You a little late on that one." The train was chuckling: "You-a-*lit*-tle-*late*-on-*that*-one, you-a-*lit*-tle-*late*-on-*that*-one."

I tried to study on something else, but the train went right on, laughing up from the green Lake water. It plain wouldn't stop. And the coldness I felt inside was only Mama's old fear, stretching-young again in me, showing me the unborn shape of what it was that froze her breath.

I watched where the surface of the Lake was stroked white by a wide breeze; then the foam jumping up to touch the long pillars under another bridge that ran alongside of ours, empty, a good ways away. I imagined how the same foam would be reaching and spraying under us, sight unseen, without a face to wet or an ear to fuss at. Wasted lone foam. Wasted sound; no sound. Only: "You-a-*lit*-tle-*late*-on-*that*-one." Right then I would of changed anything to have Dan with me.

(*Course* you can feel the future, everybody can. It's as much a part of a person as the past is. You just don't look at it if you don't want to. You go on feeling it, but you don't look. And you better off like that, anyhow. Because by the time you could understand it, you *are* too late.) "You-a-*lit*-tle-*late*-on-*that*-one." A little late for Clarence. I didn't want to let myself think that it was a little late for Dan too; maybe a little late for us all.

Marbelle was watching me, sideways. She said: "Che, did I go and make you sad?" She pulled her purse from behind her, and opened it, and took out a chocolate bar. The chocolate was mashed and squishy inside the paper from her having leaned on it, but Marbelle picked her gloves off and peeled it open. Then she tore it in two, and gave me the biggest half. "Now," she said, "I only eat stuff like chocolate when I ain't anyplace but alone in my own house, or traveling, account of I weigh one hundred and eighty now, and I don't care to do it in front of nobody which I know. Personally, I can't stand to watch fat people eat, so you just go on watching out the window do you want to, if you follow my train of thought."

I took it from her, and then I don't know how I got started, but suddenly I was sitting there and crying, with the chocolate bar in my hand. Marbelle put an arm around me, and I got chocolate on my dress front, and Marbelle had to drop hers to keep from getting it on the sweater. Then I had to drop mine too, because it was full of angora hairs, and afterwards we both wiped our hands on the hand-kerchief I had used to cry.

I should of felt better, but I didn't. Marbelle thought I did, though, and she looked pleased.

The day was graying. All the lump-belly clouds had loosened and slid together—killing their own shadows; smearing out the blue and the orange sunlight; sludging the answering green in the Lake and turning the water dark, and darker where it rimmed the sky. The whole thing was getting to look like a sad black-and-white picture you see after a Technicolor cartoon.

Out over the Lake, the two bridges ran straight: the high one we were on, for trains only, and the other low white one, only for cars. I couldn't see from the window where the other bridge ended or began. Just a long, perfect cut—a line-burn in the water—and the gray water swelling on either side.

When Marbelle took her arm from around me she had to brush the whole back of my dress for two minutes to get the pink off. Then she pushed her sweater sleeve way up past her elbow and put her arm inside mine.

Still the train chuckled: "You-a-*lit*-tle-*late*-on-*that*-one, you-a-*lit*-tle-*late*-on-*that*-one." But when we finally got across the Lake on land again, another beat came in the rhythm of the tracks, and the song stopped.

Across the Lake there is a big change from the land around New Orleans; you have to be careful, though, if you want to see it right off. After you pass the two or three thick-slushed miles that edge the water, there's a trembly look to the ground, as if something was waiting underneath to suck it in. Even where it's dry or rocky, you get the feeling that's only a crust—a sun-baked scab over the earth, holding the juices. And the growing things have deeper colors; brighter, but deeper. Like sometimes you will see a swamp flower flash purple against the dirt, as if it had roots below the crust and on below the marsh, down into the veins of fresh blood that pump way under.

But you don't sense it all at once, unless you know. At first you can hardly feel the colors darken a shade, and you only begin to get a wonder of the wet. I thought then it was all in the switch the day had made, same as the Lake lost its color when the sunlight faded.

Caytown is the second stop; Taxon is before. Taxon is lots bigger than Caytown, and it really is a town. Caytown is just a busy street.

When we got to Taxon, Marbelle said: "I would get out and stretch, but I ain't going to, if you follow my train of thought." She meant about eight more people had got on for three that had left, and the seating was worse. I almost stood up for an old lady with noplace to sit, but across the aisle a man finally moved over for her. He didn't look very happy about it.

Then on to Caytown is just twenty minutes. Marbelle was talking again, but nothing you needed to listen to very hard. I was thinking how it is you can meet somebody like that on a train, and be with them, and matter to them, and have them matter to you. And in an hour it's all finished, and you never see them again.

I was thinking: this is the first time I ever met Marbelle, and this is the last time I will ever see her in my life. This is the last time I will be with these same people on this same train going in this same direction—it is the last time. Then every new day is a last day, and every fresh start is a finish. It won't ever be the same as today, or yesterday, or like tomorrow. Not for me. My hellos are my goodbyes; my breath goes as it comes. And all the noise in my time is just the sizzle of a burn that seals each sore it makes.

Jesus above, I thought, my whole life don't amount to much more than one surprise hello, and one surprise goodbye, with lots of little hellos and goodbyes mixed between. And once I had it, I had it; and once I said it, I said it—and if I don't like how I had it, or if I ain't happy with the way I said it, that is going to be the biggest part of one enormous shame. So I better get started quick doing it right while I'm here.

I heard Marbelle say: "We coming in to Caytown, che."

The train was slowing down, but you couldn't see nothing yet. The train kind of had to slow down or it would of passed Caytown before it got there.

"Miss Marbelle," I said, "I really am glad you sat next to me."

Marbelle held on tighter to my arm before she let go. "You give my regards to Cousin Wila," she said, "and you tell her I think she's making like she should."

After that, we didn't hold no more conversation till the train was almost stopped. I thought maybe Marbelle would ask me to look her up was I ever in Biloxi or something, but she didn't. She only patted my knee and said goodbye.

It was when I stood up to get my coat that she told me: "Che, don't you go worrying none how to live. If you know enough to worry about that at your age, you ain't *got* nothing to worry about." She looked back at the men crowding in the aisle and she added: "Walk careful, Lucille, if you like to follow my train of thought."

I kept having the feeling when I left her that there must of been a kindness I could do or say to be nicer. But all I did was to pull my box out from under her feet and make her uncomfortable all over again before I went away.

2

I KNEW the house was named Will-o-Wilds, and the people Pharr; if Cousin Wila wasn't at the station to meet me, I had the number to phone her up and say I was there.

The wood station house is across the tracks from Caytown and from where cars can park. So, while a train is in, you can't see but the open side: a dirt road that winds past three shacks, one of them made into a store and all stuck around with tin signs for Jax beer and Coca-Cola and Seven-Up. The road has two deep ruts dug out by tires and wheels, and in between you can see crab grass lacing, burnt brown by the sun. There, the earth looks even drier than on top of the levee, rusty and cracked.

When the train pulled away, I saw Cousin Wila waiting on the opposite side. She was standing next to a tall colored man in a mahogany-stain uniform, toned redder than his skin, but about as dark. A thin man, with long legs, and too much shoulders for his high-sewed jacket sleeves. Thin only because he was so tall, but powerful. Big hands; easy muscles, fatless. He stood crooked, one shoulder up and the other hip out, angled all over to keep you from taking a notice of his longness. The sleeves was so pointed on top they made him have a set shrug, peculiar and stylish enough, I thought, for a chauffeur in any magazine.

Cousin Wila looked up and waved a pencil she kept in her hand. She had been writing with it on a piece of yellow paper. I remembered her by her glasses and by the twist that pulled the whole right side of her face down, just like I expected. But there was more than just that. There was a way about her I remembered from when she used to look at our father while he was talking—a kind of happy frown, and eyes that came out of her face like a turtle sticks its head out for friends. I could tell right then that Cousin Wila's ugliness was a very unlikely place for Cousin Wila.

I hiked up my box and crossed the tracks to meet her.

She came up to the edge of the first rail, and put her left cheek against my forehead, and kissed me. Her hair was greased back tight, stringed with silver, and she smelled of clean lemon brilliantine. "Che," she said, "you twenty-four minutes later than time." She said it like I should of known not to get on a train that was going to be late. Then she put her arm around me and walked me to where the man was standing, next to a new maroon station wagon. "This is Mr. Charles Leroy Merrill," is what she announced, "Charles Leroy is the butler and chauffeur, like I wrote you, and he used to have family in Jackson, Mississippi, and he still has some in Biloxi, and he is related to us and you going to call him Charles Leroy just like everybody else does. This is my cousin, Miss Lucille Morris, and her father was one of my closest cousins, and you going to watch your step around her so help you Jesus, will you shake her hand while I'm talking, for God's sake, like a gentleman, or where was you brought up?"

Charles Leroy pulled one hand out of his back pocket and gave it to me. I thought his face was too full of bones and hard, and he didn't seem very nice. He looked in his twenties, only I knew it was hard to tell with people who have bony faces. He reached over and took my box from me; he opened the back of the station wagon and set it on the floor, even though both of the back seats was empty.

Cousin Wila said: "That what you using for a suitcase? I'm going to give you a suitcase."

"Oh, no, I . . ."

"Now, don't put me up no argument, first thing," she said. "Just don't put me up no argument at all."

She made me sit in the middle, next to Charles Leroy. I had enough room ahead of me there to stretch my legs straight out if I wanted to, but when Charles Leroy sat down his knees peaked up high in the air, way separate. A muscle hardened along the outside of his thigh as he stepped on the pedal. The car hummed, quiet and rich. I sat with my hands in my lap and looked through the glass at the bright silver bird growing out of the hood.

Cousin Wila said to Charles Leroy: "Don't forget to pull in at Manley's, now." Then to me she said: "We got to pull in at Manley's, and we were going to before you came, but we figured there wasn't no sense in it because we didn't want to be late for the train. But you got in twenty-four minutes later than time." She took and put another word on the yellow paper with the pencil. I saw she was making a list.

Charles Leroy said: "Two cartons Parliament, five tubes Colgate, and I don't remember what-all else."

"Four toothbrushes," said Cousin Wila, sounding like it wasn't the first go-through, "black pig's bristle; a roll of two-inch adhesive; a bottle of hydrogen peroxide; two square yards of black oilcoth; six bottles of Sani-Flush. One of the things you *ain't* got is memory. No memory at all. *One* of the things." She kept the list hanging beside her while she was talking, so I knew it was about something else.

We had passed down the street that was Caytown, and it seemed like we were going to cross over the railroad tracks right away and join onto the highway. But before we got that far, Charles Leroy turned in by a two-story building with a screened gallery hanging out the second story.

Up underneath the gallery, I saw a long sign with "Manley's General" printed on it in thick black paint. The letters was real little, and spaced apart so they would stretch all the way across the building. They was so far apart, when you came close you had to spell them out to read them. And if you kept further off, they was all shadowed dark by the gallery, and too little to read anyway. It was just not a very good sign.

Charles Leroy stopped the car and unwound hisself out of it and went into the store; he slammed the door as he left, without looking. Cousin Wila saw me watching after him, and she said: "He ain't so dumb, you find out. The reason he ain't got much common sense, he ain't common. But he ain't dumb."

I tried to turn around and smile at her, only I was sitting too close. I didn't want to give us more room, though, because I didn't want to sit on Charles Leroy's part of the seat.

Cousin Wila shoved with her behind. "Slide over, che," she said, "I can't look at you how you is."

I moved over a little on the slick maroon leather.

Cousin Wila pushed forward and turned to me. She looked down to the floor on my left, and then back up my right. Her glasses was all crystal-glass with only one line of gold wire along the top and on into her hair, but without no bottom rim. "Lucille, you is powerful light-colored."

"Yes, ma'am," I said.

"Not ma'am. Cousin Wila, or plain Cousin, or plain Wila. But not ma'am. I didn't remember you being so light-colored. Your papa was darker. You remember your papa?"

"Yes, I do, Cousin Wila."

"That's right. Your papa was a good man. Your mama always seemed like she had pinchbugs in her vitals, but your papa was a good strong man. You powerful light-colored, ain't you? That ain't a question, I'm just commenting. Manley's is the general store, you want to remember that. Like a drugstore. No medicine, but everything else." She leaned closer. "Lucille, you going to do all right. You do fine. What you not looking so happy about?"

I tried smiling, but it wasn't much, because Cousin Wila was staring at me too hard. Her eyes doubled behind the thickness of the glass, and you could see the whites full of tiny red crisscross, like an enamel washbasin after somebody cuts theirself.

"No," she said, "no, indeed. You want to smile, you got to start it in your stomach, you can't just jerk it out of your face. How would I smile, with a face like mine?"

I did smile then.

"That's right," said Cousin Wila. She gave me the list. "This is what you got to do," she told me. "Most every day. Sometimes there going to be things besides. But then you get told. Right off you start doing these every day." At the top of the list she had written in all capital letters: "THINGS EVERY DAY." While I was reading it, she picked it out of my hands, and turned it over, and put it back again. "Now there is what you got to do one time a week." On the top of that list was written: "THINGS ONCE A WEEK." Cousin Wila explained: "I ain't made no list of the sometimes things, because they could be most anything. But you always get told. You study up on the list tonight." She folded it and slipped it inside my skirt pocket. "I be here to the end of the first week," she said, and she slapped me twice on the leg and left her hand there. "In a week, you won't need no kind of a list at all." Then she shut her eyes, and pushed her glasses up, and pressed her fingers over the dents the pink plastic nose-clamps had made on either side of her nose, in the soft part of the bridge. Then she leaned back.

I sat and squinted at the M of Manley, starting to glisten in the dark glare that crept under the gallery. The black enamel paint was put on so thick, every hair of the brush had left a different stroke to dry and make shaky corduroy lines inside the letter. One drop of paint had crawled down the first part over onto the white board, and dried whole. Somebody must of wiped it earlier in the morning, and it shone harder than the letter, like it was trying to make up for not having a rightful place there.

Charles Leroy came out of the store with two long paper bags in his arms. He wasn't looking at us, so I watched him go behind to put the bags with my box. He walked in different sections, separate-boned. It was a walk I already knew. When he stooped down to climb in the car, I pushed against Cousin Wila again, and he didn't even touch me.

We drove across the tracks and followed the highway a distance. All of us kept to our own thoughts. (So I wouldn't fidget, I had to stop my mind from spreading out wild, and I took to wondering how Charles Leroy could hold his foot so steady on the pedal with his knees spread like they was. I knew it was a silly thing to think about, but it worked.) Cousin Wila still had her hand on my leg, and she would squeeze it every little bit. I guess she figured that made me feel better. And it did. Cousin Wila had a strong hand.

Then we swung off the highway, and went on a narrower street that didn't have no white line down the middle. The steel of the sky had gone soft and mushy—building up to rain. On the left, a gray wire fence started, running next to the road. Inside the fence was a tangle of high trees and moss.

Cousin Wila said: "You got Charles Leroy here. Then you got Cousin Celeste the cook, and Cousin Ernest the gardener, and Mademoiselle the upstairs maid who don't count, like I wrote. The general cleaning help once a week ain't always the same, when they come, which ain't always. Just the five of you steady. Cousin Ernest got a woman in Caytown he lives with, so you won't be seeing much of him. Then in the house you got Mr. and Mrs. Pharr, and old Mr. Sage (that's Mrs. Pharr's father), and you got Mr. Robert (that's Mr. Pharr's brother). He going to look you over a couple times, but he ain't going to do you nothing more than that. Just don't take no notice." She leaned around sudden, and looked at my chest. "Che, is you wearing a brassiere?"

I tried not to look at Charles Leroy to see was he laughing.

"Better take it in two, three inches the first month," said Cousin Wila. "Flatten you." She glanced over at Charles Leroy, and added: "Best do your watching out for him. He ain't looked you over at all, which means he ain't going to, but you watch out for him, che, just the same. Never trust no man that don't look you over."

Charles Leroy was grinning now, I could see out of the corner of my eye. Cousin Wila sat back again, and I pushed down in the seat and stared ahead.

The rain had begun. A few big drops hit the glass, and some of them splattered wide. The wind kept the pieces from running down; it held them, trembling and shivering. But there wasn't enough yet to turn on the wiper.

Charles Leroy braked, and swung in between two short brick columns that made an opening in the fence. On top of one of the columns, a black iron grillwork sign spelled out Will-o-Wilds in fancy writing, with a black iron cutout of a horse-and-buggy under it. Then we started down a white driveway made of clamshells, another fence on the left, and on the right even rows of bare, dry-looking trees, without much moss. The rain began to come down harder. Charles Leroy turned on the windshield wiper.

Cousin Wila told me: "This is it, che."

I couldn't see a thing except the trees and the white driveway through the rain.

"Them is pecan trees," she said, "all of those there. They got five acres of pecan trees."

We kept right on going, crunching over the clamshells, and passing row after row of trees. I must of started counting about midway, and I made twenty-two before we came to the last and swerved sharp around.

Then I looked up and saw the house, wet and slippery, standing in the cold. It was a real imitation of a plantation house, and it was all tarnished white, with white columns, and green shutters, and ivy, and an upstairs gallery that went completely around. The only trouble with the imitation was they hadn't been able to spoil the newness of it, not even with the yellow-brown patches of dirt they had let weather over the walls. It was a very expensive house, but you right away felt sorry for it.

We passed it by, and I saw a black strip of Bayou Liberté curve out beyond the last green of the winter lawn. Then some azalea bushes got in the way, and standing next to one a life-size old iron deer somebody had painted to look older. It dripped there, heavy, but hollow. There was a tone to that deer under the paint made it look proud, and hurt, and shock-puzzled—like a once rich old man who has to beg for his living being funny, afraid he don't quite know how. Ernest the gardener told me later, referring to that deer, he had very special orders never to clean the bird droppings off it.

We drove into the garage, and stopped alongside a low, bulging Cadillac that was parked there. We all had to get out on Charles Leroy's side, not to make a scratch in the back door of the Cadillac. I waited next to it, with my fingers crossed together in front. I was feeling real dumb and young. I don't know why.

Cousin Wila said: "Che, you look like you ain't even circulating." She came and put her hand on the small of my back and rubbed me.

After that, Charles Leroy opened up a black umbrella over all of us, and we walked out under it close together, Cousin Wila in the middle. We tried to keep on the stone steps that led through the winter-grass to the kitchen door. And we just walked along like that in the rain.

3

IT took me upwards of a week to be able to live at Will-o-Wilds without feeling clobbered and mildewed in—oyster-fleshed with the staleness there. It wasn't a thing you could name. Not *the way* the house was made: everything inside was dry and put together careful to keep out the wets of the swamp and the sky. And the Pharrs was generally nice as they knew how to everybody, and old Mr. Sage the same. It was something that wanted to live with them, in them, and in the house. Something sticky that reached and spread around you, like the smell of molded molasses, from the air they breathed out there. I got used to it finally, same as you get used to any wrong smell if you live in it long enough—only I couldn't forget; I just stopped paying it much mind. But that first rainy week, with the electricity and the dripping water shutting us all in, was the worst.

It was a bigger house than it looked from the drive, but you could tell it wasn't as big as the plantation house it was supposed to be. There was just two floors. Upstairs was the bedrooms with their little dressing rooms, and two different living rooms, and the dining room, and the gallery outside everything. Downstairs was for the kitchen, and the pantry, and the game room. There was another building, one-storied and narrow, that attached by the kitchen door; all the help's quarters was in there, except for Mademoiselle's. Mademoiselle had her own place made from an extra dressing room in the main house, on the bayou corner of the second floor.

Mademoiselle was a *personal French maid*. White; about fifty. She didn't do anything but take care of Mrs. Pharr and Mrs. Pharr's things. She sat all day in her shoebox-room, and sewed and pressed and had her meals brought up on a tray, and talked French at everybody in a squeak that happened back of her nose someplace. She could talk English fine when she wanted, but Mrs. Pharr didn't like her to. I think the only reason Mrs. Pharr had her there was to be

French. Once every morning she would come out and dust Mrs. Pharr's bedroom and make her bed, and go back again. Sometimes, if the weather was specially nice, she would sit on the gallery outside her window and sew there. But not often, because Mademoiselle didn't think very much of the American weather. She never mixed with the help, and Cousin Wila only called her the *upstairs* maid to keep her from thinking she was too personal. They was pretty good friends, though, ever since Cousin Wila got rid of the Cajun gardener. (Celeste said every time Mademoiselle heard him muttering around down below in his patois, she would get the heebie-jeebies and not eat for two days.) She always dressed in black same as Mrs. Pharr, only with pointed black boots that laced up high, and thick dark brown cotton stockings. She was just puckered skin over bones like needles, as if she might of had the water and the meat pressed right out of her.

All the rooms in the house was full of antique furniture and stuff, with curlicued edges sticking out all over the place, and more squiggles than a sick snake. But only some of it looked really old. One of the living rooms was named the Japanese Room, and in there everything was antique and Japanese. Course, you couldn't really tell if it was antique *and* Japanese, it just looked Japanese. To anybody, Celeste said, but a Japanese. That was a guess, though. There was a black screen with little slant-eyed mother-of-pearl men fishing in it (most of them had fish hanging still and dying on their lines or in their nets, and they squatted and grinned at you, like they had done what you asked them to). And lamp shades made into Japanese roofs, with the lamps made into houses, and green china dragons with holes in their backs to put cigarette ashes in, and green china frogs where you got the cigarettes out of. By the fireplace was a long silver tube of matches, with each match over a foot long. Mrs. Pharr didn't allow nobody to use those matches, they was just there. And there was six Japanese chairs spread around not to sit in, account of they fell apart. The other living room was supposed to be all French, but it looked about the same to me as all the rest of the house, except for the Japanese Room. It was called the Music Room. It had a piano that they kept out of tune, and a tall gold harp. The piano keys was streaky amber-colored, and the top parts had peeled off most of them (Mrs. Pharr kept the tops in a yellow cardboard box on the bookshelf); the gold paint was chipped and peeling off the harp in places, and you had to watch yourself dusting it. The wall behind the harp was a solid mass of books. I always took my time to dust there, after I started reading the end book on the bottom shelf. It was named *Beekman's History of Europe*, and sometimes I could get through as much as a page a day. It was awful old, and full of big words, but it was a real book. I would of loved to open all the others too, only I was afraid somebody would come along before I had a chance to stick one back, so I didn't. On the mantelpiece over the fireplace in the Music Room was a high porcelain vase that had belonged to old Mr. Sage's dead wife. It was shaped like a twisted leaf—solid pure blue—and I thought it was the only beautiful thing in the house. Sometimes, I would go in and just look at it when everything else got to be too much, and if there wasn't anybody around. Then, over the mantel, was a painting of Mrs. Sage herself, before she died. It ruined the vase if you looked up that far. She had been a very famous player of the piano, which was what she was doing in the painting; only she had her hands in the air, and she was glaring out so fierce and nasty, it kind of made me wonder if the painter had come out with a dirty word; she wore a long black velvet dress with a white lace collar and an orchid on her shoulder. That was another thing. They had taken a plaster cast of Mrs. Sage's right hand, up a little past the wrist, after she died. And on every mantel in the house, was this bronze hand laying palm down in a carved wood holder. On every mantel, even in the dining room. Used to make me kind of lose my appetite to have to pick each one up and dust it and put it back again. When I could, I generally left them till after lunch.

I don't know why I never even began to enjoy it, the richness of it all. I hadn't seen anything expensive or fancy as that in my whole life. But right from the start, I took a disagreeable sense to it. After all those years of imagining what might be inside the big beautiful houses on St. Charles Avenue, and here I was back in a tightness and a waste of air would of made Mama happy. So I sort of took to wondering if maybe there wasn't no real world, not for me, not like I wanted. Because I couldn't believe. I plain couldn't see where a person might *like to be alive*, and fit into a house such as Will-o-Wilds. In fact, the only difference I *could* see between the Pharr's house and Mama's was that they had so many more things to rot there than just people.

I remember later on in the fall, we used to sit and eat pecans from the lines of trees that dropped them in heaps and patterns all over the ground. Ernest collected as many as he could. But mostly they had to stay where they fell; Mrs. Pharr didn't care enough about saving them to have extra help for gathering. When you crack a bad pecan, you can tell right away. It breaks in hollow, and if you have it up close, you get a puff of funny-smelling air—sweet and rotten together—the smell of *not*. The way the world would of smelled if God hadn't invented life. And inside the shell, there is a transparent film of woolly fluff, the not-color of the sky on a day when it might of rained or it might of cleared up but it just ain't going to do nothing at all, Then you kind of wonder if there ever had been a real pecan inside that shell. Or if it wasn't born empty and dead—to keep a catch of not-being that God forgot.

The house was the same: like an empty pecan shell. It was a house made to hold nothingness, and to pretend that something had been there alive.

Mrs. Pharr was the lady of the pretend. Mrs. Nora Sage Pharr. *Sage-Pharr*, Mademoiselle said it, and she pronounced Sage her own way, sort of like *lodge*. Mrs. Pharr wasn't much taller than Mademoiselle, but she fooled you, she stood so straight. And I never did see such a little woman with such a heavy step. She wouldn't put one foot in front of the other without planting it there. You even heard her downstairs in the kitchen when she moved around, making dead wood thuds, slow and sure as night. She didn't look much older than forty, but it wasn't because she tried not to.

Mr. Pharr's brother, Mr. Robert, spent more time living in his apartment in New Orleans than he did across the Lake. And sometimes, when Mr. Pharr's business got the better of him, he spent a couple nights there too. Celeste told me they had two women living in the apartment permanent, one for each. She said Mrs. Pharr and old Mr. Sage both knew about it, but that they didn't seem to mind any. And Charles Leroy told me about once when he drove Mr. Pharr and his brother into town, and then carried a case of liquor up to the apartment. He said the two women was spread all over the living room, complctcly dressed just like it was their own place. They was cutting long strings of paper dolls and listening to "Ma Perkins" on the radio when he came in, and they went right on, and one of them told him where to put the liquor.

Old Mr. Sage was supposed to be dying, but he wouldn't go ahead and do it. Mrs. Pharr nursed him along, wheeling him in the house, or around the gallery outside if it wasn't raining. He couldn't walk. According to Celeste, it was him who had all the money, from back when his family sold the real plantation. According to her, Mr. Pharr and Mr. Robert didn't make enough out of their business to pay carfare home on a duck. She said she heard them arguing once every so often, and she always made a particular point of picking up the entire conversation. But Celeste was the type of person got to know most anything there was to know about everybody.

I kind of liked old Mr. Sage. He smiled a lot to hisself, and you got the feeling he thought the house and the people in it was all very funny. One day when I was cleaning, I found him sitting by the fireplace in the Japanese Room. He had one of his wife's bronze hands in his, and he was giggling like a little girl. When I walked in, he put his free hand over his mouth and giggled harder, looking at me as if he expected I should know the joke. I giggled too, just to make him happy, and then he doubled up and laughed so hard he choked. I was afraid to leave him there in case he might laugh hisself into an attack or whatever, but he was all right. The trouble with him, he was a bottom-pincher. He plain liked to pinch bottoms. You couldn't ever turn your back on him, and when you didn't he would find a way to get a couple fingers around there. I can't figure who he might of pinched before I came. Celeste pretty generally kept to the kitchen—and he couldn't of done it to Cousin Wila more than once— and a door wouldn't of pinched Mademoiselle. Anyway, the first morning he saw my behind, he practically had to wipe his chin, which makes you think he must of been missing one quite a while, mine not being a very special kind of a thing for a man who is truly interested in the problem. Mrs. Pharr saw him do it to me a few times, but she always looked in the other direction.

Cousin Wila followed me around all the first week, and showed me what to do, and saw I did it right. She was on half pay then (didn't nothing pass by Mrs. Pharr in the way of money); only when I said I would make it up to her out of what I got, she laughed and pulled at my hair. "Che," she said, "what you think I do my living for?"

She couldn't see to spit without her glasses, but while she wore them she saw more than most people. She toned up to me by the second day, and from then on she could tell how I would feel about a certain thing or a certain person before I felt it myself. People who know how to care can do that. For instance, the afternoon Mr. Robert looked me over (like she told me he would) she said right off: "You going to go and feel dirty just because a man wants to know do you fit your dress?"

". . . Not so much *dirty*," I said.

"Oh, yes," said Cousin Wila. "You feeling dirty. Yes, you is, don't put me up no argument. I can tell." She could, too.

The reason she saw so much with her glasses on, they was cut extra-strong, much more than she needed. She said she got that done because if the Lord Jesus had meant for her to have a twisted face and wear glasses all day, she might just as well take some advantage out of it. She really could see a lot. When she didn't have anything else to do, she used to stand back and read little print at you from wherever she found it. Then if she couldn't locate something special, she would prop the newspaper against the wall and walk three feet away and fire that off like she'd written it. Course, she got these terrific headaches all the time, but you never dared to tell her it was the glasses.

There is a certain sort of girl would go crazy about Mr. Robert, and he knew it. Not for his good looks so much—more because of how he acted. He had a way of talking to you that was too polite, and at the same time it showed you exactly what he was thinking underneath. And the lower he thought you was, the politer he got—which must of made him feel like a better man, I guess. The way he did it, if he treated a person with the back of his hand, then it was a person; but if he was very, *very* nice, you knew he wouldn't of noticed your funeral. He had a quick smile he made at you, too, that was just a wrinkled face with lots of teeth. It was the smile bothered me that day, not his looking me over.

Cousin Wila said: "Anyway, he done paid you all the mind he's going to, unless you let him think you trying to bug-eye him."

I had finished my waxing in the dining room, and we had just come into the kitchen. "How you mean, bug-eye him?" I asked her.

Celeste looked over from the macaroni she was turning. "Bug-eye," she said, "b-u-g-e-y-e. You don't get her meaning?"

"How lovely," said Cousin Wila. "Do I ever need any spelling help, I will *always* know where to direct myself."

"I was trying," Celeste told her, "to be nice . . ."

Cousin Wila explained: "When I say bug-eye him, I mean play up to him. Nuzzle around with him, you know honey, there's some girls would plain try to nuzzle around with him."

I was helping Charles Leroy polish the silver. He didn't look at me or talk when he handed me something to wipe, but it wasn't careless: he kept a feeling of our doing the same work there, and he would put each thing right in my hand.

"*Patent applied for,*" said Cousin Wila.

Celeste said: "I sure do hate to grate cheese. If there is one thing you can say I hate, it is grating cheese."

Cousin Wila backed up two steps. "*Patent applied for,*" she said, "I can even see it from here."

"You done read that calendar eight million times," Celeste told her, "you could even see it with your eyes shut."

Cousin Wila puffed up. "I am *reading* it from where I am standing. Whether I done read it before, or whether I ain't, is all *highly immaterial.*"

Celeste said: "A quarter-pound I got to grate. Just as soon scrape my teeth on the sidewalk."

"I heard you the first time," said Cousin Wila, "ain't no call to go around repeating everything that I know of." She grabbed the cheese from Celeste and started rubbing it on the metal grater.

Celeste was four years older than me, but shorter. Cute-looking, and chunky, like she was carved out of wood. Putting a chair under Cousin Wila, she said: "This house ain't going to stand up right after Sunday." (Sunday was the day Cousin Wila had to leave.)

"Yes it will." Cousin Wila was pleased though. "Got to be on my new job in two weeks. Got three more cousins in New Orleans be ready to work by May."

Celeste leaned over and scratched her leg. "Friend of mine used to have this very good girl friend in Sante Fe, New Mexico, wanted to get herself a job around here. Poor thing. No family, all dead."

"Name of what," said Cousin Wila, "how come you ain't spoke about her before?"

". . . Just didn't happen to cross over my mind. May Cain."

"Cain," said Cousin Wila. She cleaned her hands on her apron, and went over to the sideboard drawer, where she kept her carrying-copy of the family tree. She took it out. "Cain." She always opened it up on the floor, because it had about sixteen pieces of paper pasted around in different directions, pretty worn, and some of them was already beginning to tear. Before she would, though, Cousin Wila slipped off her apron and swept across the floor to make sure there wasn't no dirt. Then she knelt down and spread out each paper real gentle with the tips of her fingers. She did it the same way a woman smooths a blanket over a sleeping child.

Celeste turned around. "What you doing?"

"I know I got a Cain here someplace."

"That family tree," said Celeste, "is approaching to look more and more like a weeping willow."

"Shut your mouth," said Cousin Wila. "Cain."

Celeste said: "Who, *her?* You ain't related."

"Che, ain't you got some business to do?"

"I'm doing it." Celeste was singeing a chicken.

"Well, see can't you pay a little bit extra mind to yours, and a little bit less here to mine."

"I'm just telling you, you ain't related."

"Cain," said Cousin Wila. ". . . *There*, I knew it. Shane. Hildegarde Shane, from Jackson. Must of changed her name. Same family, though. I remember her talking about these relatives she had in Santa Fe. What part of Mississippi is Santa Fe?"

Celeste said again: "You ain't related. And Santa Fe ain't even in Mississippi. It's west from there."

Cousin Wila stared at her. "Hildegarde Shane," she said, heavyvoiced, "is my fourth cousin, only three times removed. Or is you in an arguing mood?"

"I'm just trying to tell you . . ."

"It's the *same family*."

"Okay, fine," said Celeste. "You related."

Cousin Wila pulled out her fountain pen and began to write. "May . . . Cain . . . Santa . . . Fe . . . How old you say this girl was?"

"Sixty-three, last time I heard," said Celeste, "and she's half Indian. Better put that down too."

Cousin Wila laid the fountain pen on the floor. Quiet, but kind of dangerous, she said: "You *told* me she was a *girl*."

"I did not, I said she was this friend of mine's girl friend that he wanted to marry."

Real careful, Cousin Wila asked: "How old you say your friend was?"

"Eighty-five," said Celeste.

Cousin Wila kept very still and repeated: "Eighty-five. He ought better to be dead."

"He is," said Celeste.

Charles Leroy dropped a spoon he was wiping, and picked it up and rinsed it off.

Almost to herself, Cousin Wila said: "Dear Lord, I am a patient *lady*."

Celeste told her: "He used to live around the corner from us. Came from Santa Fe when he was only fifty, but he always used to talk about this May Cain. Said he was saving up to marry her one day, after his wife died. Never got around to it, though. Talked about her all the time. I used to date his grandson. Nice boy. He worked for these people name of Fitch on Carondolet that had a son lived in

Boston on account of he went to college there, and this son got hisself into trouble driving his Chevrolet convertible with white-wall tires over this woman who owned a five-and-dime up there, and she was going to sue him for twenty thousand dollars, but they got her to settle for half without even taking it to court, because they didn't want nothing to get in the papers, and it would of, if they'd allowed it to get into court."

Cousin Wila was gathering the tree together. "*And* how you know all that?"

"I found out."

"The most tremendous unhappiness in your life," said Cousin Wila, "is going to be that you can't cook for the FBI."

One of the papers had come loose. Celeste reached for it. "Here, let me help . . ."

"You keep your hands on your chicken," said Cousin Wila. But she took a hold of the paper so quick, it ripped straight across the middle. Cousin Wila swallowed. "Nobody's fault," she said, "that's all right. Nobody's fault at all." She sat down on the floor where she had been kneeling, and put the two halves in her lap. "It don't matter, she said, "that's all right. Just my carrying copy." She lifted her chin up. "I got the *real* one in Biloxi."

Celeste told her: "I do know this one girl in New Orleans . . . crippled girl, not much older than me . . ."

"You write down her name, and her age, and her address," said Cousin Wila, loud, "and you put it in my room tonight."

"Okay, fine," said Celeste. "Sure."

Cousin Wila stood on her feet before anybody could help her.

I was having trouble getting a shine out of a silver fruit bowl. I didn't see how Charles Leroy could of taken much of a notice, turned away like he was; he took it out of my hands, though, and gave me a pair of grape scissors instead. Cousin Wila saw him.

"Wherever I am, you want to let me know if that man gives you trouble." She was talking to me.

"What man?" I asked her.

She blinked at Charles Leroy through her glasses.

"What man?" I asked her again. I could feel the blood flushing in my face.

"Can't see but one from here, not even with my vision."

"He ain't doing her nothing," Celeste said. "He ain't never once paid her no mind."

"I know," said Cousin Wila, "that's what I mean."

It made me feel embarrassed for Charles Leroy. But then I leaned around to get some more polish, and I saw his face in a windowpane over the sink. He was grinning again.

The morning Cousin Wila left, she mashed all her clothes into one of her two suitcases, and made me take the other. She kept talking to keep me from thanking her, and she said both suitcases was old anyway, and it was time she got rid of them. But the one she left was a slick green, without hardly a scratch.

Then she got into her traveling dress, and put on rouge and lipstick, trying to balance up the split in her face. When she was finished, she stood a long while in front of the mirror.

Course, practically everybody changes their expression and puts it the way they want it to be, when they look in a mirror. Even the beautiful people will hold their faces up at the angle they want other people to see it from. The thing is, almost nobody knows about their own face: a mirror sheens over the deepness, and turns you backwards, and you really not looking at yourself at all. To catch on, though, you have to see a reflection of somebody you love. That's when you sure it ain't right.

I hated watching Cousin Wila's face in the glass. It was pretty terrible when she wasn't talking to a person she cared about. And when she saw it, she flattened her nose and made the bottom lip longer, and it was worse. The sad thing was to watch her thinking she was better that way.

She said: "I certainly hope there ain't no men to bother me on the train. When I was on the train the last time, there was this man stared at my legs for the whole entire trip." She put one thumb on her cheek and pushed the bad side up. "You can just tell me what he saw: an ugly old lady with hairs all over her."

"*You* ain't ugly," I said, "and you ain't old. And you got other things besides."

Cousin Wila pushed a laugh. "I got spectacles to see. I ain't blind, and that's for true." She was talking high. She went on looking into the mirror.

"How long is the trip?" I asked her, to get on something different. "How long you going to stay in Biloxi?"

But she went on: "This man kept staring at my legs, and I could *not* give him to understand I was not interested. I just could *not*. He just did not *want* to understand."

I put my head back to watch someplace else.

"That ever happen to you? Course, you so young." She went and picked up her purse and her coat, and walked back to the mirror. "I certainly hope I ain't going to be bothered on this trip. You could say I am not in the mood."

I wanted to tell her not to talk so stupid to me; I wanted to tell her I loved her, only I knew she wouldn't like for me to say so—she would figure I was just trying to be nice. People won't ever admit what they need. Only what they think they want.

Cousin Wila put a hand up to her temples. "I took two aspirins," she said, "and they didn't touch my headache. I have this headache again."

I took her bag, but she looked back from the door to see herself full-length. "That's all right. Give me an excuse to shut my eyes on the train. Ain't nobody going to bother me if I shut my eyes." Then she walked out of the room and down the passage without stopping.

Celeste cried when she kissed her goodbye.

Cousin Wila got mad and shoved her away. "Who you think you treating there," she said, "your *mama?*" She waited in the kitchen with us for most of an hour, but once she decided to go, she turned quick and went out to the car, and she didn't look around.

4

SOME sunny days, I took Mrs. Pharr's place wheeling old Mr. Sage along the gallery. He liked the bayou side most, and we always stopped there for a little. The bayou made a wide curve out from the house, and it left plenty enough lawn for the big duckpond and for the fishpond too. All of the ducks had their wings clipped so they couldn't but swim around and sit on an island in the middle of the pond. The fish was brought over from the Lake.

Mrs. Pharr sometimes came out and walked with us, but only if there was a few clouds skittering by. When the sun was naked, she always left me to do it alone. Then she would just come if she had something to say to Mr. Sage, or medicine to give him, and go right back in. I don't think she approved of the sun much.

When Mrs. Pharr talked, she cut every word off exact, and said them all in the same flat voice, like she was foreign. At first, I took it for granted she must of been mostly French or something. Only, one day I took Mademoiselle up a glass of hard cider on her tray, and she got giggly and told me that Mrs. Pharr just wanted to be from the French, but that she really spoke it like a *Swiss cow*. Mademoiselle never would of said such a thing if it hadn't been for the cider, and afterwards she got wary as all get-out, and wouldn't talk to me for over a week.

Anyhow, Mrs. Pharr spoke English on its toes, and you got the feeling she would rather of been speaking French, and I guess that was the feeling she wanted you to get.

We always knew when Mrs. Pharr was going to be with us on the gallery, because we could hear her before we saw her. But once, Mr. Sage put his head back on the pillow and made like he was sleeping.

She saw it wasn't for true, though; she stood next to him and put a hard hand on his shoulder. "Père," she said, "sign this, please."

Mr. Sage kept still.

"Père," said Mrs. Pharr, only not the way she would of said it if she'd thought he was asleep. She plain sounded tired. "Take it, Père, and sign it please." She was holding out a book, with a check on it and a pen, but he wouldn't open his eyes.

"*Bon*," said Mrs. Pharr. She walked a slow step to the railing, and looked up at things. It wasn't a very bright day. "When you are finished with your game, you let me know, and I will give you this to sign, and then I can go back to my work."

"What work?" asked Mr. Sage. He hadn't even waved a lash.

Mrs. Pharr held out the book again. "I have my work. Père, please I *ask* you not to start. It is wet today, and I am not feeling in the least amused."

"Everybody in this house works. Everybody but me. That's what they do all day, they work. I was wondering."

"Will you please sign? My arm is tired."

"Will I please sign how much?"

Mrs. Pharr turned her back to me. "Today is the thirty-first, and we are not alone. Kindly make some attempt not always to tire me unnecessarily."

"Where's Henry?"

"Henry went in to the city."

"Today?"

"Yesterday."

"Robert with him?"

"I am sure you know that Robert is with him."

" . . . Everybody works." He really was getting sleepy there, with his eyes shut.

"If you are feeling ill," said Mrs. Pharr, "you should not be out of doors."

"Everybody works. Everybody works, so I can feel ill. But I'm *not* feeling *ill*."

" . . . Just as you wish. I will not put up with this kind of behavior much longer." Mrs. Pharr walked away from us, and you could feel her steps in the floor.

When she had the door open, Mr. Sage said: "Give it to me."

She waited a few seconds with the doorknob in her hand, but she finally came back.

Mr. Sage opened his eyes right at her. "You *have* to put up with this," he said. "Don't you?"

Mrs. Pharr just gave him the book. He took a long time making the signature and closing the pen, but she stood quiet till he had finished. Then she started back in.

Mr. Sage called: "Oh, creature. Are you proud of all the air you suck in? Is *that* why?"

She never answered him, though.

Soon as he let his head rest on the pillow again, he did go to sleep.

My first Sunday off, I knew Charles Leroy was free too, but I only figured he had his friends.

He showed me the way to the bus stop, and before I could thank him he got on with me. Then, in Caytown, he walked me over to the station, and explained which train takes you one station further into Lansville, where they have shops and two picture houses. But when the train came, he climbed on and sat beside me.

After you know a place well, it's hard to think back to how you felt when you first saw it; after you live in a house a good while, you don't recall about the time when you wasn't sure where a certain room was. And if you really know a person, you almost can't remember when you didn't know more than what he seemed like.

But I remember about Charles Leroy.

He practically never turned to you. In the train, he sat in the aisle seat and watched the head in front of him, with his hands loose over his crotch, bent a little forward. Charles Leroy could bend in more places than anybody I ever saw. I didn't talk to him, because he looked as if he had his own things to wonder about.

It was only a fun twenty-minute ride, but I didn't like it. I couldn't see why Charles Leroy had bothered hisself to come on the same train, if he was going to stay that way the whole time. And he wouldn't change. He kept twenty careful minutes of his own thoughts shut right up inside his own head. Not shy; you don't mind a shy person. You don't even mind a peculiar person. What you mind is a person who stays interesting just by not letting his interest out.

When the train stopped at Lansville, I thought I was going to have to step over him. But he got up, and let me by, and then followed me. I walked straight on through the station and into the town, expecting him to go off someplace and find his friends. He didn't. He went right alongside, quiet, looking out over the street, and taking in all of the sights but me. For a distance, I thought he was following my lead, wherever I wanted to go. I finally caught on that it was exactly the other way around—and when I did, I got peeved.

I told him: "I am trying to locate where the picture houses are."

"That's where we going," he said.

(We who?) I asked: "You going *too?*"

He turned his head and looked at me. "Course," he said. And then I couldn't be sure but what he wasn't smiling there to hisself; only, so what if he was?

He paid for both the tickets, and he wouldn't take the money for mine. He even picked the picture I hadn't seen, *without asking.*

Then it was the same inside. If I hadn't checked him before the lights dimmed, I wouldn't of known he was there. Except once he laughed out sharp, when nobody else did. And so I had to sit through the whole second part, going back over the first part in my mind, trying to figure just what he might of thought was so funny. Which killed that.

Not far from the colored entrance of the picture house was a colored drugstore, and there was where we went afterwards. Same thing. A slow coffee in a thick white cup, and a piece of cold pie that came in an envelope, and I could as well of been sitting next to the most powerful brain in the United States. I was beginning to think maybe he had a mind something like Miss Roberta Roberts.

Our father met fat Miss Roberta at a wake a good six months before she moved in across the street from Mama's house, and by the time she came over to meet Mama, we knew all about her. Course, some one of us was bound to meet her sooner or later, at church or on a street corner. Because anytime anybody got together for anything, there was Miss Roberta, plup in the middle of it. It didn't have to be a wake, big or little; a couple people making a sick call was enough. The thing was, Miss Roberta had two personal sections: one, she was kind of stupid; two, she liked for people to pay attention to her. So she discovered the best way to take care of both sections was to shut up. She would sit by herself in the middle of a party, and not open her mouth ever, except to put something in it. Because what Miss Roberta found out was that when people get closed in a little room together, they generally talk about the same subject, and each one likes to give an opinion on it—and if they can locate a person who ain't got no opinion, then that is the person they all give it to. So everybody gave it to Miss Roberta, and because they usually wound up talking all at the same time, they had to shout, so each one could be sure she was *really* listening to *him.* Course, it wasn't long before everybody got to thinking fat Miss Roberta was a highly intelligent specimen of a lady. She would just sit there and nod her head or shake it (didn't much matter which), and when the party was over, she got up and went home. After a while, she made such a name for herself, she had to have special visiting hours for people who wanted to go to her house and discuss their problems with her. Then, if the person with a problem was a man, nine times out of ten he finished by marrying her, because he couldn't find a friend in the neighborhood who wouldn't tell him that the quality Miss Roberta had was so much more precious and enduring than just a pretty face.

Charles Leroy knew how to do the same thing, different, and worse: the way Miss Roberta looked at you, you was sure she could tell exactly what you was thinking; the way Charles Leroy did it, he made *you* sit and wonder what *he* was thinking.

After the coffee and the pie, he smoked a cigarette. From time to time he seemed like he might be going to say something—but it was only that deep breath people take to blow the smoke way out.

Then he paid again, and we left and had a walk. Just a walk. Strictly. I might of liked to stop and look in a window, but I didn't, because I plain couldn't get over the sense of being there *with* Charles Leroy. And trying to keep in rhythm with that broken-jointed way of moving I knew so well. But Charles Leroy even pinned his own style to that: he walked in all his different muscles, doubled forward, like he was attached to hisself all over. I got the feeling I didn't know if I was traveling with the upper part or the lower part.

Finally, I couldn't stand no more. The only remark I thought of to pass: "You finding any answer to your problem?" I meant to talk hard, but my voice didn't come out exactly right.

"No problem," said Charles Leroy. Then he said: "I like it with you."

"So do I," I said, and I wanted to slap myself. It was true though. We both of us kept quiet on the way back.

5

ERNEST the gardener had heaps too much work to do alone. So the duckpond smelled, and the lawn was uneven most of the time. Way through the trees beyond the house, in a place where the grass stretched away from the water's edge, there was a mealy wood platform to fish on where nobody ever did. The platform marked the outside limits of Will-o-Wilds, only it was around the bend in the bayou, all overgrown, and hidden from sight. Ernest never had time to go half that far, and the wet ground was full of sleek chuck-weeds, like a thick satin fringe on the fancy border of the swamp.

One afternoon free I went walking, following the bayou, and I crunched on rotten wood before I saw the platform. But the part that hung over the water was dryer, and it made a good seat where I could be alone. So I sat there to think, with my feet swinging out just above the bayou slime.

I had a problem: I wanted to be a real woman.

I was beginning to see that luck was against my ever finding a woman to study on. And I hadn't wanted to copy, it wasn't that; I just all my life wanted to see what it meant to be a woman. But the only person I could remember hoping to be like from the very first was our father, and he was a man, and look what happened to him.

It was as if I had got born faced in the wrong direction, and then just grown up that way. Bumping my head down every wall—never finding the door that would open for me. Never Mama, not quite Jewel; not Adelaide. Not all of Marbelle nor Cousin Wila nor Celeste. Not Mrs. Pharr. Nobody. Little pieces of some people, but no one perfect real woman. In the early years I thought: maybe I am just *wanting* to be different, like Adelaide. But I was older now, and I still didn't see the how or the why to live that was right for me. So I thought: okay, maybe I *am* different, but the wrong way; maybe

I don't fit because I'm plain peculiar. I thought: it's better to be a half-good person than a peculiar person. And I thought: a real woman wouldn't have to study to be what she is.

Only I didn't know a real woman to ask.

All the time I'd spent in Mama's house, I never had to think so much about me. But soon as I got away from her fear, I found my own. All the time I'd spent watching my brothers take their secrets, and knowing their secrets was wrong—all that time was finished now too. The point was, they *had* secrets, and I didn't. Seventeen years and up of waiting to get out into life, waiting to live. And now I was out—and now I had no life. And I couldn't see my reason to live.

But then I knew I wasn't out at all; I knew I still carried Mama's house on my back. Because I could see that seventeen years of learning every blessèd detail about wrong—wasn't going to help me find one single one about right. And I was still shut inside with the walls and the locked doors. Still, still waiting.

So I leaned back on the mealy platform, and I thought the only thing in the world left for me to do, long as I had to wait, was to try and see could I fit all the good pieces of the people I knew into one tight sum. And I thought I would take the sum, and see if *it* would fit into *me*.

And there is how I sat my soul down in the swamp that day and hooked one long eyebrow at God.

The next time I went out to the platform, Charles Leroy followed me. He did it so quiet, I never even knew I wasn't alone till he up and said: "Slush, slush," just behind me, and I practically jumped over into the water.

I wasn't in a mood to show him he'd scared me, though. I kept right on sitting with my back turned, and I asked: "Slush, slush, what?"

"Just slush, slush," he said. On top of he had interrupted my thinking, he was going to be cute.

I couldn't call up a word to answer him. So I sat still and looked at the other side of the bayou. About three minutes passed, with nothing going on. Then, exactly when I started to figure he must of got the message and gone away, he sat down next to me and scared me all over again.

I said: "Charles Leroy . . ." I had something else to say too, only I forgot it soon as I opened my mouth.

"Who you think it was?"

"I knew it was you the whole time." Which I did.

Charles Leroy tried to hang his legs over the water, same as me, but they was too long. So he turned around and sat on one of them, and stretched the other out. "What we using here for talk?"

He was getting me peeved again. "Like for instance?"

"Like for instance. Like for instance, seems to me I might even get to love you."

That was Charles Leroy. When you wanted him to make words, he was a dead oyster, and when you didn't he came up with a pearl. He was *obliging,* is what he was.

I stopped swinging my legs. I leaned forward and put my hands under my behind, and sat on the palms. "Look," I said, "Charles Leroy." Then I said: "Man, don't . . . don't fiddle with me."

He had his head dropped back on his shoulders, looking up, watching the moss move in the creeping wind.

I explained: "I mean to say . . . what I mean to say . . . I got enough with my own problems. Please . . . don't . . . *heckle* at me." But that wasn't what I meant, neither.

Charles Leroy studied the moss, and he held off a time before he said: "I'm sorry."

"No," I told him, "why? Why you sorry? . . . Ain't no call for you to be *sorry.*" I was staring at him, but you wouldn't of said he knew it. Over his head, I saw a tree lizard standing in a spot of sunlight on a branch.

I did my best to keep from getting mad, but I couldn't help it. Not being able to talk right, just when I wanted to—not being able to tell him how I felt. I thought: course, the only reason you can't tell *him* how you feel, is because you ain't sure your*self.* That did it; I got up.

"Come on, let's go back." My voice was wavy, and even I heard the anger under it.

But he held still.

"Come *on,*" I said.

He looked at me. "Ain't no hurry. You go back do you want to."

We had a look at each other, and I rocked on the balls of my feet. Then I sat down again like before, facing the bayou. I told him: "I plain *don't know.*"

And I could of swore he understood a little of what I meant then, because he didn't answer me at all. He let me be quiet for a while, with the wet wind reaching to us through the trees.

Finally, he said: "You don't have to be scared with me."

"I know," I said, "I ain't scared. I got problems."

"On my account?"

"No, boy. Living problems."

"I saved up some money . . . "

"It ain't money," I said.

"You got a man?"

"No," I said, "I ain't got no man."

" . . . You had one."

"No, I didn't."

Charles Leroy kept his mouth shut.

"I *didn't*," I said.

"Okay," said Charles Leroy. And he told me: "If it's something you rather not say, you don't have to."

I shifted around so I could see him. "You make me feel silly. It ain't nothing like that."

"Skip the subject; I don't care." He sounded like a little boy who had dropped his gum.

"Look, Charles Leroy. Sometimes you want to figure out things. Sometimes . . . you know you ain't right inside. But you don't know if it's because of where you came from, or because of where you going, or maybe because there ain't no place *for* you to go. Sometimes, you think your brain's gone pasty, and you can't remember why the world began."

Charles Leroy lay back down and half shut his eyes. "Is that what it is, is wrong?"

"That's what. Mostly."

"The trouble with you," he said, "you ain't got no trouble."

Nothing came in my mind to say to that one.

"Look at it like this." Charles Leroy had opened his eyes real wide, and he was swirling them around slow.

I waited, but he didn't go on. "Like what?" I asked.

"Lay back down, same as me."

That didn't make much sense.

"Lay down."

The way he said it, it was an order. I flattened out on the other side of the platform.

"Look up, like I am."

I did that too.

"What you see?"

" . . . Everything."

"Everything *how?*"

Then I got what he was talking about. The trees was miles taller, and they had swayed in over us way at the tops. They seemed as if they was stuck in the sky, all endless and off-balance, rounding out a place for us to lay. And the moss and the bushes, the gray and the green, all of it was leaning in, making a curved hollow of the land for me and for Charles Leroy. The flatness was gone. Looking up like that gave you a place to be.

"I see it," I said.

"Feels better, don't it?"

" . . . It feels right."

I watched around-and-over-and-down, around-and-over-and-down. What I wasn't watching was Charles Leroy, when he rolled sideways and kissed me.

I didn't think it was fair: I had my arms to my sides, and I hadn't even known he might be going to. He took a long time, and when he finished, he just stopped the kissing, but he kept his face there. I felt him breathing on me, and his eyes was so near I couldn't see into but one at a time. But that eye looked like it wasn't kidding.

I said: "You stuck your tongue out."

Charles Leroy took his head further away. "That all you can think of to say?"

"Yes." It was, as a matter of fact.

Then Charles Leroy came down and did it again. His chest was over mine, and he had one arm around me; I was still laying on my back with my hands down, so I couldn't move. I wondered whose heart was pumping between my breasts.

When he was through, I said: "I feel like a fish."

He rolled on his back, and left me there. "Nobody ever kiss you before?"

"Couple boys. Not like that."

Charles Leroy got up. "Let's go," he said, "the time is late."

But I lay quiet and watched him upside down, like the trees.

"Stand on your feet, Cille." He gave me his hand to help me, with his foot against mine.

I stood up then, and brushed myself clean. The wet had seeped up from the platform and made my slip all stick to me in back. "Have to take a shower bath," I said.

He was standing right next to me, but when his hands closed behind my waist, they could of been another person's. He said: "Cille, it's like this." Then he took my arms and put them in back of his neck, and fitted our mouths right. While he kissed me, all his body tightened and hardened, as if every one of the separate pieces suddenly knit together.

I tried to kiss him back, like he wanted. Afterwards, I asked: "Is that the way?"

"Sure," he said, "but don't talk so soon. You shouldn't always talk so soon."

I slid down. "That was fun," I told him.

"Good," said Charles Leroy. He smoothed some hair back off my face. "Who was the first person ever told you you was pretty?"

"Charles Leroy," I said, "don't be stupid."

"Stupid to ask?"

"I ain't what they call pretty," I said, "and I know it, and I don't need no foolishness about that. You want to kiss me, you go ahead and kiss me, but keep the excuses strictly out."

He wanted to know: "You being cuddly?"

"Listen," I said, "I could get mad. I just might could get mad."

Charles Leroy chuckled. He said: "I knew there was something funny about you."

" . . . Funny, huh? Well, I told you, I got my problems."

"Yes," said Charles Leroy, "you do." He chuckled again.

I straightened out my skirt. When I turned my head back up, he was still looking at me. "Stop watching," I said, "and let's skip the subject."

"Okay." He let one hand stay around me on my hipbone, and we started back along the bayou. Only he never quit looking at me.

"*Skip it,*" I said.

"Skipped," said Charles Leroy. But he went right on.

When we got near to where you can see from the house, he made me go first, and he waited. I didn't feel right about that.

Celeste walked into the kitchen through the early white sunlight and said: "Good morning to all who is concerned." She meant Charles Leroy and me. It was seven o'clock, and I had been there a half-hour, but Charles Leroy had just come in, puffy-faced from bed.

The June morning air breathed dew around you, and long drops glistened over the dark yellow lawn, basting it for the later sun. Out the kitchen window you could see a little of the bayou on the other side of the trees; the water was smooth and dead and black, with angled strips of white cut across it, shining back up at the sky.

Nobody answered Celeste, and she said: "I am so glad to see that everybody contains such a lovely humor."

"Good morning," I said.

Charles Leroy finished his coffee, and left to clean the night's cigarettes out of the living room ash trays, and get started in the pantry.

I told Celeste: "He's sleepy. He ain't given to talking much so early."

"He ain't given to talking at all no time," she said, "he just likes to be a presence."

I looked out the window and thought about that.

"Is you two going to get in serious?"

". . . Who?"

"Who. You and Booker T. Washington."

"About what?"

"Oh, Lord," she said, "let it pass, let it pass."

I scratched a piece of soap off my fingernail. "What makes you think to ask?"

"Nothing of a particular nature. You been cow-eyeing around for a while."

Now I wouldn't of thought that was true. I went and took the broom and the dustpan from the linen closet; then I came back and sat down again. I wanted to know: "Was you ever in love?"

Celeste had part of her head and one arm in the oven, wiping it out. "Certainly, che. Lots of times, and once really."

"What's the difference?"

"If you ain't sure, then you ain't.

". . . I might could be."

She stood up and passed the rag down her arm to get the black off. "Che, love is one of them words means what you want it to mean. Like sonofabitch."

I tried hard to think what it meant to me, and what I had heard somebody say about it that was important.

"You can't do nothing but sit around, honey. Can't push it. Can't even know what it's going to do you. Take me: I thought I was going to be swimming in syrup."

"And you wasn't?"

Celeste sort of cough-laughed.

I said: "But I want to know *now*."

"Okay, che," Celeste said, "what you want me to say? Loving is taking a man and making him a part of you, in you. That what you want me to say?"

It didn't sound right. Almost, but it didn't sound right. Somebody had put it better.

Celeste said: "Anyhow, don't matter a peanut what I tell you, one way or the other. You still going to have to find out for yourself. Part of life. Like getting toilet-trained."

"Foo, no. Not like that." I was tying my white cap on, and I had it over my eyes.

"Listen," she said, "just listen. Now listen here. All I ask is for you not to get no rose petals on me. I don't mind you talking it over, I always was a person with half of her interest in other people's problems. But keep me out of the rose petals, that's all. I'm four years older than you, and I'm a big girl, and I been through it left and right and sideways, and I done taken so many baths afterwards, I can get depressed just thinking about it."

"Why baths?" I asked.

Celeste yawned. "You'll find out. Sweaty business."

I leaned the mop against the window and got up to stretch. "Celeste."

"Huh?"

I said: "I want to know something."

"Such as?"

"Well. Am . . . am I . . . *pretty?*"

"Oh shit," she said, "here we go."

"No . . . I mean . . . I want to know, am I . . . am I what people would call a . . . a pretty person?"

"Che," said Celeste," you a nice gal, and a sweet kid, and I like you very much. Leave an old lady in peace. Do not screw around."

"I ain't. I ain't the type. I just want you to tell me."

"Honey, there never was a woman born didn't know whether she was pretty or not, before she was out of diapers."

"I . . . I don't know."

"Lord," she said. "Oh, Lord. I knew this would happen the day they went and emancipated Greta Garbo." She turned to me and bowed. "Yes. You is pretty."

I put my hand up to my face. I told her: "Thanks, Celeste."

"Don't mention it," she said. She knocked the used coffee grounds and chicory into a half sheet of newspaper, and folded that up and threw it in the violet enamel trash can. Then she put the percolator in the sink. "You a catch, ain't you?"

" . . . Catch?"

"A *virgin*, honey, a v-i-r-g . . . Well, a *virgin*."

"ɪ-ɴ," I said. "Yes."

She asked: "Play with yourself?"

I just about couldn't answer.

"Don't, do you?"

"No."

"Should, che." Celeste had a big paper bag in front of her, standing on its edge with the weight of the potatoes. "Gets you ready for a man; gives you a chance to tone yourself up while you waiting." She took the paring-knife and started to peel one long potato. "Kind of breaks up the time, too."

When I went upstairs to sweep, I started to think it all over; but the more I figured, the less I thought out. It was the way Celeste talked about taking that threw me. Because she had it right, only she said it backwards. Loving is giving, and Marbelle was the one who told me that. And it don't mean what you want it to. It means what you are.

Course, I really knew all along, only my mind wasn't ticking very well then. It's just when you need words for life that they don't help.

6

THE first thing I took a notice of was how I wanted to watch Charles Leroy all the time. Not to make him look at me. I was happiest when he didn't know I was watching him, and I could just see him moving around and doing things his way. Like sometimes you would rather sit and study a kitten play by itself than grab it and hug it. I had to haul off and stop, though, because I was getting so I couldn't be in the same room and look at anything else.

Charles Leroy must of known real well what was happening. Some whole days would go by without him raising his head from work. But there are people who can say more by when they don't look at you than by when they do.

The other things that got unusual was how I liked to wake up in the morning, and how the house didn't bother me so much.

Then old Mr. Sage began to make up excuses for me to be with him. He wanted a cup of coffee in the middle of the morning—or when I was cleaning his room, he said: "Sit down, honey, you get me nervous."

I told him: "I can't, Mr. Sage, I got my work."

But he didn't care. "You make a fresh smell when you come around."

"Airing out," I said, "and cleaning."

"No. This place won't air out. Won't clean either."

And then another time I was in the Music Room when it was getting dark, and he told me to go stand in a corner.

"Sir? In a corner?"

"Go on. Now move over there."

I went where he pointed.

"See?" he said. "You do glow."

"Mr. Sage?"

"You glow. All over." He studied me hard for a little. "Turn around and look at that painting of my wife."

I wouldn't of had to, to remember it, but I did.

"Like that painting?"

" . . . Don't know, sir."

"That's right," he said, "it's a bad painting. It shows the way she was, though, you can tell the way she was. See what made her daughter? *See?*"

"Yes, sir." He was right, it almost could of been Mrs. Pharr. Only older. And there was another thing . . .

Mr. Sage said: "But she won't ever learn to be as mean. Not dry enough. Likes suffering better. Some people like to suffer. Think it gives them dignity."

That was it. Mrs. Sage's face could of cracked the canvas, and the eyes was stony and alive. It was the way Mrs. Pharr tried to look, but didn't. I said: "Yes, sir," again.

"Yes, sir. Glowworm. Who is it, is it Robert?"

"Mr. Robert, sir?"

"I said Robert. Well . . . is it Robert you glowing for?"

"No, sir. It ain't Mr. Robert." I smiled when I told him.

Mr. Sage sat back and squinted at me; then his face broke, and he giggled. "I *thought* you had some sense. You wouldn't waste juice on a man like Robert. All right now, go on away."

When I had passed into the hall, he called: "Hold on to it, honey, keep that sense." And I heard him giggle again and say: "Now will you please look where the sense is going these days?" I figured he must be talking to Mrs. Sage's painting. He went right on giggling.

I counted the days till the next Sunday we both had free. Before, I hadn't cared what day of the week it was, not since that last afternoon I brought my books home from school. After that, I always used to get them mixed—sometimes even my Sundays with the River. But now, I kept the calendar checked exact in my mind, and I counted.

I didn't ask him about what we were going to do, like whether we might go to the pictures: I didn't talk about it at all. When Sunday came, soon as work was finished, I put on the wornest of my two dresses with my old easy-walkers and I left by the side door so he wouldn't see me. I ran to the bayou, where the trees began.

There wasn't no path to the platform, and I liked to follow the swing of the water, treading light to keep my feet dry. Last year's leaves had made a spoiled covering over the ground there, in a strip that was wide as the length of a man, and long as the bayou. Across the surface, the strip was light brown, with fuzzy pieces of green fungus reaching out from under it in little hills. The leaves held a filmed glaze of dirt that sealed them together, keeping their tops shiny and crisp. But if you put your weight on your foot, the softness squished under the crust—and if you kicked, you made a gaping hole in the darker leaves for the wetness and the worms to feel the air.

I walked, and I wondered when he would come after me. I thought: maybe he did have a friend to see this time; maybe I should of asked. But I didn't think I should of had to ask.

The clouds looked like stuffed slugs, too heavy to move, their bellies dulled and swollen. They kept still over the swamp, but I knew they had decided not to rain. They was going to sit there and mildew instead. Looking up, I thought: Cille, someday you better figure out just exactly what it is you have got against clouds.

In the swamp, the smell of damp decay has a special perfume that sops into everything. It runs on every breath you take, and stays behind in the bone of the head, pushing. It makes your eyes feel soft and spongy. And it makes you think of slick black animals, crawling hard through the sinking mud, in a hurry to die.

But the swamp is a land for itself. Death is personal there. Because they don't need nothing new for food in the swamp: their private death is what makes their private life, and green lives on green's own rotten mother. That is the why of the deep quicksand pits: graveyards for visitors. And that is why the swamp laughs at you—laughs at anything strange might come to join it—the way the bayou laughs at the rain.

There is the kind of a place for beautiful things to happen.

I was walking quick, because I wanted to be alone a while before he followed me. I wanted to think into words and be able to tell him why I was like I was. Then we could talk, and forget about those last two weeks, with the quick looks and the quiet and the feelings all past. He'd understand then, and we would be able to think back together and see it all from the outside.

When I got around the bend, I walked slower to the mossy branch that shut off the platform, pretending I didn't know what was behind it. I was just a person who was wandering along, and I was going to find the platform all over again, by accident. I wasn't going to take a notice of it till I stepped down, the same as before, and then I was going to be very happy, like I had made this discovery. I used to do that kind of a pretend once every so often, to order up my mind.

I didn't push the branch with my hand, because I couldn't know it would move. Course, when I stopped and leaned against it to rest, it did, and that was when I was ready to find the platform. So I swung right on through.

And Charles Leroy caught me, and eased me down against his body.

He didn't kiss me. He held me there, and our heads crossed, and I held him. It wasn't easy keeping my eyes open, but I wanted to. I don't know how long it was before I said: "You got here first."

"Sure," he said.

When Charles Leroy holds a person, he leans over them, and the person bends back till she thinks she's bound to fall away. But he keeps the balance for everybody.

After he spoke, he let go. He let me fall back, and he put one arm under my legs, and flipped me up in the air. Then he sat me on the platform, and straightened up and hooked his fingers over his belt behind him. He laughed, soft.

I lay down, my hands under my head and my ankles touching.
"Charles Leroy," I said, "I wanted to talk. I did want to talk."
"Talk," he told me."
"There ain't nothing. It all went away."
"Miss Mysterious."
"No, I ain't. I want to get the feelings out."
"Love me?"
"No," I said, "oh, no . . . I love the way you walk."
"*How* do I walk?"
" . . . Like a person I knew once."
Charles Leroy knotted up his face as if he had a terrible problem.
He said: "Your father?"
I sat up fast. "How you know?"
"Oh," he said, "I kind of figured you for that." He put his foot
against mine and lifted his toes, playing to get my shoe off. "Easy-
walkers. Wonder why I care about you."
Then I remembered. "You don't. No, man, you don't. Not like
you think. You just interested, because I ain't all clear. That's the
thing I wanted to say."
Charles Leroy sighed, and fell forward on the platform next to
me, face down. He did it stiff, buckling at the last second to stretch
out loose and long; he put his head inside his arms.
"Don't get sad now," I told him, "that don't mean you might not
like me fine after I'm all cleared up. Just because I ain't a person now
don't mean I ain't trying hard, you know. Charles Leroy. When I
get all the bits fitted into me, you can always come back and take
another look."
He kept his head buried, and whoosh-breathed to hisself.
"Please don't get sad, I told you. Charles Leroy. Don't get sad."
He wouldn't move.
I got on my side and took his arm away, and I pushed his left
eyelid up with one finger. The eye was rolled way down, so I could
only see the round white, pink at the rim, with a red string in it
that came to the surface and went back again, like the mark a shooting
star leaves. "Charles Leroy. Stop being like that."
Then he took my hand and put it for his chin to rest on.
I felt over his cheek, and found a spot where he hadn't got all the
beard shaved off. "Hey. Open your eyes."
"No."
" . . . Why?"
"Because. Don't want to."

A big bird swooped into our hollow, and floated out slow, and then circled up and around and did it again. It was looking for something to eat. "We ain't dead, bird," I said, "and anyhow we ain't from here."

The clouds must of been moving after all, because the sky had cleaned right above us. There was ash in the blue, and you could make out the higher clouds way up, streaked across like somebody had combed them.

My arm was going to sleep from the position, but I didn't want to say so.

Charles Leroy opened his jaw and closed it, twice, gnawing on the air. He told me: "The flat of your palm is hard."

"I used to do washing."

"When? How old are you?"

"Not quite eighteen," I said. "Still jailbait."

He pushed his chin out and grinned. "Funny I don't know a thing about you yet."

"That's just what I think," I said, "we don't know nothing about each other at all. Now, why don't we just lay here and talk for a while, and see if we can't get to know what the other person . . . "

"Cille."

" . . . What?"

"Shut up."

"Why? Don't you think it's important for . . . "

"Cille."

"*What?*"

Charles Leroy said: "We got time."

"It ain't a question of time," I said, it's a question of . . . "

"Hey."

"Charles Leroy," I said, "I am getting most powerful tired of being interrupted."

Then he kissed the inside of my hand.

I made a fist and shivered. "Quit that," I said.

"No, che. Ain't nothing else important for a while."

"What you mean?"

"Just what I said."

"Ain't nothing else *important?*"

"Not for now."

"*Why?*"

"Because," he said, "that's the way it is."

I said: "Men."

The grin came back. "And what-all is wrong with men?"

"Everything," I told him, "you finally come across one looks like he might have something to say, and he won't say it."

"Cille."

"What now?"

"Lay back down."

" . . . Can't." But he lifted his head so I could take my arm away. When I was on my back, I said: "Okay, here I am."

Charles Leroy opened his eyes, and swung his chest over me, with his elbows straight. He let them break out, and he eased on top of me, easy with his weight. He asked: "Hurt you?"

"No," I said, "you only on the top part."

Then he really laughed. Not noisy, but his stomach bounced. "Che, you sure is lucky I ain't somebody else."

"Count of what you might do?"

"Baby. Oh, baby."

"Stop bouncing," I said, "what would you do?"

"Want to see?" He said it in a strange way, teasing and anxious.

"Sure. But I already know how you going to start off. You going to kiss me."

Charles Leroy shook his head. "Lucille," he said, "where did you get all them different *words*?"

When he kissed me, I wondered if that was going to be all. It was enough, though; what I didn't know could happen with just a kiss. What I didn't know could happen at all.

He did it longer than before. First he just stroked his mouth over mine, gentle, letting the force come only a little—and then more, and more, like he couldn't hold back. He kept one arm under my head, holding me to him; the other was on my side, smoothing me through my dress.

I wasn't used to breathing so quick, and I tried to keep it in. But when he finished I saw the color of his face, and I knew he was the same. I said, "You meant that. Didn't you?"

He lay his head against my throat. "I done told you not to talk so soon."

I had to, though. "Charles Leroy, tell me what it is."

"Ain't nothing to tell, if you couldn't sense it."

"I could," I said, "I sensed it." Then I said: "Charles Leroy, I do love you."

He lay still, and his lips moved on my neck when he asked: "How you know? You ain't even a person."

"I do. I do." I wasn't saying it to him so much, only I had just found it out myself, and it was very new.

He didn't say no more.

I took his head and lifted, pulling him up. He was heavy, not helping much. I said: "Do that again."

"Wait a while, honey."

"Why?"

"Wait a while."

I told him: "Please do it now."

Charles Leroy leaned away on one arm; he put his fingers in his hair. "Cille," he said, "quiet . . . Cille."

Then he came down.

I remember the noise of a heron behind us, and something that made light slaps in the water, like the sound of wind-waves when they skim across the Lake and break over on its cement sides.

Up, the sky and the trees blurred all together, changing to a gray, orange, green, spotted curtain that beat fast around my eyes, soft as a grackle's wings.

The platform was rocking us, warped and cradled to hold our breath till it could soak into the wood.

Charles Leroy, Charles Leroy, Charles Leroy, Charles Leroy. He had dragged his body over against mine; our legs tangled, and he took my knee in his thighs, holding me there with his warmth. We strained close, squeezing the air away and trying to grow into each other, into the whole of one flesh. I got dizzy, and sharp, and dizzy again. Lost; gloried; starved for the new thing I was knowing drop by drop: wanting to reach quick through to the flood and the spring that pulsed under it, where life starts.

When the buzz came in my head, I crossed my arms behind him, and caught his moving back-muscles in my hands. Then I was drifting—my mind dark—zooming. And all the time I held to the strength that lifted me, blind, out of my old world.

I recall how the heat began wherever we touched; I recall suddenly needing to have him under my armpits, and in all the other places that never got used to warm anything ever before.

But I can't recall thinking when I reached to hold my hand down on him, on the hardness that burned through my clothes—feeling with my hand for the center of the whirlpool and of everything.

He grabbed at my wrist, and he broke away and sat up. He said: "Cille. Be still." And he said again: "Be *still*."

I lay alone then, by myself. I felt like a weak part of me that wasn't right by itself, with the need that was so young. I was angry for a second, and I could of laughed. But I asked him: "Why?"

"You don't even know what you doing."

"I don't *care*."

"Better think, Cille."

Think? I wanted to tell him: all the time I spend every day thinking, and how far does it get me—and just when I was going to find out one thing that might be true, you stop for me to think again.

Then he asked: "You a virgin, ain't you?"

I pulled my skirt out and sat up too. "Charles Leroy," I said, "you shouldn't always talk so soon."

"Ain't you?"

" . . . Sure," I said. "Everybody been asking me that."

"What I mean, che, you better think . . . "

"If you use that word once more at me, I likely could get angry."

"Right," he said, "skip the subject."

One of the big clouds had moved overhead, shaped exactly like the opening in the trees. But it didn't make no real shadow, not for us anyway. The day just wasn't a day for shadows.

I fixed a loose hairpin on the top of my bun. "Charles Leroy."

"Hey."

"What we going to do."

"What you *want* to do?"

" . . . I ain't sure no more."

He stood on his feet, facing the swamp. "Want to go for a walk, for right now?"

"I ain't interested in right now," I said, but I got up.

After he tucked his shirt in, where it came out behind, we wandered a little. We went on the other side of the platform, letting the trees pass between us, making space for them because they didn't matter.

"Know when I said I love you?"

"Course."

"That was true."

"I know."

Then I asked him: "You worrying to yourself?" He looked like he was.

"No, che." But he just said it to say something. He was back to being quiet, like his usual-person.

We finished the day like that, without touching each other again, walking through the trees.

Only that afternoon couldn't really finish, not in my mind. Because it was when something finally cried out from my insides—something real—something I didn't know I had; it was the afternoon a fresh life called to repeat in me, before my own life was weaned.

It was the afternoon Charles Leroy gave me a different way to love.

Going up to the house, I saw Mrs. Pharr on the gallery. (Charles Leroy was standing down by the bayou till I got inside.) She wasn't faced in my direction, but she was watching me, turning her eyes without moving her head. I didn't like the way she kept it up. I knew she would wait to see Charles Leroy follow after me, and I was upset with him for wanting to sneak about nothing, like Mama might of done. I let it go, though.

I didn't see him again before supper.

We all three ate at the kitchen table, after the Pharrs had finished. Celeste did most of the talking. Charles Leroy and me held that silent thing, alive in the room.

Celeste tried to bust through it a couple times, but she couldn't. She asked me: "You got no appetite, che?"

" . . . Not much."

"Then why don't you just leave the soup sit in the plate, honey?" she said. " . . . Instead of spilling it all over your dress?"

I looked down, and took a dishcloth and wiped at the spot.

Celeste hammered with her fingers on the table top for about half a minute. "A person certainly never could get bored sitting at *this* table."

Charles Leroy's hand was moving on his coat lapel while he ate.

"Cille," said Celeste.

"I'm here."

"That is so nice to know," she said, "you could of fooled me."

I stared a long time at this piece of bread, and I saw the platform and the dark water.

Somebody had turned on their radio—Mr. Sage, I guess; tinkling of a piano, a long way off.

"Cille."

"Huh."

"Goddam," said Celeste, "goddam. Honey, either put the spoon in your mouth . . . or put it down in the plate . . . *but stop holding it up in the air like you was feeding me.*"

I put it down. "Sorry," I said.

Celeste decided to have another try. "Look at this, che. Stick out your arm here next to mine."

I did, real slow and careful, and I knocked over a glass of water.

Charles Leroy mopped up fast with the dishcloth.

"If I was a Catholic," Celeste told me, "I swear to God I would cross myself."

I felt a little stupid. "What about my arm?" I said.

"Look," said Celeste, and she put hers alongside. "Look at that difference."

"Sure."

"Well, now, listen at her . . . 'sure.' It certainly is nice to hear you keeping up the heavy end of the conversation."

"Well, what about it?" I asked. "Only a lighter color."

Celeste told me: "I was just going to remark, know what sitting here next to you makes me feel like, aside from dead?"

"What?"

"Shit-brindle brown," she said.

Charles Leroy went on eating, and Celeste sat back and gave up.

It was a hot night. A black breeze from the bayou drifted in the open window to edge around us, tightening the circle of light over the table. It blew in the lightest waves, and you could feel it whisper —hotter than the air inside the house. The swamp was sleeping with its mouth open.

A good fifteen minutes must of passed before Celeste said: "I sincerely hope I won't be disturbing no atmospheres if I make this request for somebody to pass the salt."

Charles Leroy and me reached for the Morton's box, and we both put our hands on it at once. I laughed then. I was happy.

About ten o'clock Mrs. Pharr rang from the Japanese Room. She pushed the button twice, for me, only Charles Leroy figured she made a mistake so he went instead. When he came down, he told us she wanted coffee and a plate of ladyfingers, and she wanted me to bring them. He didn't make it sound strange or anything; he said she probably just got a yen to ask me about the criminal cases in the newspaper.

Mrs. Pharr was always the first person to take the paper in the morning. While she read, she made a pencilled outline around any articles she could find on people who had broken the law and was going to get punished for it. I used to hear her talking about them at mealtime to Mr. Pharr and Mr. Robert and old Mr. Sage. Then after they was all through with the paper, she gave it to me or Charles

Leroy, or sometimes she went down to the kitchen and gave it to Celeste. She said: "There is a most interesting article here I have thought would be worth the effort of everyone to read," or: "I am sure that I hope you are following the case which I have been marking to bring to the attention of everyone." We really had to study them, too, because like as not she would ask us questions about them the next day, and it wasn't nice to be around her if you didn't know the answers. She always found some excuse to ask all three of us, at least once a week. Celeste said it was her way of making sure that none of us got an urge to go astray; leastways not until we really knew the field.

Only, this time I had an idea she wanted to talk about something more than the criminal cases.

At night, the house was a place for echoes that wouldn't sound. The carpet had been taken off the stairs to be cleaned, so I walked on wood; but my footsteps hardened and faded out soon as I heard them. The electric lights along the wall was made to look like stiff bunches of candlesticks. I felt sad for those lights, put there to make believe. They threw a strangled, yellow sheen on top of the wood, slick from the morning's wax.

The tinkling music had stopped.

Mrs. Pharr was alone, sitting with a book on the sofa in front of the Japanese screen. She was quiet while I put the tray down and poured her coffee. One Japanese fisherman winked a pink eye at me when I straightened.

On the floor to my left I saw three crooked squares of moonlight fallen in from the gallery, like clean white bandages patched over the sickness.

She said: "I am sure you know why I called for you."

Not why. I knew what about, but not exactly why. I told her: "I ain't positive, ma'am."

She put a piece of sugar in her coffee with the tongs. There was no splash. "I am quite sure that you *are* positive . . . do you understand? I should like this not to be either difficult or prolonged in the least."

I had forgot that she didn't use cream, and she stared at the pitcher as if it might of crawled up there on its own. Then she took the cup in her hand, and leaned back and crossed her legs. She stirred it and said: "Outside of the servants' quarters, I do not *permit* a lack of respect either in my house or within its grounds. Kindly serve me a ladyfinger."

"Ma'am? Respect?"

"Put the plate there. You do not know what respect means?"

". . . I think so." I had to clear my throat.

"Respect is a certain attitude which is required in this house. I think you will find that it is also required, to a degree of more or less, in most *decent* homes where you might wish to be employed. Personally, I am very particular about it. To speak quite simply, I *demand* it."

Seemed to me she was taking way too long. I said: "Please tell me what I did, Mrs. Pharr."

"That is what I am attempting to explain, although as I say, I am sure that you already know. You are very young, are you not?"

"Nearly eighteen, ma'am."

"That is not young? But perhaps not, as you were brought up to believe."

"I don't feel very young, ma'am. Most of the time."

"No, quite obviously, you do not. *Bien sûr, bien sûr.* Very well, I shall speak with you as you *feel* . . . Lucille, I witnessed a very disagreeable spectacle this afternoon. You should be extremely thankful, however, that I have seen it alone. Had there been anyone *else* present with me, you would be dismissed and on the train back to New Orleans at the moment."

"Can I say something, please, ma'am?"

Mrs. Pharr sighed, tired. Then: "Go on," she said, "I am waiting."

I told her: "Ma'am. It ain't the way you think." That was all I could come up with.

Mrs. Pharr smiled: "By which you wish to say?"

"The way you think about me and Charles Leroy."

"I am not sure I understand you when you say the *way* I think."

It wasn't right to speak like I wanted—not to her, and not there. Anything might go bad in that room. I said: "I mean, we couldn't of done wrong. Nothing that was *wrong* could happen between us."

She jerked a little, and put her cup down, empty. "I am afraid that I find your attitude insulting."

"But, ma'am . . ."

"Is it possible that you imagine it is of any importance to me what you may or may not do with Charles? *Or* how you see fit to justify these actions?"

"I thought . . ."

"But you thought incorrectly. For me the importance is entirely limited to the outward conduct of the married and *unmarried* servants whom I employ, during the time when they are *not* confined to their own quarters. Nothing more."

I couldn't help saying: "Yes, ma'am, my mama would understand that."

Mrs. Pharr took another ladyfinger. "Well, I can see that your mama has some intelligence. Is she, by the way . . . colored?"

"Oh, yes indeed, ma'am," I said, "and how."

"I beg your pardon?"

"She's very dark, ma'am."

"I see. And your . . . uh . . . *papa?*"

"Colored, ma'am," I said; "and dead."

"I see."

I told her: "It was my great-grandmother, and my great-great-grandfather, ma'am. They both got born wrong. On a plantation. A real plantation."

". . . I . . . *see.* I am . . . not interested."

"No, ma'am," I said, "I didn't think you would be."

Mrs. Pharr flicked a feather from the couch off her black taffeta sleeve. It settled next to her, and she pressed her finger on it.

I said: "You don't want us to walk no more."

". . . *Who?*"

"Charles Leroy and . . ."

"*Oh,*" she said, and looked up. ". . . I forbid either one of you to make use of my grounds together for any reason whatsoever."

She made a time for me to say: "Yes, ma'am."

"I am rearranging your free days in such a manner that they will not coincide with those of Charles Leroy, either on Thursday afternoons or on Sundays, ever."

". . . Yes, ma'am."

"If these arrangements do not suit you, your are free to give immediate notice of your departure. That is to say, you are free to leave."

I thought: *Leave?* Leave Charles Leroy? Or even leave *with* Charles Leroy? *Why* should we leave? There ain't nothing between us that's not right, nothing that ain't more than right. Nothing to run away for.

I made my back a little straighter. I said: "*Yes,* ma'am."

"Yes, what?"

"Like you telling me, ma'am. I'll stay."

"Just as you wish." Mrs. Pharr uncrossed her legs and stood up. She waited for me to pull the coffee table out of her way, and she went over to the mantelpiece to take a cigarette from one of the green china frogs. After it was lit, she turned around. Then she creased her forehead—like she wanted to give the idea she never expected to find me still there. "I am sure I have finished, unless you wish to say something further?"

I did wish. I said: "Excuse me, ma'am, but it wasn't wrong. Nothing about us is wrong."

"To *whom* do you . . ."

"*Please,*" I said, "*I want to say it wasn't wrong.*" I was talking too loud. Much too loud.

But Mrs. Pharr suddenly laughed. Her voice was excited, like a person who has just found some new answer. Or like a person who is mad with her own hurt. She said: "I actually believe you are *not* pretending. Then why did you come back that way, one by one? Do you only know guilt in *spells,* you colored people?" She turned towards the mantel and laughed again, standing hard.

I thought: I will not cry now. Course I will not cry.

She was there, without talking, for a while. Then she said, quiet: "Go downstairs, Lucille. You may go downstairs immediately. And be very careful in the future how you are seen to behave here. Be very careful."

When I had taken the coffee tray and I was out in the passage, I could still hear her saying: ". . . Be careful . . . Be very careful." But most probably that was just in my ears.

7

THE world keeps its shape, whatever you might think. Even though in your mind it could go flat as a squashed bouncing ball, or oval out too long. That's in your mind. So keep your pain out of the world; sing yourself a song when you ache. It don't matter if you can't recall any music, make your own music, that's what you here for. Sing your own why-songs to live. Wait for the right reason if you have to—but never fight time if the reason won't come when you want it. The time scale is different for every person, and quickness ain't rightness. Wait, wait. Just be sure to make your own music while you waiting.

Charles Leroy was sad when I told him what Mrs. Pharr had said. If he was angry, though, he kept it deep inside. I wanted him to shake with disgust against her, against all of them upstairs. And that he didn't do.

The first big change started with him watching me all the time around the house. The second came when I was the one who wouldn't look back. I could feel his eyes following me along whenever we were in the same room together. Only I felt something sneaky and shadowy about the way he did it. And I wouldn't sneak for my love.

Next, I even had to stop reading the history book on the shelf in the Music Room when I dusted there. Because I just would not sneak in that house.

It was only when Mrs. Pharr was with us that I looked at him— turning myself straight where he was so she could tell. I stared so blind then, I had to fight not to let my eyelids bat till I could swerve my whole body away to something else. I stood, and I bent over each exact piece of work, stiff with my pride and my shame.

If Mrs. Pharr went away, I let my blood run again, but I never turned to him alone. If he asked a question, I would answer him, short—and loud.

And once when I came out of my room in the helps' building, I found Charles Leroy standing waiting for me down the passage. When I tried to get by, he took my hand, and he said: "Lucille. She don't mind if we together *here*." I ripped free so fast I skinned my arm on the wall; then I had to run all the way back in with Celeste, and slam the door, and lean on it. Because I had almost slapped him.

So I was even more careful than Mrs. Pharr told me. Only, never for the reason she thought.

Living like that I expected the next month would be easier—but it just got worse as time passed. Somewhere around then, I stopped saying my prayers at night, and made a list instead. There was four things not to do, in my list, and one thing to do. They went:

> Number 1. Don't you feel dirty.
> Number 2. Don't you be afraid.
> Number 3. Don't you get angry.
> Number 4. Don't you look to blame.
and Number 5. You got to wait.

Some nights I added:

> Number 6. You can go on loving Charles Leroy;
> that part is all right.

Midsummer came so early it got ripe too soon, and the ripeness spoiled, and passed. By August, everything was limp and open— jellying in the heat. At night the house made a big, sucking yawn for the mosquitoes to whine in and sing circles around your sleeping blood.

Most weekends, Mr. Pharr and Mr. Robert took a couple extra days and drove to a beach hotel on the Gulf Coast. They usually went on Thursday afternoon and came back on Tuesday night, but sometimes they stayed later. Mr. Robert got real dark, and his teeth glistened when he talked. Celeste said they had moved the two women to the beach in July.

We all got white uniforms, and Mr. Pharr and Mr. Robert and even Mr. Sage dressed in white against the summer.

But not Mademoiselle nor Mrs. Pharr. Mrs. Pharr wore black because Mrs. Pharr wore black, and it could of been five thousand degrees in the middle of hell: Mrs. Pharr wore black. She stomped slow, up and down and around the house, only no slower than her winter stomp. Mrs. Pharr was not a seasonable woman.

One Wednesday afternoon, she sat on the piano stool in the Music Room until Mr. Pharr passed through from the gallery, and she told him: "We . . . we might all go to the beach . . . for a day."

I was dusting in the dining room with the door open, and I wondered how *her* voice could sound shy—and what had happened to the funny accent all of a sudden.

"Too hot to drive him. He's old, and he's too sick." Mr. Pharr wasn't going to stop walking, and he almost passed right across the open doorway; he hardly ever stayed with her unless Mr. Robert or Mr. Sage was there.

"Don't you think . . . ?" She waited for him to stop and listen. Then she said, softer: "Don't you think the fresh air, the fresh sea air, would be nice for him?"

"Nora, my God, he's dying. What do you want to take a dying man to the fresh sea air for?"

". . . We might all drive out one day, only for one night, and we could drive back the next day."

"Five hours out and five hours back for one night?"

"Or for two nights. We might all go for two nights, that would make three days in all."

"No."

"Why do you . . ."

"It would kill him. That would probably kill him."

"I rather wonder why you are so considerate of Père at this moment." Some of the softness had glassed over, even though she was trying not to let it.

After a beat he said: "Well, what *else* do you want? Go on, drop it, don't sit there and stare at me, if you have a load to drop, drop it."

". . . I don't think a drive would be particularly bad for Père."

"Oh, hell."

"*What* did you say?"

"Nora, he sleeps all day. He's tired from dying. He's so tired he even hates to write a check."

Mrs. Pharr was quiet.

"Well, he does, doesn't he?"

"Not because he's tired."

". . . No?"

"My father is spending large amounts of money."

"Whenever you start talking about his money, you stop saying *Père,* and you start saying *my father.*"

"That happens to be the case."

"*Meaning?*"

"I only say he is spending large amounts of money."

"He's got large amounts of money to spend. Unless he wants to bury it with him, like a pharaoh. Besides, this is his house. You built it for him, and you put it in his name."

"The house is the least of it."

"No, sure not. It's the money I take with me on a weekend. That's what you're getting at."

"I haven't said . . ."

"You *never* say what you mean. Make you feel better if people talk about Mrs. Pharr's husband who goes on weekends like a poor nigger?"

"If people talk about your weekends, I rather doubt that it will be because of money. Besides, there is no reason you should ever be poor, with or without my father's aid. You have your business."

"I've been trying to explain to you for the last year: *business . . . is bad.*"

"Please, I ask you not to shout."

"You *make* me shout with those damn silly ideas you grab onto. Christ, you get some idea, and you push it, and you push it . . . Now we have to take everybody out to the *sea air.*"

"It was . . ." Mrs. Pharr's skirt swished when she got up and moved. "I thought . . . I haven't been able to . . . to sit on a beach since I was very small, I . . . I could . . . even hire a nurse . . . to be with Père for only two days . . ."

"What?" A chuckle edged under the word.

It was in that second that Mrs. Pharr knocked the blue vase off the mantelpiece. The vase made one hollow crash that hushed almost before I heard it. But I knew right away what it was.

Mr. Pharr quit leaning on the door. He put his hand up to his mouth, and chewed on a fingernail.

There was a thing like a wild babiness, and something more in her voice, when she said: "I would *like* to go to the *beach*."

Then the sound of his laughing sank into the heavy carpet and into the walls of the house. It would of echoed in any other house as big. It was that kind of a laugh. He said: "Honey, what would you do on a beach?"

". . . Don't . . . don't say *honey* to me."

"What would you?" He put his arms out and walked from the doorway back into the room, smiling and laughing at once. "You feeling like a beach girl? Is that what you want to be, a girl on a beach?"

"Don't . . ."

"Now, come on, give me one of those little peck-kisses . . ."

"*Stand where you are.*"—There was the accent, and the right voice too. She didn't shout it exactly, but her tone was a tone felt like it might of come from that hard face in the painting. She said: "If there are any orders to be given in this house, I will give them. If I decide to take a few days to go to the beach, or to go anyplace at all of my choosing, I will take such days, and I will go. I am not sure where you think you are, and to whom you imagine you are speaking. I say what I *wish* here."

"Okay, okay." He wasn't laughing at all now. "Say it."

". . . I have said I want to go to the beach, to . . . to a hotel. Some weekend."

"Which weekend?"

"I will see, I do not know at the moment."

"*I've* got to know, I have to set my plans."

"Yes, I'm sure you do."

"Well? Which weekend?"

"I will inform you when the idea particularly pleases me."

". . . Want to go tomorrow?"

"No."

"Why not?"

"I do not want to go tomorrow."

"Okay. Well, you tell me."

"I will tell you."

"You can feel *free* to tell me."

Mrs. Pharr coughed. "I will tell you."

"Okay. Right."

He had gone out into the hall before she asked him: "Do . . . do you have enough money for tomorrow?"

"I think so. Should I go and look?"

"Yes," she called. "Yes, my dear. Yes, of course, you go and look."

For a while, there wasn't no sound at all. Then her skirt swished again; it stopped sudden, as if she'd caught it with her hands.

I wasn't going to go right on in and clean up the vase, because she would be sure to see I must of heard. So I went down to the kitchen and spent about five minutes trying to fight off Celeste (she hadn't heard but half of it, with her head in the dumb-waiter); and then I went up to the Music Room carrying my dustrag like I didn't know what had happened. I was feeling pretty bad about the vase, and a little sad for Mrs. Pharr, busting that wonderful thing herself. I was even going to tell her how sorry I felt, whether she understood or not.

But when I got upstairs, Mrs. Pharr was sitting on the piano stool again—and before I could talk, she really started to play.

I plain stood and watched her—with my mouth open, I think; I certainly wouldn't of said she knew how. Mrs. Pharr just hadn't seemed to me like a woman who knew how to play on anything, and get music out of it. The tune was sort of whiny and awful, because the notes that did make a noise was all sour. But even so—there it was. And there was two stranger things besides. First, that she never watched what she was doing: she stared straight out the window onto the gallery, and she didn't even know I was there. And second, when I looked down at the fireplace, I couldn't find a single piece of the vase left anywhere.

Backing out of the door, I let my eyes pass over the bronze hand, delicate and clutching in its black wood holder—then the painting above. I was thinking: *she* wouldn't ever of played on no sour piano. But I had to hold still then, and squint. Because, in the darkening room, one last heat haze from the sun warmed over Mrs. Sage's neck and the bottom half of her face. And I wondered how I could of seen her there so many times every day—from so many different angles—

and not once taken a notice of her teeth showing. And I wondered too, how a person could keep such a nasty expression on their face —*and* grin.

Then I got this pewpy feeling right on the back of my neck, like you get when you go outside barefoot, and step on a caterpillar. It was a good thing Mrs. Pharr had enough to do inside her own mind, account of I couldn't help to put my hands up and my own face must of been a study for a second.

I went back down the stairs, slow; listening to that awful tune.

The next weekend, Mr. Pharr was away for longer, till Wednesday night. And the Friday after, Mr. Robert and him left alone again. While they was away, Mrs. Pharr went and called up some nursing service in New Orleans on the phone, and hired a nurse. But she only made me call up again at nine o'clock Monday morning, soon as they opened, and cancel the order.

She never did go to the beach.

The last week in August, the heat was so solid it made you bend. My afternoons off, I couldn't stand to do anything from the waist down. So I generally took a big pan of butter beans from the kitchen and walked out and sat by the edge of the pecan orchard. Over the fence there, one big oak stretched three of its branches in a cup-shape —and the moss and the leaves made a place that was always shady. Shelling beans and checking rows of naked pecan trees, most times I fell asleep.

Once on my way out, all oily and logy in the choked air, I met Charles Leroy. I saw him soon as I stepped down from the kitchen. He had the Cadillac standing outside, and he was polishing it.

It was always a special thing to be near him, even though it happened so many times a day. Now I kept on the stone path, and I felt the air thicken up against my body as I went closer: I had to push through the stillness to pass him by. I could tell he was watching me, and I hoped he wouldn't talk.

But just as I got there, I knew he was going to.

"You come across the water pitcher?" he asked, "I been looking for . . ."

"In the kitchen sink," I said.

"*Hey.*"

I stopped.

Charles Leroy raised one foot and rubbed his shoe on the other pants leg. "Where you going?"

"It's my afternoon off."

"I know that."

"Going out to sit. See if I can't find some cool in the shade."

"Cille," he said, "what's wrong?"

"With what?"

"You."

"Oh," I said; "that's a heavy story for a summer's day."

". . . Why you mad at me?"

"I ain't mad."

"You been mad for a good while now. Ever since . . ."

"I ain't mad," I said.

Then Charles Leroy told me: "Cille. We could get married."

I studied a path some snake had wriggled out in the hot mud—while I shook my head no.

"Why not?"

I made my fingers flat; then I lifted my arm and put them on the top of my head. "My hair is just boiling," I said. "Just from the two minutes I been in the sun."

"Why can't we?"

"We can't. It ain't right."

"*Why* ain't it right?"

I said: "Now you talking like my little brother used to."

"*Why ain't it right?*"

"Charles Leroy . . . it ain't, that's all. I won't let her make us do that."

"Make us? Who, Mrs. Pharr?" He turned away and spit. "If you don't want to, you plain don't. Ain't no more about it."

". . . I do want to, Charles Leroy." I spoke low, trying to make it sound simple, without no importance.

But he told me: "You can just drop your fool hand *down* when you say that."

I let it fall.

"If you do," he said, "then how come you care what she thinks?"

"I care," I said.

"You making up excuses."

"Charles Leroy," I said, "I ain't got no call to make up excuses. Only I won't get married that way."

He leaned over me. "*What* way?"

Then I thought. But there was just one kind of thing I never could explain to him—the kind that needed explaining. I said: "Like we *should*. Like something was wrong. Like . . . something was dirty."

"Ain't nothing dirty, Cille."

"I know. But it would make it dirty to get married that way."

Charles Leroy rubbed his chamois once across the black metal, and left it bunched up there. The streak behind had circles of rainbows, shimmering and changing as it dried, like oil on water. But when it did dry, the rainbows dried with it.

I blinked in the heat waves that swam out from the car. They made the pecan trees swerve and ripple all at the same time: rows and rows of hula dancers tatooed on a white sailor boy.

"Cille. If you don't want to get married to me, why don't you just say so?"

". . . I done told you I do want to."

"Well . . . just *what* is it you waiting for, then?"

That was even harder to say. "I don't know."

"Oh, you *don't?* You don't know, and you asking me to wait here too, while you . . . mealy around trying to find out."

"Charles Leroy," I said, quiet. "I never asked you to wait."

"Lord, will you *shut up?*" He made a stinging slap with his whole arm on the roof of the car. It was going to leave a mark.

I stretched my shoulders back, and held on tight to the pan. "*Listen,* Charles Leroy," I said. "I never asked you to wait, and I ain't asking now. Yes, I want to marry you. Because I love you. But the other thing I want is for you to go ahead now and do exactly what you think is right, just like I'm *not* doing what I know is wrong. And whatever you do, for pity's sake, *leave me alone.*"

Then I hiked the pan up higher, and went on out through the orchard to sit under the oak tree by the fence.

8

CELESTE held off till we were alone in our room that night to ask: "What you needling him along for, che?"

"Ye gods and little fishes," I said.

"Ain't none of my business, course," Celeste told me, "only you plain can't crawl in and out of yourself fast as you been doing without cutting some of the corners on my curiosity."

We were flopped on the beds, naked, drinking these cups of weak coffee that wouldn't keep us awake; Celeste had carried them up from the kitchen.

I put my cup down on the floor, part way through a swallow. "All you-all make me want to laugh. Or cry."

"You a silly one," she said, "if you get to capture my meaning of the word. You act like the type of a person was hanging pretty far out to have herself one good time . . . but you don't act like you was having it. Much. I don't think."

I undid the bun on the back of my neck, and shook it out. Then I brushed my hair into two halves, and started to braid it for the night. I said: "Don't nobody understand."

"*Can't* nobody understand. You ain't human. *Plain not human*: you want to have your cake, and you don't want to eat it." She rolled over on her side and put down her coffee.

Nothing I could think of to say was worth the while.

"If you don't want to get married," Celeste asked, "why don't you just go ahead and give it to him anyway? Got to sooner or later. Can't just go on putting it in cold water."

"Give him what?"

Celeste lifted up her shoulders and her eyebrows, like she was talking to a foreigner or a very dumb person.

"No," I said. "I could of before. But I can't now."

"Why not, you sewed up or something?"

". . . Not there," I said.

Celeste told me: "You ain't one to be scared. You ain't chicken-shit."

"No," I said, "I ain't."

She sighed, and scratched her tummy. "Don't rub the heels of your hands in your eyes," she said, "it ain't the least little bit good for them. Why don't you make it easy on him and tell him you plain decided not to? None of my business, course."

"I ain't decided not to do nothing. I ain't *decided* nothing."

". . . Better not tell him that."

"He knows."

"What he say?"

"You heard him," I said, "you was practically making a dent in the screen door."

"Didn't hear the last part."

"What happened, was there an earthquake?"

"No," said Celeste, "the peas was shooting out the hole in the pressure cooker."

"Lord. Could of exploded."

"It didn't could of," she said. "It did."

". . . Messy?"

Celeste said: "Oh, brother."

"Got to watch that."

"Anyway," she said, "what he say?"

I wrapped a rubber-band around the second braid. I told her: "Don't know, che. I think . . . I think maybe . . . he still wants to marry me."

"Even after you done told him about all them things that are activating in your brain?"

". . . I think so."

Celeste stretched, and put her chin in one hand, and breathed deep, looking at the ceiling. "Most serious boy," she said.

I yawned. I was wishing that she would go on to sleep, so I could be by myself. I all the time wanted to be by myself now, to wipe my mind.

Out of the night, moths and mosquitoes and other bugs batted against the window screen, hungry for the yellow light. Maybe there was thirty of them there, pushing to get in. Sometimes you could see the flick of a bat that flashed across to eat one.

Celeste wanted to know: "If you ain't happy, why don't you get out of here and go back to New Orleans, che? Or go anyplace. Go get another job."

"Go *where?*"

"Lots of jobs."

"I ain't got noplace to go and no reason."

"That's all right, don't get mad."

"No reason to run away from *nothing*. I ain't going till I *know* where I'm going." My voice kept getting louder.

"I see exactly what you mean, now let's just skip the subject."

I all but yelled: "I plain *don't feel like* going away."

"That's okay, honey," said Celeste, "you do like you want. That's okay."

We had stripped the light bulb clean of any shade, so it wouldn't shine so dull: it was the only light in the room. It hung on a black cord from the ceiling, like the one on the gallery of Mama's house.

There was a flat bug walking around it now, making monster-shadows on the wall. Looked like it would be too hot for no bug. I said so.

"What does?" Celeste asked.

"The light bulb."

"Let him alone," she told me, "that bug don't mind."

But it made me mad to see him there, stepping so quick and busy around the bulb—thinking he was going one long way—and the glass getting hotter. I stood up and hit out with my hand.

Soon as the cord started to move, I could see the room was full of lots of different shadows I hadn't known about. They had been there, though, just the same. They was pinned under all the furniture legs, and they reached way out and back, swinging in opposite time to the bulb, keeping away from it.

Except for the one biggest shadow; the biggest one of all. It moved with the light. Because the bug didn't fall off. He squatted and stuck, fighting to hold there, in the heat that would finally burn him—instead of flying away to live. That dumb bug.

Celeste stretched again, and kicked the sheet to the foot of her bed. "See," she said, "it ain't no use."

I sat down to cut my nails, and Celeste looked over the newspaper and read me the two criminal cases Mrs. Pharr had marked. After that, she turned out the light.

Alone with the blackness, I made my list. Then I lay and watched till I could see the moon-fog, where it bent through the window. I tried not to think of the things that hurt in my life. But I couldn't remember nothing that was easy and nice to think about instead. So I tried to wash my mind with the heavy August moon, watching till the darks of my eyes opened to let it in, and I could find time to go to sleep.

Sometime in the early morning, I couldn't stop dreaming:

Much as I dusted everything, the more dust came, and it was my fault. I passed my rag in fast circles over the black-top table, but every time I cleaned to one end, the other end had already filmed over. And while I tried to clean this table, all the rest of the furniture was a shame. I was in the Japanese Room. Somebody had thrown open the windows and the curtains to let the sun reach into the staleness, and tons of silver dust swirled through the orange streams that cut across to burn out the damp and bake the rot away. The dust moved and twisted up, laying soft on every surface, hardening in the air. But it was my fault I couldn't clean that dust away; I was just not doing a right job, and it was all my fault.

Besides me, there was two other people in the room, and more kept wandering through the house and around the gallery outside. Mama sat on the floor next to Mrs. Pharr's feet, looking up at her. Sometimes I saw them through the dust, and sometimes I only heard their voices. But that was all right, because otherwise they would of seen how bad I was cleaning the dust away.

They said:

MRS. PHARR: I am sure such a very interesting case as this one, is going to be worth some of our time.

MAMA: Oh, yes, ma'am.

MRS. PHARR: Last week there was a most interesting case in the *Times-Picayune* which I am quite sure you did not read about.

MAMA: No, ma'am.

MRS. PHARR: You must be more careful to read these interesting articles. Else, why do you imagine I trouble to bring them to the attention of everyone?

MAMA: Yes, ma'am.

MRS. PHARR: Yes, indeed.

MAMA: Yes, indeed, ma'am.

MRS. PHARR: I did not mean for you to copy what I say.

MAMA: No, ma'am?

MRS. PHARR: No indeed, no indeed.

MAMA: Oh, no *indeed,* ma'am, no *indeed.*

MRS. PHARR: Stop that. Now I am sure you will agree in such a case as this we must leave it all up to the Coroner.

MAMA: Ma'am?

MRS. PHARR: To the Coroner. If the girl has done a bad thing they will put her in the morgue, and if it is a very bad thing, then they will have to bury her.

MAMA: Bury who, ma'am?

MRS. PHARR: Bury Lucille, dear.

MAMA: Oh, yes, ma'am.

MRS. PHARR: Eat one of my fingers.

MAMA: Oh, no, ma'am.

MRS. PHARR: *Eat* one.

MAMA: Yes, ma'am.

MRS. PHARR: Not the one with the ring on it, for God's sake.

MAMA: The Lord God is all good.

MRS. PHARR: *Bien sûr, bien sûr.* What are you doing?

MAMA: *Ma'am,* breaking off all my fingers too, *ma'am.*

MRS. PHARR: Ah, no indeed, dear, no, no, no. *Lady*fingers are *white.*

MAMA: Oh, course, ma'am.

MRS. PHARR: You might just as well throw yours away, dear.

MAMA: I did, ma'am, already.

MRS. PHARR: Well, I can see you have some intelligence. I am sure we will have no trouble with you. If the girl is bad, better to bury her.

MAMA: If the girl is bad, she is dead.

MRS. PHARR: Well, I can see you have some intelligence.

MAMA: I had a son who was bad, and he is dead too.

MRS. PHARR: Well, I can see you have some intelligence.

MAMA: When your child is bad, your child is dead.

MRS. PHARR: Ma'am.

MAMA: Ma'am.

MRS. PHARR: Well, I can see you have some intelligence.

MAMA: Oh, I'm scared.

MRS. PHARR: How do you say?

MAMA: Save me, save me. Dear Lord God, save me.

MRS. PHARR: Better have one more ladyfinger.

MAMA: The Lord is punishing me for being born black.

MRS. PHARR: There, I just *knew* you had some intelligence.

MAMA: The Lord is punishing me for the color of my children.

MRS. PHARR: *Bien sûr, bien sûr.* Like it says in the newspaper.

MAMA: The Lord is punishing me for my husband's blood.

MRS. PHARR: Watch me, now. Look at here, I'm a Swiss cow. No moo, but the best French on the bayou.

MAMA: Save me. Dear Lord God, save me.

MRS. PHARR: *Pew*py-*dew*py, *rum*py-dumpy, shit-brindle brown.

MAMA: Save me, save me, save me. Dear Lord God, save me. Forgive me, dear Lord God. She's out of tune, and I can't read, and *I hate ladyfingers.*

I saw Mama then, between two dust-drifts. She was sitting with her legs out at the foot of the couch, in front of the screen. But the couch was empty, and dust was already settling over the cushion where Mrs. Pharr had been.

I ran to Mama.

ME: Mama, get up, now. She ain't here no more, Mama, you get up and don't be scared, now. Get up, Mama. Get up.

But I couldn't touch her. When I leaned down to take her arm, the dust flashed in a sparkling cloud, and each tiny piece reflected the sun into my face, so I couldn't even see her. When I straightened, she was gone.

CLARENCE'S VOICE OUT OF THE DUST: Hurry and clean.

ME: I'm trying. Where's Mama?

MAMA'S VOICE: I'm here, honey, I love you. I love all my children.

CLARENCE: That's a laugh. Hurry and clean.

ME: Mama, it's not true what she said. I *ain't* bad.

MAMA: I'd love you even if you was bad.

Clarence laughed.

ME: Don't laugh, man, she means it.

CLARENCE: You'll see.

ME: Mama, tell Clarence.

MAMA: Clarence? . . . *What* Clarence?

ME: My brother Clarence.

MAMA: You don't have no brother Clarence. Your brother Clarence died.

CLARENCE: Hurry and clean, you ain't got much time. Hurry and clean.

Then we were on the platform, in the swamp. The platform was really the gallery of Mama's house, sticking out over the bayou. The dust still poured through the air; but it was all gathered into separate white clouds now. Cloud after cloud passed around me, hundreds of them. I had to clean the sparkling gray dust off the bark of the trees that edged the gallery. "Thank God for a Garden" echoed from somewhere, louder or quieter, however it felt. The Coroner was dressed in a black robe with a black hood, digging a grave in the quicksand next to me. It wasn't easy, because the spade kept sinking down out of sight, and the grave filling with water.

Something was wrong, and I knew it, and I felt it. And then I saw it: everything and everybody there was different shades of black and white—the same as in a moving picture. It was just all black and white. Except for me.

THE CORONER: I done told everybody to go home, except for her. Dead is dead.

ME: Who's dead?

CLARENCE'S VOICE: Don't ask questions. Hurry and clean.

THE CORONER: I mean to tell you, I am sure this has been a very interesting case; but now we know her father is dead, and now we know her brother is dead, and now we know *she* is dead, school is out.

ME: She who?

CLARENCE: Oh, hurry and clean.

ME: I want to know who's dead.

THE CORONER: I am quite sure you better tell her not to talk. It ain't fitting.

ADELAIDE's VOICE: I would just like to inquire why the poor thing died.

THE CORONER: She died because she was bad.

ADELAIDE: Oh, the poor thing.

ME: *I* ain't dead.

THE CORONER: Now don't start.

ME: I ain't, and I can prove it.

THE CORONER: You can't prove nothing without no friends.

ME: What do I want friends for?

THE CORONER: To prove you ain't bad. Dead, I mean.

ME: Ask anybody. You can ask anybody. If Charles Leroy was here . . .

THE CORONER: Charles Leroy?

CHARLES LEROY: All I said was, she wouldn't marry me.

THE CORONER: *You* wouldn't marry *him?*

ME: It wasn't right to, like that.

THE CORONER: But it *was* right to go walking with him? *Like that.*

ME: Then it was different.

CLARENCE: It ain't no use, honey. Try to get your cleaning done while you still here.

THE CORONER: Is that all the friends you got?

ME: You can ask anybody. Everybody knows I ain't bad.

THE CORONER: This is mucky going. Slush, slush. Name a name.

ME: Anybody. You ask Celeste.

THE CORONER: Celeste?

CELESTE: What I'm referring to, I told her to get off it before she got burned, and I hit the light bulb so it swung way out and back in the air, but she got mad, and squatted and stuck there, and she wouldn't fly off.

THE CORONER: You mean to tell me you wouldn't fly off a stinking light bulb?

ME: I didn't feel like it. Anyway, where was I going to fly to?

CELESTE: Lots of light bulbs.

ME: But I ain't done nothing to fly away for.

THE CORONER: Talk, talk, talk. I really do think this is one big waste of time.

CLARENCE: If you don't hurry with that dustrag, you going to have to leave your cleaning half-finished.

ME: I don't care about the cleaning.

CLARENCE: What else you done on earth?

THE CORONER: She even talks to herself.

ME: I was talking to my brother Clarence.

THE CORONER: You ain't got no brother Clarence. Your brother Clarence is dead.

ME: He ain't dead. I was talking to him.

THE CORONER: Clarence?

On the other side of the Coroner, there was a row of coffins. They made me walk along and look into each one. The first coffin was the marble bathtub from the white cemetery, and laying inside was our father's body. All the rest was regular wood coffins. Adelaide's mama was in one, and there was a little drawer-coffin for Jewel's baby. I hated to look in the next one, because I knew what I would see. But I had to: it was Clarence's body. The next coffin was empty.

ME: Clarence, you get up.

THE CORONER: How is he going to get up, if he's dead?

ME: He ain't dead. Mama . . . please, Mama, tell him to get up. Please, Mama.

But I couldn't find Mama. But I saw Dan standing alongside the Coroner, with a Mardi-gras mask on his face. The mask was made to look exactly like Dan, and it was smiling some.

ME: Dan, where's Mama?

Dan wouldn't talk.

ME: Take that mask off, and tell me where Mama is.

THE CORONER: What mask?

ME: Come on, Dan.

THE CORONER: I done said what mask?

I reached up and ripped the corner where the white elastic attached. It snapped free and I lifted the mask away. There wasn't no head behind it; Dan's neck ended in a clean stump with the bones sticking out.

ME: Dan . . .

DAN: She killed the fish, the ass-fool, she killed it with a stick.

ME: Listen, Dan . . .

DAN: Then she put the hook in my heel and she killed me.

THE CORONER: You ain't dead. It says here: My son Daniel has went crazy like I said he would.

ME: Mama didn't say that.

DAN: Oh, yes, she did.

THE CORONER: You convinced now?

ME: I ain't convinced I'm bad.

THE CORONER: Dead, you mean.

ME: But all I was doing was waiting.

THE CORONER: Waiting? Waiting for what?

ME: I don't know. If I knew, I wouldn't of waited.

THE CORONER: The trouble with you, you should of been dead a long time ago.

ME: Now look, I had to find out where I was going.

THE CORONER: By *waiting?* The only way to find out where you going is to go.

DAN: Ass-fool.

THE CORONER: You shut up.

ME: I had to find out my reason for living.

THE CORONER: Then why did you stop living to wait?

ME: Well, anyhow, if I don't have no reason to live, I got *less* reason to die.

The Coroner laughed.

THE CORONER: Sweetheart, *you don't need no reason for that.*

ME: But who would want to live here? Just tell me, who would want to live in this stupid world here? Look at it. Look at yourself. Look at everybody. It's all black and white. The whole stupid thing, it's black and white.

THE CORONER: Naturally, it is. Well, listen at her talk, with the fool color she's got.

ME: Like a picture. All of it. You just stupid people in a stupid black and white picture.

THE CORONER: Here now, don't you go calling me no names. Technicolor riffraff.

ME: I don't care about you. I'll get out of here, I will. I don't care. I'll go on up to New York City and do modeling work, I will. Up there a person can be any color she wants. Up there a person can be free.

THE CORONER: Before or after she gets embalmed?

ME: I ain't dead.

THE CORONER: Course you is.

ME: I ain't. You so stupid, you don't know what you talking about.

THE CORONER: Lord, I swear I never saw such a sassy cadaver. I must be getting old.

ME: I don't give a hoot what you say. I *ain't* dead, and I don't *want* to be dead.

THE CORONER: You want to be dead because you can't live. Comes to the same thing. Slush, slush. Slush, slush. Slush, slush.
I ran to our father's coffin, and knelt down in the mud beside it.

ME: Father, please. Please, I got to know how to live, now.

OUR FATHER: I'm dead.

ME: Tell me anyway.

OUR FATHER: You want me to read to you?

ME: *No.* Not now. I want to live. I want you to tell me how I can live. Tell me what I can do.

OUR FATHER: Do? You can't do nothing. Not likely. Not in this flat land.

ME: Well I don't care. I'll get out of here, I will.

OUR FATHER: Fixing to run away?

ME: No, not that. I ain't done a single thing to run away for. I ain't done wrong.

OUR FATHER: Then you *can't* get out of here. Can you? You can't even leave; you can't do nothing at all. Not in the likes of a place like this.

ME: I told you, I don't care.

OUR FATHER: Oh, but you got to. You was born to care.

ME: But I won't. I promise I won't. Not anymore. Just let me live.

OUR FATHER: Live? In a place . . .

ME: *Slop* on the place.

OUR FATHER: You can't slop on the place. Only on yourself.

ME: Slop on the white people.

OUR FATHER: You can't.

ME: Slop on the colored people.

OUR FATHER: You can't. You can't even slop on God.

THE RECORD: Thank God for a garden,
            And for the fish in the sea;
            Thaaaaaank God for a gaardeen . . .

OUR FATHER: In this flat land?

ME: Father, please. Please, *I want to live.*

OUR FATHER: Don't be ridiculous.
I heard voices, and I stood up and turned around. The dust was thinning out. Between the trees, I could see most all of the people I ever knew, and other people I didn't know yet; people I never would know.

ME: All of you who can say I ain't bad please raise your right hand. Nobody did.

THE CORONER: And she *will* keep right on saying *bad*.

ME: All right. *Dead*, then.

Nobody moved. Then another cloud lifted, and I saw the Upward Brass Band in the middle of everything. They was the ones had been playing "Thank God for a Garden"; it wasn't the record, it was them.

ME: Cousin Wila ain't here.

THE CORONER: She couldn't come to the wake, she's working for some Indian in Santa Fe. She ain't a real cousin, anyway. Sent the band, though. Such a lovely woman.

ME: Marbelle ain't here.

THE CORONER: Who-all is Marbelle?

ME: She's a lady I met on the train. She knows I ain't dead.

THE CORONER: Says you.

ME: It's true.

THE CORONER: Everybody met a lady on a train once. That's what they all say. Mostly the boys, though. Anyway, it don't count.

ME: Well, you just prove I'm dead. Go on, now, you just prove it.

THE CORONER: Read the evidence.

Our father's voice was the voice that did it. It was only one stanza, but he read it slow. Much slower than he usually read.

THE CORONER: That proves that. Most important piece of evidence we heard yet.

ME: Foo. If any one of you can explain it, I'll give him a nickel. I don't believe there's one ounce of meaning in it.

OUR FATHER'S VOICE: Oh, you don't, huh?

ME: What's that White Rabbit doing there?

THE WHITE RABBIT: Tea Parties. Tea for Two. Slews and slews of ladyfingers. I was just going, what time is it?

ME: You better put that watch away, Rabbit. You in the wrong dream.

THE WHITE RABBIT: Oh, no I ain't, che. No I ain't. *You is.*

THE CORONER: Talking to herself again.

ME: I was not, I was talking to the White Rabbit.

THE CORONER: Rabbit? In this swamp? *White?* You should of been dead a long time ago.

ME: Who *are* you? Are you God?

THE CORONER: Me? Sweet Jesus, no. Man, you do latch onto some rough ideas.

ME: Then who are you?

THE CORONER: I am sure you know why I wish to speak with you. Why, we probably have the same great-great-grandfather. That's what. *Pew*py-dewpy, *rum*py-dumpy . . .

ME: That's what I figured. I know who you are.

I grabbed her spade and swung it at the face hid under the black hood. I used the edge, and I hit her again and again—till I could feel the flesh go pulpy—till the blood squeezed out and ran over her robe in thick streams. Then I dropped the spade and pushed back the hood to see her mashed face.

But it wasn't Mrs. Pharr. It was Mama.

MAMA: My child is killing me. Reach me a glass of water, my child is killing me.

ME: Oh, Mama. Why didn't you say it was you?

MAMA: My child is killing me, my child is killing me. Save me.

ME: I didn't mean to do that. I didn't know it was you. Hush, Mama. Hush, please forgive me. I didn't mean it. Please, Mama.

Then I was laying in the coffin, sinking slow into the quicksand. Charles Leroy lay next to me, sideways, and we were both looking up.

CHARLES LEROY: What do you see?

ME: Everything.

CHARLES LEROY: Everything how?

ME: The way the trees bend in, way high. The way they make a place for us in the world. The flatness is gone now. I see it. I do see it.

CHARLES LEROY: How does it feel?

ME: It feels right.

CHARLES LEROY: Now you won't mind so much being dead.

ME: Hold me, Charles Leroy. I'm scared. Hold me, stay with me.

CHARLES LEROY: I can't stay.

He put his arms around my middle, and his mouth opened over mine. There wasn't much room in the coffin, so he had to lay on top of me. He put his legs exact over my legs, like he was plastered against my body, and he was heavy, but I loved his heaviness. Then we didn't have our clothes on, and I could feel the good heat that began in him, where his legs joined, and I could feel it coming into me, pushing inside myself and spreading there. I strained up and tried to make us grow into one.

CHARLES LEROY: Be still. I got to go.

ME: No, no. Not now.

CHARLES LEROY: You don't even know what you doing.

ME: I do know. *Now* I do know.

CHARLES LEROY: It's too late, honey. You already dead. We both dead. You made me my coffin too.

ME: I ain't, we ain't. Look: I got all the pieces fitted into me now. Feel there. That's Jewel. And here is Marbelle. And this part is Cousin Wila. And over here is our father. It's all right now.

CHARLES LEROY: Too late.

ME: But look at me. I've got the right pieces now. I'm so black I'm blue.

CHARLES LEROY: Too late.

ME: And I'm so white I'm blue.

CHARLES LEROY: Too late.

ME: My mama is the blue River, and I'm all right now.

CHARLES LEROY: Too late, too late.

ME: But I didn't do no wrong. I didn't do no crime.

THE CORONER'S VOICE FROM WAY OFF: She committed the crime of never staying happy. In the beginning, God created the Heaven and . . .

ME: But I *could be* happy *now*.

CHARLES LEROY: Now is too late. And could be never was.

He held my arms down and pulled away from me, unsticking the warmth between us like adhesive tape. Overhead, I saw the trees suddenly weave through each other and wind down, turning into the flat coffin-top and blackness.

ME: (*almost in Mama's voice*) Not in the swamp, don't bury me in the swamp. The swamp don't need me. Save me, come back, Charles Leroy, save me. The swamp don't care. Oh, God, save me, dear Lord God, save me, I never wanted to be dead. Dear Lord God, save me, save me, save . . .

I tried to sit up, but I couldn't. I had opened my eyes and stared for a minute at the beginning of the pale white morning, before I knew I was holding the sheet stretched across my own body.

I looked at Celeste, asleep naked on her bed. And I took deep gut-breaths of the growing day.

9

ABOUT the second week in October, summer sneezed behind a limp wrist, and gave up. By the first of November, you couldn't even smell the duckpond outside the kitchen door anymore.

Every time the seasons switch, I always get a new wonder about life. Every silly time; I plain can't help it. Did I ever really decide to slit my own throat, I would have to up and do it in the middle of one long season. Winter, probably. But if I waited till the earth began to change again, I'd forget I had seen that before, and I'd lose the urge to stop breathing, and get curious all over again. I guess life just has a way of goosing you along, if you not careful.

Mrs. Pharr was careful. She put her fan in mothballs, and took back our white uniforms, and stopped ordering the soup cold, and quit shining through her powder; but otherwise, she didn't show no difference.

Mr. Pharr and Mr. Robert moved their women off the beach and back to New Orleans. (The Celeste Dumb-Waiter News Service.)

And Mr. Sage decided he still wasn't ready to die.

The start of each season, Mademoiselle got mad with the weather. She would put her head out into the first new smell and say, annoyed: "Now, you *see*? It begins."—like God was at it again. Then she told everybody how in France it never got so cold, or so hot, or so wet. Then she shut the window and sat in her straight-backed chair, and sewed into the next season.

This time, though, my wonder for the change didn't last very long. Because I knew it wasn't going to help me and Charles Leroy get used to living like that. We kept right on knotting up whenever we had to be together, and there was no easy way for us to talk. Sometimes I would meet him by surprise, head-on—and the bones in my breast circled tighter with the want. But I made my muscles hard and held my breath not to let it show.

And some mornings, I woke with my mind empty and clean— dizzy against the sleep-logged hurt that stretched inside, groping its way through me to take hold again. I could feel it moving. But if I lay very quiet, I could sometimes stay numb and stop from remembering where I was or why I should be sad. I would tell myself: don't you worry, it's just a little hurt—maybe something that somebody said yesterday; or it's an old hurt trying to come back—like the one when you had to leave school. Only, if I could lie to myself about that for a minute, I still couldn't stop from thinking about my love and my one big happiness. And then I would remember how the hurt and the happiness both came from the same place, and that they was the same thing. The hardest time in life is when you really learn you can't separate all-good from all-bad, and you begin to wonder why no silly woman ever had to eat no goddam apple in the first place and find out the difference between them, if she wasn't going to be able to keep them apart. And then you can't understand: if she was so set on discovering *good* and *bad*, why couldn't she of learned a little something about *right* and *wrong* while she was at it, and passed *that* on?

The thing that made me maddest was Mrs. Pharr's believing I acted like I did on account of her teaching me to do right.

Once in the upstairs hall, she said to me: "Lucille, it is necessary that I tell you how pleased I am to see the way you are behaving. My very first impression of you was a pleasant one, and it is always nice to know we are not mistaken in our first impressions."

I said: "Yes, ma'am," and waxed the floor harder.

Mrs. Pharr kept on: "It seems that many colored people have bad instincts, because of the manner in which they have been instructed, or because they simply do not know. However, I do see that you have taken my lesson seriously, and after all, the examination of a strong person is not how much she may know, but how well she is able to fight off the bad instincts she has, when she is *told* she has them by someone who *does* know."

I had to fight off a new one right then that was instructing me to clip her over the head with the wax-can, so I shut up.

But when I think back, I can't be mad with poor Mrs. Pharr. She was Queen of the Not, but she *was* a queen, and that was what she wanted to be; that was her reason.

A time of hers came on a morning in January, two weeks before I had to leave Will-o-Wilds.

I was cleaning in the Music Room. Mr. Pharr and Mr. Robert was there, playing a game of checkers on a card table they had set up in the corner by the French windows. Winter sunlight drooped over them, cold and wet and clear, breaking on hard furniture edges to thin and splay out in the steam-heated air. I passed my rag, gentle.

Mr. Sage and Mrs. Pharr was talking in the Japanese Room, and when he started to shout, I sort of figured I better go down to the kitchen. But I didn't want it to look like I was going for any special reason. And anyhow, Mr. Pharr and Mr. Robert went right on with their checker game: they wasn't paying no mind at first.

Mr. Sage's voice wavered and grated when he tried to make it loud. He was saying: ". . . I don't give a damn if they do hear me, somebody should hear me while I'm still alive, I think. Nothing but sit and make believe, every day, every week, every year . . . I *will* shout if I want to, damn it. The same sad story, and everybody grins up and down, and we all know, but nobody says a word. Each person talks his part, according to the way the game is supposed to be, and goes to bed and sleeps in peace with his lying soul. Living on the surface like tadpoles waiting to change, only here nobody's going to change, because you all like it just the way it is. Living like people in a kitchenmaid's thriller."

Mrs. Pharr's "Père, please, Père," was tired, but it sounded uncomfortable too.

"Don't you understand *you* are the one who has to change it? No, don't shake your head that way, it won't do any good . . . you can stop shaking your head like that, I say, I will shout if I want to, and I will shout till I'm finished. It's you who should shout, you silly ass, you hollow silly fool. Every day I expect: tomorrow she won't be able to stand it anymore, and she'll explode, and she will scream out; someday, she will tell them all to go to Christ-God knows what hell, and she will tell me too, and I'll be happy, because I'll know then . . . I'll know my daughter has some of the strength her mother had and I had. Not strength to sit and take any kind of life a man wants to give you . . . you think *that's* being strong? Don't you close the door, I'm going to open it if you do, and I'm going to shout louder so they can all hear. Do you think what matters is to hold on to the past, and if the present slaps you in the teeth, you can just let it slap? What kind of a child did I make, then? You think you are worth so little? Well, you're not, because if you are, I am, and *I am not.* You let your husband whore and live off my money with his brother, and you wait for me to die so he can do the same thing gold-plated . . . you let him do exactly what he wants, *anything* he wants, just so he stays married to you. Is that how much you think you are worth? *Is it?*"

Mr. Robert stood up and squeezed his hand dead white on the

back of his chair. But Mr. Pharr never budged. He only said: "Sit down, it's your move . . . *sit back down.*" And Mr. Robert slid into the chair again; he put his fingers together and cracked his knuckles, and they went on with the game.

Mr. Sage's voice shook: ". . . Old Japanese, old French, old accents, old ways, I wouldn't be surprised if you used your mother's old toothbrush. And an old, shriveled, dried-out prune of a heart in you trying not to feel. What in the name of hell do you think you're doing, protecting the past? You think the past needs protecting? You think because a table was black, and the wall was full of candles, you have to keep painting the table the same color, and put electric lights in the same kind of candlesticks? You think that helps? Didn't you ever learn that *was* and *is* and *will be* are all just as good? Even if you take that table and make it red with purple polka dots, it still *was* black, you muffling idiot. Time can't touch the true values, you think *you* can? What in God's name do you imagine you are? You know what's happened to you? You're so much in love with your past, you've gone and got yourself stuck backwards like a crayfish that gets stepped into his own mud . . . and the present is laughing in your face. Your husband laughs at you, and if you *had* any friends worth spitting at they'd be laughing too . . . and the awful thing, the thing you won't see, is that I'm laughing too, and your mother is laughing out of her grave, laughing at you just like she always did. And the table snickers when you paint it black. But you don't hear all that, or you presume not to. You just go right on cheapening the past and thinking you're doing it a favor. Only, thank God, you can't really cheapen it any more than you can protect it. Because you *can't get near it.* All you can soil is your own private memory, but you don't ever touch what *was.* And you can't manage to live decently with what *is,* you can't face the present. You don't belong anyplace. That's why you went and built this disgusting house for me, so you could . . ."

"*You have said enough now.*" Mrs. Pharr spoke loud, and loud was all. She had pushed up her voice to top his. "*You have said enough and you will be quiet.*"

In the silence, Mr. Pharr's checkermen clicked exact on the warped board, making it rock.

Then Mr. Sage said: ". . . That's it, see? . . . You *can* shout. Now why don't you go in and shout into your powder-glass before it's too late? Show me I have a daughter before I die, for God's sake."

"I repeat: *that is enough.* I will not have any further discussion.

You are a very old man, Père, and you do not know what you are
saying."

Mr. Sage's voice barely came through to the Music Room to tell
us: "Yes . . . I am . . . a very old man."

Maybe two minutes went by after that before I heard Mrs. Pharr's
footsteps hitting down the passage. When she walked in, her face
looked a little gray and bony, but nothing more.

She stopped soon as she saw me. "What are you doing, Lucille?"

"Ma'am, cleaning here."

"So *long?*"

"I'm finished now."

"Then you are ready to go *downstairs*, is that not correct?"

"Yes, ma'am," I said, going.

As I passed her, Mrs. Pharr turned to where both of the men sat
staring down at the checkerboard. She pulled at the sash of her dress
with her folded fingers. It made her neck stand up long and straight.

"Well," she said, "considering the hour, I rather believe we may *all*
go down. I am really quite certain that dinner is served."

10

WHEN I got to the kitchen, Celeste was practically laid out in
a chair, fanning herself with the spatula.

I asked: "What happened?"

"She'll be all right," said Charles Leroy. "Got her head stuck."

"*Head?*" Celeste let the spatula drop on the floor. "If he'd went
on much longer, I would of crawled up."

"That's what it seemed like you was fixing to do," Charles Leroy
told her, "when the tray fell." He went out to the pantry.

"Lord," said Celeste, "what an *old house*." Then she leaned forward. "Where was you?"

"Music Room," I said.

"Anybody see you?"

"Everybody. Except Mr. Sage."

Celeste sighed. "That's fine. That's just dandy-do. That's three
more jobs we better start looking for."

I didn't understand: "Why?"

"Honey, Mrs. Pharr ain't going to have us around after hearing that. She'll hold off a while, but she'll find some reason to get new help. Ain't the first time, she already had to clean house here once before."

"Go on," I said.

"Go on yourself," Celeste told me. "You watch now. Watch, honey. You just wait."

I had no time to wait. The next Monday week, I got a letter from Dan.

dear lucille

you beter come home now. Somethen hapen mama says I aynt supose to tel you becaus she says she will rite you herself teling it to you when she sees a reeson only she says she dont see no reeson so I am riting to you any way becaus I think you beter come home to her now. mama is fine and plese dont tel her I rote to you teling you this she dont know I am riting this way. I am fine to and I hope you fine. from your loving brother

Daniel

When I read it, I didn't want to let myself think what might of happened. But I knew. Only, I don't really have this ability some people got, to *unsee* when they want to.

Celeste was right. Soon as I told Mrs. Pharr I would have to go home for a couple weeks on account of the letter, she said I should stay there, account of she didn't want to come between me and my family, did they need me. She said she had been remarking anyway for a long time how the bayou climate wasn't keeping up with my constitution, and she didn't want to come between me and my health neither. She said it all in a way there wasn't a thing I could answer to.

The letter came on Charles Leroy's day off, and he was in Lansville. He walked into the kitchen that evening while I was telling Celeste about what Mrs. Pharr had said and about my leaving the next day.

He took his coat off, and lay it across the end of the table; he was standing crooked. I quit talking to Celeste, and then I started again, and then I quit again. She finally took a notice, and she turned the gas off under the cabbage, and went on out to our room.

I only had to walk three steps to a chair, but my knees shook. Then I sat down straight, and watched a cold, off-season fly crawl up the wall. I tried to wonder where it is that all the flies go in the winter.

Charles Leroy held like that, his shadow bending over me. Once one of his bones popped, but he had only shifted his weight. In another part of my eye I could see his right hand hanging at his side. It was a fist.

"You want me to cry?" I said. "I can't. I just can't." And I told him again: "I can't."

The fly was crawling right back down.

"What's wrong with you, Cille?"

"Wrong? . . . With me?"

"What makes you act like you do?"

"Well, let's see now. Like *how?*" My voice whipped free.

"Why didn't you tell me you plain had enough, without putting on no act?"

I began: "*Charles Leroy* . . ." Then I stopped. I said: ". . . I should of. Yes, I should of told you that."

"You must be sick inside."

"Sick. Sick is the word. Sick is the way I am."

"I'm ashamed for you."

"Be ashamed."

"I hate to think of your life. Of the way it's going to go."

"That's right," I said.

"Going to keep on lying to every man you know. All your life."

"Do you want me to answer you different?" I asked, "like I been doing? Or do you want me to just say *yes* once every so often?"

"Say what you goddam well want."

"Yes," I said, "I'll say yes."

"Going to have yourself a hell of a time, ain't you?"

"Yes."

"Going to breeze through about ten years."

"Yes."

"But one day, you going to wake up and be an old-young woman. All alone. Without no age. And no more men."

"Yes."

"Alone. All alone. One old . . ."

"Yes."

"Bitch."

"Yes."

"One old . . . dirty old nigger bitch . . ."

"Ah," I said, "not that word. You hush your mouth before you use that word that way to me." I had stood up, and I was rocking so hard I had to put my hand on the table.

Charles Leroy turned to the window with his arms in front of him, and watched the blackness through the black screen.

Then, in half a minute, I got so sleepy my eyelids pushed down and my body went weak and cottony. It was only to shut out the pain and to keep from thinking. But I knew that, so I couldn't help to walk around the room—trying to get my muscles back—trying not to let go.

"Be still," said Charles Leroy.

I went on walking. I had to. Over by the pantry door—back to the table—around the table—walking and walking.

"Can't you be still?"

"No." I really couldn't.

Charles Leroy smashed his fist down on the sideboard. He got his shoulder in it, and one cup jumped off and bounced into two pieces across the floor. Just a kitchen cup. He left his hand, loose, where it had hit, and he looked over at the cup like he was wondering how on earth *that* could of gone wrong.

Suddenly I was there with him, and I put my hands up on his shoulders and gripped them, and pressed my whole body against his. When he wouldn't move, I said: "Hold me. Charles Leroy. Hold me for now." And he did. He lifted up his arm slow, as if it weighed more than all the rest of him, and he put it around me; then the other one too. We kept standing, each making ourself strong for the other person to lean on. But nobody leaned. We were like two different things that grow up together and then touch: like two chuck-weeds under the wind.

Celeste had her radio on low, and some sweet, namby music wheedled in wisps through the door and around the kitchen to remind me of the forget-me-not cologne water Adelaide's mama used to put on her. There was so much to say to Charles Leroy, it amounted to nothing at all. So I only told him: "I'll write you from New Orleans." And even that came out phony and no good. He didn't answer me.

When we went to the helps' quarters, I walked ahead along the narrow passage, past my room. I saw Celeste's feet naked on the white cover, beating easy time to the music. I went on into Charles Leroy's room and sat down on his bed, doubled all over myself with the weakness of my body. He lay down behind me, and after a time he pulled me back with his hand, and with that same hand, the one that broke the cup, he reached in my uniform and took one breast and held it in his palm. He kissed it, and he licked across my mouth. His other arm went up to the light switch, but before he found the wall I said: "No. It's all right." I said: "Leave it . . . It's all right, don't. Not like that." And I was sideways next to him, and he lifted my skirt and pulled my panties all the way off and touched me there for the first time. But no heat began in me, so I could only hold him closer when he got anxious, like any woman has to hold a baby tight—no matter what she is thinking—if it's going to nurse. He went on wetting over my mouth. Then he put his wide, hot hand around my bottom, and he came into me quicker than he meant, because he couldn't do it easy. I remember now how much it hurt, but I didn't care then. I was wandering alone through my mind in a half-dream of separate times and colors; I was a separate person, giving him what I couldn't feel. Just at the end, when his face got so beautiful, was when I started to cry. And afterwards I went on crying, more and more, but without sobbing; only letting the tears run. Charles Leroy patted my head and pulled it against him, and he put his lips in my hair. And I knew he didn't understand. But there was no way for me to explain to him that I wasn't crying about the pain between my legs, or even about the thing that had torn in my heart; but only because his face had looked so beautiful there while he was finishing, and because none of it—not even his beautiful face —had meant anything at all.

Then I got up. I took my panties and went out, down the hall to the bathroom. After I washed myself, I walked back and climbed into my own bed in the dark, account of Celeste. I think I cried most of the night. I wanted to, though; I wanted to let it all run. I felt like a sponge dragged out of water and left on a hard board to be light and dry before dawn. Only, I didn't ever wake up from that half-dream, so when I finally went to sleep I never knew the difference.

I was on my feet, ready to pack, fifteen minutes before Celeste's alarm sounded. My face was still shiny from the tears. But the heaviness was gone, and the night had passed. And there's something new about any morning.

Mr. Sage was in one of his slumps when I said goodbye; I don't think he exactly connected that I might be going away. He sat and frowned up at me, and nodded his head, and then giggled at something that was his to giggle about.

Mrs. Pharr looked like she wanted to make a speech, but she didn't. The air in the house was too much on everybody that day; not just on me. She paid me for the whole eight months and three weeks, less what I had got each month to send home to Mama, and less the cost of the telegram she'd let me phone in the day before so that Dan would know I was coming home. Then she gave me a sealed envelope with three dollars in it as a bonus. It all came to twenty-two dollars.

Mr. Robert smiled his awful smile, and Mr. Pharr was too busy to leave his room.

Mademoiselle gave me three bony sewing-fingers, on loan.

Celeste got the trembling-chin, and did it real well. (Celeste had the trembling-chin down to a fine point, account of she was convinced it was one of the best details about her, and it looked so wonderful whenever something sad took place. What she did, she had a muscle below her bottom lip in the crease there that she could twist a certain way, and it would set to twitching by itself. Always did look pretty good, as a matter of fact. The trouble was, not enough slightly sad things got near to Celeste, and nothing very sad ever did. So she had to save it for coming out of the Bette Davis pictures, and such.) It seemed sort of useless this time, though, because she was just through telling everybody she'd decided to come to New Orleans one week after me. So there wasn't no call for her to be sad.

Mrs. Pharr let Charles Leroy drive me to the station. When we rolled out of the garage, I saw her standing behind one of the upstairs windows, a high chiffon collar curled around her neck. It was almost as black and transparent as her eyes, and it fluttered at me when she turned away.

Charles Leroy wanted me to talk. If I looked over, he shrugged and smiled and shook his head, with pain and a question in his eyes. He wanted me to show him that something big had happened between us the night before—something to make us closer than we had ever been. So I tried only to watch the sky, and then the road with its dark green on either side. Because I couldn't hurt him, by letting him see that nothing had changed for us, or even in me, the way he thought; or that what we'd done, instead of cementing us together, had cemented us apart.

Once, I told him again I would write. The station was full of people, and we shook hands to say goodbye.

I disremember the train ride back.

SIDE FOUR:

*Third and
Fourth Movements*

FOUR years later was when it all started to end. The wrongness, I mean.

Dan and me and Celeste and Adelaide had been working at the Jenkins' over half that time.

It was Celeste who placed us. She was part-time cooking for an old lady turned out to be Mr. Jenkins' great-aunt when the Jenkins came to New Orleans and built their house (they'd just got through living for two years in Rio de Janeiro, Brazil); and they stayed a while with his aunt till the house was finished, and when they moved in, Celeste went with them. But they wanted lots more help than just a cook, so that was when she grabbed a hold of the rest of us. Celeste and me had always kept pretty good friends ever since she came back from across the Lake after I did.

Those four years was long, but they was empty too. They dragged by like a slow, sooty freight with nothing in it, when you waiting to cross the tracks on a hot day. (First you start to count the cars, and you get nervous; but then when you can't even see the end of the train, you forget about it, and you stand and sweat through the dust, with your mind wandering over this private train everybody has of thoughts that don't matter. Course, when the real train finally passes, and the black-and-white bars go up, you got to be so occupied with nothing at all that most of the other people walk right on past you, and you wind up being the last person to cross over.)

Little stuff happened in the meantime.

Jewel's father died, and she went off with some man, and came back alone a while later. She wanted a baby bad, but the new doctor said she'd had so many abortions she couldn't no more. Then she decided she wanted to get married. So she found another man, and did. It wasn't no use, though. She spent all the money they both made on medicines and on anything anybody told her would make her pregnant. Sometimes she spent too much, and they didn't have enough to eat; but I or a couple other friends always helped out. It got to be the only thing she lived for then, after she had killed it in herself. She cried a lot, most every time she saw a kid in the street. Then she took to drinking, and she couldn't of held a job down after that if she'd wanted to. Her husband loved her, though, and he stayed with her. He knew it wasn't his fault, and he knew why, but he never said a word about it. They lived that way.

Adelaide got herself engaged to a boy name of Howard that had some ideas about going up to New York City and making a pile of money. But he wasn't very serious, and he was just standing and dreaming and waiting for the freight too. So Adelaide kept after him and nagged him on with his own ideas, which must be the worst kind of favor you can do for a man. Because Howard finally caught fire and really did up and go to New York City and make a lot of money, only he forgot the part about coming back for Adelaide or sending for her, account of Adelaide wasn't there to remind him of that. So he wrote home and thanked her so much for all she done for him, and then he married some other girl name of Fidley that was probably exactly like Adelaide, except Fidley was there to tell him.

Adelaide got in bed for a month or so with the unhappy news, and when she got up afterwards, there was her mama all over again. She and the unhappy news gave birth to this bad stomach-trouble, which she said came from having a very delicate disposition, and she nursed it and took care of it till it was a real big thing, and something to be proud of in an awful sort of way. Grown-up Adelaide was thin and long and bone-lovely, with tiny wrists, and fingers that never ended on her beautiful hands. She walked her pain slow and careful, speaking so quiet nothing took place in her throat, and she had to keep clearing it to get the natural phlegm out. She worked as a second maid, and she was forever getting fired, because of the way she went around: just for Adelaide to make her hair smooth was an effort that hurt to watch.

But the way Dan took her over and fell right in with her, hurt more.

I don't know if he'd ever gone out with a girl, but I don't think so. If he had, it wasn't where I or Mama could see. Only, course, Adelaide always was Mama's one yes-person.

He started by bringing her some flowers from the shop where he worked. They was about as wilted as Adelaide, but he fixed them up almost nice. Then she had him bring her special things for her stomach-trouble, like bouillon cubes, and a bottle of sassafras-root powder. She let him go on like that, and being two years younger than she was, Dan thought her sadness was all holy and wonderful. Except, I guess he would of thought so no matter how old he had been; he would of loved her just the same. On Sunday afternoons they would go for little walks together: Dan and Adelaide and her stomach-trouble. And he protected it for her, like a man *should* protect the poor, fatherless baby of the woman he loves.

I watched them, and I waited. Because I knew that she was waiting too. I knew what she really thought of Dan, and I knew she hadn't ever changed inside. And I'd already seen Adelaide change her skin once before.

Celeste never got any different, but then she didn't have to: she was all right like she was. It was good to have a satisfied friend who stayed strong on her feet. I think that was mostly why I liked her so much.

The happy way Mama got proud and righteous about Clarence being killed in the war, made me sick. The first thing I saw when I got back from Caytown and walked into the house, was the telegram the government sent her. She had bought a white enamel and gold frame for it, and put it up on the wall so it would stand right out for anybody that opened the door. She wouldn't talk to us about it, but when some stranger came in and asked, she would bend her head and smile before she told them, like a person who has a very particular, very expensive thing she don't want to seem *too* proud of. The same as when our father died: one less person to have to be scared for—one more person she had turned over to God. People said it was wonderful the peace she got from it.

Dan met me at the station that day, and he let his face break enough to stutter when he told me. But when I saw he was shaking, and went to put my arm around him, he quick picked up my suitcase and walked ahead—and by the time we got home he was stony again. The fear and the hate in his love for Mama had grown and mixed and set then, but I think I was the only one who saw it. Watching her out of the corners of his eyes sometimes, he would remind me of Clarence—only there was a sealed-in spark there, a little different from the white heat that Clarence had known how to let out.

Two weeks from the time I got back, the bank sent Mama a check for six hundred dollars in Clarence's name. Mrs. Merle down the block told us it was life-insurance money just like the four hundred they sent her on her boy who was killed overseas. But a week after that, the real life insurance came: *a whole ten thousand dollars.* I knew then what Clarence had done with his life, and how he had made it worth something.

Nobody we knew back of town or anyplace else had owned one quarter that much money at once, and for a while people came over nearly every day to bless Mama. She always stood next to the telegram and bowed, very quiet—and when she did that, I plain had to walk out of the house. I didn't like her making what was left of the payment on our father's grave with it, either, but there wasn't a thing I could do. After that, Mama went down with me and we put the rest in the bank, in her name, and from then on she called it just: "the insurance money." She wouldn't spend a penny of it (Clarence's big numbers hadn't ever meant much to her); but it did make something to lean on that was new for Mama.

And Clarence, never spoke of between any of us, in his five-and-dime gold frame on the wall, was again the first child in the house—and again Mama's pride and her joy.

I wrote to Charles Leroy. I told him about Clarence, and that I was going to get a job in New Orleans so Mama would quit washing —and all the other facts that didn't have a meaning or a place from me to him. Nothing else of what I kept inside came out on paper any better than it would of if I'd seen him then. Course, I wasn't one of these tied-up people who can empty theirselves out to other people if they are alone; I was a whole lot better tied-up.

Charles Leroy answered to tell me he was going in the army. He said they hadn't called him, but the only close family he had left now was his old aunt, and he could take care of her all right with what they paid him. And he wanted to fight.

I read his letter all one weekend, and every time I looked away I saw the gold frame that already got a chip on its top right corner (Mama had touched over that part from a bottle of gold paint she bought for keeping it new-looking). And I wrote him a three-page letter telling him please not to do it. But then there was no sense to stop from saying why not, and I had to tell him he didn't only have his aunt, he had me too—and I couldn't say that. So I burned the letter and I wrote another just saying I was awful sorry. That sounded bad and cheap when I read it over, but I sent it just the same.

A while later, he came to New Orleans for half a day on his way to the training camp; I had started a new job the week before, and they wouldn't let me off to see him. Then, after a little more than three months, he got a leave before he was sent overseas. He had to spend the time with his aunt, but I saw him in the waiting room at the station for most of an hour when he was leaving again for California and then for nobody knew where. There was lots of colored soldiers and sailors with their girls and families. Charles Leroy held my hand, and we watched the others—the ones who wasn't crying and carrying on. But I didn't cry till after the train was gone. Good old me.

He wrote from Los Angeles, California, and he wrote from some foreign places in those four years, and I answered to the address he gave me. Same kinds of letters, both ways. It didn't matter: my insides went back to working whenever the mailman showed up with one, or just didn't have no telegram. Then I remembered that it wouldn't be sent to me, it would be sent to his aunt—and she lived in Biloxi and didn't even know me. So I had to live on the real letters. And I still only wrote him about the few things I did, and what the weather felt like, and how chubby Celeste had got. And that was all; and that *was* all.

I lived on in Mama's house for the almost two years before Celeste came up with the Jenkins. I hotel-maided through that time instead of looking for a private house, because it didn't seem so personal. I tried not to do two things: make friends, or care. The first was always easy around Mama.

Celeste was real excited with the new job. She came over and talked to us for upwards of three hours the night she found out about it. She said the Jenkins was very fine, rich people, and that we would all have steady work at a good salary for as long as we wanted. Mama wasn't convinced enough to let Dan leave the flower shop, but I gave notice at the hotel soon as I heard the Jenkins had a maid's room that Celeste and me was supposed to live in. Then, when we'd been working there long enough to know it was all right, I got Dan to do the same, and he brought Adelaide with him.

The Jenkins built the first house called a *modern* house that anybody ever saw in New Orleans. It was completely flat and squared off, except for Mr. Jenkins' study bubbling out of one wall. The whole thing was made of white cement, just like a sidewalk, with navy-blue metal strips around the windows and the outside doors, and navy-blue railings on the three terraces upstairs. I don't know what type of navy-blue paint they used on that house, but after the first good rain, all you had to do was creep past for it to come off on you. The Jenkins had another coat put on seven, eight times every year, but it didn't do no good. It got so they wouldn't ever go on the terraces except when they was wearing their old clothes; then, it turned out the only old clothes they owned came from a sports store in New York City that made some very special kind of old clothes which navy-blue didn't go with, and we kept having to send everything to be washed so it would look old the right way. Then the Jenkins stopped going out there at all, so they got three great big dusty dogs name of Afghan hounds sent over from New York City, and put one on each terrace. A little blue looked okay on them. Those dogs was kind of a mess, though, because they used to howl at each other from terrace to terrace, and they never learned to dump anyplace else. So after a while, they was got rid of.

The house was just outside the city limits, in Metairie. Course, Metairie wasn't as built-up when the Jenkins moved in, but it was just as fancy, and you still had to have an extra-extra lot of money to live there, even for a white person. It had a golf course, and a Country Club, and heaps of trees and green and honeysuckle all over. The driveways was clamshell; the roads was gravel and dirt, a lot like the ones around Mama's house, except much wider, and out there they was supposed to be a very swell thing. There was special acres of weeds, too, to make the country look more countrified for the Club.

The Jenkins place had two acres of ground, exact, with straight rows of high bushes marking all the lines. Inside was the house, and a badminton court, and a beautiful lawn, and another little house built just like the big one, only it was called a playhouse. They had one son, name of Mr. Stone, and the playhouse was where he was supposed to recreate hisself. Only, he never did. He never played at all.

Probably one of the reasons he didn't was that Mr. and Mrs. Jenkins played so much. They had people over for card games on Thursday nights, and badminton games on Friday nights, and they went on hunting trips, and then they got a sailboat. Mr. Jenkins right off bought hisself a whole slew of books on sailing, and spent about four months studying them. He must of had fifteen, at least. And he sent off for different kinds of sailing clothes from the New York City sports store, with sailing shoes and caps and stuff. It wasn't nobody's land in the kitchen for a while, because he got to using his new sailing words on the help to keep him in practice, and there was a time you had to port and starboard your way all over the house. Then later on, they had a tremendous birthday party for Mr.

Jenkins on the boat, and they took along two big vats of crayfish bisque Celeste cooked up for them, and six shakers of martini cocktails. The thing is, on a sailboat, when you want to make a right turn, you supposed to holler: "Ready about," and when it's to the left you supposed to shout: "Hard to lee," so everybody knows which way you going and what to do. Anyway, the guests was sitting around the vats eating lunch when Mr. Jenkins got it backwards and said: "Hard to lee" when he was supposed to say: "Ready about," or the other way around—and we had to go out next day and scrape crayfish off the deck and out of the cabin. But most all the guests was lucky and got knocked overboard, so there was only one burned bad enough to go to the hospital, and didn't nothing make the papers. He wouldn't of mixed it up like that, except the real sailor he had working on the boat went up front alone with one of the martini shakers, and got stuck under a sail; and by the time Mr. Jenkins had brought him to and pried him out, they was both pretty upset. It wasn't long after that he got rid of the boat.

Mr. Jenkins was this actual live *poet* whose father left him an awful lot of money so he could write poems; then he married a beautiful millionaire-wife, who understood him. I thought he was awful wobbly and skinny-looking, but Celeste said a heavy day of poem-writing does that to you. Only, after the way our father made the reading sound, I was a little disappointed that the writing could come out of a thing looked like Mr. Jenkins. He shut hisself into his study from nine o'clock to five o'clock every day, just like it was an office—except on Wednesday and Saturday afternoons when he went to a gymnasium to build his shoulders up, or unless they was off on a hunting trip, or he had to go sailing, or something important like that. It was his wife told him that his shoulders needed building up, and he went to the gymnasium twice every week for a year till they got where she wanted them, and then he started parading around town and trying them out on other women. Celeste had friends working in a lot of houses, and she used to keep a list called "Ladies Mr. Jenkins Went Visiting." According to her, poor Mr. Jenkins was only trying to prove to hisself and everybody else just how much of a man he really could be. But what happened was, he got stuck with one rich society lady name of Mrs. Harriet Laverne, who was very famous for helping men to prove that kind of thing to theirselves. Mrs. Laverne used to come over all the time, and she made real good friends with Mrs. Jenkins, because Mrs. Jenkins was the only person in New Orleans who didn't know what was going on between Mrs. Laverne and Mr. Jenkins. (Except for Mr. Laverne, and Celeste found out from their cook that he was sweet on his poodle-dog anyway, so most anything went by him.) Mrs. Laverne was sort of frog-faced and tall and not pretty, and I couldn't ever see what Mr. Jenkins saw in her with his own wife being so beautiful. But Celeste said Mrs. Laverne had so much experience with men under her belt, that Mr. Jenkins figured if she thought he truly was a man, she must know.

It used to make me unhappy to see little Mr. Stone try to make up to his father, because all he ever got told was "Good morning," or "Good evening," or "Don't roughhouse." Only, I guess if poor Mr. Jenkins was having trouble proving he was a man, he didn't have no real place for a son.

Inside the house, there was all *modern* furniture, and the rule was that everything had to look like what it wasn't used for. The beds looked like sofas, and the sofas looked like beds, and the ash trays looked like plates, and the plates looked like nobody *knew* what *they* was for. There was eight slats in the living room wall, and every second one was a compartment for keeping something, with a sliding door that didn't look like a sliding door. Then, each slat was cut from the same design, so you generally had to open all eight to get to where you was going. The radio-phonograph was so well hid it never got cleaned for the first couple months. Course, things was really quite interesting in the beginning, because you never could be too sure just exactly what it was you was dusting. Celeste spent the first day around the kitchen pushing buttons and watching objects react. All the floors was black linoleum that wouldn't stay clean, and on the outside walls there was big sheet glass windows that you couldn't open, and the inside walls was made of glass brick with no doors that you couldn't close. But we weren't the only ones had trouble at the start: even the Jenkins would come wandering into the kitchen once every so often to ask where the bar was (it flipped out of one of three things in the living room that looked like chests of drawers); and Mr. Jenkins kept walking upstairs and into the linen closet, because he never really got convinced it *was* a linen closet, on account of from the outside it looked just like the guest bathroom.

But what didn't make sense to me about the house was this: most of the lamps and the furniture and the book ends was just as mysterious and unusable as all that squiggly *antique* stuff in Mrs. Pharr's house; the only difference was that it was a different kind of a mystery. The ceiling lamp in the living room was really a case. It pushed out in every direction anybody ever thought of and one, and then it sort of played with itself out there and forgot to come back. I couldn't see what the sense was in making it all *modern,* if it was going to look that peculiar. I mean, I can see why a person might like to take some of them real fancy old lamps, for instance, and shave the squiggles completely off, so you wind up with a lamp that plain looks like what it gets used for, without no extra gook. But if you going to shave it clean, and then turn it around and pull it out and twist it and fuss it up so it don't even look like an honorable, law-abiding giraffe—what have you got when you finished, and what you done? You could do the same thing with your grandmother, if she could stand the strain; it wouldn't make her any younger, though. What you got to do is make yourself a *new* baby, and work on *her.* And stop screwing around.

Celeste and me lived in the house, but Dan stayed on with Mama, and Adelaide only came four times a week.

Mr. Stone took to eating with us a lot when the Jenkins was out. He didn't have no friends. He was a too-quiet little boy unless he got used to you, and if he did, he was sometimes too wild. But you never could say anything to him about that, because he would just shrivel right up and go off alone.

We ate on the aluminum sideboard in the kitchen. Adelaide always spent a good hour more than she had to, on account of her stomach-trouble, and Dan watched her and was careful not to go any faster: he chewed each mouthful at the same time she did, and kept the same painful look on his face.

Then Adelaide got into the habit of belching real loud every so often. When that happened, she shut her eyes, and pressed her napkin hard over her mouth—like she was *hoping* to stop the blood. She would gasp: "Please to excuse me," in such a very low voice that it almost didn't sound up from a whisper.

"You excused," Dan would say, quick as she talked. He held his hand up to his mouth too.

Celeste told her: "Don't holler so loud, honey, you giving me a headache."

Adelaide took the hand with the napkin off her mouth, and put it on her forehead—her eyes still shut. "Gas is a terrible thing," she whispered, "a terrible, terrible thing."

"Oh, I don't know," Celeste said, "after the sick way your voice comes out when you talk, you ought to *frame* them burps."

Adelaide said something that ended in: ". . . my condition."

"What she scream?" Celeste asked.

Dan told us: "Says you got to be very careful the food you give her in her condition."

"Yes, I know," Celeste said, "I know: her gastric juice don't squirt proper."

"Well, you got to give her the kind of thing will *make* it squirt."

Celeste looked over at me. "I certainly would enjoy to," she said.

2

IN the white clamshell dust of one summer after another, the same old problem began to tear at me again.

First, Celeste got to asking why I never went out on dates. She always had one steady she liked best, and two or three more she kept waiting their turn for when something bitched the steady. But my afternoons and Sundays off, I would only go home and sit with Mama—rocking out time on the gallery and watching every layer of cloud that rose or fell or broke over the camphor tree. Lots of boys asked me to go out, but I wouldn't.

Celeste asked: "What's the matter, che, don't you like *men?*"

"Sure," I said.

"Got a hold of one I don't know about? Ain't none of my business, course."

"No," I said. "Sure it's your business."

"Then what's the matter with you?"

"Matter? . . . nothing."

We were walking to the streetcar from work. It was nearly a mile on the glistening cement sidewalk that curved around the golf course to the Canal. Different color dragonflies and bees was buzzing up a hot hum that stayed in the air when the afternoon died—leaving one singing note to go out with the last heat waves, so the locusts could catch the sound of the day.

"Want to come and eat oysters with me and Jackson?"

"No, hon. Thanks."

"We just going down to that oyster bar Stupid Hanley runs by the market. Jackson could get you a friend of his."

"No," I said. "Mama's all alone."

"Everybody's alone after they goes and gets born; come on down and eat yourself some oysters."

". . . Thanks just the same."

Celeste took her chewing gum out and shook it off her hand into the weeds. "Ever hear from Charles Leroy?"

"Sometimes."

"You didn't marry him, did you?"

"No."

"*Did* you?"

"No, che."

"Bumped you that last night, though, didn't he? Ain't none of my business."

I looked out at the golf course. "I didn't marry him," I said.

"Well, even if you going to, you got to get in a *little* more practice."

"Why?"

"Good for you, for God's sake."

"I can't," I said.

"Trying to be a one-man dog?"

"I ain't trying," I said. "I just can't."

Celeste reached over and ripped out a baby sourweed to suck. She asked: "Know what messed you up?"

"What?"

"Rose petals," she said.

". . . Don't get you."

"I warned you, che. Never say I didn't do my best to warn you. A girl plain can't crawl out of her shell and spread rose petals all over hell and gone like you was doing, without expecting one of them to get shit on. But that still ain't no reason to crawl back inside head first and ruffle up your ass-feathers. A girl's got to live."

"Sure. If a girl knows how."

She took my arm with hers. "Listen, che, answer me this one question: did you ever come?"

"Come?"

"Did you ever feel anything down there?"

I could tell the blood was running into my face. ". . . I guess so."

"No, ma'am," she said. "Ain't no guessing. What was it like?"

"I don't . . . know."

"*How* don't you know?"

"It was all right," I said.

Celeste took her arm out, and patted me on the back. "That's what I thought," she said. "You ain't't."

I wanted to know: "Did you?"

"About a year ago," Celeste said, "the first time."

"How it happen?"

"Well," she said, "I was just laying there, and pling."

"You mean you wasn't expecting it?"

"*Expecting* it? I couldn't even of told you who it was."

". . . What it feel like?"

"Didn't feel *like*. It's a feeling all by itself. Sort of a holy itch. But suddenly, all them baths got justified."

I thought about Charles Leroy and me. "I can wait," I said.

"You a fool if you do."

I told her: "Friend of Mama's says she was acquainted with a girl once who died from too much playing around with men."

Then Celeste got this dreamy look on her face. Almost prissy, she said: "What a lovely way to pass on. Just to goof off."

We were coming to a beer joint that had a colored entrance. It looked kind of empty.

"Want a Coke?" I asked.

"*Hell no*," said Celeste. "I want to get on to them oysters."

We took the same streetcar, but she got off to transfer. Before she did, she said: "Study it over, che. You ain't a woman; not yet." And she got down and left me sitting there.

And then I couldn't help going back over it—all of it—all of my life. It was as if the film that was healed over the hurt in my brain had been ripped off, and I had to unhush the hurt to think again.

Sitting on the gallery with Mama, rocking, rocking till the blood in my veins felt clotting-thick. Thinking till my ears buzzed and my eyelids edged down to where I could only see one bent branch of the camphor tree, or the hard white of one cloud. Watching till the white burned a haze around my eyes that softened to a darksilver pool, dented with the outlines of spots: circles of eyelashes slipping in still water.

Mama said: "If you going to sleep, take yourself inside. Get a cramp like that."

"I ain't asleep."

"Then open your eyes. It ain't good for a person to shut their eyes wide awake. They likely might turn in on your brain."

"I wish they would," I said.

"Lucille, what's wrong with you? I ain't never seen you the way you been acting lately."

I was getting terrible tired of that question. "What could be wrong with me?"

"I don't know," Mama said, "I'm beginning to wonder. I used to think you was the strong child in the family. I used to think you was strong like me, and . . ."

"No."

"See? You *see*? There you is. You answering me back before I even get a chance to finish what I'm talking here. You getting uppity; you never been uppity."

"I'm sorry, Mama. What was you saying?"

She got up and pushed her chair over and sat down again. It was a brand new rocking chair Dan had bought her. "Don't matter none at all. I can't remember."

"*Please*, Mama. *What* was you *saying*?"

"Don't you sigh at me that way, I don't like the tone of your voice."

". . . I'm sorry, Mama."

"Don't nobody force you to come and sit with me here on your day off. I never asked you to. You don't even live here, you don't have to come and sit here. You don't have to come and sit with an old lady just because she worked most of her life to make you what you is."

"What am I, Mama?" I asked.

"Huh?"

"What kind of a person did you make in me? What am I, Mama?"

"Don't you go poking no fun at me."

"I ain't," I said, "I want to know."

"Don't you know what you is?"

"No, Mama. No, I don't know."

". . . Is you been to church lately?"

I didn't answer.

"When did you stop going to church?"

"A long time ago, I think. I can't recall."

Mama stood on her feet. "Oh, Lord," she said, "my own child. Oh, Lord, what did I ever do? Didn't I take you to church every single Sunday? Didn't I teach you to go every week and pray to the Lord for your everlasting soul? Was you lying to me all them Sundays when you went out in your best-dressed? Where did you go?"

"I did go to church," I said. "But then I missed a while. And then I stopped."

"Don't you believe in your everlasting soul?"

"I don't want to believe in that. I want to believe in me."

"Don't you talk that way, don't you . . ."

"Sit down, Mama," I said. "Sit down." There was a soft wind had begun to sift over the tops of the houses, and move, dusty, into the trees. I said: "Listen to the wind."

Mama began to rock herself too quick; her feet scratched every time she came forward. "I'm going to pray for you. Two times in the day I'm going to pray to the Lord Jesus to bring you back to His right hand, like I left you, where I put you soon as you was born. I'm going to pray."

"That's right, Mama," I said. "You pray."

It was the same summer I got so I couldn't sleep at night. I would lay on the bed every which way, moving again whenever the sweat on my body soaked into the sheet and made it stick against me. Then I would get up for a glass of water, or to go to the bathroom, or just to walk around—and when I went back I would lay down slow, sensing the sheet come up to meet me and lick against my skin, like a cool, fleshy tongue. I would study the wall patterns of the moon and the street lamp: how they doubled and slid away when a late car threw its headlights into the room; how they came out in the old place after it had crunched by. Sometimes, laying there, I would touch myself down below, and I would try to imagine where the wonderful feeling began, and what there was in me that could make it so wonderful. And I would want to ask God if I really had the same parts as other women, or if maybe there wasn't something missing in me—some little thing that stopped me from being what I should of.

Celeste never understood why I laughed so hard the morning she said: "Get a move on, che. You look like you got a piston left out." But I laughed and laughed all that day. I laughed till my eyes filled up. I really laughed.

Then on one Thursday afternoon off, it got so bad I knew I couldn't go and sit with Mama, rocking, and twisting inside.

Only, where could I go?

I stayed on the St. Thomas car, past Millicent; I sat next to the window, watching the people and the houses and trees clip along, my eyes out of focus. The sky was a sweaty smudge, like some baby's forehead had rubbed across it, and underneath everything moved fast in a long stream of patches—a crazy, cutout world for my fuzzed eyes. The car rackety-racked to each stop, swinging hard from side to side, keeping me awake.

When we came to the end of the line, I got off and walked the five blocks that was left. I hadn't been there since I was twelve, except in my dreams. But I could of done it blind.

Some old lady had put up a flower stand at the gate with empty beer cases. She looked like she wasn't doing much business. I bought half a dozen dying carnations that cost a nickel, and I gave her a quarter for them. Then I went in.

Five rows straight ahead; three to the right. Seventeen graves over.

There was no green, and the earth lay mealy under my feet. No stone city. No color, except for brown—the same on top as underneath, it was only fair. No softness to the mealy earth, too much salt for that. Not a place for tears.

I stopped and looked down at the crusted dirt heap, splotched with a little yellow to mark its secret difference; and the dried crayfish hole next to it.

I thought:

He was a man. *Bones now . . . the crossed bones of hands that disremember mine.* He was a wise man. *And the voice that turned the day for me, plain turned itself to mud.* He was a gentle man. *The magic mouth that could kiss the cold of my cheek into a warm tingle, just kissed its little maggots into flies and buzzed away.* He was a good man. *The mind that couldn't hate is an empty, hateful smell for the roots of dandelions.* He was a loving man. *The wonderful, wild heart that never learned how not to care, got very taken care of by the worms.* He was a walking man. *The legs that ran so tender out from life, only click now when they tremble.* He was a real man. *And the whole body that hid its white mistake between those legs, has had a fine chance to rot in peace in its own particular, private grave . . .* all paid for.

Then I said to him: "Father, you ain't in much shape to listen to any questions. Are you, now?"

And when there wasn't no answer at all, I swung away and walked out of the graveyard.

I walked all the way to the Farnay car, and took it, and bought a transfer. I got off at the corner of St. Charles, and switched cars. Then I rode, standing up, to the first stop on Canal Street. The car pretty near emptied there; I waited to be last.

Canal Street downtown was crowded. Most everybody had their

afternoon off on Thursday, even the white workers, and bunches of people packed the doors of the orangeade places, and the department stores—pushing and turning so you didn't know if they was going in or coming out. I crossed over and walked on down near the curb, trying to keep a space for myself.

I walked past the picture house that's too small to have a colored section; past the railway station, full of parked cars, and puffs of dirty steam, and grit that blew into my hair.

Down to the River.

And then I stopped and listened to the hoos and haws of the big ships, and the bleeps of the shrimp barges and oyster boats. I stood on the wharf and stepped empty shrimp heads down between the slats of tar-black, splintered wood, already full of broken clam and oyster shells and dried pieces off the backs of crabs.

The port is where men made the River a cemetery toilet. Where her dead lay out to burn and stink up into the air—where the boats empty, dropping oil and men's dirt into the clean mud of her water, changing the deep warmth of her color to a slick, cold gray. But the River don't care, because the River can take anything, and she can take that too. She just slides by, still as clean and warm as a dog's mouth, no matter what she eats.

I love the bad smell of the River-rot and the water and the tar. It's full and hard, and there's no sweetness to it like on the bayou. I love the smell of life shuffling easy over death, waiting to follow it away. And living a while, even if you have to dirty up and die; not being afraid to finish what you began. I wanted to be a part of life that way, for the River to see.

Only, the River didn't pay me no mind. She left me to stand there in the rich, rotten air, with the hollow screeches, and the empty shells of things.

I turned and walked back up Canal Street on the same side. When I got to where the neutral ground turns green, I crossed and came down again, to be with the people. Then I turned left on Bourbon Street into the Quarter.

The sky had gone dark into night, but there was no stars could shine over the hazy, speckled, jumping neon colors. I walked on, and I went right on one corner, and left on another, stomping through the old streets like I had someplace to go. Twice I had to step across to the other sidewalk: when some white men, half-drunk and laughing, jumbled out of a bar behind my back—and when two colored boys with a bottle started to shout at me. I thought about some of the stories you read in the papers of what happens to girls that go around there single at night, and I set my teeth together and went on walking.

I passed the open back doors of restaurants, through the hot smells that blasted out with the noise of talking and of slopping dishes and the clink of hardware. No matter how fast I went, I could always hear two radios, sometimes three, screaming off the galleries where women had to laugh louder if they wanted anybody to hear them and look up. I saw a spasm band, with a bunch of people to stare and throw pennies at the three little colored kids who danced for them. A juke box, and a baby crying, and two deaf men swearing at each other. And through it all, each sound came by itself, sawing into the tight black space, and bouncing back alone. So there was no big living sound; no one hum or clash that is made up of everything, the way it is in other parts of the city. The sound of the Quarter is like a picture negative; or like the echoes of millions of memories that won't come together, trapped in a drunk man's dream.

I was going so fast, when I turned the next corner I bumped shoulders with a colored sailor who had his head up, watching the sights. I said: "Excuse me."

The sailor picked up my purse, and wiped it off before I could stop him. "That's all right," he said. "Look, you scratched your pretty bag."

I grabbed it away from him. "Ain't nothing in it. No money."

Then I cut out quick, making like I didn't hear him laugh and ask: "What that supposed to mean, flower girl?"

When there was time to wonder about what he'd said, I looked down and saw that I had forgot to put the six carnations on our father's grave. I unlatched my purse, and stuffed them inside.

My stomach was shivering, and my arms was too stiff to move in rhythm as I walked. That made me mad: I don't like for no part of my body to kick up without me. So I slowed some, and when I came to an open penny arcade, I went in and stood there.

I kept both hands on my purse, and tried to blink out the cigarette smoke that streaked down into my eyes from a cloud with a flat bottom, just overhead. The different whites of flickering neon tubes and screaming bulbs mixed on the yellow walls and washed away the silly, lollipop colors of the pinball machines. I watched four couples buying their fortunes with a nickel.

Two white men in shirtsleeves leaned over a South Sea Island peep-show box, with opposite hands on their belts, talking. One of them flipped his cigarette on the ground and looked around the room. "Hey, nigger," he said.

I watched where he had looked, but I couldn't find anybody he might of meant. Then I saw that I was the only colored person in there. When I turned back to the man who had spoke, he was staring at me.

I wasn't going to back away, so I put one foot behind me and pivoted on it till I was facing the street. Then I went out, but not fast, and not shaking so hard anymore. I walked on down the street in the same direction.

From behind, a man said: "How you doing, sugar?" He came up alongside me—a big colored man dressed in brown pants and a faded red shirt. I started to cross the street, but he took my arm. "Watch them cars," he said.

I unhooked my arm and ran across the street. When I got there, he came right up again. "Don't be scared, sugar," he told me. "What you scared for?" He wasn't too drunk to talk clear.

No use my walking faster, he was too big. I said: "Go away, man. *Go on*," in a tone like my old schoolteacher.

But there is a type of person, if he knows you plain don't like him, then is when you got a friend. "You *ain't* scared, is you? What's wrong with me, sugar? What's wrong, think I don't got no dough?"

There was a lot of people passing us. I stood still. "No, I ain't scared. Now get on away from me."

He pulled out a roll of bills from his pants pocket. One of them fell on the sidewalk, and he stooped to get it, wavering some. I tried to walk by, but he caught up. "See that there?" He pushed the money in front of me, under my face. "I got plenty dough. Look at it, see all that?" I had to stop again, if I didn't want him to touch me. "Come on, sugar, don't fool around."

Five or six white people had stopped to watch us, and one girl was giggling. Then another colored man came and stood on the other side of me, and started to be funny for the crowd. "Go on, sugar. Sugar, go on." He had a wheezing laugh. "Go on with the man. What you waiting for?" He laughed again, and slapped his knees.

I said: "Leave me alone, I'm with somebody. I ain't by myself, I got a friend. You better leave me alone."

The clown said: "Where's your friend, sugar. Where's your friend?"

More people was stopping, and we had a ring around us—some

of them giggling and some just eating popcorn and watching, like we were a spasm band or an accident.

On a second-story gallery across the street, two white women in purple silk robes leaned over and jeered at me. "The girl's got herself a friend, can't you hear? That girl's just got herself a friend. Where's your friend, honey? Where's your friend, huh? Where's your friend?"

I said: "If you-all don't leave me alone . . ." Then I saw the colored sailor I had bumped into, standing where the crowd was thinner. "Serge," I said, "what took you so long, Serge? Where you been at?"

"Oh," said the clown, "oh, Serge, what took you so *long*, Serge? *Oh, Serge.*"

The big man said: "I don't see no Serge."

I put my hand out ahead of me, and wedged through the crowd to the sailor. "Come on, Serge," I said, loud. "See what you got me into, waiting for you?" I took his arm, and started him down the street.

Everybody was laughing and shouting at us, but the gap where I had come through must of closed, because the two men stayed where they was. I held to the sailor's arm and rounded him into the next street. Some of the people came after us, but they straggled behind on the corner, gibing. When we reached the end of the block, we turned again, and the voices faded.

I quit walking, and let go the sailor. I said: "I'm terrible sorry, mister. Thanks a lot. I'm really grateful for what you done."

"That's okay." He was smiling, very wide-lipped. "It's a heavy town."

"Well," I said. "Thanks again."

I gave him my hand, and he shook it. But when I started off again, he came along. We walked a while towards Canal Street, and I waited for him to say goodbye or just drop back.

"Had your supper?"

"Sure."

". . . Bet you ain't."

"I'm late," I said. I pulled out a strand of hair that was blowing in my face, and picked up some speed.

"Live around here?"

"No. Not around here."

"Where you live?"

"A ways away. Nowhere around here."

"Big hurry?"

"Pretty *big*," I said.

But he kept right with me. "I know a restaurant got pretty good food."

"Thank you, but I ain't hungry. I'm late."

"Funny girl."

I figured the best way to get rid of him was just to let him keep talking, and walk right on, without lending any attention.

"You got a date?"

I let it pass.

"Honey, *you got a date?*"

"I don't keep no dates."

"Well, what you late for then?"

"Got to see my mama."

"Ah, come on, don't give me that."

"Look," I said, "I ain't giving you nothing. I'm very sorry if I caused you trouble, but you wasting your time."

"No, I ain't. You wasting it for both of us. Only got till morning."

I thought about Charles Leroy. The same age, about. Probably doing the same thing—but better. Then I turned and took him in: sweet-looking, real dark, and a face too young for the body. "Sailor, sailor. Go find yourself another gal."

". . . Don't want nothing for free. Got my pay yesterday."

I sighed at the empty street in front of us. There was two more blocks out of the Quarter, and I could see people milling under the big lights with the traffic. Grinding of streetcars and the metal mewing of horns seeped through the black air to meet us. "Turn around now, man. Plenty gals back there."

He put his hand on my shoulder and stopped me so short I nearly went down. He told me: "Come on."

"Let go my shoulder. Let me go."

"Why don't you get some sense?"

"You going to *let me be?*" I snapped free, and swung my purse up to hit him on the side of the neck. It opened, and everything fell out, clinking on the empty sidewalk.

He frowned and shook his head, before he went to catch the sliding comb and the rest.

I followed him with my eyes. My body was quiet; all the shaking had gone out. And I knew that the thinking and the hurting had gone too: there was only a cleanness that blew through my mind, empty as the dark street. One loose cleanness—a notch wider than worry, a whole lifetime faster than thought. And nothing else.

The sailor came back. "Your mirror's busted," he told me. "I'll pay you for the busted mirror."

"Don't matter. Just leave the flowers there."

". . . Why?"

"Put them where they fell. Go on, leave them there."

He shook his head. "Ain't no reason to," he said, "they ain't so very mashed. See? . . . You could still save them, you could still . . ."

"*Sailor.*"

He looked up.

Gentle as I could, I said: "If you want me . . . you just leave those flowers there."

He stared a second. Then he reached up with a long arm, and threw them straight out. They fanned, separating across the night on their way to the pavement.

"Like that?"

I said: "Like that."

"What you going to do now?"

"We going to have something to eat. Ain't we?"

". . . Funny girl. Nice, funny girl."

"Yes, indeed."

"I'm sorry if I hurt you."

"That don't matter. Don't nothing matter in this world."

"The restaurant I was telling you about, it's back that way. Right back where we came from."

"Don't tell me, man. Show me. Run me there, all the way."

"What you want to run for?"

"I feel like it."

Smiling: "Funny girl."

I turned, and trotted up the street to the dark cloud and the sparkling rainbow lights.

But he didn't have to run to keep up with me; he took quick, long steps, like a man walking a pony in a dream-circus. "Hey, hold on," he said, "you don't even know where it is."

"Don't talk, man," I told him. "*Run.*" And I said: "We got to run."

Then I stumbled, but he caught me, and we went on. We laughed and went on, hurrying—rushing against the turn of the earth—running back into the Quarter.

3

THE restaurant where we ate was a room on a sidestreet. The kitchen didn't have a door, and the hot, heavy air of cooking pushed out, slicking around the shiny walls on its way to the open windows—too strong for the taste of the food. All the air was thick with okra as the soup, where it slimied off my spoon and fell back with a greasy plop.

Or anyhow, it seemed like that to me.

He was from Alabama, Georgia, and his name was Best Edward Poole but you could call him Best. I didn't, though.

I said: "Best Edward Poole, this is the first time in my life I ever ate in a restaurant."

"No, it ain't," he said.

"Oh, yes it is, Best Edward Poole."

"What-all you been drinking?"

"You be surprised, man. You be surprised just how drunk I am."

"You ain't very, but you had some."

"Sure. Certainly, certainly. B.E.P. Can I just call you old B.E.P.?"

"What makes you want to?"

"I don't want to," I said. "You wouldn't exactly say I *wanted* to."

The waiter came with some other food. He asked: "Finished, honey?"

"Course I am. I was finished before I up and got born. Know that?"

"No," said the waiter. "That I didn't know." He winked at Best Edward with his far eye.

When he went away, Best Edward asked: "What made you so excited all of a sudden?"

"Nothing. You. You made me excited. You made me free, man."

Best Edward smiled his smile. "Not yet, I ain't," he said. "You wait."

I couldn't eat my food. I squished it around for a while, though. Best Edward saw me, but he didn't make no comment.

The room had six tables in it; only three of them was being used. There wouldn't of been much call for a colored restaurant in that part of the Quarter, if it hadn't been for the war. I leaned around and watched another couple eating in a corner. Soldier and a girl.

Best Edward said: "I sure am glad you don't paint yourself up like that and do that to your hair."

"Think I'm all right the way I am?"

"Sure do."

"Think I'm all right without no lipstick?"

"Sure. Why'd you take it off, though?"

"I didn't, I never wore no lipstick."

". . . Look awful pretty against your color."

"My color," I told him, "seems to do so well by itself, I just *hate* to go and make it *common*." That's it, honey, I thought; Adelaide or bust.

Best Edward said: "It ain't common."

"Oh," I said, "you just so full of *compliments,* you just making shivers run all up and down my little old *spine*."

"It ain't. It really ain't."

"Now you stop that. You silly boy."

Best Edward put his spoon down in his mashed potatoes. He said: "Your color . . . *ain't* . . . *common*."

"Man," I said, "you are making me giggle all over. I bet you say that to every girl you meet, too."

"I do not."

"You do too."

"I do *not*."

"You do too."

"You know," said Best Edward, "you puzzle me."

"I have a puzzling character."

". . . You a funny girl."

"Cootchy-coo me some more," I said, "I just love it."

"Well . . . you very pretty."

"That's it. Come on, now. More."

"You one of the prettiest girls I ever saw."

"Well, now, I would like for you to *show* me how pretty you think I am."

"You wait. You just wait." Then he said: "How much they pay you around here."

"Best Edward, I think the way you eat mashed potatoes with a spoon is *darling*."

"How much they pay you?"

". . . Pay me?"

"You heard what I said."

I took my spoon and rubbed at it with my napkin. "Seems to me that ain't no proper way to ask."

"It's my way. I like for everything to be straight from the beginning."

"Well . . . I don't know."

"Course you know. Ten . . . fifteen? You ain't never made more than fifteen on one night."

I thought: okay, now; okay, here we go. Black molasses-voiced, I said: "You don't mean on one night. You mean on one man."

Best Edward laughed. "I like you. I plain like a girl that don't frig around."

"That's my way," I told him, "I like for everything to be straight from the beginning." My spoon was shining so hard I could see myself upside down on the inside.

"Tell you what. I'm going to give you thirty dollars for the night."

I breathed on the spoon and watched the cloud fade out. "The *whole* night?"

"You wasn't going to work anyway. You was going back to your mama, like I heard it."

I said: "Sixty."

"No," said Best Edward.

"Sixty," I said, "I'm expensive."

"Nobody's *that* expensive."

"You don't know me."

Best Edward moved his legs around and sat the other way. "Lady right where I'm staying told me she'd get a girl for me cheap. It's that kind of a house."

"Go get one."

"Well, what makes you so special?"

"You already named it."

"Your color?"

"There's my boy."

". . . That all you got?"

"No," I said, "that's just all I'm selling."

"How come?"

I sat up straight. "All right. All right, Best Edward Poole. You win. You found me out, and you absolutely right: my color *is* all I got. It's all I got in this whole world, it's the only thing I have. *Take it or leave it.*"

Best Edward sniffed. Deep, he said: "I take it." He reached across the table for my arm.

I pulled back. "Ah-ah. Got to put the nickel in first."

But he didn't laugh. "I make you one last offer to thirty-five."

"You ain't offering," I said. "I am."

"Know how to make your business, don't you?"

I told him: "I come from a long line of salesladies."

"Okay. Forty. Ain't going no higher. Last chance."

Then I chuckled loud. "*My* last chance."

"Say, who you think you is?"

"It ain't who. It's what."

". . . Had a lot of practice?"

"Experience," I said, "is what I got more of than anything."

Best Edward put his hands in his lap and looked at them. "When I pay here, and pay for you at the boarding house . . . I maybe have fifty dollars left." He sounded young as his face, then.

Only, I wasn't studying on him. I slapped my purse on the table by his plate. "You put them fifty inside."

"Oh, no. Not now."

"Now."

"I been rolled once before."

"You don't have to leave me by myself at all. Put them fifty inside."

Best Edward watched my arm against the tablecloth. Then he grabbed the purse and held it below the table. When he put it back, I took it and counted the money.

"Better be some good," he said.

"You ain't ever seen nothing."

He held out a cigarette at me, and I opened my mouth and let him push it in. He lit it, and then I blew the smoke right in his face, like they do in the pictures.

Best Edward coughed. "What that for?" he asked.

I blew some more, and dropped the cigarette over my shoulder, with my little finger stuck up in the air.

Best Edward waved the smoke out of his eyes. "You sure is a funny girl," he said, "I swear to God." After he paid the bill, he told me: "I still got enough for a drink, maybe."

"I don't need no drink."

He smiled a little. "You don't know. *You* don't know *me*."

I got up. "Well, come on. Let's us go see about you."

"Right now?"

"Sure, right now. You got me all hepped up."

"Go on."

"For a fact," I said. "That's why I made you pay me now."

"Don't get you."

"Well, man, if you do me like I think you going to do, I ain't going to be much good for collecting when you get through."

"Is that right?" He followed me out.

"Course. Why you think I wouldn't go with you soon as you asked me to?"

"Don't know."

"Well, because I was just sure you could make me go crazy. I said to myself that's a man could just rub you crazy."

"Hey, you making it up."

"Going to show you how much I'm making up. I got a lot of friends, Best Edward Poole. Lots and lots and lots. So many I couldn't even count them. But I ain't been with one could make me feel like you going to make me feel. You better get yourself ready."

"You a funny girl. You look funny when you say that."

We were in the street, and I put four fingers around the upper part of his arm. "Lots of muscle," I said. "Make some muscle now."

"Hey, don't pinch. What's wrong with you?"

"Ain't nothing wrong with me. Just watch and see."

"Don't shout like that."

"Take me where we going."

"Sure you don't want a drink?"

"I want to go where we going."

"Okay, okay. You a funny girl."

It was a house on the other side of the Quarter. We didn't talk again till we got there; we didn't have time. I walked so fast he was always a piece behind me, and four times he told me to slow down. But I went on, leaning over ahead of myself, walking so that people made a path for us when they saw us coming. Twice he had to yell at me because I kept heading on down a wrong street. When we came to the house, I was panting some, and I couldn't stand quiet.

Best Edward pulled this metal handle that was on a string, and a bell clapped inside. After too long, a fat, middle-age colored lady opened the door, and I went first and waited. When Best Edward was in, she slipped the catch to and said: "Be five dollars extra with company."

Best Edward said: *"Five* dollars?"

The lady pushed up her shoulders and grinned gold.

"That's more than double what it is for one person by hisself."

"Price goes up with outside company. I done told you I'd bring you a girl."

Best Edward thought some. "Can't pay no more than three dollars extra."

Without turning, the lady reached in back and lifted the catch. She went on grinning.

"Here," I said. I peeled a five-dollar bill off the money in my purse, and held it out.

She looked strange at me while she reached and took it. When she let the grin come back, it wasn't quite the same. "Go on up," she said. Then later: "*Honey.*"

I stopped and turned. She was still standing by the door, just the same, waiting. I went back to her.

"Do you ever need a place to go, I always be here."

"I'll keep that in mind."

"I approves of the way you act. You high-class, and you know it."

"No," I said. "Not high-class. *Special-deluxe* type."

". . . Uh-huh. Yes, you is. I approves of that. I just approves of the way you act. You want to come back and talk some time, maybe we could fix something up."

"I'll remember," I said.

"Lot of steady customers come here. I could set up a heap of business for a girl like you. Girl who knows what she's worth. I respects that."

"I'll remember."

"I treats my girls right. Ask whoever you want. I treats my girls according to the way they walk. I approves of the way you walk."

"I'll remember."

"You do that." She patted her fat hands together, and started looking me down to my feet and back up again. "Nine-eighty Garvine Street. You do that. Nine-eighty Garvine. Yes, honey, you do that. Just remember Garvine, corner of Forquette. I'm the only red light on the block except Mrs. Gaiter, and she's white, so she only runs a colored house on the side. Anyhow, her husband's a policeman, so she takes you for more."

"I'll keep it in mind."

"You just do that, honey." More gold.

I left her, and went after Best Edward.

I followed him through a passage to this square courtyard that had a flight of steps leading off one side onto a wood gallery. No electric bulbs. Some of the light from the night sky touched there, feeling its way into the Quarter. We passed a raised goldfish pond with the moon in it, and I marched over sad little sprays of star-gray grass that tried to grow between the bricks and the tiles. Overhead, the Milky Way hid behind the city's sheen—so faint and delicate you could only sense it—like a streak of crumpled tissue paper from God's last Christmas.

The stairs was hollow, and they gave under my feet, bouncing me up; the wobbly bannister held out the beginnings of splinters for my hands. At the top, we went on along the gallery, and the third door was the one.

Best Edward went in to flip the light switch, but I followed him before he had time. Then the room came out yellow, and he clicked the door shut behind me. I waited, with my purse in my hands, and my feet together.

Back of my left shoulder, the edge of a table and a chair under it; front of me on the same side, a dresser with four drawers and a door; across in the other corner, a washbasin, and an oval mirror, flecked with spots of toothpaste; back of my right shoulder, the foot of the bed. All the furniture dark wood, but the bed (metal, color of an old dime). Black streaks on the ceiling from bugs. Tight, small room; dead-yellow walls like the penny arcade to make it seem bigger. Slave quarters for my grandma.

Best Edward stepped around in back of me. I made myself hard for his hand, not moving.

But he sat on the bed. It creaked, loud. "Smoke?"

"No."

Scratch of a match, and the flame's first whistle. Louder creaks.

"Always like to take my shoes off on a bed."

"Take them off," I said.

"Just did."

I looked at the ceiling. My fingers felt cold.

"Sure you don't want a smoke?" He sounded kind of awkward.

I couldn't turn. "No."

"Well," he said, "here we is."

"That's right."

Whining of a mosquito; I watched it settle.

"Boy, you sure was in a hurry."

"Course." The mosquito and me kept still. You could of heard any sound.

"Don't smoke much, do you?"

"No." I could hear my heart. Hands was starting to jump. Mama would say: Not enough exercise, it ain't good for a person to not get enough exercise, keeps you from breathing. But what would our father say if he saw me now? Would he say: . . .

I swung around so quick Best Edward dropped his cigarette. I gripped my purse, and I asked him: "You want *me* to begin, or do *you* want to begin?"

"Lord, man." He was laying on the bed, brushing the ashes off his pants before they could burn. "Scared the shit out of me. You the funniest girl I ever did meet in my life."

I waited for him to get clean.

"How long you been doing this kind of thing?"

"Since I was . . . fifteen."

"How old you now?"

"Twenty-nine."

He looked up. "No you ain't."

"It don't matter," I said. "You wasting time. Let's get started. Who's going to begin?"

Still looking: "Honey, for chrissake, what you think this is, a poker game?"

I lifted my eyebrows. "At fifty dollars a night, every minute counts."

"Not that much it don't." He pointed at the chair. "Sit down over there and relax yourself a while."

"I don't want to relax."

"Well, I *do*."

"At fifty dollars a night . . ."

"At fifty dollars a night, you going to do like I tell you. Now sit down over there."

I went to the chair. I didn't want to look so tensed and shaky walking, so I swayed my hips out and put both hands up to my hair. But I forgot I still had my purse in one of them, and when I sat down I hit myself with it in the eye.

"Bang," said Best Edward.

"Nothing at all. Didn't hurt none at all," I said. The eye was tearing pretty bad, and I had to blink some before I could keep it open without its burning. "I am *always* hitting myself there."

Best Edward was leaning over on his elbow, watching me. "Must get sort of *painful* after a while."

"It's a bother," I said, "I am *always* doing it."

We stayed quiet a time.

"Well. I'm sitting down."

"I can see you," said Best Edward, "from all the way over here."

"I don't get why you have to relax."

"You would," he said, "if you wasn't in such a calm state yourself."

"*Me*? I'm fine. Ain't nothing to upset me."

"That's helpful to know."

"Sure. Business is business. Make a penny here, make a penny there . . ."

". . . A *penny*?"

"Well, you know what I mean. It's the idea."

He shook his head.

"Best Edward."

"What?"

"When are we going to begin?"

"Lord," he said. "I don't even *feel* like it any more." He lit another cigarette with the old butt. Then he put his head back. "You ever been in Alabama?"

"No. I never been there."

"You wouldn't take to it."

I was supposed to ask: "Why?"

"Because. Different kind of a life. Everything goes slow there, nothing like this. Same thing the other way around, my girl couldn't live hereabouts."

"You got a girl?"

"Sure."

". . . Nice girl?"

"Sure she's nice."

Across the courtyard in the house, a victrola started up. Dance record—tinny. Like when I was little and I pinched my nose to hum.

"You didn't marry her?"

"No. Not yet."

"Why not?"

"Well," he said, "after the war."

I stretched and leaned back in the chair. "You didn't want to, or she didn't want to?"

"Didn't neither of us, but I wouldn't of cared. Mostly her."

"Uh-huh."

"What that mean?"

"Nothing. She say why?"

"Just didn't want to yet."

I breathed deep.

Best Edward rolled over on one elbow. "I wish I could spot you.

Don't know what it is." He rubbed his little finger on his bottom lip, thinking. "Something the matter with you."

"Weird you should say that," I told him, cuddly-cute, "nobody else ever did."

"You lived here all your life?"

"Mostly. I been across the Lake."

"Some man was over there?"

"Yes," I said, "some man was over there."

Best Edward rippled his toes. "Don't you get awful tired sometimes?"

". . . You might say."

He watched me some more.

Just for talk, I said: "Got no picture of your girl?"

"Sure. Want to see?"

"Yes."

"Why?"

"No reason."

He swung his legs over the bed, and sat up. Then he reached in his back pocket and pulled out a brown wallet. It was dull, and sticky-looking; shaped like a new moon, from sitting on it. He came and stood next to me and dropped it in my lap.

I said: "She's pretty," before I even had it open. But she really was. Wide, sloping cheeks in a smooth skin, dark as he was. Thin eyebrows, long and perfect, but not pencilled. Big, sunken-back eyes. Then I saw Best Edward's white pants close next to my face.

He put his hand on the back of my neck, under the bun, and stroked there. I tried to make my body hard like before, not to shudder. I think there was just time.

Best Edward pulled my head over and pressed it against his groin, easy. The wallet slipped out of my hands and flapped open, by the table leg. One side of it curved up; it closed all by itself.

I said: "I dropped your picture."

". . . Okay." He breathed in quick. The hand went under my arm, and he lifted me up against the full firmness to his head, bent over me, waiting. He had his mouth wide apart, and when he kissed me, his lips seemed like they covered half my face.

I opened my teeth much as I could, like it was supposed to be, and felt around him. I was shaking a lot, but his body was all solid and round, and I held tight to it, to keep from pulling away.

His hands went down over me, pressing me in; he was getting stiff there, and it felt awful big. When he had enough of the kiss, he swung his head up and looked at me, gulping in air. Then he backed me to the bed till my knees buckled and I fell; he kept a hold of me till I was down, and he lay on top of me, his arms spread wide and his legs around mine. He kissed me on one eye, down my cheek to the mouth again.

I couldn't quit shaking, and it got worse there under him. But he thought it was something else. He took his face away and said: "All the others make you hot as that? Do they? Huh? All them queers?"

Then his wide lips again, and his big tongue filling my mouth, slipping in and out faster now, fast as the beat of his chest. He began to move down below, in grinding circles, and the stiff, selfless thing on the inside of his leg twitched against my thigh. He passed an arm under my hair.

I could barely cross my hands behind him, but I dug my nails into the skin of the other wrist. I told myself: *feel it, let go, feel it . . . let go now, let go, you here now, it's all right now . . . let go, let go, feel it.* I kept my eyes open and fixed on the light bulb, till it stained a dark yellow, and the ceiling pulled back into nothing. *Feel it, feel it, feel it . . . you got to feel it, you got to . . . you got to feel it . . . open up and let go and feel it, make yourself a woman, feel, feel, feel, you got to feel it.*

I must of tried to talk out loud once, because he reared back and said: "What, love?" hoarse-voiced; he put one hand down and began to unbutton his pants.

That was what finished it. Finished, done. Scissor-clipped.

I pushed his shoulders back and turned away, peeling out from under him. Then I slid across the bed and jumped up. I swayed some, and my dress caught between the mattress and the thin metal. I tore it free. He grabbed at me, after his surprise, but it didn't take. Nothing would of took: all my insides and a long time's nerves went into that, and I was strong.

"What? . . . what . . . what you got?" Voice of a kid who wakes up from a happy dream, frightened that it *was* only a dream.

"Never mind," I said, "just you lay there a minute." I took my purse and went to the washbasin, stumbling. I rubbed water on my face and back over my hair.

"What the hell?" Still sprawling on his stomach, I think. I didn't look at him. "What you doing? You crazy?"

"I don't know," I said, "I guess I must be. I must be crazy."

". . . Something hurt you?"

"No, indeed," I said. "Me? Something hurt me? Never in the world." The words came out in pieces on my broken breath.

"What the hell?" He got up and came for me.

I was combing my hair, but I turned. "*Look.*" I pointed the comb at him, and said: "You get over there." And my voice held together now; it was Mama's.

He checked hisself sudden, and sat down on the edge of the bed. Then he shook his head till his lips rattled, like a horse. "I don't catch you. What's the matter, what's wrong with you?"

"Everything." I tore at my hair with the comb. "Everything that was ever wrong on earth is wrong with me. *That's* the answer to *that* question."

"What I do? Ain't you . . . ?"

"Ain't I what?"

"You ain't no hustler. You ain't no real whore."

"Inside I am. Inside I'm *worse*. You shouldn't ever believe what you see with just your eyes, Best Edward Poole. The world even has purple toothpaste now."

He got up again. "What you figuring on doing?"

I quit combing my hair and stuck the comb in my bag. Then I took out his roll of money and set it on the washbasin. I had ten dollars of my own, and I put seven of them with it. "Fifty dollars," I said. "And two dollars for my dinner. The five I paid downstairs will hold for the night, if you Cajun-talk the lady. That's a present. Go get yourself some fresh company."

". . . What?"

I walked past him and put my purse on the table for a minute to pull my skirt down. I said: "Best Edward, I'm sorry. I really am sorry. You shouldn't of got mixed up with me, I ain't a very nice person. I told you to find another girl. I'm sorry, Best Edward. I hate to hurt anybody, but I plain can't help it, seems like. I didn't do it on purpose. I'm just . . . that way. And I'm sorry."

Best Edward started to the door. "Hey, don't think you just going to clear out like that. You ain't clearing out of here, honey. Not like that, you ain't." He circled behind me and stood.

I picked up my purse and turned. Mama's voice said: "Oh, yes, Best Edward. I am." And I pushed him aside, and opened the door and went out.

Along the balcony; down the stairs; back across the courtyard, darker and green-mooned now. I spun around there and looked at him. He was standing uncertain, with one foot out of the open door-way—a make-believe shadow of a sailor dangling in the ugly yellow light. I said: "Young sailor, good luck. And stay away from the ones like me." Then I went along the passage and let myself out the heavy grilled gate onto the street.

There was nobody in sight. Nobody for blocks. Only the green moon, fading upwards—and some street lights that didn't take no notice—and the smell of old wet—and the sound of my own footsteps slapping against the buildings and jumping back to clatter on ahead of me till they died into each other. Once a she-cat screamed behind me and went on screaming, fearful-high and grating, like a baby being ripped in two. But it was all part of the night, and nothing more could bother me.

Something of a glow mixed into the black, and a juke box called out to me. I was getting near to that part of the Quarter. Then a couple talking—another one necking—a whore standing alone in the middle of the street, leaning over with her hands on her hips, being sick. Then some men.

It wasn't how quick I was walking, it was the way: as if I was crunching down on bugs and liking it, just hoping for some person to fall across my path. I never had to go slower or change my direction. People, men might shout things at me, from a distance, or from across the street—but any man who saw my face knew to leave it alone. Only one drunk stood in my way, and reached to grab me. I straight-armed him, without stopping, so hard he swiveled and sat down on the pavement.

I remember walking through the glow and the noises and smells that highed into the night, and then feeling them back of me. Eating the pavement with my feet along Canal Street till a late streetcar caught up with me; sitting so upright on the wood seat, every clack of the car knocked me off balance. It was twenty minutes to the end of the line, but when one of the conductors started to switch the seat-tops around, it seemed like I had just got on.

I didn't take the transfer bus. I walked by the cemetery; across the bridge; past the gas station to the golf course. All the way to the Jenkins' I sailed along, letting my body carry my legs, swinging my legs to keep up with my body. Not sensing nothing. (While Mama sat home and worried her handkerchief till morning when she could go over to the drugstore and phone up to find out if I was truly dead, or only partly mangled and ruined worse. But I never thought about that.)

I went to the back of the house and pulled the screen door wide. I had my key pointed exactly right, and the blue wood door opened so easy I never had to stop moving. Up the back stairs, in the dark, and into my room; undressing without the light, not to wake Celeste; putting my clothes on a chair.

Naked, I went into the bathroom and closed the door soft, pulling it till it snapped to. I switched on the light.

And then I finally stopped.

I held quiet in front of the mirror over the basin. For a long time, I looked at my reflection, almost a real brown against the shiny white tiles. I watched the tears that had spilled down my face and neck, and I watched them still come, and I wondered when I had started to cry.

I raised my fist in the air and hit myself with it in the face three times, slow and vicious.

I said: "Goddam it, goddam it to hell, you couldn't even do that. You couldn't even whore. Learn, honey. Learn, learn, learn. Worse than a nothing, learn. Worse than a filthy, shitty stick, worse than a dead thing on show, worse than any person you ever met in your life, *learn*: you can't do right . . . *and you can't even do wrong.* Learn what you ain't, and stop trying to be. Quit the fighting. Quit the heartache. Give up." I watched myself sob out loud, and I said: "Go on, have fun with it now. Cry all you want to. Make it good and sad. Because you ain't never going to cry again. You ain't going to feel sorry for yourself, because you don't have no self. You going to shut your mouth, and you going to shut your mind, and you going to quit pretending you have a heart to shut too. And that's *all* you going to do. Unless you want to fuss up God for leaving the soul out of you. You want to fuss up God, you stupid jackass-fool? Think you can fuss up a fight with God? Go on crying, go on. You so dumb you make me want to laugh." And when I said that, I did begin to laugh—hard, from the stomach.

But all the same, I knew I wasn't listening to my own voice. Because through the sobs and the laughter, another part of me just kept right on repeating: "Goddam it. Oh, goddam it. You stupid, dirty, simple bitch. You couldn't even do that."

4

MR. JENKINS was scared of lightning. Really scared. So scared, if there was an electric storm, he would find a place to go and close hisself in where he couldn't hear it or see it. The trouble was, when they built that house, they forgot about Mr. Jenkins and the lightning, and they didn't even make one inside room where a person could hide. There was big square windows all over, and where there wasn't windows there was glass brick. And not one room with four plain walls.

So, with the start of the rainy season, Mr. Jenkins took to marching into his bedroom closet whenever the sky lit up, and shutting the door, and reading the storm away. It wasn't long before Dan decided to fix up the closet so it would be nicer for him.

Dan thought Mr. Jenkins was the most wonderful man he ever met. Which wasn't going very far, he hadn't met hardly any at all, white or colored. Anyhow, after the way Mama talked about the white people, he probably expected to have his fingernails torn out and thrown at him for lunch. So when Mr. Jenkins started telling him "Good morning," same as one person would tell another person, Dan used to walk back into the kitchen looking like he just got introduced to a gardenia. Didn't even seem to matter to him that Mr. Jenkins was so occupied with his poem-writing when he first came downstairs, he would say "Good morning" as much as three different times to anything that moved, generally including the Siamese cat they had, name of Mathilda.

So from then on, Dan was always dreaming up special things to do for Mr. Jenkins around the house, by way of making that poor man's life easier on him. The morning he got the idea about the closet, he asked me to come and help; he wanted it to be perfect, because it was a surprise.

I hadn't got much of a chance to be alone with Dan lately, living away from Mama's like I was, and with Adelaide and Celeste and Mr. Stone always in the kitchen. I said: "Che. Seems to me you thinking about getting married someplace along the line."

It was hard to tell if Dan heard you when you said something to him. He never creased a muscle in his face except the ones around his mouth if he was eating or talking. Even when he laughed at a joke, you didn't know whether to believe him or not—it was just his mouth that moved.

He told me: "Try putting the table on the other side of the chair. Here, hand it in my hand."

I picked it up and swung it over to him. "You only twenty years old. I was saying you act like you was thinking about getting married."

"I got what you said." He stepped back to see how everything looked.

"Well. Are you?"

Dan spoke to the chair, and he let his voice come out on his natural breath: "We ain't made up our mind yet."

Grated my nerves, the tired way he used to talk. *"We?"* I said, loud.

". . . We ain't made up our mind yet." Just like when he was little, and he would singsong the same old thing to tease you. Except it wasn't play now.

"Well, if I was we," I said, "if *I* was *we*, which I ain't, I wouldn't make up *our* mind till I was about five years older." Fool remark to pass, only he could still irk me.

He went on working.

"I guess Adelaide gets in on that we."

He was on one knee, pushing the chair around.

"I guess Adelaide gets in on that we."

Dan flipped his head and looked at my ankle, to show me that he heard, and that he didn't like what he heard. But he wasn't going to talk no more.

Getting angry was making me angry. I held myself down. What I really wanted to say: "Dan, you best think about it some. Adelaide ain't conditioned to think none right now. She's sick, and . . ."

"Let's drop the subject, please."

"You don't have no business dropping the subject with me, man. You got a problem there. Adelaide can't . . ."

"I done told you . . ."

"Adelaide can't help you to study it out. And Mama's no good, you know that."

He stood up and dusted his hands. "What's wrong with Mama?"

"She's old, and she's sick inside. You know that. She always was."

"According to you, everybody sick around our family."

I meant it when I said: "I think that's the way it is."

"Well, you just take care of *your* sickness."

There wasn't much answer to that. I tried to tell him: "All I mean is, Adelaide ain't ready to . . ."

"You keep off Adelaide . . ."

"But she ain't . . ."

"Adelaide's the best person you ever going to meet long as you live, you keep off her. She got that stomach-trouble right on top of a sorrow is the only thing wrong with her, account of she has such a *delicate physical structure*."

". . . A what?"

He turned away from me and set the lever on the edge of the closet door.

"Where in the name of Samuel did she pick that one up?"

Dan kept his hand high on the door, and he put his head on it. He talked with his back to me, choked and uneven, out into the watery daylight of the room: "Adelaide ain't the way she seems to everybody else. She ain't what everybody thinks. She's . . . Adelaide's . . . wonderful."

Then he was quiet so long, I was afraid he wouldn't go on. But I shut up, to give him a chance.

Finally: "When you really know . . . she's got . . . like glass growing inside of her . . . But . . . but the thing is, she . . . she don't even know it herself. But I do. And I have to take care of her, so nobody won't ever smash . . . what she's got. She's so perfect. Sometimes . . . I feel like I should get down on my knees. I don't know how . . . how the Lord picked me to take care of her. I don't know what I ever did for Him. I don't know . . . she . . . she's so . . . beautiful all inside . . . I . . . I ain't never in my life had nothing to take care of like that. Sometimes I don't know what to do. I think . . . I ain't got the right hands . . . I . . . I ain't used to being around nothing like her. I just never seen a thing was like that. It scares me to plain touch her. Just to help her down some stairs. I . . . if she was ever to fall or . . . hurt herself, I . . . I don't know what I'd do. She's so perfect. I think I would rather see her dead than . . . if she was hurt. She don't . . . she can't understand about things that is wrong. She don't know about people. She don't see how things can be wrong inside people, because she thinks everybody must be perfect, like her. I wish . . . the Lord would help me to take care of her, till she dies. If He picked me, He should . . . He should show me how to do. I pray at night for Him to help me keep her like she is. I ask Him to make me right . . . fix my hands so I know how to touch her. Teach me how to build a glass house all over. To keep her breathing and walking, and . . . to give *her* the good air."

He might of gone on some more, only I couldn't hold back. I slipped my arm around him, and held. "Dan," I said. "Dan . . . oh, Dan."

But he pulled out and walked into the room. He took his dustrag and slapped it on the bedstead twice, till the air shone white. "What you making?"

"I . . . thank you, Dan. I'm grateful to you for telling me." I was afraid to go close up again.

" . . . You my sister, ain't you?"

"Yes, Dan."

He waited. I think he wanted to see if I was going to say something else. Only I couldn't, right then.

He wiped his nose on the back of his hand. "I'm just telling you: you keep off Adelaide. You just watch how you talk."

I said: "I won't . . . I never meant . . ."

It was too late, though. Too late again. "Ain't nothing for you to mean. Closet's all right like that. I got to go."

"I hope you . . ."

"Got to serve lunch." And he gave me the dustrag and went away downstairs.

What should you do when somebody you care about throws his care away? How can you tell him that his everything ain't much more than sad? How can you show him that there's more wonder in him to be able to love like he does than could ever grow in the awful thing he loves?

What is the good in caring?

Later on in the kitchen we were eating lunch, after the Jenkins got through. Dan and me and Celeste and Adelaide.

Young Mr. Stone sat by the sideboard, spelling his name out with matches. "It's not omni*p*otent," he said, "it's omni*p*otent."

Dan told him: "Well, I ain't heard it said that way."

It was Adelaide had come out with the word. Dan hadn't heard it said no kind of a way, any more than the rest of us.

Celeste said: "I never heard it no kind of a way. Which magazine did you see it in, honey?" Trust Celeste.

"No *magazine*," said Adelaide. "I don't remember where I *first* heard it, I'm sure."

"Anyhow," said Mr. Stone, "it's om*ni*potent."

Dan put his fork down. "Let's drop the subject, please," he said, "while we eating."

Mr. Stone explained: "Oh, it's not *that* kind of a word."

"It ain't the kind of word it is. It's the discussion." From Adelaide. Then she held off a second, and burped loud. Then she whispered: "Excuse me," and went through the hand-on-the-forehead-with-the-napkin act.

". . . Going to be all right?" Dan fiddled with his thumb on the back of her chair.

Celeste looked at me, and raised her eyes to God.

"It sure is a lovely stew," I said, fast, "what-all you make it from?"

"All kinds of crap," she said.

Adelaide shuddered, and slipped the napkin down over her eyes. "You watch your language," Dan said.

But Mr. Stone wanted to know: "What does crap mean?"

Dan told him: "Forget it, it ain't important."

"I just want to know what it *means*."

"Never you mind, honey," Celeste said, "it comes to about the same thing as that other word." She went and scraped her dish into the ash can. "Anybody want some more?"

"Not me," I said.

"How about you-all?"

Dan said: "No."

Adelaide pushed her plate aside, and leaned on the sink to get up. Then she turned to face us. "Thank you kindly, but I have had an *ample sufficiency*." Came out like she'd been practicing it all day.

Course it didn't get by Celeste. "My Lord," she told her, "don't let a little thing like that bother you, honey. I had one of them too. Just take a fast shot of Pluto Water before you go to bed tonight. Dear."

Dan took his plate over and began to scrape the food off, loud.

Adelaide made a weak step forward and then stopped. "I plain hope I ain't going to be sick at the stomach, with all this discussion."

"Sick at the stomach *how?*" asked Mr. Stone.

"Upchuck, she means," said Celeste, heavy.

"Heaven above," said Adelaide. "What a word."

Celeste screwed up her face and leaned back against the stove. "Which word," she said, slow, "would *you* use *this time?*"

Dan wasn't looking at Adelaide's face when he stood up, proud. "The right word for it is *vomit.*"

Celeste shook her head. "Not for me. Saying vomit makes me just see it there on the sidewalk."

Mr. Stone said: "But it is too the right word, though. Of course, a lot of people will say upchuck when they *mean* vomit, but vomit is the way they teach it in school."

"They teaching that now?" Celeste asked.

"It's definitely vomit," said Mr. Stone.

"It might be," said Celeste, "but it's still upchuck to me."

Nobody was paying any mind to Adelaide when she put one finger between her teeth and rushed up the back stairs. Dan was so surprised he just stood there.

Celeste smiled. "One thing I appreciated about that girl from the first day," she said, ". . . always willing to try something new."

But Dan suddenly went up to her so fast he kicked over the ash can. "You shut up, do you hear? You shut your mouth with Adelaide. See what you did now? Next time something like that happens . . . you going to be sorry." His face had drained very pale, and blotches stood out in it while he talked. The way his eyes stuck wide and his bottom lip shook open made it a thing I hadn't ever seen before.

Celeste said: "Ah, I was only fooling." He'd scared her too, though.

"You remember what I said." Dan stared down at her, near sobbing with his breath. Like a little, little boy that plain could not say what he wanted and spill it all out. He stayed the same for about fifteen seconds, with his mouth moving, and a string of spit sliding from the left corner over onto his chin. Then he backed away and ran upstairs.

"Gee," said Mr. Stone. "Gee."

Celeste let her breath out. "What-all is the matter with that man?"

But I didn't answer. Because I could still see him there: his bottom lip twitching; and that little boy staring—out of place and horrible—in my grown-up brother's face.

5

BY the time the rain started, the weather had already turned cold. It began on a Saturday night, and by Sunday afternoon the puddles in the gravel road that passed the house was joining together to make one solid channel. Cars sizzled by in it, throwing a heavy arc of muddy water high into the air.

The rain was steady and slow, straight down. There was no wind. After three days the muck got so thick you couldn't hear a splash—only a gutsy plopping, like the rich thud of pouring beer. Outside, the two baby magnolia trees that had just been planted bent their arms down and their tops back under the beating, and shook a few leaves away: two hustlers taking a shower, and shimmying some while they was at it, for God. The badminton court ran red into the lawn and mixed with the gook, settling over the first feelers of smooth winter-grass, not long seeded. And water seeped through into the house and trickled there, to show us for the hundredth time where the builders hadn't fitted another window exact into its frame, or where they had used the wrong kind of glue to fasten a rubber strip under a screen door.

One day of the rain, Mrs. Jenkins rang me up to her room on the second floor. She was laying on her pink and iron-colored bed, reading. It was right after lunch, and Mr. Jenkins was there too, instead of in his study. He was sitting along the sofa with his feet up, making marks with a pen in some book. It was very dark outside for that time of day, and they had the electric light switched on and all the curtains drawn.

Mrs. Jenkins took off her glasses. "Lucille, would you sit with us for a moment?"

". . . Yes, ma'am." I went and sat on the edge of the stool under her dressing table. The pink sheet-mirror sent out a warm flush around the room. Through a crack in the curtains, I could see the swollen gray glare of the sky.

She smiled. "I feel that I should talk to you for a bit . . . *if* you don't mind?" Mrs. Jenkins had an honest, right kind of voice; but she didn't know that, and she generally tried to make it sound so true it got phony.

"No, ma'am, course not." I tossed that off, like it was all just a natural thing.

She said to Mr. Jenkins: "If we disturb you, dear, we could go into the other room."

But Mr. Jenkins didn't hear. He turned over a page in his book. Like Clarence.

"Frankly, I prefer that my husband be present. I want to talk to you for the family."

"Yes, ma'am." Then something was wrong.

"I have begun to feel," she said, "that something is wrong."

I kept still while she lit a cigarette. The smoke came out of her nose in two blue streams.

"And . . . I want to put it to you in a way that will be clear. And try to help you if I can. You see . . . we are not accustomed to the mores of life in the South."

"Yes, ma'am. The mores?"

"The . . . habits. The ways of looking at things that are in practice here. My husband has been away from New Orleans for a good many years, and I have never been here before. But from what I can see, and . . . uh . . . from a few unimportant incidents that Stone has told me about . . . I feel that there is a certain . . . well, *tension* among all of you downstairs."

I was swallowing, so I could only nod my head.

"We . . . uh . . . what we don't want any of you to imagine . . . you see, we know, everybody knows, that there are certain laws in effect here governing the distinction and separation . . . of the different . . . well, *races*. However, we want to make it very clear that we wish no separation of that kind in this house. What I mean is . . . we don't want you to feel *awful* simply because you are a *Negro*." She frowned and smiled at me at the same time.

"Yes, ma'am."

"You understand what I mean?"

" . . . Yes, ma'am."

"Everyone in the South seems to go under the ridiculous impression that because a person's skin is darker, the person must be dirty or whatnot. Of course, that is *just plain silly*. Now we want to do all we can, in our small way, towards correcting this mistaken idea. So we don't want you to be ashamed in any way while you are with us. There is nothing *wrong* in being a Negro. It is perfectly *all right*."

"Yes, ma'am."

"You see, Lucille, I've decided that you are the one to whom I should speak, because you and your brother are actually rather light in color. Celeste and Adelaide are much darker. And I and my family are all white. That puts *you* in a very fortunate position. And I think you should take advantage of that position, and that you should be the one to . . . cement the good feelings between white, and . . . uh . . . black."

"Yes, ma'am."

"You see, if any of *you* feel that there is something wrong about the fact that *you* are *Negroes,* then, of course, I must feel that there is something wrong about the fact that *I* am *white.* Now, do you want me to feel that there is anything wrong about the fact that I am white?"

". . . No, ma'am."

"How do you want me to feel about it?"

"Well, ma'am," I said, "don't you worry about it none."

"*There,* you see?" The smile got so big her ears wiggled. "Now, I have made you say to me just exactly what I have to say to you: don't *you* worry about it either."

"No, ma'am," I said, "I'll try not to."

"Good girl. I know we are going to get along very well, indeed. You see, if one goes about feeling that one is . . . well, inferior to someone else, just because of a little thing like color . . . one . . . well, one develops certain *subconscious fears.* Now, fear can be an awful thing. We want you to realize that there is nothing to be afraid of in this house. Everything is safe and easy here, and we want you to feel just as free and secure as we do. Now, is that clear?"

Before I could answer, there was a quiet little growl of thunder from a lightning flash that must have been too far away to shine through the curtains. Mr. Jenkins jerked straight up and looked around.

"Now, Vincent," said Mrs. Jenkins.

Mr. Jenkins frowned into the air before he bent to pick up his glasses and his book from the floor, where they had fallen. "Electric storm's starting," he said.

"No, it's not dear, that was just two clouds bumping together way over Baton Rouge or somewhere."

"Don't be silly," he said. "And it *wasn't* a long way off."

"Vincent, you just do your work, dear, and don't worry. We're going to finish our conversation."

Mr. Jenkins opened his book and began to find the page.

"Now, you do see what I mean, don't you? We want you and all the others to feel just as secure and happy here as we do. Because as soon as you and I get these little misunderstandings straightened out, there is really nothing to feel *in*secure *about*."

"Yes, ma'am." I said.

The curtains glowed white for half a second on the far side of the room. Mr. Jenkins dropped his book on the floor again, and jumped up. He started to count: "One, one thousand, two, one thousand, three, one thousand, four . . ."

"*Heat* lightning," said Mrs. Jenkins.

"There is no such thing as heat lightning, and you well know it. Five, one thousand, wait I skipped a little that makes eight, one thousand, nine, one thousand, ten . . ."

The thunder grunted hard.

"Only six and nine-tenths miles away," said Mr. Jenkins, "and getting closer every second."

"Oh, now dear . . ."

"It *is*," he said, "it is getting closer every second. And I *know* it is, so you needn't bother making up any stories about it."

"Well, now, dear," Mrs. Jenkins told him, "I didn't plan the storm."

Another flash, double this time; the two thunders mixed into one long one. Mr. Jenkins made his hands into fists and looked as if somebody had put a live goldfish down his back. "If I'd had any idea this was going to start, I'd be at Harriet's house by now."

"Why *Harriet's?*" said Mrs. Jenkins. "Bill can't even be home from work yet."

Mr. Jenkins mumbled something about Harriet having thicker curtains.

"Now, dear," she said, "just relax. Just remember that magnificent passage you were reading to me from Berkeley the other day, about all the choir of heaven having no substance except in the mind. Well, now this is a part of the choir, dear, and if you don't recognize it as being out there, well, it just simply is not out there."

Mr. Jenkins got a brand new expression on his face, sort of like you see on a puppy when he remembers where he's left a bone. "Not out there," he said. "*Not* . . . out there."

More thunder.

"Oh, yes it is," said Mr. Jenkins. He picked up his book, and walked fast into his own room.

Mrs. Jenkins called: "Shut the closet door tight, Vincent, and

you won't hear a thing at all." She turned back to me. "You see?
. . . we all have our little problems. My husband is an artist, and
so of course he needs all our assistance in his dealings with the
outside world. The important thing in life is that we be *aware* of
our problems, so that we can move on into the future with a better
understanding and a newer outlook for all concerned. Well, I think
you and I understand each other now, don't we? Mr. Jenkins and I
want to share some of our happiness and security with you. We
want you to feel that you are all members of the same large block
as we white people. White and black together."

"Yes, ma'am."

"Right you are. And now that that is cleared up, I know you
will find any serious problems you might have thought you had
here will clear right up with it. You can't really have any more
serious problems in this house now, can you?"

". . . No, ma'am."

"Good *girl*. We are all equal, and we are all people, from now
on. If we don't do things like eat together, that is because each
of us has a different place in the house, and each of us has different
work to do. But the difference is not in our equality. We are all
the same. Some of us do one kind of work, and some of us do another
kind of work. But we are all just *workers together*."

"Yes, ma'am."

"Right you are. Well, back to work. And please remember to tell
the others that we are all part of the same family here. We don't
want anyone feeling like a *Negro* or like a *servant* in this house.
Will you remember to tell them that?"

"Yes, ma'am."

After I opened the door, she said: "No more *tension*, now."

I went out and shut the door behind me. While I was walking
through the passage, lightning glared once through the glass brick:
ugly, naked white. The thunder crashed right away, hurting-hard,
and much closer than before.

Something below my stomach felt it, and twisted to answer.

Downstairs in the kitchen, Celeste was drinking a cup of coffee.
She said: "You took so long, I finished that piece of sewing for you.
Didn't have nothing else to do."

"Thanks, che," I said.

"What she want?"

"Nothing special. Just to talk."

"Talk about what?"

"I ain't sure," I said. "She wants me to tell you, you ain't supposed to feel like a Negro or a servant."

Celeste spit a swallow of coffee back, and gagged. "Oh, happy day," she said, "oh *happy* day."

I sat down.

"You kidding, ain't you?"

"No."

She slapped the coffee cup onto the stove. "That's just fine," she said, "that's just lovely. Oh, happy, happy day."

I told her: "Foo, she didn't mean it that way. She really meant it nice."

"I know, honey, don't tell me, I know. I used to have this boy friend would do all kinds of crazy things you never expected. Always meant them nice, though. He really always meant them nice. He was the one I was in love with for true. Used to live right here in New Orleans, till we had that last little disagreement."

I didn't see much point in it, but I asked her: "Where does he live now?"

Celeste poured out some coffee and handed it to me. "He don't," she said.

6

THE rain kept on for two and a half more weeks, and then stopped for three, and then started for three more. When it stopped that first time, you could tell it was only taking a breather: the sky was a gloomy, wrinkled cloud that sat heavy on the land, smoothing as it filled to break again.

The smell of wet lived in everything, and held, frozen, in the dead air. It got back of your nose to clam up there, and the whole world smelled flat. Celeste said if little Columbus had went out of his mama's house on a day like that, and took one good whiff, there wouldn't be no cowboy pictures.

It was in the second to last week before the rain started again that Howard Crawford came back to New Orleans for Adelaide. He drove up to her house one night in a big red De Soto with his name written on the side in silver. Ten days later, she quit her job and took him in to live with her.

I knew it before that. I met Jewel on the street, and she told me Howard done had a fight with his wife up in New York City, and had come to stay with his mama for a while. The whole back of his car was full of presents for the old lady, and she took to sitting out on her gallery and then going in to change her dress every hour. And pins, and hats, and rings. Jewel said the gallery was always full of people who went to watch the show.

Right off, Adelaide started to walk different. She found her backbone, and she lost her stomach-trouble so sudden Celeste figured there was something wrong with the cooking. Because Adelaide even began to ask for second helpings.

Dan was sweeping out the garage. I said to Adelaide: "Howard's in town."

". . . Is?" she said.

Celeste turned around and spilled two peas on the floor.

"That's right," I said. "He is."

Celeste said: "Now I wonder why nobody ever told *me*." Celeste had a regular spy system, and she hated it when anything slipped through.

Adelaide bit the thread from the button she was sewing on one of Mr. Jenkins' shirts. She pressed the shirt out on her knee, and began to thread the needle again. "I really don't see how Mr. Jenkins can lose *all* his buttons like he does."

"I thought you would of known," I said.

Adelaide sucked the end of the thread, and studied on pushing it through the needle. Then she looked up. "Oh," she said, "you speaking to me?"

I told her: "I was speaking to you. I said I thought you would of known."

"Known what, che?"

". . . About Howard."

"Oh, you mean about his being in town? Why, yes, matter of fact, I did know." She made a double knot in the thread with her left hand.

Celeste picked up the two peas and put them in the ash can. "You wait till I get hold of Alfred," she said. "Poor Alfred ain't going to have a very long expectancy." (Alfred was Back-of-Town Agent Number One.)

"Must be kind of painful for you," I said, ". . . *Adelaide*."

She kept her eyes on her sewing.

"I hope it ain't *too* painful," I said, "I wouldn't like to think you was suffering none."

"Thanks, che," she said. Then quiet: "That's a real nice thought."

Celeste muttered: "Alfred better start adding up his assets."

"I wonder why Howard didn't bring his wife Fidley down with him," I said.

"He didn't *what?*" asked Celeste.

"Well," I said, "she'll probably come along later."

Adelaide swung the shirt around to sew at it from another angle. "I don't believe . . . from what I been *told,* I don't believe his wife is coming down. From what I been *told,* seems to me he must be going to get a divorce from his wife."

"A what?" said Celeste, "he going to get a what?"

Adelaide sighed. "Otherwise, what would he be doing here? I mean, seems to me a man like that wouldn't want to come back to no town like this if he didn't have a very *special* reason. Course, I really don't know nothing about it at all."

"What seems to you to be wrong with this town?" I asked.

"Oh, nothing, I suppose." She sighed again. "Course, it's one thing for the people who never thought of getting out of here. But, it seems to me, for a man like that who is a more important man than most of the white people in a place like New York City . . . well, he wouldn't exactly be crazy to come back . . . unless . . . ."

"Unless what?"

"Well, you know." She broke the thread by wrapping it around her finger, and started to fold the shirt.

"No," I said, "I don't know. I don't understand about a man who's got hisself a wife and a home someplace else, and walks out just like that."

Adelaide curved her lips and showed her upper teeth a little. "Seems to me anybody can make a mistake. Course, personally, I don't . . . ."

"Know nothing about it," I said.

"That's right," she said; "that's just what I was going to say."

"Lord," said Celeste, "I don't know what-all's been happening to me. I feel as if I been living in the middle of the Sahara Desert with all them sand scrips."

I meandered over next to Adelaide. "Pretty bracelet you got on," I said.

She covered it with her hand before she could think. Then the teeth got some more air. "It *is* pretty, ain't it?" She held her arm out under my face. "Look at it close up, che. Got my mama's name written on the back."

I didn't touch it. I asked: "What was your mama's name?"

"Why, *Adelaide*," she said, "just like mine."

Dan wiped his feet on the mat outside the door as he came in. He told us: "Still is going to rain."

Celeste leaned over the sideboard, real sad, and put her hands under her chin. "I plain do not comprehend it," she said. "Alfred was such a good friend."

Dan walked through the kitchen; he barely touched Adelaide's shoulder as he passed. "I better clean off the back porch anyway." He went on into the pantry and left the door swinging back and forth.

I said: "Adelaide. Don't mess him up."

". . . Why, I don't know what you mean, che. You mean Dan?" She got up and stretched.

"All that crap aside," I said. "You do what you want. Everybody should have a chance to do what they want. But do it right. Don't mess him up."

She yawned. "Lucille, I ain't never meant harm to nobody in all my life. I'm a person just couldn't do something that was bad." She believed it too, you could tell.

I told her: "Sometimes it's hard to know what's bad."

But Adelaide yawned again, and walked away with the folded shirt over her arm. She'd forgot all about the needle, and it must of been left hanging by the thread off her sleeve because when she brushed past the wall it jabbed into the flesh of her thumb and stuck there. She held her hand up, and ripped it out, and threw it way across the sideboard. And she kept her teeth together when she whispered: "*I hate needles.*"

She went on, but she stopped on the second step and looked back over her shoulder. "Cille, honey, I just live my life," she said, "the best old way I can."

I think Adelaide probably spoke to Dan on their way home the day she left, but maybe she did it later that evening. (She had already told Mrs. Jenkins early in the afternoon, and made up some excuse to get her pay without notice.) She wouldn't tell Celeste, and it was my Sunday off, so I didn't find out till the next morning. And I never found out exactly what she said to Dan. Wouldn't of made no difference, whatever it was. The same things would of come to pass no matter what she said or how she said it: reasons go deeper than that. Yellow and blue make green; yellow and red make orange; yellow and black make mud. Colors blend or colors clash according to the way they was set up in the first place. And if you start out by mixing certain kinds of people in a certain kind of world—certain kinds of things are what happen.

When he came in the morning, Dan went upstairs to take Mr. Jenkins a new reading lamp he'd made for him. On the way back to the pantry, he passed me. I was hoovering the living room rug.

He told me: "Better get a move on, you got a lot of work to do today."

"Not so much," I said, "about like every Monday. General cleaning is all."

Dan lifted his foot to tie the shoelace. "More than every Monday," he said.

Then I began to see. I switched off the Hoover. "Adelaide ain't coming today?"

"No. She ain't coming back no more."

I wet my lips. ". . . Dan."

He dusted off his pants leg, and then straightened. "What?" he said. Like a man would ask any question. Nothing in his voice, and nothing under it.

"Dan, I . . . I wish . . . I could help."

"Help? What? Oh, sure, I plain forgot, Mrs. Jenkins just said for us to start looking around for another part-time maid to . . ."

"I don't mean help Mrs. Jenkins," I said, "I mean help you."

"Me? Don't nobody need to help me."

"Adelaide . . ."

"Adelaide's better off where she is. Lots better off."

I said: "You don't mean that."

Dan laughed out loud. "Course I mean it. Ain't I telling you?"

And I believed him for that minute. It was so simple, the way he talked, and so easy. The way anybody might talk the day after they cut away a sore from off their soul. I believed him without ever thinking what he really might of meant. Because his eyes was clear; because he didn't know it then hisself; because anyhow, I *wanted* to believe. He stood at the other end of the room and giggled across at me—the fine young man who had just got rid of a terrible problem—and I reached out my arms and giggled with him so loud Celeste heard me all the ways in the kitchen.

And the wrong that was inside him tricked us both.

7

WHEN the rain began again, it took one day to settle into the crust of caked mud and clamshells drying over the earth, and turn that back to a moving swamp. In the center of town it took longer. But after two weeks, even there the streets ran higher than the sidewalks, and you couldn't walk around without high boots on. They got the business section drained off for two hours every morning, but it always filled right up by the same afternoon.

On the third week, it only rained in the evenings and all night. By that time, the River had swelled so high it sloshed over the levee in five places. They sandbagged it, and four of the places broke over again. Then they put warnings in the newspapers and on the radio, only not much of anybody found out what the warnings was for, because the papers didn't get delivered, and the electricity kept shutting off. On the twenty-seventh of November in the evening—just when Celeste got through telling me she was going to get on that ark if she had to cackle and lay eggs—the rain stopped for good.

The sky looked yellow right away, but nobody took it for true, including Celeste. Course, Celeste was awful superstitious. She said the only system you could really use to tell about a change in the weather was to watch a live oyster and see if it farted. According to her, the oysters will always do that, account of they can't go along with no kind of change, good or bad. The way she explained it, it takes any oyster a real long while to get used to things like they are. So by the time it does, everything got different again. So, it gets disgusted. So it farts. Celeste said she didn't see why the weatherman don't lay off balloons and just set up a diving bell and go down and watch for bubbles. She was so convinced, she went and bought herself an oyster, and put it in a bucket in the kitchen. She walked over and looked at it every five minutes, but nothing ever happened. Then Mr. Jenkins heard about it, and he called me in and got me to tell him the whole story. I had one pretty embarrassing minute, but I made a quick substitute of a hiccup for a fart, and got through it all right. He looked most interested, and turned to Mrs. Jenkins, and said: "These folk superstitions always have some basis in reality," whatever that might mean; then he ran and got his stop watch, and took to coming into the kitchen every two hours on the nose, and sitting over the bucket, taking notes. Which went on for four entire days, and between Celeste and Mr. Jenkins, the poor oyster never got any privacy at all, so personally I didn't think it would of passed gas even if it had wanted to. And besides, I kept telling Celeste it was dead, she just wouldn't believe me. She finally had to give up, though, what with the smell and all, and she fed it to Mathilda the Siamese cat. Then Mathilda got sick on the living room rug, and Celeste said that was some kind of a sign too. Anyway, the rain stopped.

For those three weeks, I stayed close to Dan as I could. I studied his face and the way he acted and talked—because I would think: it can't be so easy; it must come out *some* way you can see.

There was nothing. He smiled; he made jokes. And when he looked at me, a freshness shone out that made me want to run and skip with him, like when we were kids together by the River. So all I could do was be with him and try to show how glad it made me that he was a man now.

You could tell the good difference from one day to the next. He was opening up and getting lighter on his feet; the mask was beginning to crack through and slip aside. It was like Adelaide took the weight from him when she left. Like all the soul-gritting years that knotted him inside had come to a head and boiled away with his love. After the rain, sometimes he would go outside and stand with his mouth open, stretching so hard his bones cracked. He made you think of a butterfly, ripping off its cocoon, waiting for the sun to dry it and bring out the colors. A butterfly of a man that blinked back at the straining new sun—free for the world at twenty.

He had a deep cough then, and I got some medicine sent over from the drugstore the Jenkins used. He made a game of letting me give it to him off the spoon: wanting to see it spill over us or drip on the floor. If I held it way out, he craned his head down and stuck his tongue in it first. Then we giggled, and I tried to keep my hand steady, and when the dark red syrup oozed over, Dan plain guffawed.

But his youngness wasn't at all like the horrible little boy I had seen that day in the kitchen. It was a nice, natural young—what

Dan should of been. In the evenings, I bundled him up tight and I held my palms on the sides of his neck a minute, hugging to him, before he walked off quick down the drive.

And one morning he came late, and he was carrying a bunch of fresh jonquils that he'd bought for me with his own money from the flower shop where he used to work. I put them in a glass in my room, where the sunlight could hit them. That was when I started to forget about myself and my own problems—thinking I could help somebody I loved, and loving the world through him. Because my brother Dan, with his ton-deep suffering and horror that nobody knew—fighting a dying king's battle on one lost acre—was showing me the sun.

I couldn't understand why his cough kept getting worse. But when I told him he should stay with Mama for a couple days, he only giggled and played the game of taking his medicine off the spoon, and then some pills Mrs. Jenkins gave me for him to swallow once every four hours. And I got Mama to feed him hot soup with supper and a hot lemonade when he went to bed.

Nine o'clock one Wednesday night, five days after the sky began to clear, I was finishing up in the kitchen with Celeste. Mr. and Mrs. Jenkins was out, and Mr. Stone was in bed asleep. When the phone rang, I ran to it, not to let it wake him, and I grabbed a pad of paper and a pencil off the pantry shelf to take the message. But it was for me.

Adelaide sounded shaky, only she always spoke so low, I couldn't really tell if it was her or the connection. She asked twice who-all was in the house before she would say anything—and then she just asked if I would meet her the next afternoon at the drugstore down Millicent from hers and Mama's house. I had Thursday off, and she knew that, but I said I didn't see why unless there was something very particular. Course, I was already pretty sure there must be, or she wouldn't of called me up. She told me it was important, and not to tell Dan; she wouldn't say no more. We made a date for four o'clock.

I walked slow into the kitchen, and sat back against the door of the grocery closet. Celeste had been listening on the backstairs extension, and she said I shouldn't worry: Adelaide probably just got a diamond nose ring she wanted to show off with her new clothes. But that night, I turned around for hours in bed, shivering without no cause. The little clock between the beds clicked its seconds out like a flapping fly swatter in the heated room.

In the morning, I did the early work, and yelled goodbye to Dan from across the kitchen. He was stacking plates in the pantry. I felt like a sneak, and I didn't want him to see me too near. I slipped out of the house before he could dry his hands.

Sitting with Mama made me feel worse, so I went and walked a couple miles right after lunch. The stream in the streets had gone down, and humps of muddy gravel stuck out of it, washing away. I had to pick my way careful when I crossed them, my knees bent low to make my step lighter. And even so, the thick water came halfway over my boots, and my stockings got dotted. It smelled bad too, because the flood had backed up the sewers and left the dirt to run all through back of town, where nobody would come to fix up that kind of mess. I kept the same speed going over the broken pavement, and my feet made loud splats whenever they hit a level on the cement. I walked up and down our neighborhood, hurrying nowhere, asking somebody the time often as I could. I went in the drugstore a half-hour early, and sat at one of the sticky, green tables in the back. The other two was empty; the Thursday people wouldn't start coming in for another hour at least. I had a cup of coffee.

Adelaide came at ten minutes to four. She saw me right away. She wore her hair slicked into a tight bun, with a black silk scarf tied over; it pulled her eyes up and made her face thinner. And she had on a black dress—new, but plain—with a black patent-leather purse, and black boots. No jewels, not even a pin. Not even the gold earrings she always used.

She sat down soon as she was near enough to the table, awkward and fast.

"You look nice," I said. She did.

"Oh, thank you, che." She was upset, but she couldn't help running her long fingers over her hair and pulling her neck out to match. She had stopped using polish, to let her nails grow. "I just put on this old dress, last minute."

"It's a pretty dress," I said. "Not old."

George the soda jerk hollered over what was it going to be. Adelaide kept her back turned and pointed high at my coffee. Then she took a blue compact out of her purse, and made out she was powdering her face till he came with the cup. When he had gone, she snapped it shut and put it on the table.

"Lucille . . . I wanted to see you."

"That's what you said." I waited.

She took a sip of coffee. Then she put one elbow next to the cup and picked at the front of her dress with a hooked finger. "Thank the Lord it stopped raining."

"Yes."

"I don't know what we would of done. I mean, we couldn't even walk out of the house for a while."

"Sure not."

She moved in her seat and took her arm down. "Must of got worse up to the Jenkins', with the shells and the court . . . and the grass and all."

"That's right," I said, "it did."

"Well, it was pretty bad here too." She cleared her throat. "You get over to your mama's in the rain?"

"Days off. Like always. Mama was okay."

"Well, I'm glad of that. Course, she had Dan staying with her. Didn't she?"

"Course. You know she did."

"Did Dan . . . was he working all that time?"

"Sure," I said, "like always. Adelaide, what you got to say to me?"

She put her hand up to fiddle with her dress again, and took it away soon as she saw me staring at it. "I'm . . . trying to give the nails a chance to grow."

"I saw that."

"Cille . . . I don't know what to say. I don't . . . know how much *you* might know."

"About what?"

"Well, about . . . the way I'm living, and . . ."

"I know how you living," I said.

"It . . . it ain't that exactly. Cille . . . I'm . . . worried about Dan."

Then I sat back and laughed. The flower lady, dressed in black and scaring me to make herself feel important. I swallowed at the anger that came with the relief. "Don't you worry none about Dan, honey. He's just fine, and he ain't worrying his head none about you."

Adelaide put both hands around the table edge and leaned towards me. She said: "Yes, he is."

"No, he *ain't*," I told her. "He is *not*. Dan is better off than he ever was, and he done forgot about you like a spoiled fish. Why you did him a big favor, che. You took all the bad out of him when you left." Then the set of her face cooled me off. "I didn't

mean it like that, honey. I'm sorry. But you really ain't got nothing
to do in *them* parts."

Adelaide wasn't peeved though. She looked scared. "Cille, he
. . . you don't know. He comes to the house at night."

". . . He *what?*"

"He comes to the house at night. No, please, che. Don't laugh.
Che, listen. Don't; now listen. In the morning, early, about three
o'clock, he comes. Every night."

"Excuse me," I said, "excuse me, but ain't those kind of strange
hours to drop over for a cup of coffee . . . *and a smile?*"

"He don't come for coffee. He don't come in. I wish you would
listen to me. He stands on the gallery stoop for about two hours.
Watching. He just stands there and he watches."

I quit laughing to stand up. "Adelaide, I ain't got this kind of time
to waste. I was going to the pictures this afternoon, and it begins
in . . . twenty minutes."

"Please don't go, Lucille. Don't go."

"Honey, look, I'm sorry. I'm sorry do you want to make a big
deal out of this for yourself, but I ain't going to help. And Dan
ain't going to help. You plain got to get it into your head that
you finished and forgot about, and you got to start new with Howard.
If he won't pay no attention to that stomach-trouble, or whatever it
is now, I'm sorry. But don't come running back to us for that or
for anything else. We took care of you, and we nursed you along,
and you left. And you going to *stay left.*" I was out of breath, but
I had said it all. I got ready to leave.

Adelaide sat very still. She said: "If you go away now, I swear
I will call the police."

I pulled my hand back to slap her, but George the soda jerk
came around from behind me. "What's wrong?" he asked, "something wrong?"

Adelaide said fast: "It ain't nothing. Thank you, but it ain't
nothing at all."

He looked at us both. Then he pulled one end of his mouth down.
"Don't make me no mess around here. I ain't having no fights." He
walked away.

Adelaide told me: "You better sit down."

I bent and slid into the chair. I took a deep breath. "Honey . . ."

"Listen, Cille. You got to listen. I know you never did like me,
and you don't like me now, but that don't make no mind. I ain't

trying to start a mess for you. All I want is to be left alone, like you said. Howard and me getting ready to leave town, but we can't do it before three weeks. We planning to leave right after Christmas Day, or maybe a little later. But you got to stop what's going on before then. It's the truth what I'm telling you."

". . . Tell it again," I said.

Adelaide swallowed. "Dan comes to the house. Every night he comes. He comes to watch."

"Since when?"

"For two weeks, I think. Maybe more. Two weeks ago I got out of bed to fix the window. It was three-thirty or four in the morning. The window didn't close right, it . . ."

"I don't care about the window," I said, "finish what you got to say."

"He was standing on the stoop at the far end of the front gallery, in the shade of Mrs. Thompson's crape myrtle. First I thought he must be a trick the moon made, with the rain, and the branches moving. But I watched him a while, and he didn't move with the shadows. Then I saw the buttons on his raincoat shining, and . . . I just about screamed."

"Why didn't you?"

"Because. I knew it was Dan."

"*How* did you know, could you see his face?"

". . . No."

"Then *how?*"

Adelaide said very quiet: "I know Dan."

"You do, huh? And the night after that, did you see his face?"

"No. I ain't got no reason to lie to you, Cille."

"I ain't saying you do. I . . ."

"You said it before."

"Well, I ain't saying it now. You know what's happened to you, Adelaide? You got so sick in your mind trying to dream up a sickness for your body that you plain can't tell no more where the dream stops. Better catch hold now, honey, while you still able. It ain't so serious . . . yet. *Everybody* dreams."

Adelaide shut her eyes. She didn't talk for maybe a quarter-minute or so. Then: "Yes," she said. "Oh yes, I dream. I dream about my mama the way she was before she died. That whole last year, when she laid in bed and kept calling to me to tell me how much longer she had. Feeding her soup, one teaspoonful every quarter-hour, so she wouldn't vomit it up. Being careful not to give her any-thing sweet, so she wouldn't say I was trying to make her diabetes worse and kill her sooner. Mixing sugar with the salt in her soup because the doctor said she had to have it. Getting it in that way so she wouldn't know about the cancer, so she would go on thinking she had diabetes. I dream she's still there, dragging it on, taking forever to die. Calling to me and telling me next month and next month and next month, and never, never doing it. Never dying. I dream about taking the money she'd saved and spending it on morphine so she wouldn't feel nothing. Not knowing if the pain was real or if she was making it up like she always did. The doctor said I was giving her too much of that morphine, but how could I tell if the pain was real? Getting the prescriptions from him, and giving it to her myself so the money would last longer. Doing what I had to do with the doctor to make him give me those prescriptions. Doing it with him for the first time not to spend her money. Knowing that was all the money we had because I never could learn to do embroidery. Praying she would die soon, praying to God to make my mama die before the money ran out. And praying to make Him kill my father too, wherever he was, for leaving us like that. Asking God what my father looked like, so I could go out and find him and kill him myself, after she died. Only, in my dream, she never dies. She just goes on like that. Calling to me." When Adelaide opened her eyes she already had them set on mine—and the voice that came out was real and clear, without the sick sheen that hushed it. "Sure, honey, I dream. One night. Maybe two. But not fourteen nights in a row. And not about your brother. Not about any man in this whole, wide world, honey, would I dream. Just about my mama and about not having enough money. That's all. That's all I got to dream about. I don't care what happens to Dan, and I don't care what happens to you. I don't even care what hap pens to Howard, just so he gives me every single thing I ever need, and enough to live on till I'm one hundred and five years old and get ready to die, and then enough to die on. So you can stop think-ing I would make up a story about your brother, while I was awake, or while I was asleep, or no kind of a way at all. I told you once, honey, all I want is to live my life. Just get your little brother out of it, will you, che? Just get him off my front stoop."

For a time after she finished, I couldn't push any words out. When I could, I only said: "Adelaide. I wish I knew you before."

I got my hand over to her, but she snatched hers away and hid it under the table.

"You know me now," she said, "and you know what I want. What you going to do about it?"

I didn't answer till my head cleared. I was wondering how a person can pretend she's got a thing like a phony stomach-trouble to make you feel sorry for her, and close up the real pain that makes you want to cry. How can a person want to be soothed where she don't hurt?

Then I remembered my own pain. Sometimes you have to. I said: "Was . . . was it really Dan?"

"Yes. It was Dan."

I laid my head in my hands and held it there. "I don't understand," I said. "Jesus, I don't understand. I don't know what to do."

Adelaide told me: "You better do something."

I saw it right away. "Oh, sure. That's how he got the cough." It was the only thing I could think of.

"Going to get worse than a cough if Howard finds out."

"Howard don't know?"

"I never woke him. I'm telling you first. Maybe you can do something."   ✎

"Thanks, Adelaide," I said.

"Keep your thanks, just get him away from me. I don't want no trouble."

"Don't be . . . scared, che."

Adelaide chuckled. "I ain't scared no more," she said. "Thank *you* for that."

I sat, breathing through a crack in my hands.

"Well." She got up. "I can't stay here."

"Okay," I said. "That's okay." I let my arms fall in my lap, and went cross-eyed staring at the table.

"Goodbye." But she didn't move.

I told her: "Don't forget your pretty compact."

"You like that?"

"It's a pretty compact," I said.

"From New York City. Blue always was my favorite color."

". . . I remember."

"Cille. You can have it."

"No," I said. "You keep it, honey."

"I got lots more. I don't like that one anyway. It don't suit me."

"Sure it does. It . . . suits you."

"No. I can't use no heavy compact. My hands is too thin and delicate."

I said: "They are?"

"That's right," she said. Then: "You ought to start using a compact. Lucille, I'm going to leave it there."

"You are?" I stopped staring at the marks in the green table top, and rubbed my fingers in my eyes. "Oh, che, well . . . thanks, I . . ."

But she had already left. I watched her walk away out the door. Tall and thin, but her whole body sized right to it. When she turned onto the street, the light curved up her black dress. I could see the muscles moving soft under the black.

I guess I just hadn't ever really chanced to notice before that Adelaide was beautiful.

8

I DIDN'T go back to Mama's when I left the drugstore. I went on the St. Thomas car, and transferred, and rode out to the Canal. Then I got off and walked across the slush back to the Jenkins' house.

I tried to think of what I could tell him, but no thought came. I only wanted to be close to him a while. To take his head in my arms and hide his face against my breast. And maybe understand.

The air was cold with the wet rising up to the bleary sun. You couldn't see the sun all by itself—just a harder yellow in the haze, that burned through your eyes when you looked at it, and left dark blue splotches right ahead of them when you looked away. There was colored men on parts of the golf course carrying long crossed sticks, like rakes without teeth, scraping off the mud to show the caked grass, uneven and dull green under the brown. But you had to squint to see that, because everything looked yellow under the sky.

I walked on the near side of the sidewalk, so the cars wouldn't splash me when they passed.

I knew I would have to go with Dan to Mama's house that same night, and live there from then on. I would have to keep from sleeping in the dark, and see did he try to get out. And if he did, I would have to stop him.

I looked for some excuse to tell everybody, so they wouldn't think it was queer my living back with Mama. Some reason that Dan would believe, and Celeste, and Mrs. Jenkins too. Celeste could stay on to be there with Mr. Stone when they went out in the evening. Some excuse.

But I never needed an excuse. When I got there, Mrs. Jenkins was in the kitchen. She'd put Dan to sit on the kitchen stool, and she was feeling his pulse. He had a high fever.

She said for me to take him to Mama's and put him to bed; she would send the doctor over, and if his fever wasn't better the next day, Dan might have to go to the hospital. I told her how white doctors don't take to going into the colored section, but she said this one wouldn't mind, he was a friend of hers. Then I told her I'd do Dan's work in the house and mine too, but she said not to worry about it, because she had to get a new part-time maid anyhow, with Adelaide gone. And she said not to come to work at all till Dan was better, so I could take care of him proper—and that she would pay all the doctor bills and the medicine. I couldn't thank her. It always seems to me I can't say enough when people are like that. So I usually wind up saying nothing at all. But she didn't mind. Nice people just like being nice. That's why they sometimes do it all wrong.

Mrs. Jenkins herself drove us to Mama's front door. Dan had his overcoat and one of Mr. Jenkins' old sweaters on, but he was chattering. He put his head on my shoulder and let me hold him there. I listened to Mrs. Jenkins talk, and I wondered what Dan was thinking, and what he was going to do.

Mama came shuffling out, and stood pushing the air with her arms. I had to tell her what was wrong three times, and she wanted me to whisper so Mrs. Jenkins wouldn't hear in the car. When I'd got it through to her, she bent and looked in the window, bouncing her head up and down, and trying to smile. She kept doing that, even after the car was two blocks down the street.

I tucked Dan into bed with the sweater over his pajamas, and I laid three blankets and his overcoat on top. He was trembling so hard by then, the coat took to slipping off, and I left Mama in a chair by his bed to hold it there. I went in the kitchen and made him hot soup for when the fever went down. Mama was praying steady, and she only quit to tell me something I should of done, or what I was doing that I shouldn't. I kept busy, not to let her get on my nerves; Dan was too sick to hear.

His fever went down, and up, and down again. The white doctor finally came. He was young, and one of his legs was turned in so far, it made a clump when he limped. He told us Dan had pneumonia, but that there wouldn't be room in the hospital for at least two days. He gave Dan an injection, and said he'd be back in the morning early.

After he left, Mama told me she wasn't ever going to allow them to take Dan to a white hospital, no matter what. I explained to her about the colored ward in Charity, but she said she didn't care: the Lord and His medicines was the same there as anyplace else, and the only good of a hospital was to operate on people, and she wasn't going to let anybody do that to Dan, account of this wasn't no time to worry about his appendix. Mama thought all operations was about the appendix. I didn't argue with her, because you couldn't argue with Mama, and because I knew when the time came I would get Dan to the hospital.

At one o'clock he was more unconscious than asleep, and I convinced Mama to go to bed by telling her she would have to take care of him alone all the next day if I went to work. I took her clock and put it underneath Dan's bed. Then I shut the door and sat and kept the bedclothes on him while he turned from one side to the other. After a while, he lay still. A little past two-thirty, he sat straight up and asked me the time.

I had been waiting for it. I said: "Six o'clock in the morning. Lay back down, Dan." I put my hands against his shoulders.

"*Six* o'clock?" He frowned. "No, it ain't."

"You lay back down, Dan."

"Got to go."

"No."

"I got to go. I'm late, I got to go." He leaned forward, strong.

"Dan," I said. "*Dan.* She was here."

". . . Here?" He stared at me.

"She came here to see you while you was asleep. She said: 'Tell Dan not to get up out of bed till he's all well. Tell him not to get out of bed. *I don't want for him to get out of bed.*'"

"Said . . . said that?"

"Yes. She said that."

". . . Why didn't you tell me she was here?"

"You was asleep. She didn't want me to wake you."

Dan went on staring, and then looked at the door.

I told him: "Lay back down, Dan. Do like she said."

Then his body slumped; I pushed him back. I took the sweater off, and his pajamas, and dried him quick with a towel. I buttoned a clean shirt on him, and the sweater again. Dan lay there with his eyes wide open.

"Go to sleep, Dan. How you going to get well if you don't go to sleep? You can't get up till you all well. Go to sleep now."

Flat-voiced, he said: "I ain't going to get well."

I stopped, with the towel in my hands. "Oh, yes."

"No, I ain't."

"Why?"

"I just ain't."

"I done asked you *why*."

". . . Because."

I reached over and slapped him across the face, once with the whole inside of my hand, and once with the back.

I said: "All right, now, listen to me, Daniel Morris. *Listen*. Nobody was ever born with the right to say that. Nobody. Who in all hell do you think you are to lay there and say a thing like that? You think you can chicken off, and leave Mama and me to bury you and go on by ourselves? Well, you can't. No, sir. No, mister man, no sir, no indeed, you *can not*. It's a darling little idea you got there; only, it's too easy. It's just too simple and easy. Been having fun all this time, ain't you? It made you happy, didn't it? Opening up . . . laughing . . . singing a song to life, because you thought this is goodbye, this is all, this is going to be the end. Well, friend, it ain't quite so simple as you thought. Life won't let you laugh, not that way."

Dan's bottom lip was sagging, and after I straightened up I saw the little boy was back. The horrible little boy, set in his face like a dead baby's skull. Dan's flesh shook to give it room.

The little boy whined: "I hate it. *Mash* life, I hate it."

"Sure, you hate it," I said, "sure you do. And *so what*? Who asked you to be happy? You can hate it all you want, and you still have to see it through. You have to suffer, and you have to burn with it. You have to let it hit you and twist you and smash you up against the wall till it gets tired and goes on to somebody else. You have to let it play with you till you plain played out. And after that, you have to let it throw you away. But you can't fool it. You can't trick it or laugh at it . . . and baby boy, *you* can't throw *it* away. Oh, no. No, you don't. That's dirty cheating, that ain't part of the game. Maybe you catching on by now it ain't a fair game. Don't matter one single damn, you still have to play. Think you can cry like you was a month old, and spit and die just because you finding out all of a sweet sudden that the rules are against you? You poor thing. Let them be against you, you can't do nothing else. You can't break the rules like that, just because you think life does. Anyway, you wrong, life don't. Life don't have no rules on its side. It can play a free game, and it can do whatever it wants. The rules are just for you. It ain't fair? That's right, it ain't. It certainly ain't. You knew that when you was a *real* baby, only you let it pass. But you took one breath of air when you was born, and you used that breath to cry. Remember? Then you started to grow up, and you thought the trees looked pretty, and you forgot. You forgot the whole thing, you forgot what life really is. And you had to find out all over again. And so now you want to cry again. Except now you want to do more than cry, now you want to take life in your sticky little fists and toss it off somewhere. Man, even a real baby don't try to do that. It hollers and it kicks and it wets and it dumps, but it lives . . . God damn it if it don't live. You bigger and you stronger now, sure. You can do more now. But, friend, no more foolishness. You don't get the right to do no more foolishness than when you was a baby, to yourself, or to anybody else. Account of it ain't according to the rules. The rules don't stop *you* from suffering . . . you can suffer all you might like. They just say you can't *make* suffering. Life can. You can't. Because if you use the bigness and the strongness for that, it means you ain't even worth the rotten space you took up for twenty years on earth, or the rotten food you ate, or the rotten air you breathed. And you got them years, boy. You can't get rid of them. You was already in debt when you first blinked at the air, but it's twenty years worse right now. You got twenty rotten years to account for. Not to God; not to me; not even to yourself. Only to the shadows of all the lucky little sonsofbitches that might of got born and didn't because you did. *They* the ones going to need to hear about it. And every second you breathed away is one more second to explain to them. See, they don't know what it's like . . . they don't know how awful it is . . . they don't even know how lucky they are . . . *and they wouldn't believe you if you told them.* So you going to have to prove to those boys that you used every step of your years: to suffer or to sing or any silly way you could . . . just used. And just so you did it according to the rules. You don't like it? You hate it? That's too almighty bad. You should of thought of that *before* you was born."

But the fever had taken over again. Dan's eyes was closed, and he was asleep.

I sat with him all night; he didn't wake up again. When I got so my eyelids weighed too heavy, I went in the kitchen and drank a half a pot of black coffee without no chicory, and with plenty sugar. Then I sat back down by his bed and listened to the house knock, and to Dan cough in his sleep, and to his mumbling. I knew he was saying the same thing over and over by the pattern of sounds his voice made, but he ran all the words together, and I couldn't hear a separate one. I left the light on next to his bed so I could see when he turned over and shook the covers off. About six o'clock he was sweating so hard I changed his shirt again. He didn't even stop his voice.

Pictures of people and pieces of times ran through the night in my mind and jumbled, making no sense:

Our father and those two gentlemen; our father and Florabelle; the preacher, telling lies over his grave in a liquor-steady growl; Jewel and the nice fish sandwich; Mama sneaking to Jewel's with a bowl of soup; Mama putting Dan in the potato sack; Dan and the dead cat-fish; Dan in the white cemetery, and Clarence chewing the sugar cane afterwards; Mama and Clarence, the night he left, and Dan watching them and being sick; Dan when Mama looked at him; Dan when he looked at Mama; Mama and Adelaide; Mama and "Thank God for a Garden"; Mama, Mama, Mama, her muscled hands wandering, jerking, waiting to jump and grab us—tearing us apart to keep us safe.

Then Charles Leroy, fighting and being killed—fighting next to Clarence, and already dead; Marbelle telling me not to worry; Mrs. Pharr flicking a feather off her sleeve; Mrs. Pharr breaking the blue vase, and playing that sour tune; the White Rabbit and the wrong dream; Celeste and her questions; Best Edward, and the fat lady who called me back; Mr. Jenkins shut in his closet; Adelaide moving inside her black dress; Dan's face when it was a mask; Dan's face when it looked free; Dan's face when it was that little boy; Dan's face in my dream, when I ripped the mask off and nothing was there.

And Charles Leroy, holding me under the trees that curved in to make us a place, so it didn't matter how the other people looked or what they said, or who they was. Not caring about anybody, in the heat from his arms—not having to care about anybody ever again in my life.

Except: Dan.

Mama got up at seven-thirty, and the doctor came at nine with a message from Mrs. Jenkins that I was to remember not to come to work that day. Another injection. "No, Mrs. Morris, it's a bit early to say anything definite . . . now, I wouldn't take that attitude, no indeed I would not, I always believe in keeping the chin up about this sort of thing . . . Yes, I'm sure you must be . . . Yes, I'm sure you do . . . Yes, I'm sure you always did . . . now, now . . . now, now."

When he left, I lay down on Mama's bed for two hours; only I knew I wasn't asleep because I could hear her praying in Dan's room. Then I thought I heard Dan say something, and I got up and went in, but he had only coughed. I didn't feel very good, so I washed my face and drank some more coffee before I sat with him again. After an hour, he started to cough in a way that he couldn't stop. It woke him, and he kept doing it till he turned a dark purple and gagged and spit up what he could. Then I fed him half a cup of hot soup, and a teaspoonful of the new syrup the doctor left. When I lay his head down he was panting like he had been running, and whistling in his chest.

Mama talked and prayed. I tried not to listen. I was all right till she went in her room and I heard her winding up the victrola. But that snapped me. I ran in after her, and grabbed the record; I threw it hard as I could, edgewise, against the wall. It splattered over the room, and a big piece of it bounced back to catch in my skirt. I took that piece and broke it twice more.

A thin line of blood opened across my palm.

Mama held her hands out stiff. She said: "What you doing what you doing what you *doing?*"

I slipped her handkerchief out of her sleeve and wrapped it over my cut. It came off right away, and I wound it tight again and made a knot.

"Cille. *Lu-cille.*"

"Hush up, Mama, you going to wake him."

"Don't you dare tell me to hush up." But she was already talking lower.

"Shhh, Mama."

"I said don't you . . ."

"Yes, I heard." I took the winding-arm out of the slot in the victrola, and put it inside. Then I closed the box and pushed it back under the bed.

"Lucille."

"I'm here."

". . . Well, I never." Mama was shaking.

"That's just about what you did," I said. "You never."

"My record, my own daughter . . ."

"Look," I said. "You got two more of them hid around the house someplace. If you want me not to do the same thing again, they better stay hid till Dan gets well. And if Dan *don't* get well . . ."

"What you think you talking, girl? You in *my* house. You think you talking to some *friend?* Don't you *dare* to . . ." The words was gargling in her throat, and she had to stop.

"Mama, I've hushed you twice, and I don't count on doing it again. And I don't care whose house this is. While Dan is sick here, things are going to be like I say. Just exactly like I say."

"No, they ain't."

"Oh, yes," I said, "they are. Even if I have to send you out to live with Miss Roberta, and stay here alone and do it all myself."

"Even . . . *even if you have to send* . . ."

"All right, Mama, you better calm down. You might just as well calm right down. You know me, and you know all my life I've done what had to get done in this house. And not for what you said nor how you acted. There's a new job now, and I'm here to do it. And you can do some of it, *if* you act proper. Now lay down a while. I'll call you when I need you."

"What? Lucille, what? *What?* . . . Breaking . . . break . . . breaking my record . . . the Lord's record, and . . . ?"

I told her: "Mama, that was just another little bit of work. That's finished now. I was only finishing what somebody else started once."

Then she squinted. "You trying to be like him?"

"I got some of him in me."

"You fixing to wind up like he did?"

"No. I ain't that much like him. The big difference between him and me is that you can't wear me out."

"Your father knew I had the Lord on my side. He knew it. He was scared of me because he knew . . ."

"No, Mama, he was not. He wasn't ever scared of you."

She flattened her shoulders and swallowed. Then she said: "If . . . if my . . . *other* son was here . . . you wouldn't dare to talk to me like you is."

". . . Other son? What other son?"

"My son . . . my . . . my son . . . *Clarence.*" The word didn't sound right in her mouth.

I asked: "Here?"

More swallows. She was looking into a corner.

"Here? In this house?" I leaned towards her. I said: "Mama, would you care to have him on the wall in *every* room?"

"*My* boy," she said.

"Sure."

"*My* boy."

"Sure he was."

"*My* boy, *my* boy. The only thing I had left in my life after . . .
after . . . my mama died. And now they both gone . . . gone up to
the comfort of the Lord."

I thought: on the same carfare. But I didn't say it. I only said:
"Shhh, Mama."

She raised her head then. She raised it, and turned her mouth
down, glowering. I could see she was wanting to look like before—
like the Mama of a long time ago. But she couldn't; she was older
now, and different.

Or maybe I was.

I thought: is that what did us like it did? . . . Is that what made
creeping animals out of my brothers, and froze the blood inside them?
. . . Is that the look used to make me think I was born bad? . . .
How can it be?

Mama said: "You watch what you doing, Lucille. You remember
who I is. If you *ever* do a thing like that again around me . . ."

My mouth opened to yawn, and I stretched back over my hips.
"Oh, Mama," I said, "please just shut up. Please, Mama, be good
now and shut up."

I could hear Dan coughing some again, and I went in and closed
the door.

It took him one more day to almost die, and then seven to get well
so quick that didn't nobody understand, not even the doctor. They
never took him to the hospital: by the time there was a free bed in
the colored ward, Dan was sitting up to eat, and the fever was gone.

The first day, when I thought it must be near over, I let Mama sit
with me in his room. I held the covers down against his trembling,
and I waited for the trembling to stop with his life. His temple
blood bumped the skin out fast, picking up speed as I watched it,
and Mama prayed to match.

But I couldn't pray. I tried to once, but I plain couldn't. Because
I thought: *how*, how can I, after all this time? . . . And anyway,
saving Dan ain't up to God, not now.

I had long ago stopped feeling sure just what God might be, or
what-all He does. But I was getting more and more familiar with

practically the whole list of things He can't do, and saving people from theirselves is number one. Number two on down is saving people from other people, or from anything else.

If a person ever takes a good enough gander at God's can't-list, she either gets so scared she leaves off counting, or it stops her from being scared at all. Depends how she felt before she began. Sitting on Dan's bed and hearing Mama rattle words in time to his pulse— waiting for him to die—there wasn't nothing more I could do. So that was when I first began to number the things God can't do.

I must of spent about two hours checking off one after another till I got back to where the only thing I really had left for Him was setting up the world and filling it. Which made me feel sort of stupid, because it was the second time in my life I'd been back that far, and because if I'd went and begun from the beginning this time, instead of plowing through it the same way, I would of looked at it from His point of view right off, and that would of been that.

Well, so it did take me a while; but when I got there, this is how I thought:

God set up the world. Okay. Then He filled it with all kinds of silliness, including people. Not *as* hot, but still okay; anyhow, that's the way it is.

But after God made His bed, He just had to send everybody out to sleep in it, and figure the strong people would be the ones to rustle up and live. Because it was natural for Him to make a couple mistakes along with the world, taking off from scratch like He did; only, being God and all, once He made them mistakes, they pretty well stayed made. So from then on, all God could do was expect that the strong people and the good people would be the same people. From then on, all God could do was hope.

Hope. Hope for what, though? Come on, now, hope for what? Is He truly hoping, or is He just passing the buck? What can a person do that her God can't do?

Then I thought: no. It don't make sense. No, indeed, Sir, if You couldn't why should I try? What am I struggling around here with, if You already gave up? What is there left to do? Where does a person get off trying to outdo You?

There, I thought, see? Look what I been banging my head on all my life. Look what I been messing around with, big muckity me. Thinking I was big enough to light up on my own power, in a storm where even the Lord blew a fuse. That's a heap more than sassy, that's downright stupid. I might just as well of crawled up on a cross and tried to hold the position. Me, I can't as much as walk on water, and here I was trying to sit right in the world. A world that never cared; a world that never even had a place for me.

And I thought: well, there's my answer. No more fooling around with *that* problem. No wonder I got so acheful and twisted around. Better say the wonder is I didn't squeeze my brains out. Anyway, I'm free now. Free as the Lord. If I never knew it before, I know it now: I can't where He can't, and I ain't got no duty where He ain't liable. Maybe I'm littler than I wanted, but I'm free.

And when I thought that, it was as if I'd cut a band from over my breast, and my whole self like to loosened and pushed out. I opened my eyes and my ears, and I flared my nose, and I knew that whatever wrong went on around me, I wasn't expected to fight it. I knew that I belonged to myself, and only to myself, and that my soul was just as private as my pain. I held Dan's hand through the covers, and I wished I had told him about that instead of what I did tell him; I wished I had given him that peace instead of slapping his face and shoving him on. I wished I had done my one last thing right, for my brother.

His breathing went slower now, and Mama's prayer with it. Under my mind, her words came mumbling, over and over: "Our Father who art in Heaven, Hallowed be Thy Name. Thy Kingdom come. Thy Will be done on earth as it . . ."

So truly without meaning to, I heard: "Thy Will be done on earth . . . *Thy Will be done on earth* . . ." And then all of a sudden, all on its own, my mind cocked to one side, like a dog's head for a new smell.

Oh, goddam, I thought; goddam, goddam, goddam. Oh, *goddam.* Here we go again . . .

9

ON the morning of the seventh day, Dan was weak and worn out, but you could tell that his body had won. His eyes had stopped watering and dried shut, so I took a piece of cotton and boiled some water to wipe them clean. He smiled for me. Then I brought him a cup of soup, and he drank it all. When the doctor came later and told us Dan was going to be all right, I already knew.

I went to work the next morning, and left Mama to take care of him. I kept on coming back to the house at night to sleep, with my bed just outside the open doorway between Dan's room and the kitchen. I slept light, and I trained to get up for the least little sound. If there wasn't any, I still got up every two hours or so to see did he need something. Most times, I found him on his stomach, with the covers pulled up over his ears. But once, I woke up easy, without stretching or rolling over. When I put out my arm, I found the lamp switch right away, and I flipped it on. And Dan didn't have time to lay down fast enough to keep me from seeing that he had been leaning on one arm and watching me in the dark.

Mr. and Mrs. Jenkins drove over one evening early on their way to a party. They sat with Dan for a quarter of an hour. Mama walked in and out the room, rubbing her hands together, and fixing the curtains, and bending over to nod whenever one of them looked at her.

Dan hadn't ever quit thinking Mr. Jenkins was some kind of a superman. He squirmed under the covers while they sat there— ashamed at the attention, and at not being able to stand up. Then Mrs. Jenkins asked after Adelaide, and there was a second of quiet in the house. I said she was fine, and wasn't it wonderful how fast Dan was getting well. After that, I kept them talking about other things till they left.

I got so tired from not sleeping enough that I waved dizzy over my work, and sometimes I plain had to sit down. Celeste told me to ease off on the worry, be what it might, and Mama thought I was taking over Dan's sickness. More than anything, I wanted to talk to somebody—but who? And what would I of said about my brother? How much would I of wanted to remember?

A week before Christmas, he was already doing a half a day's work at the Jenkins'. They wanted him to hold off till the first of January, but he came anyhow. He ate a lot, and started to fill out quick and get healthy-bodied. I stuck right on with him much of the day as I could, and all night. He was heaps better, and he slept quieter, and he never tried to go out again. Even the youngness had faded: there was a gentle peace about him now, like a person who finally faces up to their own secret privateness. I got to thinking I was going simple, worrying for a thing Adelaide told me. One goofy thing I was trying to make important, when everything else you could see in Dan was all right. Looking to find the shadow behind a post, hot and glow-ing with the sun on it. What does a shadow matter? Everybody's got one; everybody who stands in the sun. (Yes, but that ain't the matter. The matter is, Dan *don't* throw no shadow. Not the kind to make a mark.) Oh, so what? So stupid what? Cille, you getting to be like Mama.

The war had been over for four months, and the soldiers was beginning to come home. But my last letter from Charles Leroy was dated April tenth. I'd studied not to think on it, ever since the day in August when all the people ran out in the streets with rattles, and made noise and hugged each other. Miss Roberta's brother came back married to a white girl he met overseas in the war. He left her there, and he was going to have her sent to New York City; then he was going to meet her and live with her up North where it wouldn't make no difference. He said he expected his kids would be white, account of he wasn't so very black hisself, and he showed you a picture of a yellow-haired girl about twenty-five, plain and shy-looking, and so white she made no outline against the sky. He always had it out to show around, but he never let anybody touch it. Every night he got drunk saying his goodbyes to the colored people, and the picture stained dirty and dark in his hands.

I never got time to wonder why I needed Charles Leroy so bad now, or to know that I was changing in some way. I had Dan to worry over. So I only asked the sun that shone over Charles Leroy not to let him be dead. I didn't want to ask for too much at one time, and I didn't add nothing about having him come back *to me*.

Every Christmas, the grocery store sent two turkeys for the help to the Jenkins' house. They did that because we were the ones phoned in the food order every day, and they wanted the business. Usually, I took those turkeys home to Mama, and let her cook them up for Christmas Day. We would all get off from work early then, and Celeste and Adelaide would trot on over to Mama's house for a party. But this year, Mrs. Jenkins had a lot of company coming for late lunch, and she wanted to know would we mind having Mama join us, and making our party in the kitchen. Mama was scared to at first, but when I told her Mrs. Jenkins had *ordered* it that way, she gave in.

I asked Celeste over on Christmas Eve, only she had to go to her new boy friend's, with Alfred. So Dan and me took the streetcar for Mama's in the evening soon as he got through serving dinner to the Jenkins. Mama made us go to church with her, and then we went back home and ate hot pot roast and cold blackberry pie she'd cooked up. We had bought her a black sweater and a black wool coat with mother-of-pearl buttons for a present, and we hid them in a box under her bed so she could find them and wear them the next day. I had an overcoat for Dan too, hid in the Jenkins' linen closet, and a purse for Celeste. It was strange and new being able to buy presents like that; I wasn't sure just how Mama might take it.

She and Dan ate their supper quiet, and kept to their own thoughts. I laughed a while, trying to make us three a family for once, but it didn't work. Mama didn't think it was a time for laughing. Course, Mama never laughed. She was always too busy thanking God.

I can't recall ever seeing Dan look as happy as he did that night. I quit trying to make it a party, and I was happy with him, sitting there and eating in the stillness that comes at the end of a long fight. Because I could tell then that Dan's fight was really over. He went to bed right afterwards, and slept straight through to morning. And after a month of gritted nerves, I slept easy too.

10

THE Jenkins' house came to life for Christmas Day. They had a tree in the living room high as the ceiling, glittering gold and silver and gay colors of red and green and blue and orange and yellow— covered with strings of lights and lead tinsel and angel-hair. The tree was planted in more than a foot of packages that piled up to the bottom branches, and each package was wrapped in the same silver paper, blue-striped, with a silvery ribbon. There was at least two hundred of them. They had presents for everybody, and one for each of us, and even one for Mama.

By one o'clock Mr. and Mrs. Laverne was there, with their three boys—all a little younger than Mr. Stone. They ran up the front stairs and down the back, all over the house; and Mr. Stone finally let up acting like an old man at his own funeral, and joined in on the third round and ran even faster. There was food to serve before lunch, and at lunch, and after lunch—so much that Mrs. Jenkins told Celeste we should save both our turkeys for some other day, and just eat what they did. She even brought us in a bottle of champagne to drink, and when Dan opened it, the cork powed and there was a gold swoosh that made a fizzing, bubbling puddle on the floor the color of the day.

Mama came at one-thirty. She sidled up the drive, trying so hard not to be seen that you couldn't miss her. I watched her from an upstairs window, and I ran down to ask her why she hadn't put on the new overcoat or the sweater. She said she'd found them, but it wasn't right to put them on while her old things was still good. Meaning if there wasn't any holes too big to patch. But it didn't matter—nothing did. When there's too much joy running wild, you forget about happiness: you don't want to let anything that real wet you down.

The only real thing that stayed with me was Charles Leroy; the shape of his face kept catching me in the middle of a laugh. But after a little champagne, I made up my mind I could only feel so close to him if he was alive. On a day like that, you like to fix the world right, in your mind.

The Jenkins had sent a letter to the army camp outside New Orleans telling them to send two soldiers over for Christmas lunch. Must of been a mix-up in the camp, because the soldiers came late, while everybody else was in the second course. They was very long-backed, and they didn't talk none. And when I looked through the window in the pantry door, I knew they had already ate their lunch: they was stuck to their chairs, pushing the shrimp cocktail down piece by piece, still scared to spoil the war effort and turning sort of green. But Mrs. Jenkins didn't get on to it, and she just couldn't give them enough food. It was okay, though, account of after lunch one of them went and threw up in the downstairs bathroom, and then they helped each other out to the back porch and got blind-drunk and had a wonderful time.

Then it was one big party, the same for the soldiers on the porch and the Jenkins and the other company in the living room and us in the kitchen. Like somebody had blown the house full of fun-gas, and put a match to it. If the soldiers got to guffawing at some joke, the Jenkins or somebody would hear them and join in, and we would hear that and do it too. Maybe nobody knew what the joke was, or maybe there wasn't no joke. Nobody cared. If people up and decide they are going to have fun, they generally don't like to stop till they had it. And if you ever let the ball touch the ground—the game will be over.

A while after lunch, the air was so full of joy, even Mama had to breathe it in and let it carry her along. Celeste was nice: she sat and told about funny things that wouldn't fuss her, and laughed for both of them. We put Mama on the high stool, higher than anybody, and we made out she was directing the party for us all. Celeste started us giggling whenever Mama made some comment that didn't mean nothing, till we had her practically chuckling with pride. I bet she never felt that good or important in her whole life, not even at our father's wake. And I know she never did again.

Around seven o'clock, Dan really began to laugh. I disremember what got him started, but it wouldn't of had to be much. He laughed and sputtered, doubling up like a washrag you wring into a knot. Celeste and me caught it from him, and for a time only one of the three of us could hold enough wind to make any noise, while the other two choked and waited for it to come back. Mama's voice kept jabbing through it to say: "Stop that . . . Now you-all stop that," partly scared at seeing us let go that hard, and partly wanting to do it herself and not knowing how. Course, the more Mama told us to stop, the worse it got, because laughter only grows and swells on a reason to die. So we went on choking and wheezing and dragging our whole selves with the *ha-ha* that pulled into one long *haaaaa* before it burned out on its own to leave us weak and worn.

Dan was the last to stop. While Celeste and me panted, he wiped his eyes, and hid his face in his handkerchief—peeping at us over the top to see if he could get it going again—asking not to let it end. But the ball was down: the game was finished. And dead laughter is deader than a baby's tears.

He got up to kiss Mama on the cheek; when he walked away, she pressed both hands over it and watched him. He walked past Celeste, and fingered the top of her head, looking at me. Then he took me in his arms, tight till it hurt. He stood back, grinning wide—a real grin—free and happy for hisself, and sorry for me and for all the rest of the world that couldn't feel that way. And maybe just a bit sorry for something else too. After that he went back and sat in his chair and looked down at the ash can.

"Hit me Henry," said Celeste, "this is what I call a for-true Christmas."

Mama folded her hands and pouted. "Thanks to the Lord," she said. "The Lord been too good to us. Shouldn't be taking no advantage of the Lord."

Celeste asked: "What advantage? Who is taking His advantage?"

"You-all is. Folks like us can't go laughing like that just because we might want to. What the Lord going to think?"

". . . But we feeling good."

"That ain't no excuse. If you feeling good, you keep it to yourself.

Don't show it off none; don't wave it in the Lord's face. The Lord don't like for the colored people to feel too good. It ain't our place. If He sees us acting like this, no telling what He likely might do."

"What He got against us?"

"Be careful how you talk," Mama said, "be careful."

Celeste rubbed her elbows. "You sure can make Him sound peculiar."

The same instant Mama had her mouth open to answer, Mr. Stone banged in so loud from the dining room he made us jump. He shouted: "*Where did they go?*"

"Boy . . ." Celeste flopped in a chair. "Boy, don't go around scaring a body that way." She looked over at me. "I swear to God, I practically thought it was the Lord."

"Where did they *go*, did they come through here?"

"Did who?"

"Billy and Jess and Edward."

"Them is those three little . . ."

"His little friends," I said quick. "No, they ain't been in here."

Mr. Stone hit one fist in the other hand. He was bright red. Whatever kind of a game it was, he was playing it hard as he could, to make up for all the time he never played before. He said: "They must be upstairs."

"You look like you having fun," Celeste told him.

Mr. Stone thought that over. "Not just fun," he said, "it's a very serious game. It helps a person to build up his perception."

"His what?" said Celeste.

"Perception. Perception means . . ."

"Don't matter what it means," she said, "you ain't going to build it up much standing here and talking."

"That's true," said Mr. Stone. Then he asked: "What happened to Dan?" And he turned and ran out again. The swinging door clapped back and hit the aluminum sideboard loud.

Mama said: "What-all he say about Dan? Ain't nothing happened to Dan."

But I saw what Mr. Stone meant. Dan was still sitting and staring down at the ash can, same as before. Or nearly the same. Only there was a new angle about him now that wasn't quite right. He was just not sitting quite right. Not for Dan.

I crossed in front of Mama. I said: "No, there ain't nothing. Mr. Stone likes to fun him up." Then I told Celeste: "You shouldn't use the Lord's name like you do."

It reminded Mama. She called Celeste over to the high stool and started off on a lecture about the Lord and the colored people. I waited till she got into it, and I squatted down by Dan. I said, half-tone: "What is it, man?"

He didn't talk; he stared right on through my middle with his big, shiny eyes.

"Dan," I said. "Dan, what is it?"

Nothing. He wouldn't look up.

I patted his knee. "Hey," I said. "Dan. You feel sick?"

Kindly, he said into space: "More than sick. Lots more than sick."

"I told you you shouldn't of come to work," I whispered, "not right after being in bed like that. Come on, you come up to Celeste's room now and lay down, and you'll feel better later."

He moved his head just a tiny bit to shake it. "Not later."

". . . What?"

He moved it again.

"Come on, man. Going to be all right."

"No," said Dan, "it ain't."

"What? Oh, sure. You come on upstairs and lay down now, for . . ."

"I can't. I can't lay down." Neat and perfect, like if he was telling me the time.

"Hey. Ain't nothing the matter with you." Suddenly it seemed pretty important to make him believe that.

Then he raised his chin just enough to look at me, and he looked down again. And, I'm glad he did, because it's the way I can always see Dan whenever I want to.

He said: "That's what you think."

The buzzer rang twice from the living room. It seemed a lot stronger than usual, from the quiet voices we were using. Twice was for Dan, but he didn't budge. He acted like he hadn't heard it.

I told him: "They buzzing you."

Mama had stopped talking.

I got on my feet. "Think I'll go myself," I said, "sort of like to see what they doing." I made Mama tie my apron in a fresh bow, and I told Dan from there: "You stay where you are, man. You let *me* go." I went and propped the door open, and skipped on out through the pantry.

I crossed the dining room, all dark around the long black table. Part of Dan went ahead of me, high up and faster. "Foo," I said, "you just tired."

In the living room everybody was talking at once. The voices chittered together, and sawed apart—like cricket music. The people was busy enough not to take much notice of me; colored lights from the tree licked around their white faces and settled down into Mrs. Jenkins' diamond pin, sharpening there.

I had some fool thing to say if she asked me why Dan hadn't come. But she only touched the empty cookie dish. I nodded and picked it up. When I was going, she said: "Lucille."

I stopped and turned.

"Is everyone having a good time?"

". . . Everyone, ma'am?"

"Yes. All of you in the kitchen."

"Oh, yes, ma'am," I said. "Thank you so much. Yes, ma'am."

"That's nice." The two ladies on either side of her smiled. One of them was Mrs. Laverne.

A man said: "Merry Christmas," a little drunk.

"Thank you, sir. Merry Christmas to you, sir."

Then they all quit their conversations and said it to me. I nodded my head, doing my best not to look like Mama; I walked out sideways, nodding up and down.

In the pantry, I put the dish by the sink and filled it from the pan of chocolate brownies Celeste had made. I couldn't hear any talking in the kitchen and I called out: "They ate up all your brownies, che. They sure did take to your brownies." When nobody answered, I said: "They told me Merry Christmas. All of them. They the nicest people. They real nice."

Still no answer. I was beginning to wonder if everybody might of gone up, when Mama said: "*Oh*, Lucille. *Oh*, Lucille." She sounded gaspy, as if she was being sick; I ran into the doorway, one last brownie in my hand.

Mama wasn't sick. She stood next to Celeste, against the stove, and she was curved way back over it, like she was trying to get away from something. Both of them watched past me into the corner where Dan had been sitting.

I made myself go forward another foot, and looked around the edge of the bright metal cabinet to see.

Dan was kneeling on the floor. His body was iron-straight, right to the top of his head. He held his arms out, and his hands wound together—woven into a ball—pale around the knuckles. He pumped them to an even beat, like a praying mantis, clobbing his own chest. And his body swung in a slow, painful circle, around and around and around.

Mama said again: "*Oh, Lucille.*"

I told her: "All right, Mama, it's all right." But my voice didn't mean much there. I went and knelt down next to Dan, and I put my arm around him, gripping his shoulder. "Come on, Dan," I said. "You come on now."

Celeste wanted to know: "What is it, he got gas? I been asking him if he got gas."

"Dan," I said.

He went right on swaying, like my arm wasn't even near, and pounding his chest.

I raised my other hand to stop him, but it already felt full. Then I saw that I still had the brownie, squeezed in my fist now, and the thick chocolate edging out between my fingers.

"Is it gas?" asked Celeste. "Hey, Dan. Is it?"

I said: "Dan. Dan, listen to me."

But he wouldn't. He shook free of the straightness, and sat back on his heels. His hands fell apart, hanging loose, and he made a long arc with his head till it hung down too. He said: "Yes, yes, yes, yes, yes."

"Yes, what?" said Celeste. "Yes, you got gas?"

". . . I don't have no gas." He moaned the words through his nose, like a wore-out preacher who has to finish his sermon. I got the voice, though. I bit my tongue and leaned forward. Then I had to look away. Because this time the little boy wasn't set in Dan's face; he *had* Dan's face, all changed and molded for him. And it was then I first recognized that little boy, and his way of staring. It was then I remembered. And it was then I knew I'd already said goodbye to my grown-up brother Dan.

Only, I pretended not to know. I had to pretend something. I said: "Dan, what is it?" Then I said: "Please tell me what you going to do."

He knocked my arm off, and raised his own over his head. "Die. The Lord done made up His mind to take my life and let me die." He said it deep, and very phony.

Mama sighed aloud with fear, and Celeste laughed.

"Laugh," Dan said. "Laugh at me. All you-all."

Celeste told us: "It's the champagne. He done drunk too much of that champagne."

"I never had no champagne. I been talking to the Lord."

"Oh, hush up," said Celeste. "I bet you had a shot of something out there in the pantry too."

Dan yelled: "*I never.*"

"Course you didn't," I said. I batted with my hand in back of me for Celeste to keep quiet.

"I never drunk nothing. I never. I been talking to the Lord."

"Course," I said.

Dan swung around to me, his mouth open rounder than his eyes. "What make her say that?"

"She ain't going to no more."

"*What make her say that?*"

"Forget it," I said, "forget it, Dan, she didn't mean it."

Celeste said: "Certainly I did. What you greasing him up for, can't you see he's soaked?"

Dan lifted his eyebrows at me, much too sly. "You-all going to see. Laugh at me, go on. Say whatever you want. Wait till tomorrow. Wait and see."

Mama began to beat on the hollow top of the stove with her palm. She said: "Stop him. Stop him looking like that, I can't stand to see him looking like that."

I told Celeste: "You best take her upstairs."

"I ain't going noplace," Mama said. "Stop him looking like that." She shoved Celeste aside and stepped out. "Dan, baby . . . *change your face.*"

"Keep still, Mama, it's all right." I stood up between her and Dan, and I asked him: "Will you let me take you home now, Dan? For a little while?"

"Home? I ain't got no home." He spread his hands out and looked over the room, as if he wanted to give the idea he was searching for his home. The whole thing was like a big, put-on act.

I said: "You can come with me to *my* house."

"No." He shook his head from shoulder to shoulder.

"Why not?"

"The Lord didn't say nothing about that. No. He told me to wait for *Him.* Going to take me up to *His* land."

I asked: "When, Dan?"

He wrinkled his forehead and made to remember. "In . . . some hours."

"That gives you time to come with me for a while."

"No."

"Oh, fiddle, give him some black coffee," Celeste said, "give him some strong tea. Give him a nice glass of hot milk with some bicarbonate in it."

"*No.* I ain't drinking none of your dirty poison. You can't poison me, the Lord is taking me Hisself."

"You might have to, Dan." I was thinking about Mrs. Jenkins' sleeping pills in her bathroom cabinet.

"No, I ain't. I ain't taking nothing."

"Dan . . ."

"I ain't taking *nothing.*" To Celeste.

"If he was my own sweet brother," she said, "I would sock him so hard his eyeballs would switch sockets."

I looked at the silly doll dressed up like great big Dan. I told the doll: "Maybe I should do that."

It opened its arms and lifted its face to me. Like this picture I saw once about Joan of Arc. "Hit me, go on. Hit me. Just hit me all over."

I said: "Not all over, little dead boy." Then I leaned back and slapped him with my full weight. "You recall when I did that a few weeks back?" And I took my other hand and hit him again, just as hard. I had forgot about the brownie and my fist being so tight; it cracked against the corner of his mouth, leaving crumbs and pieces of chocolate mashed over his lips and into the teeth.

Mama squealed, short.

"Go easy, che," Celeste said. She jumped in front of me.

But Dan was snickering. Kneeling there, dribbling brown and red saliva over hisself, and snickering. He wiped the end of one finger across his mouth, and held it out. After he saw the streak of blood in the chocolate, he turned his eyes up, and said: "Look, Lord. Look what they doing to me. Look what they doing to Your son." Then he dropped his head. "Hit me some more. Hit me like that again for the Lord to see."

The buzzer sounded, sudden and nasty, twice, like before.

I side-stepped Celeste. "Watch Mama," I told her.

"You going back there now?"

Running, I said: "Got to. Can't have her coming here to look for me."

I turned the faucet on in the pantry sink, till my hand was clean; I dried on a dishrag and smoothed down my uniform, and ran out with the plate of brownies.

I put the plate on the table by Mrs. Jenkins, without serving, and I told her: "They wasn't ready before, ma'am." I backed off.

"Lucille."

"Ma'am?"

"Is everything all right?"

"Everything," I said, "is fine, thank you ma'am. Everything is plain fine."

She said: "That's good."

I put my left foot behind me.

"Lucille. I was just telling Mrs. Laverne about that nice talk we had the other day."

". . . Talk, ma'am?"

"Yes. Well, some time ago, actually. Of *course* you haven't forgotten."

"Forgotten? Oh, no, ma'am." I tried to keep from inching away.

"We cleared up a very delicate problem, and we made everyone at peace in this house, regardless of color or creed. Didn't we?"

"Yes, ma'am."

"Will you tell Mrs. Laverne what we decided?"

I said: "We decided everyone was going to be at peace in this house."

Mrs. Jenkins passed the brownies to Mrs. Laverne. She said: "You see?"

I bowed quick. Then I walked out, kind of crooked from wanting to do it even. I didn't start to run again till I was inside the dining room. A green Christmas light pointed through the darkness and reflected off the aluminum strip that edged the glass-brick wall; it fell in a spot that moved along the shiny top of the long ebony table, following next to me, following me right along.

Past the swinging door into the pantry; on into the kitchen. I saw Mama shaking her fists, and praying high. Celeste held her arms, clucking at her to be still. They stood close: two tiny statues of wild people on a book end.

I said: "Where's Dan?"

Celeste nodded upstairs, still holding Mama. She told me: "Leave him alone, now, honey, he be a whole lot better if you . . ."

I ran all the way up. At the top, the door to Celeste's room was open, and her bathroom door too. He wasn't there. I went down the passage, stepping so fast over the black linoleum my shoes didn't even make squeaks or suction pops when I took them up. I went into Mr. Stone's room and the guest room. Both empty.

Just as I got to Mr. Jenkins' room, I knew that was the one. I heard him whine: ". . . sneaking here to spy on me. Sneaking here to do me dirt."

Mr. Stone was crying. He tried to say: "Dan, it's just a game."

But I had to figure the last word for myself, because he didn't finish.

I leaned on the door; it was tight shut. When I turned the handle I was still leaning, so I stumbled out into the room. I looked at both their faces, and I had to keep my throat closed, forcing down the thing that rushed out of my stomach.

Only the bed lamp was on. Dan part-turned to see, but he kept a hold of the boy. He was sitting on the stuffed footstool, facing a window. He had Mr. Stone by the neck, and he was choking him.

Finally I had enough breath to say: "Let go, Dan."

Cute and baby-toned: "But I caught him *sneaking*."

"Let go."

"Just hiding here to do me . . ."

"Let go, Dan."

"But *look*."

Mr. Stone's face was puffed dark. Not pretty to see. His tongue and his eyes swelled out, wet. He was doubled so far back on the corner of the magazine table, he looked V-shaped, like he had his head on backwards.

On the bookshelf by my right hand there was a spiral glass ash tray, thick and green, with bubbles inside the glass. I knew where it was and I knew how heavy it was, exactly; I had to dust it every day. So I don't think I even took a real notice of picking it up as I walked to Dan, with the air buzzing around me.

I told him: "You going to let go right now."

"The Lord ain't said so."

"Oh, yes, Dan."

"Look, look at his color, look at that. Look there: he's darker than me."

I could tell from Mr. Stone's face that I had no right to wait. I lifted the hand that held the ash tray high as it would go. Then, in all my world, the only uncloudy spot was the sheen on the kinks through Dan's black hair.

A locust's scream can take a long while. It mostly depends on how you living.

Dan's face flipped straight up into my watered circle of truth, where his hair had been. He saw just what I was going to do. He said: "No, I didn't hear the Lord, I didn't hear the *Loooord*." And then he put both his hands over his open eyes.

In the buzz, I heard Mr. Stone slide off the table, taking a magazine with him. He didn't make no noise when he hit the carpet, but I could hear the magazine fussing its pages open. And I knew he was there. And it was all the same to me.

Because, for one lone second, the only thing I wanted to do was to mash those hands into that face and kill my brother Dan.

Mr. Stone's breath, fast and rasping: a file on soft wood.

Time. Time to wonder. Time to feel a real little life under me. Time to look. Time to live.

And time for a second to pass.

He was laying on his side, moving just for air. I watched him, my arm cemented stiff over my head. Something was very funny about him there, only I couldn't think what.

Mr. Jenkins' bedroom was right over the living room. I let the weight of the ash tray take my arm behind me about three inches, and then I tightened all the muscles in my belly and bent forward. It went clean through the window by the open curtain, and bounced off the blue railing outside. Glass spit into the night, and fell loud, breaking again on the terrace. Just one more piece kept tinkling after I was sure they had all stopped, and I didn't see how that much glass could come out of a single jagged hole, not a lot bigger than the ash tray.

Before it was finished falling, I sat down by Mr. Stone, and took his head in my lap. My shadow hid him from the lamplight, and a cool whiteness came out over his face. I glanced up and saw the moon, sticking halfway into the hole I had made, cut and twisted out of shape. When I looked at Mr. Stone again, I saw what it was that made him so funny: he was curved too far back, terrible-still, like a person who goes to sleep in the middle of a long stretch. Like the twisted moon, except the moon was only sad. You got to have blood to be funny.

He had quit panting now. His breaths came a mile apart, none of them hurrying to tell me he wouldn't die. I listened there.

Dan lifted his hands off his face. He saw us, and he yelped: "Oh, I'm dying."

"Not you," I said, "sit still, Dan."

"I'm dying. Yes, I'm dying."

". . . Better shut up now, Dan."

I hadn't left off watching the side of Mr. Stone's face; but I never knew when he opened his eyes. It was the patch of light under his eyelash that I caught first, and it didn't make sense right away.

I counted for his next breath. Then I said: "Mr. Stone."

Not a move; not one move.

"Mr. Stone." I felt of his cheek.

Dan groaned: "Look at *me*, look at me *dying*."

I think I said: "Shut up" again. But all I really remember is the buzz that blew up to fill the frozen air. And the face in my lap when it started to pull together and frown.

Probably it took him about three minutes, but there are some things you just can't measure on a clock. His whole face began to work at once with the effort. Then he snapped out of the curve, and made a short grunt that turned to a whine in his mouth. His hand felt around and pressed into the small of his back. And his eyes strained wider under the gauze-white dream that held him, till he ripped through and coughed awake.

He asked: "What? What is it, what . . ."

The buzzing in my ears had gone. I said: "Okay, Mr. Stone. Don't you worry, everything's okay." I wiped the damp hair off his forehead. I'm pretty sure I chuckled then.

Dan moaned and said: "Look at me dying, look at me dying, look . . ."

Mr. Stone sat up. "What is it?" he said. "My back hurts me."

"It's okay, Mr. Stone. Lay down now."

"No." He watched Dan. "What's the matter with him?"

"He's sick," I said.

Another while, before: "He wanted to choke me. Didn't he?"

"He's sick," I said. "You lay down."

"No."

Dan stopped making noises. There was a hush. Then footsteps from down the passage. I got on my feet when I heard Mr. Jenkins clear his throat and say: "Hello?"

I called: "In here. It's in here."

Mr. Jenkins came into the doorway. "We thought we heard a crash."

"That's right," I said, "you did. Yes, sir, you heard a crash."

Mr. Stone told him: "Daddy, Dan is sick."

"What?"

But Dan was already on his knees facing Mr. Jenkins. "Oh, Lord, You done come for me now? Come for Your son, oh Lord?"

". . . Huh?"

"Tell them who I am, Lord. Tell them that, Lord, please tell them that."

"Dan . . . what . . . ?" Mr. Jenkins scraped at his neck.

"Lord, oh Looord."

Then I knew nothing was going to take place till I made it; it was still up to me. I said: "Mr. Jenkins, sir." He wouldn't look over, and I made my voice louder than Dan's. "Mr. Jenkins, Dan is very, very sick. Mr. Jenkins. He hurt Mr. Stone."

Dan was wailing something, and I said again: "He hurt Mr. Stone. You better call a doctor. And you better help me get my brother out of here, please sir."

Mr. Jenkins muttered: "Stone . . . ?" But he had his eyes on Dan.

Mr. Stone jumped up. He still kept his hand behind him, on the pain. "I'm all right," he said. "Dan didn't mean it. He was only *playing.*"

"*Lord.* Listen at what they saying about me . . . Lord."

I felt like yelling then. Like a fog was all around us, and nobody was theirself. I wanted to send out yells into the fog and make me see everything real again. Yells to wipe the air. (*Yell, honey, yell . . . if you can.*)

Mr. Jenkins said: "I think you had better get my wife, will you?"

I breathed out, and drooped over. "Yes, sir," I said. And I walked by Mr. Jenkins, out of the room, and left them there.

The stairs didn't feel like stairs. I was whistling along a slippery black marble chute, waxed clean for Christmas, and a tum-tum-tarum, down we sliiide . . .

Downstairs. Standing outside the living room. Hearing the voices. Calling: "Mrs. Jenkins . . . Mrs. Jenkins," in time to the voices.

"Yes, Lucille. Come in."

Come in. Go in. In and watch them all scattered around the colored lights, making joy.

She was still sitting by Mrs. Laverne. The drunk man was drunker. He said: "Look who's back. Hey, Merry Christmas, damn it."

"Merry Christmas," I said. Listen to them laugh; laugh with them all.

"Yes, Lucille?"

"Could I please speak to you, ma'am?"

"Why, of course. You *know* you can always speak with me." She smiled at Mrs. Laverne as she got up.

The drunk man sang: "Deck the halls with damn boughs of hol-lyyy . . ." sloshing a gulp of his highball on the warm green carpet.

Mrs. Jenkins crossed to me, the beautiful tree behind her coloring the haze around her body. "Fal-la-la-la-la . . . la-la . . . la . . . la," she said, "what is it, Lucille?"

What is it? What Christmas did I hear a preacher say: "In this time of joy and . . ."?

"Yes, Lucille? What is it?"

What is it? (*What is it?*) Shake the fuzz out of your head. I thought you felt so clean and empty. (*I do, I am all empty.*) Then shake the thoughts back in. (*Thoughts?*)

"Excuse me, ma'am," I said. "Please excuse me, Mrs. Jenkins, but my brother Dan just went completely crazy out of his mind."

II

DIDN'T nobody believe it at first. It was hard to believe, because Dan was acting so phony. He wailed each word in that nosed-up preaching voice, and knocked his fist on his forehead like a movie actor who wants to make you feel what he can't feel hisself. They said he was just drunk, and then they said he had hysterics and was drunk, and then they said he just had hysterics from having *had been* drunk.

Then it turned out the man downstairs at the party that really was drunk was some kind of a doctor, and Mrs. Jenkins sent me for him. So he came up with his highball, and he took one look at Dan and said what he had to say: he said Dan was drunk.

Every time somebody said that, Dan would start to holler for Mr. Jenkins to tell them it wasn't so, and Mr. Jenkins would pat him on the head and say naturally it wasn't so.

The three young Laverne kids who had been playing the game with Mr. Stone crawled out of the linen closet where they had been hiding for the last half-hour, and all three started crying at once account of they had to be kept away from the room. Mrs. Laverne came up after them, and Mr. Laverne and his poodle-dog came up after Mrs. Laverne, and the doctor's wife came up because she got left all alone. The two soldiers had gone.

I stood in the corner, watching the whole thing, and I think I was the only person to take a notice that Mr. Stone kept his hand pressed hard against his back, or that he limped a little now. I let everybody do what they wanted for Dan, because I knew that my real brother wasn't there and it didn't matter.

Mr. Jenkins had to promise to drive us, for Dan to agree about going to Mama's house. Then Dan got up off his knees and made Mr. Jenkins hold his hand and lead him down the back stairs to the car.

We all followed, and that was when I stopped Mrs. Jenkins behind and told her to call the doctor right away. She said: "Oh, now, Lucille." But I told her real easy what Dan had done to Mr. Stone. She didn't want to believe me, only she knew I wasn't lying. When she said: "Now, Lucille, you should not *exaggerate*," I guess I must of looked at her exactly the way I felt, because she dropped her cigarette, and she was a long time picking it up. Then she ran on ahead to the garage, and took Mr. Stone back in the house.

Mama sat on the edge of the rear seat, alone, and shivered down smaller and smaller. It was her first ride in a motorcar. Dan sat up front, between Mr. Jenkins and me. We drove quick, spattering gravel till we hit the asphalt road into town.

Dan wailed and sang, but he kept still for a little whenever Mr. Jenkins asked him to. Then he had to be led out of the car to Mama's house. I felt the window shades go up around us, and I saw a few people standing in the street to watch the white man lead the big colored man by the hand.

12

THAT night and the next day pieced off into a neat packet with its own careful order of things—clicking as each one passed like a nightmare machine.

Mr. Jenkins left soon as he had promised Dan he would stop by again on his way to heaven. He let me know at the door that he was sending the doctor over to "make everything all right."

I figured Mama to throw a fit once he left, but I was wrong. The second we were all inside the house, she had gone and wedged herself into the corner between her bedroom and Dan's. She stood like a suit of clothes on a hanger—her arms down by her sides, and her head set proper on her neck. She wouldn't allow me to take her coat off, or give me her purse to put away. She watched everything, and she never said a word, not even to answer a question. She stood there all night.

For the first two and a half hours, Dan knelt on the kitchen floor, and I sat with him. By then he knew I wasn't going to force him to, so he eased up on a chair of his own accord, and blew spit bubbles till I had to dry his throat. He let me do that.

I listened for the old dog that still slept under Mama's gallery, waiting to hear him crawl to bed on his stomach. And I listened for the silence that made every late noise stand out sharp and glassy, like rhinestones on black velvet. The night noises began slow, and I thought how morning was a long way off—hoped it would be, because I couldn't think as far ahead as the next day. But time runs quick if you count it in heartbeats. And love, not time, is the watched pot.

The doctor came at midnight. He talked to Dan for twenty minutes in an easy, too-reasonable tone. He didn't get Dan to trust him, and when he took out the hypodermic, I saw it was useless. He went ahead and tried some, but Dan cringed back from him, hissing and spitting in his face. Then I was sure from the way the doctor got up that he was going to do it anyhow, and I made ready to take Mama into her bedroom. He decided not to, though, and he put the full hypodermic back in his bag. Going out, he said to me: "Best to let him calm down first without this. It'll pass . . . it'll pass."

Dan heard him. After the doctor's car had sighed off, and I had sat down again, he said: "It won't pass."

"I know, Dan," I said.

"It *won't*."

"I know."

Later, he asked: "Who was that?"

". . . What?"

"That man?"

I said: "The doctor."

"That wasn't no doctor."

I crossed my arms, but it didn't help much: my shoulders ached from their own weight.

"The Devil sent that man. That stupid man."

"All right, Dan."

"Coming here to keep me away from the Lord. *Listen* at what I say."

"I'm listening."

"No, you ain't. You faker. Sitting there pretending I'm right about everything."

"I'm sorry, Dan," I said.

"You don't have to always agree with me."

I put my hand over my eyes. I said: "Tell me how you want me to be."

"You don't have to be no way. You just don't have to be no way."

"All right, Dan."

"I *ain't* going to be all right."

"I know that."

"I ain't never, never, never going to be all right."

"I know, Dan," I said, "I know all about it. I know."

Then he looked past me up at Mama in the corner. "Tell *her*," he said.

I slipped around in the chair to ask her did she want a cup of coffee or some water. But when I saw her I couldn't ask. On account of I didn't, no matter what might of come on earth, expect to see Mama looking like that.

She was standing and waiting, quiet; staring back at Dan as if he was a long ways away. Three messy hairs tangled on her forehead, hanging and touching where they wouldn't of dared to touch before. And the fear—the powerful fear that was as much a part of Mama as her color—was completely gone.

It left her a new face. The tired muscles that she never learned to use for anything else, had dropped loose, letting the skin fall smooth and jowly over the edges of her bones. The rows of wrinkles I knew her by had nearly disappeared. Only shadows of the thickest ones stayed—the ones that cut deep into her flesh; they swung down now, lower than they should be, a little clownish. So in the end, our wild mama, the fright of our whole family, looked the most peaceful of us all. And it was almost nice to see how the only thing more peaceful than a very young face that hasn't felt life yet, is a very old face that won't be able to feel it again.

But something bothered me too. Because there, in the drooping, wilted skin of a life's finish, I saw the beginning of another person: a person that maybe might of been, a world ago. I sat and asked myself why those eyes should look so familiar—and why they should scare me—and where, where in twenty-two years and seven months I had seen those eyes before.

Dan said: "Tell her how I am. Tell her about me. Go on."

"Hush up," I said. "She knows."

"Tell her anyhow."

But I didn't. I was trying to remember about those eyes.

At one o'clock, Celeste's Alfred knocked on the door. He said Celeste had too much work to get over herself, but she wanted to know could he help us. I said no, but thanks, and I said goodbye without letting him come in. Course, he kept on peering over me to see Dan. But I knew Celeste wouldn't care how I acted, so I wound up shutting the door in his face.

Around three in the morning, Jewel came. She didn't knock; she opened the door and walked right in and stood, dangling an old cloth purse in one hand. Jewel hadn't ever once been as far as Mama's clothesline. But it wasn't strange. Nothing was strange any more.

She saw Mama first, and she planted her feet wide apart, and rocked from one to the other. She was half-drunk, but Jewel had got pretty used to her liquor by now—it mixed in about right with her blood. When she saw that Mama wasn't going to throw anything at her, she turned and looked at Dan. She asked: "Is it true what they told me?"

"Most probably," I said.

"Shoot," she said. "I swan. You don't ever want to be too sure."

"No; you don't."

Dan asked: "Who is *that?*"

"Just Jewel, honey. Remember her?"

"What she going to do to me?"

"I ain't going to do nothing," Jewel said, "you watch." She had her coat off, and she threw it on the drainboard with her purse on top. Then she rolled up her sleeves.

Dan told her: "I ain't taking none of your poison."

"Don't have a mind to give you none," she said. "All the poison I can afford, I appreciate to take myself."

Dan tipped his head to one side. "The whole world is trying to hate me alive."

Jewel laughed up a storm, and went to get a chair, slapping him on the back. She said: "I know just what you mean, man. I got born too."

I started with: "Hey, listen, che . . ."

"You go to bed," Jewel told me. "You and your mama get in there and go to bed."

"Everybody wants to kill me," Dan said.

Jewel sat down. "No, they don't. No, they don't neither. They just want you to live and strangulate and abide."

"They hate me."

"Naturally they do," she said, "the same like me."

". . . The Lord told *me* to wait here. Planning to take me away from here right on up to heaven."

"I swan. You lucky bastard."

"Want to wait and see him?"

"Think I will," Jewel said, "I plain think I will."

I asked her: "*Why*, Jewel?"

"Don't ask a person that, honey. Don't say why in this life. Why is the ootchie-cootchie word. The baby word you got born with . . . the little old word that *never* grew up. It's just the cutest bitty word of all, and the only one going to stay in your mouth after you die, to help you crumble faster. So save it, che, and go in there and get some sleep. Have to have sleep for tomorrow."

I got up and pulled out my body. "Jewel. Thanks . . ."

"Go on," she said. "Sleep is what you need in this life. Not why. Not thanks. Just sleep. It pins the lovely days together."

Dan was watching the ceiling. "Shit on the world," he said.

Jewel laughed again. "Telling me? But *how*?"

"I'm praying."

"Okay," she said. "Fine. Let's us pray some."

I went to Mama and took her hand. I said: "Come on to bed for a while now."

But Mama raised her arm and shook my hand away. She wasn't angry. She only did it with an extra part—like a horse switches a fly off with its tail. She went on looking at Dan.

"Come on, Mama." I knew she wouldn't, though. I went in Dan's room, and lay down on the bed.

For a while I listened to the two voices in the kitchen. I didn't think I slept at all, but I might of. Hard to tell.

Along about seven o'clock I sat up in bed. It was dark out, and the voices was still. I sat five minutes or so, enough to recall I wasn't really in hell. Then I heard the crash. I wobbled when I got on my feet, but I ran into the kitchen.

The table drawer was upside down on the floor, and the knives and the rest of the kitchenware spread out everywhere. Jewel was already picking them up. Dan sat in the same chair, with his head over the back. He was doing his best to commit suicide with a spoon.

Jewel heard me coming. Over her shoulder, she said: "Sorry, che. Guess I dropped off. It's okay."

I clipped around to Dan and reached for the spoon, but he swung away and went on stabbing his chest with it.

"Let him be," Jewel said, "he ain't going to hurt hisself none like that." She was right, Dan wasn't even making much of a dent in the lapel of his coat.

I helped her pick up what was left. I said: "Jesus. With all them knives."

"He wouldn't of took a knife," she told me.

". . . How come?"

"Oh," she said, "you don't understand."

I went to the sink to wash my face. There was a Coke bottle, near half-full of some smelly whiskey, standing by Jewel's purse; a slice of cork and seven cigarette butts was in the sink. I fished them out, and splashed water over me.

"Go back to bed. You wasn't asleep, I saw you."

"No, che," I said. "Thanks." Then I got a mind of Mama, and turned. She was in the corner, like I'd left her. Exactly like I'd left her.

I made some coffee, but nobody wanted any, except me. Jewel sat back and lit another cigarette. Dan gave up with the spoon; he started to throw it, but when he didn't get a rise out of me or Jewel, he let it drop on the floor. And Mama was quiet in her corner, waiting on.

At ten, Mrs. Jenkins came with the doctor. While he sat and talked to Dan, she held a step inside the front door and bit at her lip. She had a queer sort of grin, that wasn't truly a grin, or even meant to be. And I thought she was whiter than usual, from the clearness of the ash-blue vein that curved from under the skin at her left temple up into her hair.

Then the doctor stood off the chair. Watching Mrs. Jenkins, he took a breath and let it out through his mouth, his lips shaped for a whistle. Before he could limp over, Mrs. Jenkins turned to me and asked if there was a room in the house where we could talk. I took her past Mama, and on into Mama's room. The doctor limped after us; he came in and closed the door.

The backbone in that lady showed soon as she spoke. Her words still came out nice, but only because she was nice, now: no simple syrup added for me. Her voice stayed plain, and even, and it had a new current in it that made her sound just a little embarrassed. But the voice kept true. Because Mrs. Jenkins had something to say that was important enough for her to finally quit struggling around to be a person, at least long enough to turn into one.

What she told me was that Dan would have to be taken and put away for examination. It could be done one of two ways, but it would have to be done. She and the doctor had talked it over, and she said the best way was for me to sign a paper so that Dan could be sent straight to this institution where they understood about people who had problems in their minds. Otherwise, she said, the doctor had to report everything to the police, and that was the bad way. Because they might not realize, and they might treat Dan just like any criminal, and what with him being a Negro and all, it might be kind of awful. Only she said if I signed a paper, she and the doctor was going to see to it that Dan got the right kind of treatment—and if it was called for, she was going to pay there so that he could be treated special. As she talked, she opened her bag and slipped her hand inside; then she lifted it out again and pointed it up, and fiddled with her square-diamond engagement ring.

When she was through telling me, I went and stood by the window. I watched a tree wince in the cold, and I looked past the tree and saw Mrs. Warner's two scrawny kids—a boy and a girl about eight years old, not very dark. They was sitting on the ground, digging holes in the winter mud. I thought how that mud would turn warm in the summer and cake over, streaked with cracks, and doodlebugs crawling in the warm earth. Then those kids could go out on the levee to play, pulling up chunks of dust with the dry crab grass, laughing, laughing and playing through the slug-heat of a slow summer; sneaking over the levee with their poles, and fighting for worms to fish with in the River; thinking they was doing a big, important, new thing in the mother River that plain wouldn't care. Two kids playing on the levee. Just two more colored kids.

The doctor was talking now, but I didn't listen. I looked out the window till the girl saw me there. She smiled two separate teeth, and waved. I waved back. Then I unhooked both sashes, and pulled the old cretonne curtains over the glass, and faced Mrs. Jenkins. The doctor stopped short with his lips apart; or maybe he had finished whatever he was talking about.

I said: "You can give me that paper now, please, ma'am."

Mrs. Jenkins went on working at her ring. I think she would of liked to help me now, but she had said her piece, and she knew it. She dropped her hand and took a long white envelope from her bag. Her fingers ran over the smooth whiteness on each side, and then up under the flap. Four thick sheets of paper came out to be unfolded, swishing together as crisp as sandpaper back to back. They was all buckly with lines of small print.

The doctor unwound the top off his green fountain pen and put it on the other end, with smart little movements, like doctors have to do.

Mrs. Jenkins told me: "I know how perfectly ridiculous and cheap it must sound for me to add that I know how you feel. But I think that this time perhaps I really do."

I had way too much ahead of me to bother about answering her. I took the pen and the papers, and got over to the only table by Mama's bed. I sat down on the bed next to it. I lifted the lamp off and put it on the floor. Then I laid the papers on the table and signed my name at the bottom of each one, where Mrs. Jenkins had pencilled in a cross to show me the place. I waited for the ink to dry, and I folded the papers. After I had put the lamp back, I took them and gave them to Mrs. Jenkins, and gave the pen back to the doctor.

"Thank you," she said.

The doctor barked.

I told her: "I ain't signed my whole name since the day I left school. Except to practice."

"Really?"

"That's right. I used to practice."

"Oh," she said.

I dug the rough edge of a fingernail into my palm.

The doctor scratched his nose.

I said: "Mrs. Jenkins, ma'am, *I* got to thank *you*."

"Oh, no . . ."

"Yes, ma'am. You a very special type of person."

Mrs. Jenkins had her head turned. "How much of a complete idiot did you think me to be?"

"Not . . . that, ma'am. Never."

"Yes. I hope so. Oh, yes."

I asked: "Please, ma'am, how is Mr. Stone?"

". . . uh . . . he . . . we all hope . . . he'll be all right. We . . . had X rays taken this morning. We won't . . . know for certain till we see the results."

I was careful to hold my eyes away off the doctor's bad leg when I asked: "Does he still limp?"

". . . No."

"Good," I said. And: "That's a blessing."

Mrs. Jenkins explained: "He . . . uh . . . he can't . . . walk now, you see."

I was near sure I hadn't heard right. "He what?"

"No. He was walking . . . he was walking down the hall, when . . . after you left. Going right down the hall to his own room. I don't . . . we don't . . . know exactly why he . . . fell. It was . . . he bent down to pick up a . . . he . . . it was a button, and . . . he collapsed, you see, all of a sudden . . . we don't know why yet."

"You don't?" I shook my head back and forth.

"No."

I said: "No." Then I asked: "Does it hurt him much, does it . . .?"

"Oh, no," she said, "you see . . . he doesn't really feel anything from the waist down."

I shut my eyes. I said: "That poor little kid."

Mrs. Jenkins went fast to the door. "Well, we all have our different problems."

Without thinking much, I told her: "I don't know. I kind of wonder if it ain't always the same."

"Yes, perhaps. Perhaps." And then she said a funny thing. She said: "I'm not exactly certain what you mean, but I think perhaps you are right."

". . . Ain't there something I might could do?"

"Oh, no, thank you, Lucille. Just come back to work when you feel up to it."

"Back to work?"

"When you feel able."

"At *your* house? You want me to come back to work at *your* house?"

"Why, of course," she said. "What did you think?"

It made me forget the thing that was so important for me to say. I forgot it cold. I only gulped: " . . . a very special type of person."

The doctor put in: "Mrs. Jenkins is a very *understanding* person."

She swirled around on him so fast, she made him step to the side. Her cheeks seeped red with anger. She told him: "That will be enough of *that,* thank you." And she opened the door and went out of the room.

Mama kept the same expression when Mrs. Jenkins passed her by as when that lady took the trouble to come back and say she wasn't to worry. Course, she bent her head once then, from habit, but it wasn't at all like the bobbing nod Mama was used to doing for white people. It didn't even mean she had heard what Mrs. Jenkins said. It was only something her neck muscles did when somebody who wasn't colored stood in front of her and opened their mouth.

Mrs. Jenkins let the doctor go ahead, and she watched him clumpety-clump down the three steps to the ground, practically falling over the last. Before she went after him, she shuddered.

They came at three-thirty that afternoon. Dan had been asleep in his chair for fifteen minutes—Mama watching over him from her corner like a guardian angel, fresh embalmed.

They didn't use no siren, but I knew: I had been looking from the window above the kitchen sink every time I heard brakes. There was two of them in the driver's seat. Big guys with white uniforms and wrestlers' faces, sitting and squinting at the faded number on Jewel's house. And behind them, half-a-mile of ambulance.

Jewel was looking over my shoulder. "Imagine that," she said, "brand new. You don't ever want to be too sure." Then she laughed. "We ought to be proud."

The Coca-Cola bottle was empty, and Jewel's breath came strong in my face. I pivoted away from it and around to Dan.

I knelt down by him, and I thought of some other times I had knelt down in my life. I rested my hand on his wrist. I said: "Dan." But too soft to wake anybody.

Jewel was laughing again, back of me. "And clean white uniforms," she said. "Colored men with clean white uniforms coming down the walk from my house to your house. How pretty. Why, if I'd thought they was going to be that pretty, I never would of took to drink. We ought to be proud, che. We ought to celebrate the day . . ."

"Dan," I said.

"Look at the people come running. Look at them niggers. We going to have a crowd, honey." Harder laughing. "I wished I had a flag. We ought to have a flag to wave. We ought to have balloons and whistles. This is better than Mardi gras. We sure ought to have a flag. What would you write on the flag, honey?"

"Please, Dan," I said. Only I couldn't get my voice loud enough.

Jewel went: "Ha, ha, ha, ha, ha, haaaa . . . Look at them come running, the little bastards. Come to celebrate, come to see the show and celebrate, ha, ha, ha, ha . . ."

"Shut up, Jewel," I said, "look at Dan. Look at him, he's really asleep. Maybe it's all over and he's . . ."

"Here they come, now they really coming, wheee, ha, ha, ha, ha . . ."

"Shut up," I said, "for God's sake shut up, Danny's all well, look, he's just asleep, look at him, he . . ."

"Wheee, ha, ha, ha, ha, ha . . ."

"Shut up," I half shouted, "will you shut up?"

Dan opened his eyes and sat forward.

I said: "Danny . . . Dan, are you all right now?"

But he just snickered.

"Ha, ha, ha, wheee, ha, haaaaa . . ."

I stared, and I saw it was the same face. Then I really shouted: *"Jesus, will you shut up, you cheap whore?"*

Jewel's voice caught still a second before the knocks came.

I got to my feet, heavy-slow. One knee wouldn't hold, and I had to come up hand over hand on the rungs of Dan's chair to keep from falling. When I had done that, they knocked again.

Dan said: "There's the Lord, that's the Lord now. Open up for the Lord."

I said: "You tell them, Dan. I can't."

"Open up," Dan called. "Open up, Man."

I heard the handle turn and the door squeak. Then the people outside. Lots of voices, but nothing told. Lots of whispers; lots of people.

"Is this four forty-one Millicent Street?"

"Yes," I said.

"Lucille Mor . . ."

"Yes," I said.

Dan screamed: *"Angels. Angels. Angels of the Looord."*

"Can you identify your brother Daniel Morris?"

"Oh," I said, "I seem to think so."

"Will you iden . . ."

"This is Dan," I said.

"Sorry, honey, but you'll have to be very explicit. You mean the man sitting in that there chair in front of you? See, the thing is, only last week we picked up some poor . . ."

I raised my arm and pointed. In not much more than a grunt, I told him: "This. This is my brother. His name is Daniel."

"That's okay," the man said, "now step on out the way. All you-all step right on out the way."

Dan said: "Hey, they ain't from the Lord. Hey. Hey. They ain't from the Lord."

"Step back, now. Come on, step back."

I looked past him at Mama. She hadn't moved. She was fastened there as sure as her own wood house. But I couldn't make my body go to her. I tried. I just couldn't.

Then I saw the white jacket with the straps that one of the men was holding. Not quite as fancy as our father's cooking-jacket—our father's had buttons. I put my arm around Jewel, and leaned with her over the sink. She didn't say a word, but when Dan started to shriek, she grabbed my hand and ground the knuckles together.

He never quit shrieking till he was out of the house. There was only four other sounds in this age: his chair when it crashed over the top of the stove; a pot that it knocked on the floor; one of the men, swearing; then the door, banging back into place.

Dan must of cut short soon as he saw the crowd. For a time, though, I thought he was still in the house—shrieking on a higher tone. It took me a minute to hear the difference and turn.

Mama had started exact when Dan left off, without a break. Her mouth was open far as it would go, but otherwise she never changed. The voice itself was the same as Dan's; the real difference was in the kind of shriek. There was no fear at all in Mama's. Hers was only hate. Only a collection of hate, saved careful over a lifetime, and let loose after fifty-seven years on a single pure note that didn't vibrate, but held strong on the air, zinging fainter till her breath had gone out with it—ending on a snarl.

When it was over, Mama gasped to fill her lungs with clean air. Then she grew away from the walls, and marched into her room like a woman with a purpose—taller than her natural self—stiff-legged, but straighter and more dignified than anybody I ever saw, and bending in just the places she needed to carry her forward. She didn't close the door behind her. She took her coat off, and wrapped her purse in it, and put the bundle in a chair; she stepped out of her shoes, and stripped each piece of clothing off her body until she was completely naked, standing on the bare floor. She folded them over the chair, one by one. Then she got in bed, and put her face in the pillow, and went to sleep that way.

Jewel had let go my hand, but the fingers was still pressed together. I heard the ambulance drive off, smooth and fast. And in the end of the engine's hum, I heard the voices outside, getting thick now, getting thicker. I took my other hand and separated the mashed fingers with it; I put it around my wrist and shook till the blood prickled back. I left Jewel bent over the sink, and walked out the door onto the gallery, right at the center, at the top of the steps.

There was upwards of a hundred colored people, all ages, bunched close on Mama's dirt lawn and ragged sidewalk, spilling way out in the street. They muttered and whispered low to each other, and some to theirselves. Most of them kept their backs to me, watching the dust sucked up and swirled and left by the ambulance; but a few had already turned to look at the house.

I waited where I was.

I let the soles of my shoes knit into the floor of the gallery, and I waited right there where I was. I pushed down. I pushed all my juices down—down through my body, through my legs—around the bones through my ankles to my feet. Spurt by spurt, I pushed my juices out into the splintered, gray gallery floor. And I waited where I was.

I made us one, the gallery and me. For a few chiseled minutes, while my brother drove away with his secret and erased the air behind him—for those few minutes, I lent my own juices to Mama's gallery, and softened its floor with my life; I took its gray for my own. I changed that gray to steel.

I felt the warmth run under me as the wood filled, and I felt the winter shrink off from the icy dryness of my flesh.

And while I waited in the frozen case of my body, I shone my eyes on the crowd below. Starting from the left, I found every person who was faced away from Mama's house—and I stared till I saw the whole of that person's face. I went slow over the wide crowd, weeding them out with my eyes, turning them all. I stared them around where they stood.

They nudged elbows, and they licked their lips. The mutterings thinned; a hush settled with the dust. Then a soft shiver of a sigh passed across those heads, rippling like one great enormous sheet spread from my empty hands. The nudgings stopped.

Their quiet was mine.

But I never moved. Seems to me I recall smiling, but I know I never moved. And I used no more than the thinnest blade of my voice to reach the furthest pair of ears when I said: "Shout, you bastards. Don't whisper here."

The big sun gaped at me, high over Miss Roberta's house. The feel of it was bitter on my eyes. The sun sent specks to swim over the faces down below. And the silence held.

I said: "Oh, don't be scared. You don't have to be. I wouldn't hurt you. You can say anything you want, you can holler it if you want to. You can all holler, you can throw shoes, you can spit if you want. You can even run up and tear this house into pieces, and burn what you can't tear apart. Any of that is okay; we would welcome it. I will only kill the next person who ever dares to whisper again on this front lawn."

One bush-sized girl wriggled, and a woman's arm went out and pulled her close.

I said: "Talk to me. Talk, talk to me. I'm the one. The nice lady of the house is asleep now. She's an old lady, and she's done her best to please you. And I won't let you touch her sleep with your dirty whispers. Not this time. This time you have to name it out loud. This time you have to talk with words. This time you tell me what other fine thing she can do to help forgive her children for getting born. Anything. Anything at all, except fix them to be killed or kept behind bars; you already seen her do both of those. But anything else. Just name it. The old lady is fresh out of ideas."

Still they watched, and they watched.

I said: "Then what was the mumbling about? Where did you get the whispers from? What was you wondering? This is the second visit you paid us since our father died; you shouldn't have to wonder. You mean you still don't know what's been going on in this house? Is that it? That's simple. I'll explain it to you. Once upon a time, a long time ago, there was a lady living here with three little babies. And one day, her three babies drank three little bottles of bleach water, and lost the night out of their skins. Then the lady got frightened for them. She got scared that you wouldn't take to the color of her babies. She was fretful you wouldn't let them live with a color like that. So she taught two of her babies to dance for you instead. And they danced. And they danced right off the edge of the world. That's all; that's what's been going on here."

But the crowd didn't talk. Those people just watched me; those speckled faces.

I said: "But we want you to know we ain't blaming you for nothing. We can't blame here. Oh, no, when you get stuck between the night and the day, you can't blame either one. It ain't even worth the effort. But you know something, friends? You know something?

We never would of blamed you even if we could. We still never would of done it. A blame is a whine, and we wouldn't of whined for you. That's the only music we will not step to. We'll go get ourselves a bullet, or we'll go out of our minds, stuff like that. But we won't whine. It ain't a part of our act. So don't get confused. I'm only explaining you what is what; I'm just cleaning the whispers out of you. I ain't blaming."

Some of the specks was as big as some of the faces.

I said: "All right, now. All right. The boys' dance is over now, and I'm the child who's left. The nice lady don't have any other children to offer except me, and I'm doing my own offering. They call me Lucille. Now you tell Lucille what else you might care to see here. You won't get another chance, you better speak up. You better shout it out now, while I'm asking. Because I won't ask again. You better tell me. Do you want me to dance too? Do you? *Do you want me to dance?*"

The faces looked disgusted. All of them. All those faces looked plain disgusted.

I showed my lips how to grin. And out of that grin, the cold of my voice scorched my own throat to say: "Then get away from this house with your creeping whispers. Take your whispers and take yourselves and get away from here. Get away before I come down and knock you away. Before I make you sorry I didn't dance. Before I come and touch you with the crazy bug, you get away. And do it fast. And don't let me hear the use of your mouths till every last one of you is out of my sight."

Somebody's radio sounded in one of the houses behind the garbage dump. A man talking. Talking and talking. We listened about ten seconds.

Then they ran.

But they did it like I told them. They backed into each other, and they turned, and they most all ran. They split up to go in different directions, both halves tight bunched. But even though a dog yelped, and an airplane groaned overhead—those people moved off down the street like two swarms of buzzless bees, without a sound.

By the time they was off the lawn, the specks had swelled into blotches, so I couldn't hardly see. I still waited, though. I waited because I began to hear some of them clapping their hands in the distance. The same as premium night at the pictures; the same as on the radio. Clapping their hands. I heard them clapping their hands.

Then I drew back what I had put into the wood gallery; all of it. I lifted my feet and went inside. I went right through the screen of the door.

I called: "Jewel."

"I'm here, honey."

I couldn't place her. But I asked: "Are those bastards clapping out there?"

"No, che. They ain't doing nothing, except running. You got rid of them."

"Well," I said, "I hear them clapping."

Jewel told me: "That's okay. Okay, honey. You going to faint. It's okay. You just going to faint."

I chuckled. "Foo, no. Not likely. You ought to know me by now, Jewel. I ain't the type."

"You might not be," she said, "but that's what you going to do."

And I guess she probably caught me when I did.

The first thing I knew was a bigness of brown that swung over me as I breathed, and some wet all on my left shoulder. Then the brown was the ceiling. And my face was wet too. And that ceiling wouldn't keep still.

Something about being sick.

I said: "What?"

Jewel asked me: "You want to throw up, che?"

It didn't seem like much of a question.

"Cille. You want to throw up?"

"Huh?"

"*Cille.*"

"What?"

"You feel sick?"

I said: "Wait a second."

"You better come on over to the sink."

"Wait a second," I said. "Just wait a second."

I was on a chair in the kitchen and Jewel had her arm around me. Alone with Jewel in the kitchen. No more brother Dan.

I pulled my head straight, so I wouldn't be looking at that ceiling. Only, I used too many muscles, and one of them cramped. I grabbed it.

"Hey, hold on now, come on over . . ."

I said: "Never mind, Jewel. I'm fine."

"You sure?"

"Yes."

"You ain't planning on throwing up or something?"

"No. I'm fine."

"Course," she said, "you just passed out a while."

". . . How long?"

"Shoot. Three minutes, maybe. Not enough to do you any good." She went and got me a glass of water. "Take your clothes off and go lay down."

"No. Don't have to."

"It's evening in the day, and you ain't slept."

"I'm okay, Jewel. You go on home." I drank a little of the water. Jewel took the glass from me, and set it on the sideboard.

I said: "You go on home and get some sleep yourself."

"Me? Mine comes in a bottle."

"I'm all wet," I said. I reached for a dish towel.

"Threw some of that water on you. About all I can do with water, throw it. The taste of it just turns my stomach. I would of given you a slug of some liquid made of alcohol, except I'm all out. Don't happen to have any around here, by any chance?"

"Any what?" I wiped my eyes with the damp towel.

"Alcohol."

". . . What kind?"

"Don't be ridiculous," she said, "there ain't but one kind. You sure you feeling okay?"

"Yes." Then I remembered what I'd said before. It took all the dizziness right out of me. I told her: "I'm sorry, Jewel. I was only trying to hurt somebody."

"Sorry for what?"

"What I called you."

"Oh. Don't matter. True, anyway."

"No, Jewel . . ."

"It don't matter. It's true and it don't matter. You think I don't know what I am?"

"Jewel . . ."

"Let it go, che. Take your clothes off and lay down in there like I told you."

I tucked my hand under my hair at the back of my neck. It felt very cold. "I'm fine now, Jewel. You run on home."

"Home is as home does," Jewel said. "Cille, you got a dollar?"

"In my purse."

"Or a dollar twenty-five. Better a dollar twenty-five. Get me a whole quart."

"In my purse, che, take whatever you need. Shouldn't spend it on that."

"On what?"

". . . Whiskey."

"No," she said, "I just tell people I do that. Just to keep respectable. I really save it all for doctor bills, honey. My aged grandmother has syphilis."

There was another plane over the house. The second that day. I listened to it.

After Jewel got the money, I went and took her and I kissed her. "Stupid to try and say thanks for what you done. Go on home, Jewel. Go on back home."

"Okay, honey. You want anything, you know where I am. I most generally keep conscious till Jo Jo gets home, so there'll be somebody."

"Yes, Jewel." I sat down again.

She stayed a while longer. When she saw I wasn't going to faint again, she got her things together, and touched my cheek, and left the house.

I was a half-hour sitting there, with my face in one hand. I got up to drink some more water. Then I opened the door and looked out.

The people was gone. But one of them had left an empty cigarette pack on Mama's lawn. Right across the street, I saw a tall lady with a fur coat in the shadow of a tree.

I took my own cloth coat from the room that had been Dan's, and went out. I kicked the cigarette pack into the gutter. And I crossed over to meet her.

I said: "Hello, Adelaide."

". . . Che."

"You could of come in."

"No," she said.

"It's all over."

"I know. I been here a while."

"Did you see him?"

"No," she said, "I didn't see him."

"That's good."

Adelaide took her black gloves off, and put them in her purse. She told me: "You look different."

"Do I?"

"Yes. You do. I saw you up there when you was talking."

"Oh. Hear what it was about?"

"I didn't listen," she said. "I just watched you."

". . . Not very much to see."

Adelaide said: "You a woman now, Lucille."

"Yes. I know."

We gave the earth maybe a minute to hold us. Then Adelaide asked: "Who turned him in?"

"I signed a paper."

"*You* did? Why?"

I asked her: "When you and Howard going away?"

"Tomorrow," she said. "Tomorrow morning."

"In the train?"

"Howard has a car."

"Oh, course," I said.

"Cille. It don't make no difference about that paper."

"Thanks."

"No. I mean somebody else would of done it if you didn't."

"Sure."

"Maybe I might of done it myself."

"That's right."

"If you want to, you can tell everybody I did it."

"That's nice of you to say, Adelaide. Thanks anyway."

"Keep your thanks. I'm going out of town, so it won't matter none. Why don't you say I did it? You could blame the whole thing on me."

I rubbed my mouth. "Everybody loves the same word."

"What word?"

"Thanks, Adelaide. Thanks anyway. Funny, you the last person in the world I thought I'd wind up liking."

"I never asked you to like me."

"I know. Maybe that's why."

"Well . . . I got to go now."

"Sure."

"I ain't coming back to this town no more. I'm glad I saw you."

"I'm glad too."

". . . Ain't there some way I could help?"

"No," I said. "Thanks. You already did."

"I got money. Want me to give you some money?"

"Don't spoil it, Adelaide."

She switched her purse quick to the other hand, and cleaned the sole of one shoe on a hunk of cement. "Well, I got to go now."

"Hope you have a fine trip. Have yourself a good life."

"I got it guaranteed, che. I made him guarantee that in the bank."

"What?"

She smiled. "The good life."

I said: "I guess money is nice to keep for your kids."

"I ain't going to have no kids."

". . . No?"

"I don't want no kids."

"But what you going to *do* with your life?"

"Live it," she said. "I don't know how many times I done told you: just get through it the best old way I can."

"Oh. Well, good luck," I said. "Good luck, doing that."

"I don't need luck no more. I made my luck."

"Adelaide," I said, "I really hope you always think so."

". . . Goodbye, che. Say goodbye to your mama for me."

"I will."

"Cille."

"What?"

"I never did like your mama."

"That don't make much difference now, honey."

"No. I just thought I'd tell you."

"Okay."

"Recall when I used to go over and make up to her?"

"Sure I do."

"Terrible bitch," she said.

"I know what Mama is, Adelaide."

"Not her," she said. "I meant me."

"Oh. Well, I . . ."

"Goodbye, che."

". . . Goodbye, Adelaide." I leaned forward to kiss her, but she held out her hand. She only let me take it for a second, before she got it free and went past me down the street. Adelaide never would stand for a person to touch her with love.

I leaned back against the tree, and looked out at the sky—cold washed blue, with a few crusted ridges of white stuck on it like paste about to peel off and drop away. A short-winged bird batted high out of the bright glare that was beginning way behind me. I watched it fly in a straight line, cutting exact over the city, fighting the wind to keep in one certain path. That bird had someplace to go.

I didn't stay, though, to watch the end of the day. I plain didn't want to.

I walked across back into the house. It was shadowy dark inside, and Mama was moaning some old dead dream. Her voice was muffled in the pillow. I went and stood by her. Then I took my shoes off, and sat down on the mattress with my feet up. I took her head and put it in my lap.

I'd forgot most of the words to the lullaby years past; but I made some up as I went along. I sang it twice through.

And I told her: "Don't, Mama, don't. Let it go now, it ain't no use. It's all over. Everybody's gone. Let your dream fade, Mama, don't. You did your best, you might as well let go now. A woman does her best, and that's all she can do. A woman does as well as she knows how. So they forgive you, Mama; you did your very best. Love is love, no matter how much it ruins. And you loved, Mama. And it's over now. Don't. It just ain't no use."

But she was still moaning in my lap when I fell asleep.

13

I WENT to work the next morning, and came back that night to find Mama sitting loose in the curved-top kitchen chair Dan left last. She had gone out during the day to buy some wool and needles, and she was knitting Dan a scarf to wear. The wool was flame-orange, a brighter color than Mama ever used for anything before—my private color—brighter than any of us had used in our life.

It was the next afternoon that the doctor said Mr. Stone wasn't going to walk again. Mrs. Jenkins kept claiming she didn't believe it, and referring to an operation some specialist could make. But the way the doctor acted, we all knew.

I made myself go into Mr. Stone's room first off soon as they brought him back from the hospital. They had taken his pillow away, and he was laying flat in bed. He spoke real cheerful, and he made me sit by him so he could tell me ten times over what a shame it was about Dan. Mrs. Jenkins was there, and even Mr. Jenkins came in for a couple minutes and made poem notes in a corner; he quit using his pencil once when she explained to him how brave Mr. Stone was acting, and he coughed and said: "Yes, yes, of course. Yes." But I knew that Mr. Stone wasn't acting, or being brave either. He was just natural-happy because something had come about at last to make him the most important person in the house.

Afterwards, I looked for a chance to tell Mrs. Jenkins what there was to say. I had to hold off a while, though—she didn't like to come out of Mr. Stone's room, except to sleep.

And some days and some weeks passed.

Starting the first weekend, every Sunday I took Mama to the Asylum. It was over four hours in the train, and they wouldn't let us see Dan till the third visit. But Mama brought him his clothes anyhow, and a box of food: a meat sandwich and a fried chicken and two hard-boiled eggs, and some fruit. When she had given it all to the nurse, we went and sat on a high stone outside the Asylum wall, and she knitted there till the last train was ready to leave.

The third Sunday, they let us see him for fifteen minutes. We waited a half-hour in a big hollow room, cold, with spotted windows. The colored part of the Asylum was a building by itself. There was lots of others like us, there to see a person that was kept locked up; nobody I recognized, though. We all sat together on long benches, and most all talked under their breaths. It was one of those rooms that ain't made for people—the kind of a place that stays echo-empty no matter how full it is—like a waiting room at a station.

A lady next to Mama started talking to her and me right away, much louder than the rest. She was dark and velvety, not very pretty. She told us how worried she was about her sister that was inside. She said her sister's name was Thelma, and Thelma really shouldn't be in there like the rest, because the only thing wrong with her was her getting a little upset lately from time to time, but Thelma wasn't wrong in her mind or anything. The lady was worried about Thelma being in with all those insane people, even if it was just for a couple weeks. Talking to Mama, she looked around and said how sorry she was for the people who had somebody inside that truly was *that way*.

Next to me, an old man was sitting alone and crying. He held a tin of homemade custard and a spoon in his right hand, and in the left one something black to fiddle with. When his face got too wet, he wiped it on the shoulders of his coat.

Then they opened the doors and let them come in, single file. Dan was eleventh. I went and got him, and led him to Mama; I made him sit on the bench between us. He didn't know us, and he wouldn't talk. Mama slipped over close as she could get, and she took his arm to cradle in hers, stroking it there. Dan watched that when he felt like it, or me, or out the window, or just anyplace.

He was lots thinner; the skin stretched to cover his cheekbones, and his eyes seemed set further back. He didn't know why we were there, or why he was, but he didn't care: he had his world with him. Sometimes his lips moved, and I knew he was talking things over in his private new life, with its whorls and puzzle-paths all curved in and circling around nothing, like a big personal thumbprint pressed deep into his brain.

Everywhere around us the visitors whispered—pleading, straining to make contact with eyes that didn't see and hearts that didn't want to. Making old love to new foreigners—trying to call back forgotten hurts—whispering fearsome earth-secrets to brothers who lived on the moon.

The dark lady stood in front of Dan, talking hard to her sister Thelma. She mopped Thelma's nose and the saliva that bubbled off her bottom lip, with a tiny handkerchief that got wringing wet soon as she began. She talked so quick, she really looked as if she thought her sister was listening.

The bell rang, and two uniformed men walked through, helping the visitors to leave. Say *so long,* say *so long.* Or say whatever you want, it won't matter. But you can say *so long* if it makes you feel better.

We waited outside in the late winter fog while Mama put on her coat. It was the new coat, and she put it on inside out, so I had to take it off her and turn it right. Then we followed the crowd down the walk.

The old man who had sat next to me stayed behind and kept in step with us, like he belonged there; he went right on crying as we walked along. I hadn't seen his wife or sister or whoever the person was he had gone to visit, only I knew it was a woman, because I saw the black thing he still held in his hands with the spoon and the untouched custard: a gritty black cotton ball: one glove.

A country walk to the station over a wide dirt road, spewed with ice, and greenless. Back to life.

I said to Mrs. Jenkins: "Ma'am, there something you don't know."
"Hmmm?"
"I have to tell you something."
"What? Is it important?"

"Yes, ma'am. When you rang for the brownies the first time . . ."

"I'd . . . Oh, I would rather not talk about that day." She had got to the door.

"Please, ma'am," I said. "I have to say it."

Mrs. Jenkins stopped, facing the shiny wood.

I said: "When you rang the first time, I already had an idea about Dan. But when you rang the second time, I knew."

"Yes. Is that all?"

"I lied to you when you asked if everything was all right."

"No," she said. "I lied when I asked you."

"Ma'am?"

"I . . . asked. I didn't really care."

"Ma'am . . ."

"You did not lie, you simply answered a stupid question as it deserved to be answered."

"But what I said wasn't true."

"Lucille, nothing you said or did then was important. Nothing. I want you to forget that day."

"But it was my fault . . ."

"*Nothing* was your fault."

"Ma'am, but it happened. Why? Why did Mr. Stone . . ."

"Time," she said. ". . . Years of time for such a thing to happen. Time, and chance. And my own stupidity."

"No, ma'am. You ain't stupid."

"Oh, perhaps not." She cleared her throat. "Perhaps I haven't even that excuse."

It was easier talking to her back: "I should of told you, ma'am. I should of told you about Dan then."

"Lucille . . . *Lucille*."

"Yes, ma'am?"

"I want you to forget last Christmas Day."

"Forget, ma'am? Why? And how?"

She opened the door and put it against the wall beside her. She said: "Why, because it is over, and there is nothing to be gained by remembering the past evils we are forced to live with. How . . . I'm afraid I am not the person to ask." And she went off down the passage.

The end of January was mostly rain, and Mama and me both caught cold from walking between the Asylum and the station. She went to bed with hers, and lay knitting the orange scarf for six days. The scarf was all crooked, and its edge went wavy out of line; I don't think Mama really knew how to knit. She had no fever with her cough, and she wouldn't take medicine, only she wasn't any sicker than I was so I figured not to push it. Course, we had to skip seeing Dan that Sunday. I made her lunch early in the mornings and put that on the stove over a low flame, with the plates and the hardware on a table by her bed to keep her from getting up for more than a minute. I spread word around the neighborhood that she was sick in bed, and I left extra food, just in case somebody might like to come over for a visit; but nobody came. Mama ate everything by herself on Sunday and Monday, and she even told me I was a good cook. Tuesday night when I walked in, the food was still there, burnt. But it wasn't till I saw the half-finished scarf laying on the floor that I knew Mama was dead.

She couldn't of quit breathing much before I got there, or her skin would of been cooler. I sat next to her, and I set her hand across my leg. Only, no hand ever felt so foolish; there plain ain't much sense in a thing without its use. When I lifted my fingers away, I left four light prints in the blue-black of her arm. I watched how the blood seeped back into those prints, very, very slow, doing it for no reason, but just because. It made my stomach turn to see the blood that didn't care. I got up and let the arm fall on the bedclothes.

Bending down to close the eyes, I got one more flash of the other person. One goodbye look from somebody who had eyes I still couldn't place. Eyes that remembered me, though, caught in some other time. Eyes: the only part of the body that won't wrinkle; the only part that won't grow old. And the first and last to die.

I smoothed the lids down and stuck them closed. Then I stood off and looked again. I wanted to see if people can smile sweet in death. And maybe some people can. People who have a mind to. Not Mama.

They buried her two days later. A *special-deluxe* funeral, with Reverend Segrette and a fine brass band. But first, I went down to the bank and tried to make them give me enough of her money then to pay for the funeral and the grave. I thought to pay with what Clarence had left, because it seemed righter like that. They said no, it would take three or four days to clear the account. So I used my own savings instead; I bought a plot of ground outright. There was no plot free near our father's, and the *special-deluxe* rows wasn't in his part of the graveyard anyhow. I didn't have his bones moved to

Mama's side, because I knew he wouldn't of liked for me to, and it wouldn't of meant a thing to her, not truly. They was two separate persons.

The night before the funeral, I had a party for her. The hymn-singing mourners from the parlour showed up, and ten more besides, and some of the band, and some people who was passing by. And Jewel and her husband, Celeste, Miss Roberta, a couple old ladies Mama met once. It was a sad party for that kind of a party. They was all too hungry to get very drunk, except Jewel, and she came that way.

When it was time to close the coffin, I put the orange scarf and the needles in by Mama's body. Then her left half looked bare, so I took the white and gold frame with the telegram, and set that there. I didn't feel stupid about the party, and I didn't feel stupid doing those stupid things: they seemed to be the right things to do.

The lid was heavy, and heavier still because I said no goodbyes when I let it down. But I had none to say. Mama hadn't really changed for me, by dying. I let it down slow, though, just the same. I waited on the click when it was shut, but there wasn't any. They don't make back of town coffins to click. It ain't necessary.

After the funeral, I cleaned out all of Mama's belongings. I collected five neat piles in the corner of her room, to give to whoever might need them most. It made me like a little girl again, sneaking in her drawers and her closet, in her secret things. She had more stuff than even I would of guessed. Whole boxes tied closed, with packets of old letters and scraps of paper, and bottles and jars, and the top of a pen, and the handle off a broken spoon, and all kinds of things that didn't mean boo and never could of. When I had finished piling, I stacked the letters and papers in one big box. Then I took the box and sat down in a white kitchen chair and held it in my lap for a while. After that I started a fire in the potbelly stove. When it was burning high, I dropped the letters inside, packet after packet. I never read one, and I held off till the last had flared up and curled black before I shut the grilled door and laid the empty carton box next to the full ones in Mama's bedroom.

I gave those boxes away before the next morning, to three different families. I threw the junk in the garbage fire. And I gave her new Christmas clothes, and her clock, and what was left of her victrola, to Jewel. I hadn't found the two records or her other secret treasures, but then I hadn't tried to find where Mama might of hid them. I figured that was still her business.

I got all my own things into the suitcase Cousin Wila gave me and into another I'd bought at a sale. That same day, I told the mailman where I would be, and shut the house, and went back to living at the Jenkins'. I had already decided I would never sleep at Mama's house again unless I plain couldn't help it.

I did my job well, and I got up each morning looking for a letter from Charles Leroy. It just didn't *seem* like he was dead. I don't know, it just didn't *seem* like he was. I did my job every day. On through February, into the weather that won't make up its mind.

14

A MONTH and a half after Mama died, Mrs. Jenkins told me she and the family was going to move to New York City. They had to go, so some specialist could see Mr. Stone; only they had decided to stay there and not come back to New Orleans to live. She said New Orleans meant a lot of unhappiness to them, and it wasn't the right city for Mr. Stone to grow up in.

When she finished telling me that, she said she wanted me to understand I was one of her family now. She said she wanted me to let them take care of me and help me build a new life. She said I was to go with them, and start out fresh, and not look back, ever. And they was even planning to take Celeste along with me.

Mrs. Jenkins went on talking. I saw her lips move, and I heard her voice. But I didn't take notice of one word. My thoughts was turning for theirselves. Easy at first; then faster. And faster and faster, like the chug of a train moving off in the distance—zittering away over the flatness towards new colors, and a land with great enormous mountains to rock the bleeding sun till you could taste it—and a loose air to roll in, and a freedom you could leap through and keep going till you bounced off a hillside into the wonderful new place where every person could make a screaming splash high up the sky with the insides of her body and her fingertips—and nobody would care.

I said yes before I thought much about it. I said yes while I was thinking. And I said yes afterwards too. This was it: this was my new door. Out of the dark, into my glow, and soft streams of it falling over me as I got closer. Streams of burning light to show me the brilliance that was waiting there—so my eyes could begin to get used to it—so I wouldn't go blind.

Oh, you have to squint when you get thrown into your Garden of Eden, or all that sudden glory is just too much on the eyeballs. Don't fuss up, though: you'll get used to it. A person gets used to anything, even glory. Squint the first days, that's all. It's nicer for you. Squint like Adam and Eve squinted the first days that was, till they could get used to the perfect light, till they had time to wonder. You'll get time. And maybe you'll wonder. Anyhow, squint through the first days, while you make your Garden plans. It's a whole lot nicer for you.

So I made my plans to leave. There was only three.

First I put Mama's house up for sale. I left that to a white real-estate agent Mrs. Jenkins took me to see, who was to take care of selling their place. He was a squat, round man, with droop-haired eyebrows that he brushed onto his forehead. Every expression he made he did with those eyebrows—he even smiled with them. When Mrs. Jenkins introduced me to him as *Miss* Morris, one eyebrow stood up like the tail of a dog that smells something interesting on a turd. And when he found out she wanted him to sell a house in the *colored* part of town, the right eyebrow rose up to meet the left like Gabriel had called it. He agreed to turn the house over to a colored agency, though, and even to handle it personally through them, soon as he saw he wasn't likely to get the Jenkins' business if he didn't. (I knew there wouldn't be much chance of anybody ever buying it, but I had done my part.) When we got ready to go, he let both eyebrows slip together into a wrinkled arch. The arch meant: the richer people are, the crazier ideas they get, and there is always a nigger around to take their advantage. Might of made me feel pewpy some other time. But not then. I already felt too good. Go on, mister, I thought . . . you ain't a man . . . you only a white grub with eyebrows somebody turned up under a log.

Second, I got the New York City apartment address from Mrs. Jenkins and gave it to the back-of-town mailman, and told him I would let him know when to start using it. He knew about Charles Leroy being the reason, but we both skipped over that. It was nearly a year since my last letter.

Third, Mrs. Jenkins took me to see the doctor. After we were in his office, she announced she was giving him money for anything Dan might need, and that she would pay him a regular bill to go and see

Dan twice every month. But I stopped her. I said all the money I had
in the bank really belonged to Dan, because our brother Clarence had
meant it for him. And I asked her please to take the money and
arrange it with the doctor the best way she knew. She didn't want to,
but I told her I wouldn't be able to go at all unless it was done like
that. Then the doctor grabbed my hand and practically shook the
shoulder out of joint—and I signed a check to Mrs. Jenkins for the
nine thousand seven hundred and forty dollars and fifty-seven cents
that was left to me after Mama's death—and when the doctor saw
the amount on the check, he reached for the hand again, and said
this was the finest thing he'd ever heard about, and that I'd put his
faith back into whatever it was he'd lost it out of, and so on for a
good half-hour. We finally got out, and Mrs. Jenkins took the check
to her lawyer and set up a trust fund for Dan in the doctor's name.
And I knew I was free to leave.

Going away. Lucille Morris is going away.

Evelyn, the new part-time maid, helped me to pack everything at
the Jenkins' house; only I worked so fast, I wound up doing most
of it alone. Mrs. Jenkins said she didn't see how a person could clean
out a house that quick or that neat. She kept coming to tell me I
should ease off and rest some. But ease off was exactly what I
couldn't do.

"There's plenty time, Lucille," she would say, "we have plenty
time."

She was wrong. Every hour of mine that passed had another second
chipped off it. One for every heartbeat gone wild.

And a heart set loose. A heart that could rubber out like a live
balloon, growing on the in-breath of freedom, pumping out of time.
Pumping yesterday into tomorrow into the day after—never leaving
a space for now.

So I plain had to work fast, to keep up with my heart.

I said: "I ain't tired, ma'am."

"But you must be, you must be tired. Do stop and rest, Lucille,
you *must* be tired."

"No, ma'am, I ain't." And I wasn't.

Each thing, each piece of work I finished helped me to be faster
and better for the next. Better than a machine, because a machine
can't grow.

I cleaned out whole rooms and packed them in a day. At night, I sewed, I fixed, I folded. I slept two hours; I didn't sleep at all.

I worked on.

Going away. Lucille Morris is going away.

Before it got near time for the trip, I had to tell Dan.

He didn't know about Mama dying. The Asylum doctor said for me to keep that to myself. He said Dan wouldn't hear what I was talking about, and it was useless to push with news like that. Tell him in a few years or so, he said, if he ever begins to remember.

But no matter whether Dan heard or not, I plain had to tell him I was going away.

I sat him next to me on the bench, with all the other crazy people and their families, and I explained: "Dan, everybody's gone away now, except me. There ain't but just a house; nothing left to do."

It was an even day outside. Only one thick, meshmetal blanket pulled over the sky, sponging the light behind it. The brightness was heavy, and painful to watch. It shone around the black bars of the window—a dark sky—a beaming, dark sky: old, electric, silver.

I had stopped talking to see if Dan could tell the difference. He was studying a spot on the wall, his head turned a little towards me, and his right eye partly closed. When I stopped, he kept still a second, and then he swung his head the rest of the way around and looked at my mouth. When I began again he looked down, but I knew he was leaning his mind on my voice for that while.

And I understood then about the other visitors who came back every Sunday to talk to the whirlwind minds that whistled and howled in endless circles. Wide-faced visitors, trying to make their voices reach above the sound of the hurricane. I understood why it's sometimes important only to make the contact, even where you know no current will pass.

I said: "Dan, I have to go to where they'll give me a chance. I want to see people who don't need to be afraid . . . I want that chance for me."

(Dan might ask: *A chance to what?*)

"A chance to be free, Dan. Just a chance to know people who never wore white-enamel cases to hide their white-glass hearts; or had to kink black souls to match black hair. A chance to live. Don't you see, Dan? I need a chance to be free."

(Dan made a sign with his head like: *I know. You don't have to tell me no stories. I got out too.*)

"Dan, I love you. If there was something I could do for you I wouldn't go. I'd stay, I would, Dan, I would stay, you know I would stay. If you needed me, or if there was some way I could make you need me. But there ain't. I love you, Dan. Oh, Dan, I do. But you left. You took and you left, and went off by your own self. And the doctor says that's the way it has to be. He says it ain't no use for me to come here and sit with you like this, not now, not for a long, long time. And most probably, not ever. I ain't leaving you, Dan. Not you. I wouldn't leave you. And if you need me, if you need me any time, I'll come back. No matter what, I'll come back. I promise that, Dan. Dan, I promise you that."

(Dan picked up one hand off his thigh, and looked at it, and put it down again.)

"See, Dan, there's nobody here to need me. Mama's gone, Dan, Mama went too. So there plain ain't a thing left to stay for. Nothing more to do in her house. Nothing. Not a single thing."

(Dan might wonder: *Is that why you think you going? Because there ain't nothing to stay for? You really think you can go away from a nothing?*)

"No, Dan, it ain't like that. See, I have three of us to live for now. The fight is over, the whole fool fight is past. And if you lost, and if Clarence lost, you didn't lose it all . . . because you helped me to win. But now I got to live for the three of us. And I better do a good job, because it has to be three times right. More than that . . . I got to make up for what Mama did, and for what our father didn't do . . . I got to give them reasons too. I got to start where our father quit, and breathe wide, and flush the blood through every little touch of my body, till it hurts, till the hairs move all by theirselves. So I'm going out and live, Dan. I'm going away where I can live."

(Dan might say: *It all sounds pretty fine. But away from what?*)

"Away from this part of the country. Away from the flatland. I'm going to where people ain't afraid, to where there ain't no fear."

(Dan might want to know: *Where's that, che? Where-all in the world is that?*)

I said a little too loud: "You don't understand, Dan. Danny, you plain don't understand."

But then the bell rang, and I sat back and blinked, and I smiled. I sensed two or three of the visitors watching me, and my face felt hot. I thought: poor Dan.

He was staring out the window—staring through his lashes at the gray-blare day. The wind in his mind had risen, and he was alone again.

Going away. Lucille Morris is going away.

A couple weeks more, but nearly everything done. Two whole weeks, and my heart so big my bosom swelled, and less and less work. Doing the same things twice over to keep my hands full.

Mrs. Jenkins reminded me every day about telling all my friends goodbye. She said it so many times, it made me almost laugh. But I didn't explain to her that in the whole of New Orleans, I only had one friend to leave.

I said to Jewel: "And cut down on the drinking, che."

"Sure, honey. Certainly, indeed."

"I mean it," I said, "you ain't got no excuse to drink. Woman like you."

"Sure not."

"Che, you want to face up. You young, with a fine husband. Somebody would give you a baby, if you take to acting proper."

". . . Somebody?"

"Some agency, some orphanage. Maybe some friend who can't afford it."

Jewel said: "Some agency."

"You plain have to stop drinking the days away. You got guts, che. You used to be the gutsiest person I knew. But you have to *use* your guts . . . use your heart, and your . . ."

"Snatch?"

". . . Huh?"

"Personal self?"

"Course," I said, "the works."

"Shoot," said Jewel. "I clean forgot. I used to have one of them too."

"You still got all that you ever had."

"Not no more, honey. Not no more. I screwed it all away. Know something? I made myself too slippery; got too slippery up inside. And I just up and screwed it all away."

"Oh, foo."

"Foo to you," she said, "now you go on and get away from here. Get away from this here town."

"I sure don't like to go off while you doing what you doing. Che, you running out on every solid thing you ever did have . . . or love."

"Now you get on out your way," Jewel said, and she giggled. "But honey, let me run out mine."

Going away. Lucille Morris is going away.

Ten more days; no more work. The rugs up, all the curtains in boxes, all but the heavy furniture packed. Too much time. Heaps too much time.

I walked by Mrs. Jenkins, standing alone in the passage outside Mr. Stone's room. She had her handkerchief up over her mouth. She turned and slipped into the guest room, and I went on downstairs.

It made me sad, and that showed on my face, and so Celeste had to hear all about it, naturally. After I told her, she crossed herself. (Celeste had been crossing herself for more than a year now, account of she said the Catholics made her nervous.)

"What's it for this time?" I asked.

Celeste said: "A very good omen. Yes, indeed."

"You and your superstitions."

"Superstitions hell," she said, "when a colored woman sees a white woman cry, it ain't a superstition, it's a blessing. Anybody knows that."

"Hush your mouth, Celeste. She's a good woman." I got Mr. Stone's tray ready to take out.

Celeste was mopping the kitchen floor, but the mop wouldn't separate. It kept knotting up and making puddles on the linoleum. She leaned over and pulled it apart. "Personally, I wouldn't care if I saw a white woman cry herself sick. Best white woman on earth. Wouldn't bother me. Personally."

" 'Do unto others,' " I said.

". . . Do what?"

" 'As you would have them do unto you.' "

"The balls of a fish. They been doing it to me ever since I was born. Where you been at?"

"That don't make no mind. It says like you *would have* them do unto you. Not like they do."

"Honey, so what? I know another one that begins: 'an eye for an eye,' which goes on to say, if a man flips you on one side of the kisser, you supposed to act like the Lord Jesus did, and turn the other cheek so he can flip you on that side too, and then you supposed to take a hold of him and bash his teeth down his throat."

"I said: "Well, it ain't no use discussing a point with you."

"It never was," said Celeste, "that ain't a new development." She squeezed the mop into the bucket and shook it out. "Seems to take to you quite a lot, Mrs. Jenkins."

". . . Seems to."

"I'm delighted," she said.

"You slap-happy, is what you are."

"That generally, and thank you. But right now, I'm delighted."

"About?"

"Oh . . . nothing."

"*About?*"

"Well . . . if you two get along so lovely together . . . and if Mrs. Jenkins holds like she is, and if we play our cards right and start shivering around New York City a week or so before Christmas . . . you might even be able to move her to a couple fur coats."

I slammed the tray down on the sideboard. "Shit," I said.

"Ah, heavens," said Celeste. "Profanity."

"Listen, honey: *that ain't what I'm going for.*"

"Okay, okay, don't get mad."

"I ain't mad. I'm telling you."

"Okay. Told."

I picked up the tray again.

Celeste asked: "What, by the way, *are* you going for?"

I stood and wiped at the bottom of the tray with one palm.

"Well?"

Then I started for the back stairs, fast. "You and your questions," I said.

15

I THINK I could of shut my mind on everything, if it hadn't been for my hands. All the rest went like I wanted it to. Everything was in its place, and ordered, and clean, and right. Everything was quiet.

Everything but my hands.

Lunch was a little late on the Saturday eight days before the trip; afterwards I cleaned the plates and silverware, and put them away. I knew it was the last piece of work I was going to find that afternoon. When I reached to set the last plate into place, I dropped it.

Mrs. Jenkins was outside on the back lawn, by herself—heel-deep in the soft grass. She was watching the movers take the furniture out of Mr. Stone's playhouse.

I went out the kitchen door, and around to her left. I coughed before I got there, not to scare her. But she went on watching those three men.

I said: "Excuse me, Mrs. Jenkins."

"Yes?"

"I broke a plate, ma'am."

The men was lifting a big easy chair into their van.

"Yes," she said.

"Ma'am, it was one of the good plates."

"Yes," she said, "I understand."

I stepped ahead of her, but she looked right past me. "I'm sorry, ma'am."

"What?"

"For the plate."

Mrs. Jenkins told me: "That must be heavy."

"Ma'am . . . "

"Oh, yes. The way they hold it; look at that. That must be quite heavy."

I said: "Mrs. Jenkins."

"Don't be silly," she said. "Things get broken in moving. I can get another plate. I can always get another plate."

"Thank you, ma'am."

I turned and watched with her. The men was through with the chair. Two of them went into the playhouse again.

Then I knew I had to say: "Ma'am, is it all right if I don't sleep here tonight?"

"Here?"

"For one night. I got to go back to my mama's house."

"Of course."

The grass was waving up all around the magnolia trees—touching them; feeling of the young bark. But both trees was still.

I said: "I sure didn't think I would ever have to, ma'am."

"Of course. You do as you like. You needn't ask."

"Yes, ma'am."

"You know you are one of the family now, I explained that."

"Yes, ma'am. And I'm grateful. I'm . . ."

"Not to be grateful," she said, "that is simply our understanding."

"Yes, ma'am."

Mrs. Jenkins took a cigarette from her skirt pocket, and felt for a match. "Last-minute packing?"

"Ma'am?"

"You have some last-minute packing to do in that house?"

"No, ma'am. Oh, no. Ain't nothing left to do there. I just have to go back."

She looked at me through the smoke. Then she looked at the men again. "I don't believe in it," she said.

"Mrs. Jenkins . . ."

"You do as you like, of course. I wouldn't, but you do as you like."

". . . Yes, ma'am."

Mrs. Jenkins said: "I believe there is nothing to be gained by going back. Only forwards. Only towards the future."

"Yes, ma'am."

"Oh, yes," she said. "I only go forwards." Then she told me: "That man is going to drop the badminton rackets. Just watch."

"Looks like it, ma'am."

"Look at him. You see? It really can't be helped, in moving."

I shifted my weight to the other foot. "Well, ma'am. I better get on back to my work."

"No, you have no more to do here," Mrs. Jenkins said. "That's what's been upsetting you."

My jaw swung open.

"I'm sorry we didn't plan on leaving earlier. Silly of me."

"Ma'am, how did you . . . ?"

"I'm not stupid," she said, "you know I'm not; you told me so yourself."

" . . . No, ma'am."

"Those men must be nearly finished. I'd forgotten there was so much furniture in there. I'd really quite forgotten."

I said: "Mrs. Jenkins." I couldn't make her see me, though.

"All right," she said; quiet and smooth: "You have an idea about going back. It's a bad idea, but you want to carry it out. All right, then. That's my fault, for letting you get so upset. But it's done now. I am often too late, it seems. Rather often. It's not unusual for me. No matter how quickly I might . . . "

"No, ma'am," I said.

"Hmmm? Look at the size of that table."

"No, Mrs. Jenkins. It ain't the idea. It ain't even a thinking-thing. I got to do it, that's all. I just always go on and do what I got to do. Not because I want to. Not because of any ideas. It's because I plain can't do anything else."

"There," she said, "they *are* finished. Really, I'd forgotten Stone had half that much furniture in there. He never used it."

" . . . Yes, ma'am."

Mrs. Jenkins asked: "Can you feel the breeze under the grass?"
And she said: "I can feel it."
"Yes, ma'am."
"Under the grass. It's coming from under the grass."
"Yes, ma'am."
"Oh, no," she said.
"Ma'am?"
"No. I think not."
"What, ma'am?"
As Mrs. Jenkins turned, she said: "No. Don't call me ma'am."
She turned to her right, away from me, and headed for the house.
She picked her feet up high over the grass, and she set each one
down as if it was made of china. She left me there.

16

IT wasn't raining, but it was thinking to: the cave that cupped the
earth had filled with a mess of great, dusky dragonfly wings, to sift
and curl and thicken over the city, fiercer than their own quiet. Something was choking the thunder and making it wait.

I got off the St. Thomas car, and walked around the corner along
the hushed street to the house. It was seven o'clock or so; not black
yet, but dimming fast. All the air had been sucked up to play in
those clouds, so I was the only thing that moved.

Miss Roberta's new husband was singing into the stillness, hoarse
and loud:

> "Got to strip down my muscles,
> And wipe off all the dirt.
> Got to dress up my baby
> In a bugle-bead skirt . . . "

Poor Miss Roberta, I thought. Passing fifty now, and a good
hundred and seventy on any scale. Always a good listener. A lot of
bugle-beads.

I walked up Mama's steps, and pulled her screen door wide, and
unlocked the other one. Inside, I leaned it shut. The singing disappeared.

I kept my back to the door, and I waited in the dark there for the old words to whisper back. The hungry words; all the words that never got said, except to me. (Our father: "*Hell with it. Hell with everything but the camphor tree to look at and one suit to get buried in, and two books to cuddle. Hell with it, I give up, hell with it.*"—Dan: "*Don't put me in no sack. Lord, Lord, take me out of here, rip me out of this gunny sack. Don't let me die, take me out. Jesus, take me out.*"—Clarence: "*Figure what I'm doing? Figure how I'm living? Figure what I'm making with my life? I'm whoring, that's what I'm doing. I'm whoring my life by. It's the only way I know to keep my self-respect.*"—Mama: "*I'm scared. Please help me, I'm scared. I'm sinking, we all sinking, and there ain't nothing to stand on, nothing to hold. I'm scared, please help me. Help me, help me. I'm scared.*")

I waited in the hollow kitchen, with my shoulders against hard wood. I waited for those whispers.

And they never came. The house was empty; emptiness was a house. Just clapboard memories of when the nails drove in, and the dust through the walls. No more than that. Because when fear died, she left no memories. So nothing had stayed alive, not there. Mama's shelves was never used to store the days. And all the past was only in my head.

I flipped on the light switch, and laid my purse across one of the chairs. Then I sat down next to it. I didn't count on sleep.

After a very long while, I saw a big piece of soap and a rag, under the sink. They was the only personal things left in the house, apart from some of the bedclothes and kitchenware, and two boxes of matches, half-full. I had given the extra key to Jewel, and said for her to take whatever she might want.

I stood up and got one of the matchboxes, and went outdoors; I bent to look under the gallery. It was dark there, but I lit a match, and stuck my hand out. There was a shuffling scramble, and two black and deep red ovals blinked at me. "All right," I said, "okay, now. Ain't nothing going to change for you. You can stay." The bucket was on its side, and when I reached to get it, that old dog growled at me. I told him: "Dog, you think I don't know a tremble-growl? You just tremble-growling." Then I got my fingers on the bucket and dragged it free and held it up. The match burned my thumb, so I let it fall and lit a new one. But the bucket was crinkled and jagged, with a hole in the bottom so big the dirt and even the stones was already spilling on the ground. I leaned over again, and set it there for good.

I crossed the empty lot to Jewel's house. A light was on, and I knocked. Jewel's husband, Jo Jo, opened the door. Behind him I could see Jewel asleep sitting up, her hair swung down loose over the chair.

I borrowed back the newer bucket Jewel had taken, up to the top with water, and carried it across and dumped it in Mama's bathtub. I did that five times, and I poured about half of the fifth one in the kitchen sink, for the morning. Then I went and got another bucketful; I put it on the floor by the stove. After that, I pulled every window shade in the house, and switched on every light, and I took all my clothes off and spread them on the foot of Mama's bed. I grabbed the soap and the rag, and put them with the bucket.

I got down naked on my hands and knees.

The soap was dry-cracked, crusted with dirt, and one long strand of hair running along it—mine or Mama's. I held it underwater a minute or so. When it had soaked enough, I wet the rag and rubbed them hard together. I began to wash the floor.

You wouldn't of said I had a reason, in that empty grave. And there wasn't ever what you might call a love between her house and me, never from the start. Anyway, we were alone now. No family trimmings to fool us. Nothing to pretend with. Not even any running water since a week ago; just six more days of electricity, and the money with Jewel to pay the bill. Not a whole lot to show for all those winter years.

But I washed what was left. I worked slow, sensing the night pass; careful, because I only had one bucketful for everything. Slow, piece by piece, I washed the floors and the walls and the furniture. I washed till my knees was raw and my hands felt puffy—till the water looked like a taste of my last evening sky—till every other thing shone out, discolored and clean.

One side of Mama's dresser moved with the rag. I thought: so this was where. But I left it alone to go on washing.

Maybe I spent four or five hours, I worked so careful. When I had finished, I let the rag sink into the bucket.

I went and stood in the iron bathtub. I used the same piece of soap, slippery and yellow now, smaller. The smell was strong on my body, but I liked it. I liked the stinging too, between my legs and on my nipples and under my armpits. I would of liked to rub it over my head—through the hair—all against the skin that would burn clean. But there wasn't enough water, not enough for that.

I had to lay down in the tub and turn over and over to get it off.

Mama's three towels was gone, so after I rinsed, I just pulled out the plug and got on my feet. I stood for a half-hour, right there, till I was smooth and dry. Then I stepped out.

Back in Mama's room, I put on my slip, and buttoned the skirt around it; I got into my shoes. I went and fetched the bucket and dropped the soap inside, and I took the matches again. But when I opened the door, the moon was showing, so I didn't need them.

I walked down the wood steps and back of the gallery to the side. "Quiet, now," I said, "it's just me again, keep quiet now." I couldn't hear him, though. Only the swish of the water way under the house, and a soft clink the soap made on some empty can. He was out around the night, that dog.

I put the bucket on Jewel's gallery, and cut back to the house. After the door had snapped to, I squatted by Mama's dresser. I worked the slat of wood, bumping it from end to end; it didn't give. When I leaned forward on it to keep my balance, it pushed up about three inches. I slipped my fingers into the space that opened at the bottom, and lifted it out.

The box was standing behind the drawers, on an inside beam of the dresser. I had to open two drawers to get it. I closed them afterwards, and fitted the wood slat back into place.

I went around and sat on Mama's bed, the box next to me. Right away I saw what was wrong: its not being dusty at all. Mama must of wiped it every single day, alone. Because she must of got out of bed to wipe it the day she died.

The knot opened in the fingers of one hand, and when I pulled the string away, the lid came off with it.

No tissue paper. No paper to hide the three secrets I already knew would be there: her records, her Bible, her pictures. The three things I hadn't found before. And one more thing I never would of thought to look for.

The lead of the pencil was broke off clean, so I could tell she hadn't let anybody use it. Even the teeth marks looked new. It might of been dropped yesterday—maybe a couple weeks back. Not eleven years ago. Except, Mama had known eleven years ago that there wouldn't be any real need for a particular pencil ever again.

Each of the two records had its own neat envelope, without a crease or a wrinkle. And there was a third envelope for the pictures. I took that one and the pencil out, and put the lid back on the box. Then I sat some more, and thought, before I opened the box again and put my hands around those records. I didn't feel right about doing it. But I didn't feel right about leaving them there, neither. You plain have to do what you want sometimes; because about certain things there just ain't no right.

I tried bending them towards me, but they was too stiff. So I stood up and held them over the iron bar at the foot of the bed. I hit them six times on the bar till they began to rattle inside the envelopes. Then I put them back, and slipped the box on an empty shelf in the closet. Somebody else could throw that away.

I stepped over near the lamp to look at the pictures. Two of them —not new to me. One was our father and Mama on the day they got married. The other was Mama holding Clarence, a year-old bundle. Two old pictures of two strange people. Young. Wondering-young, waiting for life to come and curtsy to them. Paper faces for the camera, trying to look their best by not looking like theirselves. And only the eyes to kiss them for.

Then I stared at Mama's, open again. Still there to remind me of another person. Still in the wrong sockets. Not quite as dead as Mama was, but no more alive than she had ever been. Still just: eyes.

I got on the bed, sitting back against the iron post, and I raised the window shade. It was black outside, so I turned off the lamp and the ceiling bulb. That helped a little: I could see enough prickly points of light to know my sky had cleared, and all those clouds had blown off to break somewhere else. May weather; silly weather— Mademoiselle was right.

While I watched, a few of the stars began to blue out behind the first fresh warning-sheen of day. I knew when the sun reflected in the side window of Jewel's house it would be seven o'clock. Only the tail of the night to go. I slid down on the bedpost, with the pictures in my hand, and I was asleep.

I can't remember what I dreamt; just that it meant a lot to me. It meant so much, I woke up thinking: I will remember this dream, exact, all my life. But the second I opened my eyes and saw the day, the dream unraveled.

The brightness had passed Jewel's window: a little after seven-thirty.

I sat up and shook my head. I was sort of woozy-stomached, so I ran and smothered my face with the cold water I had left in the kitchen sink. I felt sicker, and then I felt all right.

By about eight I was dressed, mostly ready—the Bible on the

kitchen table; the pictures and the pencil in my handbag. I'd left my hair to last, in case I ran too late: I had to be at the Jenkins' to serve nine-thirty breakfast, and I wanted to get a coffee first. But there was time for my hair.

I loosened the bun, and combed it out, and made it again. All the water was used, so I couldn't get it very neat.

Miss Roberta's rooster sounded as if he'd laid the egg hisself.

It happened when I went to the mirror to slick the loose strands on top. I had my head tilted to one side, like I always do, and four hairpins in my mouth. Before I started combing, I looked at my face, tilted that way, and I bit down on the pins so hard they bent straight up. I even dropped the comb. Because the bleary eyes looking back was set in my own face—and there was the person I knew. Miss Stupid Blossom of Galilee, hiding out in her own body. And all mine to live with.

I straightened my neck, and took the hairpins out of my mouth. I don't know why I wanted to cry. Anyhow, I didn't. I just said: "Hello. Ass-fool."

Fifteen whole minutes clipped out of my life before I thought of time or anything else. Fifteen minutes to recall two eyes in a mirror, and to wonder how I could possibly of forgot that face. Then time— only a little time—to leave.

I knew it still wasn't right to cry, so I giggled while I picked up my comb and put it in my handbag. I thought: Lucille has got a little Lucille, for company. Then I laughed so many tears out, I had to wipe them away to see. With my handbag under one arm, I switched off the rest of the lights, and took the Bible, and opened the front door. When I turned around, I laughed into that house till I shook.

I went on laughing and shaking even after I had closed the door, and locked it, and walked away down the street.

I walked the five and a half blocks to the drugstore. Different blocks. Different and the same. The branches of the trees kept singing to me as I passed under; but I wouldn't listen.

George the soda jerk wasn't even supposed to open up before nine, only he was mopping when I knocked. He had a pot of coffee on a hot plate, and he gave me a cup.

He said: "Jewel done told me about you going to New York City on the twenty-seventh."

"Did?"

"That's correct. That's in a week. I ain't charging you for the coffee."

"You ain't?"

"That's correct. For goodbye."

"Thanks," I said.

"Don't mention it. Kindly don't mention it at all. My pleasure."

" . . . Thank you."

"Say no more about it. Would you care for me to turn the radio on while you drink your goodbye coffee?"

"Okay."

"I wouldn't usually turn it on till half-past nine."

"Wouldn't?"

"No. I wouldn't. But if you care to listen while . . . Hey, what-all you laughing at . . . me?"

"Lord no," I said, "not you."

"Then what at?"

"I ain't really laughing. Not *really.*"

"You is too. What at?"

"Me," I said. "It's a secret. Got to do with me."

"You laughing at your own self?"

"Might could call it that, George."

"Ain't very bright," he told me.

I said: "Honey. Oh, honey, it's the brightest thing I ever did in my life."

"Is?"

"It is."

"Well, if you say so." He sniffed. "Hey, you on your way to church?"

"No."

"Can't be coming back from church?"

"No."

"Then what you doing out with the Bible?"

" . . . That's a good question," I said.

"You walking around town with a Bible, and you don't even know what you going to do with it? You mean to tell me you ain't got no place to put a Bible?"

"That's even better."

George wiped his mouth on the back of his hand. "You acting kind of queer this morning, seems to me." Then he leaned his mop against the counter, and straddled a stool next to me. "Pretty fine trip," he said. "Pretty fine place, New York City. A pretty fine place."

"Uh-huh."

"My father-in-law was up there once. A pretty fine place. What time the train leave on the twenty-seventh?"

"Morning."

"You packed and everything, I guess."

"Uh-huh."

"Hey. Where-all you coming from so early? I thought you was living out in Metairie with the people you work for. Where'd you come from, your mama's house?"

I said: "I never heard so many questions in four days in my entire life."

"What questions?"

"All kinds."

"Perfectly simple question."

"Simple, simple, simple," I said.

"Now I suppose you probably might tell me that's another secret too."

"No, George, I wouldn't tell you that. That's not my secret."

"I should hope not. Such a fuss. Only just asked if you was coming from your mama's house. Just a perfectly simple question. Such a fuss. Didn't ask no more than that. My Lord."

I thought hard and fast. "George," I said. "George, where would you expect I would be coming . . . " Then I started again. I said: "George, you been acquainted with me for a long time now, and . . . " But there wasn't no way to get out of it. It all came back to the same thing. There wasn't no way at all. So I plain had to take him by the arm, and put my other hand on the stool under me, and say: "No."

"No?"

"*No.*"

"Where you coming from, then?"

I told him.

"Oh. *You* have a house?"

"Yes."

"I didn't know that."

"Didn't?"

"Course, I wouldn't even of had any idea you was leaving, except Jewel said so. She said you was awful excited and happy about the trip. Only she said something else too. Bet you can't guess what else she said."

" . . . Yes."

"You can?"

"Yes. I can."

"Bet you can't."

"But I can." I got down off the stool.

"Go on, how could you? . . . Hey, where you off to now? *Hey,* you forgot the Bible."

"No, I didn't," I called. "Just keep it for me, George. You keep it for me a while."

On my way to the streetcar, I did listen to the song in the trees. I was singing it myself by then anyway.

17

I NEVER had to give my secret away to anybody. Not even to Mrs. Jenkins. Matter of fact, when I brought up her breakfast and told her I wouldn't be going with them, I kind of got the feeling she already knew that. She sure didn't act like I expected her to.

I told her first off when I set down the tray. She had been reading in bed. All the windows was open, and there was a strong draft; it pressed my skirt all around the backs of my legs.

Mrs. Jenkins made the magazine into a tight roll, and set it in the wood cage at the side of the tray. Then she took off her glasses, and folded them; she laid them next to the orange juice.

I said: "I . . . I thought to . . . "

"Is that definite, Lucille?"

"Yes, Mrs. Jenkins."

She stroked the edge of the pink satin coverlet, and turned it back.

"I don't . . . I . . . "

"That is your definite decision?"

"Ma'am . . . Yes, ma'am. But I want to say I'm . . . "

"No, don't apologize." She got up out of bed, and stood in front of me, and she held one hand over my mouth. She stared some, but I just let her, because I couldn't get my lips open to talk. Then she said: "If Mrs. Jenkins won't do, my name is Laura." After that, she walked past the tray into her bathroom.

The faucet splashed on almost right away. I waited to hear it, and it did.

So if I hadn't seen the edge of her nightgown swirl back suddenly, I still might of thought it was the wind that slammed that door.

18

I STAYED on with them up to the last minute. The day before they left I packed the rest of their clothes. Mr. Stone's new trained nurse, Miss Pentage, came in the afternoon, and I showed her where I had put all of his things.

My last pay check was about five times more than it should of been. I gave it back to Mrs. Jenkins, and asked her to make it right. But she said no, even after I'd used all the excuses I got a mind of. So I finally had to explain to her how I plain couldn't take that money, *and* start out fresh after they was gone. She was buttering a piece of toast at the time; she didn't have no comment to make. Course, I can't remember ever having seen anybody spread quite that much butter on one piece of toast. Anyway, she tore up the check, and gave me another one with just the right amount.

They left yesterday. Mrs. Jenkins, and Mr. Jenkins, and Mr. Stone, and Miss Pentage. And Celeste. I went down to see them off at eight in the morning.

I took my two suitcases, and went with Celeste in a colored cab. The cab driver turned out to be a man who was engaged to a friend of a friend of hers, which was all she needed. Long before she really finished with him, he had agreed to wait for me till the train left, and then take me over to back of town for only what it cost her to go to the station. Celeste even said it was a shame she hadn't met him a day or so earlier, or he could of had the pleasure of chauffeuring her northwards.

Seemed like an extra-far drive. Rising dew and early sun-orange across the window slicked the city through a glaze of color that didn't belong there. It looked too pretty—not beautiful or solid as it really was. Like some old whore who never got told she has wonderful bones in her face, trying to rouge the wrinkles out of her skin.

Celeste and me was close enough friends not to say goodbye. We just sat with our arms around each other, and we each had a pretty good sense of how the other one felt. She was keeping a piece of ice in her lip, because she'd said goodbye to so many people in the last week, and got the trembling-chin so often, it had went pernicious on her, and she hadn't been able to stop it for two entire days. She was furious at me for not going along, and she called me most all the dirty names she knew. And she knew enough to carry her through ten minutes without hardly pausing except to kiss me, and without repeating herself once, leastways far as I could figure. Halfway through was when she dropped the ice, and from then on I did sort of suspect she was embroidering some, from the expression on the cab driver's face in the rear-view mirror. But Celeste never had any trouble using her brain, if she really had a need for it. She kissed me about every fifth word.

Then the steam of the station, and the smells. Nine twenty-five. Standing on the platform with Celeste, under the clock, waiting.

No time; no beginning; no end.

Mrs. Jenkins said: "Oh, there you are, thank goodness, our cab had a flat can you imagine such a thing? Lucille, stand here next to me, will you, till I can get everyone settled?"

"Yes, Mrs. Jenkins."

"Good girl. *Vincent. Over here.* Lucille, there should be fifteen bags on that cart, would you count them? *Wheel him over here, Miss Pentage.* Vincent, please don't wander off, dear, I really cannot organize this if you are going to wander off, now we've been up since six-thirty this morning, and if we're not all careful, we'll be simply going around in circles. Miss Pentage, are all of your bags on that cart? Are there fifteen, Lucille? *Vincent.* Really, I've *asked* you not to wander off. Yes, I know, but not *now*, dear, you can do that on the train as soon as it leaves the station. Well, you simply *must* hold off till then, dear, please don't make things difficult, we must all do our share. Celeste, here is your ticket, do you see? We'll have to ride separately until we cross the Mason-Dixon line, I do hope you understand that this is not the way we would like it to be, but we must just put up with circumstances as they are. Now, you will be careful of it, won't you? Vincent, don't buy *Time*, dear, we *have Time*, it's in the package with the blue ribbon Lucille is holding. Now, please just stand still, dear, and get on the train. Car seven, compartments eight and nine. No, dear, this is not car seven, this is car six, car seven must be that one over there, no that's car five, well car seven is *there,* then. I do wish they'd arrange these trains in the right direction. Do I sound silly? Vincent, you'd better carry Stone, dear, and let Miss Pentage take the chair. *Lucille."*

"Yes, Mrs. Jenkins."

"Oh, yes, Lucille, just a second. *No, Vincent.* That's car five, I *told* you, car seven is that one over there. Well, I can't help the way it's headed, dear, I didn't plan the train. We must be going to back out. Now, just do as I tell you, and take him over *there. Lucille."*

"Mrs. Jenkins?"

"Yes, Lucille, just one second. *Vincent, your hat is going to fall.* Well, well. Just follow my husband, Miss Pentage, and pick up his hat, will you? Oh, and Miss Pentage, tell him *not* to flush the toilet, will you please, we don't want to create a *situation.* Oh, *is* it locked, Conductor, now that's good. Yes, I know it's written there anyway, I can't tell you how many times I've seen it myself, but my husband never reads those signs. Miss Pentage, just leave that where it is now, there's no use in having it after the cart's been over it, do you see? Well, *let* the man pick it up, Miss Pentage, whatever would anyone want with a hat in two pieces? Just wheel the chair on down to car seven and get on, there's a dear, I want to say goodbye to Lucille. No, Miss Pentage, he's right there. Well, certainly he is, Miss Pentage, I'm looking at him myself. Oh, my God. *Vincent. Don't you drop him.* Oh, my God, he's going to drop him, *Vincent. Vincent. Vincent, let him slide, for God's sake, you can't knock his head off.* Dear God. *Stone, are you all right? Vincent, don't just stand on those steps holding him upside down, get on the train.* There, Miss Pentage has him, there they go, well thank goodness for that, did you see Stone fall back that way when he saw he was going to bump his head, I don't think I ever saw anyone react so beautifully. Conductor. Now, where did he go? Celeste, run after him and ask him where your car is, will you, and get on. Celeste, what's wrong with your chin? Have you said goodbye to Lucille? Oh, now don't cry, dear, for heaven's sake, we don't want any of that. Now, Celeste. Now, now. Just please get on the train, dear. That's the girl. *Celeste, dear God,* what a word. Well, really, I do think we must keep ourselves under control a little better, no matter *what* we may be feeling. Well, that's all right, I understand, but do be a little more careful. Look, there's the Conductor over there, now go and ask him which is your car, and get on. That's the girl. *Lucille."*

"I'm right here, Mrs. Jenkins."

"Oh, yes, of course you are, I *know* I sound silly, I *feel* silly, but it is a bit difficult getting things organized for my husband, and we've been up since six-thirty this morning. Of course you know that, you woke us. My God, I sound ridiculous, I sound like an absolute flibbertigibbet. I don't even sound like *me*. Do I?"

"You never did, ma'am," I said, "around Mr. Jenkins."

"What? Look at that steam. Lucille, I've asked you not to call me that. Now, give me the packages, will you dear? Good."

("*All aboard. All aboard, please. All aboooard.*")

"Well, Lucille, I . . . I'm really not certain what to say to you . . ."

"Mrs. Jenkins."

"Yes?"

"Thank you," I said.

"Well, I really don't know what *for*, now."

"For an awful lot."

"You . . . I think you feel right . . . about your decision."

I smiled. "Ain't no thinking, Mrs. Jenkins."

"Good. Yes, I thought that. That's why I . . . well. You won't change your mind then, last minute?"

"No, ma'am."

"No . . . ?"

"No, Mrs. Jenkins."

"Right."

I said: "Mrs. Jenkins, that don't mean I'm happy to see you go."

"No. I realize. I . . . *Celeste, get on this train. Any car, just get on.* Yes, it's all right, Conductor, I'll just step on here, and walk down afterwards. I . . . "

("*All aboard, please. All aboooard.*")

"Well, Lucille . . . "

"Goodbye, Mrs. Jenkins."

"I don't suppose . . . I'll be seeing you again."

"No. I guess not."

"Well."

Then that lady leaned over right in front of everybody, and kissed me.

I said: "You a nice woman, Mrs. Jenkins."

"Yes?"

"Yes."

She scraped at one of the packages. "I'm not going to cry, Lucille."

"I am," I said.

"What? Oh, no, please."

I said: "I don't think I can help it."

"Try."

"I been trying."

"Well, keep it up. I . . . that is . . . there's nothing to be gained by . . . whoops, here we go . . . *goodbye, Lucille. No please don't cry. For God's sake, don't cry.*"

"*I can't help it,*" I yelled, "*I plain can't help it. And anyway, I want to, now. Mrs. Jenkins, I want . . .* "

But the train had started up too quick; that lady was gone.

I stood quiet a time, breathing in the steam and the grit, and the freshness. After I straightened my dress, I waved some. I couldn't see the train no more, but I did it anyway. I just felt like waving.

Then I turned around and walked fast to the taxi.

The driver was down at the end of the platform with one foot up on a fender, watching me come. He wolf-whistled.

"I know what you mean, man," I told him; "I can certainly figure what you mean."

When he'd backed the car out and swung it onto Canal Street, he said: "That was your mama?"

"Who?"

"That white lady you was kissing?"

"No. Oh, no. Not my mama. That was my Red Queen."

"Your *what?*"

"Never mind," I said, "it's a long story."

" . . . Sounds sort of interesting."

I told him: "Honey, it only sounds that way."

I had him take me to the drugstore. Back through the city—with the dew gone up and the sun in the day—through the real city, looking like itself now. Back down Millicent Street. Back to the drugstore.

I thanked him, and he drove off. I took my bags inside.

George was mopping up again. "Hey," he said. "Where you been at?"

"Working."

"Today's the twenty-seventh."

"That's right."

"Them's your bags?"

"Yes."

He rested his mop on the wall; but he wouldn't quit watching me. "Come for your Bible?"

"Uh-huh."

"Want another cup of coffee?"

"No," I said. "Thanks. I ain't got time."

He went behind the counter, and lifted the Bible out of a drawer, and slid it over on top. "See Jewel around?"

"Not since I saw you."

"Not at all?"

"No."

"Not once?"

"No, not once. But I still know what she told you, if that's what you getting at." I opened my purse.

George put his elbows on the counter. "Che, I been puzzling over you."

"Have?"

"Yes. I have."

"You," I said, "and one or two other people." I was counting all my money.

"Where's that house you told me you had?"

"Four forty-one Millicent Street. Please feel welcome."

George said: "No, no. That was your mama's house."

"That's right," I said. "That was." Seventy-one dollars and fifty cents, till my next job.

George wiped his nose. "Now, I would just appreciate for you to tell me what is the difference between your mama's house and your house. Please. If it ain't asking too much. What is the difference? If you don't mind."

"Don't mind at all," I said. "You looking at it."

"At what?"

"The difference," I said. I put a dime by his elbow, and took the Bible.

"What's this for? Hey, what the hell you crying about?"

"I ain't crying, man. I ain't *really* crying."

"Oh, yes, you is, you been slobbering all over yourself ever since you walked in here. Think I'm blind? Che, you better make up your fat mind what you *is* doing. Now, what's this dime for?"

"I done made it up. I done *made* it up, can't you tell? You look like a man would be the first to take a notice of a thing like that. You know, you look like a man was powerful sure of everything. You look like a man that was sure all the day."

"I do?"

"Yes."

"Well, I am, generally, but I ain't right now. I don't even get what the hell you talking about, half the time."

"See, that's just what I mean, George. A person can not be too sure. No, indeed. No, you take my word for it, George. You don't ever want to be too sure."

He stood back. "That's what she said."

"Who?"

"Jewel. That's exactly what she told me."

"Oh," I said.

He put his hands on his hips. "Lucille Morris, you is a peculiar person."

"Lord," I said, "the Day of Judgment has come." I stuck my Bible under my arm with my purse, and picked up my bags.

"Now, this is the third time I'm asking you what is this dime for?"

I said: "One coffee."

He looked at the dime, and I started for the door.

"Hey. Hey. *Hey.* You mean you ain't leaving?"

"What do you think?" I asked.

But I didn't wait for no answer. I was already running, running all the way, with those suitcases bouncing in my hands. They must of been heavy, but they didn't feel heavy. They must of been about the only things that kept me on the ground.

And the stupid part is, I could still hear that man shouting at me when I was two whole blocks away. He just kept right on shouting: *"Hey, I was sure you was leaving. What the hell. Lucille. But I was sure you was leaving."*

Course, I didn't bother to answer him. There wasn't much point. Some people never learn.

On Looking Back

Robert Benchley once said that the world is divided into two kinds of people—people who think the world is divided into two kinds of people, and people who don't. I don't, so I have no immediate way of determining how many writers share with me a private horror of going back and rereading a piece of work once it's finished, but there are quite a few, I think, and not all of us are novelists. Toward the end of Lillian Hellman's life, when an edition of her collected plays was about to come out, she asked one day if I'd sit with her and take turns reading the galley-proofs out loud. Till then, she'd avoided reading any of her work after its completion because, she said, she'd been afraid all her life that one of the plays would be so good she'd never be able to match it—or so bad she'd never have the courage to go on.

The feeling was familiar to me, and last week, when a letter came with a request to publish this, my first novel, on what turned out to be the book's fortieth birthday, I froze. Like an hysterical bird that abandons its eggs once they're touched, I've never gone anywhere near a book of mine since the day it was first published, before which I knew where everything was located on every page of the manuscript, and after which I couldn't even remember the plot. Looking back at a story or plot I had once loved seemed downright dangerous, since there's nothing in the world deader than dead passion, and nobody wants to turn into a pillar of salt.

I ought to mention here that no two writers use the same two words with the same meaning, so terms like "plot" and "story" tend to muddy us up. My definition of "story" is what the characters want to do, while "plot" is what the author wants them to do, and by that definition *A Place Without Twilight* has no plot at all, so I needn't have worried. About that.

About other things, yes. Ever since then, if I write a book that is reviewed favorably, I think, "Well, I got away with *that* one," and the day before my next book comes out I take to wondering whether I can fool people again. Which is, I guess, a way of saying that I've felt like a fraud most of my writing life—though less so at the beginning, when I was writing in innocence, than later on, when I knew how much I didn't know. Among the things I didn't know was that Henry James had said the morality of a work of fiction depends on the felt life that is in it. Thinking about those words alone can make you feel like a fraud.

Having said all that, I can say that I liked rereading this book more than I expected to. After forty years, there are things I would change, but there were always those things, and I doubt the years have given me the wisdom to improve what was written before I knew it couldn't be written—in the days when I was more of a chance-taker than I am now. What passes for wisdom is often, in my case, loss of confidence in a flattering disguise.

Perhaps for that reason, *A Place Without Twilight* has almost as curious a history as I do. Despite what all grown-ups tell you, the important thing in life is not getting what you want—it's knowing what you want—and if I knew as a child that I wanted to be a writer, the knowledge was rendered useless by not knowing what I wanted to be as a man. I was as uncomfortable with the idea of fathering a family as I was with being a monk. I thought of myself as an in-between person. My parents traveled a lot and my main ambition was to stay alive, having spent most of my first five years more in foreign hospitals than out of them, due to a bad burn and a Rube Goldberg series of infections that took place before the discovery of penicillin. After a while I found myself growing up quietly in New Orleans, a city I liked, but a city that had no in-between twilight to speak of, in a place where day and night were so neatly defined that it seemed to me I stuck out of it like person without edges, a child of refracted light. I had no siblings, and my parents were out most of the time, so I did my growing up in the kitchen with the variously colored people who worked there. They became the people I played with, sat with, talked with, and (in one instance) went to bed with: all in all I had a whale of a good time. The kitchen had one great virtue for me, it was the first place where I felt I belonged, but like all such places it didn't last, and when I was fifteen I moved with my mother to New York. I didn't like it there, but I weathered it till I was twenty, and then went to Spain for a month—and stayed nine years.

What Spain had in common with a New Orleans kitchen I can't explain in detail, but it had this: I belonged. And this: the Spanish didn't care if I belonged or not, since they were a mixture of so many cultures, the result of so many invasions through so many centuries, that they took no notice at all of one small arrival. I moved in with them and didn't speak English again till I was twenty-nine.

The reason I didn't speak it was that I couldn't afford to, since I didn't have a work permit—Spain's equivalent of a green card—and I needed a job that paid more than writing stories did. If you look Jewish enough, you look Spanish, so I passed as a local and shied away from anyone who spoke English, for fear that I'd be identified as an American and lose the freedom to work. I lived that way for the full nine years, and I liked it fine, because it was the last melodrama of my youth and because I was the hero of my own life. I fell hopelessly in love with *flamenco* and then with *cante jondo*, the deep song of Andalucía, the south, and then with the south of Spain itself, which seemed to me so strangely like the American South. I don't remember when I started to think of it as home because I don't remember much about those years.

But I remember when I started to write a book. By then, writing had become my only real outlet for English—I wrote at night and kept my work locked up—and one day a strange thing happened. Without warning, the only English I felt comfortable enough to write in became the English of the only other place I'd ever felt comfortable in. It was what New Orleans people of my childhood used to call back-of-town English, or kitchen English, and suddenly I could use it with more clarity and tenderness than any other language I knew. That was how *A Place Without Twilight* began, and maybe that was why I had the feeling at first that the book was writing itself.

The only other thing worth saying about it now is that since the afternoon the book was finished—on a rainy autumn day in 1957—I've been asked a surprising number of times whether its protagonist, Lucille Morris, was based on a "real" person. The answer is that she was not. But, based on my reading the book last week, she has become, for me, a very real person, and her felt life today—on a spring afternoon of 1997—gives me a certain kind of pleasure I had no reason to expect. I do have a reason to be biased, so I can only hope that she may do the same for others.

PF

Barcelona; April, 1997